C.E. MURPHY

DEMON HUNTS

BOOK FIVE: THE WALKER PAPERS

LUNA™

www.LUNA-Books.com

LUNA™

Recycling programs
for this product may
not exist in your area.

DEMON HUNTS

ISBN-13: 978-0-373-80314-9

Copyright © 2010 by C.E. Murphy

www.LUNA-Books.com

Printed in U.S.A.

Author Note

By the time *Demon Hunts* comes out in June 2010, you'll have just missed the Brenda Novak Diabetes Research auction, which she runs every May. In 2009 I offered a "Tuckerization"—an opportunity to have a character named after a reader—in the auction, and will very likely do the same in future auctions. Please keep an eye on my Web site, cemurphy.net, for information about such opportunities in the upcoming years!

—Catie

This one's for Tara.
(I think that's enough apologizing
now, don't you? :))

CHAPTER ONE

Tuesday, December 20, 4:34 A.M.

Someone had been chewing on the body.

Not some*thing*. Some*thing*, in the grand scheme of life, seemed like it would be okay. Things—cats, dogs, raccoons: choose your omnivore, I wasn't picky—were expected to chew on dead flesh. I was no forensics expert, but I'd learned a few basics at police academy. For example, a bear stripped of its skin and missing its skull can so easily be mistaken for a skinned human that the exposed meat has to be tested in order to ascertain what kind of animal it had been. For another example, humans have a very round, even cusp to their bite that most mammals don't share. So I was pretty confident it was a some*one*, and not a some*thing*, who had eaten part of Charlie Groleski's left arm.

This was really not how I wanted to start the holiday season.

My partner, a holiday himself—Billy Holliday—swung down beside me. The Christmas carol he was whistling turned into a low long warble of dismay. "Looks like somebody ate him."

"I'd noticed." I rocked back on my heels—a dangerous endeavor, since I was halfway up a low cliff, standing on a semi-sheer rock face. I was roped into a harness that was secured at the top of the cliff, but leaning back still felt like asking for trouble. "Tell me something, Billy. How come we get all the exciting cases?"

"We don't." Billy crouched beside the body, his own harness squeaking and rattling with the motion. I edged several inches to the side and squinted nervously at the drop immediately to my left. Harsh white searchlights stared back at me, the generators powering them shaking all quietude from the morning. The lights made sharp shadows of our narrow ledge, enhancing my awareness that there wasn't really enough room for two people on the ledge, much less two people and a corpse. "Daniels, he gets exciting cases," Billy said. "Drug murders, Mafia turncoats, revenge killings. We never get that stuff."

"You don't think half-eaten dead guys stuffed into crevasses are exciting?"

He shook his head. "No. I think they're weird. We get the weird cases, not the exciting ones." He pushed up and wrapped a hand around his rappelling line for balance. "Groleski must've been dead from the time they called in a missing persons report, maybe before. Too many days. I can't get anything from him."

I muttered, "Crap," and let the Sight wash over me.

Billy was right, if you wanted to get technical about it. He and I constituted Seattle's only paranormal detective team, a truth which slightly less than a year earlier I would have pulled my tongue out before believing, much less uttering. We got the weird cases, the ones that could potentially have a supernatural element to them.

He saw dead people. Murdered people, more specifically. Their ghosts tended to linger, and he was the man they could turn to, if he got there within two days of their brutal deaths. Unfortunately for Charlie Groleski, that was too short a window to allow him an opportunity to offer insight as to who'd chewed him up and spat him out.

I, thanks to an unpleasant experience which had left me with a choice between dying or life as a magic-user, was a shaman. Once upon a time, my long-term plans had involved maybe opening my own mechanic's shop. Instead, I was a healer and a warrior up at four in the morning, exhaling steamy breath into an ice-cold Seattle morning, on a case that wasn't actually in my jurisdiction.

The department—city-wide, not just the North Precinct where Billy and I worked—was being as goddamned quiet about this case as they could. Murders happened. They increased around the holidays. That was part and parcel of modern city life, and had probably been part of every civilization all the way back to Cain and Abel. As far as I could tell, it was one of the things that made humans human.

But there usually weren't a half dozen bodies found over the course of several weeks, all of them looking like they'd been pre-Christmas-dinner appetizers. Charlie Groleski had been missing for sixteen days, though aside from the gnawed flesh, his body was in pretty good condition. The media had started calling global warming "climate change" instead, and the longer, colder winters Seattle had been experiencing the past few years ran with that appellation. We'd gotten our first solid freeze in mid-November, and nothing had fully thawed out since, including poor dead Charlie.

Billy had his way of looking at a crime scene: through the deceased's words, if at all possible. Mine was different, and I'd learned early on not to contaminate what my normal vision could see by accessing the Sight right away. Once I saw the world that way, it lingered, influencing everything else.

Winter, viewed through eyes that saw the breath and life pulse of the world, was heart-achingly beautiful. The earth itself lay dormant, a dark forgiving depth scored by brilliant pulses of light that were the living things traveling on its surface. Billy stood out as a flare of fuchsia and orange, and I glanced at my own hands to see familiar silver and blue dancing over my skin. Everyone had an aura, and their well-being could be read through that burst of color.

Whatever colors Groleski had once sported, they were long gone, swallowed by death. I wasn't looking for them, though. I was looking for marks in the earth: anything that would show me something of the madman who'd killed and eaten half a dozen people in the greater Seattle area over the past two months. It took a god to actively obscure himself from the Sight, but time and the winter season could wipe away the traces a killer might leave behind. I'd never tracked someone in summer, but I had the idea that the softened earth would hold an impression longer. Someday I would probably find out if I was right.

Today, though, all I saw was the calm deep brown of the earth. There were no stains to accompany Groleski's frozen body; he'd apparently been killed and eaten elsewhere, and only removed to this location afterward. Why anyone would haul a body halfway up a cliff was beyond me, except it was in keeping with the other victims. They were all outdoorsy types. Only one or two had gone missing while hiking or trail-breaking, but they'd all been found in haunts like the ones they'd loved to spend their lives in. Groleski'd been a rock climber.

"Walker?" A man's voice rose up from below, floodlights too bright to let me see the speaker when I glanced down.

Not that I needed to. I dropped my chin to my chest and took a moment before shouting a response. "Sorry, Captain. I've got nothing."

I was too far away to hear his exasperated sigh, but I felt it ripple over my skin anyway. I was good at disappointing Captain Michael Morrison. Some days it seemed like my only stock in trade. I could have lived with that, but this was the third time in a row I'd failed to come through on this case. At least the other two times he hadn't been awakened at oh-god-thirty to call a dud shaman to a crime scene: those bodies had been found in daylight. This one should've been, too. Nobody in their right mind would be scouring cliffs at three in the morning, but Groleski's brother had found the body. I guessed a family missing a member wasn't in its right mind.

Billy jerked his thumb, and I leaned back from my stabilizing rope, bouncing the ten or twelve yards down to the ground. The harness became a Gordian knot under my cold fingers and Morrison's gimlet eye, but the rope began to draw up as soon as my weight stopped holding it taut. The forensics team would be taking our place with Groleski's body, now that the esoteric detectives had completely failed to see anything untoward. Some good we were.

Morrison waited for me to regain my balance, then folded his arms over his chest in expectation. The searchlights did him no favors, turning his silvering hair white and making the lines of his face deeper and more haggard. Even his eyes were pale and hard, as though deep blue river water had frozen into ice. "Am I wasting time pulling you two out here, Walker?"

Steam clouded around my head as I breathed out, an excellent physical approximation of the exasperation shooting through me. "Not any more than it wastes the forensics team's time, boss. They haven't found jack shit, either, but nobody thinks they shouldn't be here." I winced, not exactly an apology for my tone, but at least recognition that I should modulate it. I wasn't at my best at four-thirty in the morning, which didn't excuse mouthing off to my captain.

Fortunately, almost half a decade of mutual antagonism mixed up with more recent emotional complications had, if not inured Morrison to my smart mouth, at least prepared him for it. He managed to both ignore and respond to me, which took some doing. "Forensics works in this world, Walker. You're supposed to have some insight into another one."

I honestly didn't know which of us was more astounded that he'd be saying something like that. Billy had always been an *I want to believe* freak, but until recently, all Morrison and I had had in common was a sarcastic dismissal of all things paranormal. Truth was, my boss had come around faster than I had. Less than two months after my first encounter with the world of weird, Morrison had demanded I do what I could with the Sight to help solve a series of ritual murders. I'd kept dragging my feet for months after that, trying to make my magic go away, but the captain had chinned up and expected me to use all the talents at my disposal.

I stood there gazing at him and trying to squeeze that revelation into my rigid little world view. I'd known he was too good a cop to ignore my skills if they might be useful, but somehow I hadn't quite grasped the idea that he'd accepted my power before I had. Every smart-ass comeback I had died on my lips. "I'm sorry, boss. Everything's frozen, even what the Sight can see. I'm not some kind of mystical Indian tracker."

Morrison gave me a sharp look that I accepted with a groan. Technically, I *was* some kind of mystical Indian tracker. My dad was Cherokee, and not even I was arguing about the mystical part anymore. The only part where the description fell down was in *tracker,* which I manifestly was not. I'd proven remarkably poor at hunting down mythical bad guys—at least, poor at hunting them down as quickly as I thought I should—and had no idea if that was because my schooling was incomplete, or if I was just inept. I muttered, "Shit," and for some reason the faintest smile cracked Morrison's glower.

Billy rappelled down beside us and got out of his harness with a great deal more grace than I'd shown. He'd lost a good twenty pounds in the last couple months—dropping the baby weight, he called it; his wife had just had their fifth child—and moved more lightly for it, even though he was still taller than both Morrison and myself. "We've got to find a way to catch up with this guy faster," he said.

"Like before he kills anybody else," Morrison said, so flatly Billy and I both looked at him a moment. I'd heard Morrison's angry voice plenty of times—usually directed at me—but this wasn't outrage. It was helplessness, and that wasn't something Morrison indulged in often.

Billy recovered first, tugging his rappelling rope to let the guys at the top know he was out. The rope and harness rose into darkness as he spoke. "You know the chances are we're already too late for that, Captain. We've got at least two more missing persons reported, and we'll be damned lucky if they're still alive. But what I'm talking about is where Walker and I can help. This guy cleans up after himself. We haven't found any DNA to work with, so Forensics is at a loss, and unless we get to a body faster, Walker and I aren't much good, either. Even my resources outside the department—"

Morrison lifted his hand. "I don't want to hear about it."

Billy hesitated, glancing at me, then nodded once. "Yeah. Okay. Look, I'm sorry, Captain. Right now we're at a dead end."

I breathed, "No pun intended," and Billy gave me a dirty look. I mouthed, "Sorry," then flinched as my hip pocket began to ring. Billy glanced at his watch and arched his eyebrows, and I shrugged, taking a few steps away from my companions to wrestle my phone out. The number was unfamiliar. "Yeah, this is Joanne Walker."

"Hey, doll. Where are you?"

I pulled the phone away to give it a sideways look, though a smile threatened the corner of my mouth. There was one man on this earth who could get away with calling me *doll*. "It's pushing five in the morning, Gary. What do you mean, where am I? Where do you think I am?"

"Well, you ain't at home, 'cause I called that number twice. And you weren't sleeping, 'cause you never answer that fast when you have been, and you never sound this awake. You on a hot date, Jo?"

The threatening smile broke and I laughed. "You should be the detective, not me. No, I wish. I'm at a crime scene. Morrison called me a couple hours ago. What's up? Where are you calling from? I don't know the number."

"I'm at dispatch." For anybody else I knew, that meant the precinct building, but Gary worked part-time as a cabbie. I'd climbed into his taxi almost a year ago, and my life had quite literally never been the same since. Still smiling, I listened to him rattling on, waiting for him to reach the eventual point: "I was gonna cover for Mickey's shift 'cause his grandkids are coming in today from Tulsa, but one of the other cars just called in, Jo. He found a dead lady at Ravenna Park."

CHAPTER TWO

I snapped my fingers and gestured Morrison and Holliday over to me before Gary stopped talking. Both men creaked through the snow toward me and I echoed Gary's words, looking back and forth between my boss and my partner. "A driver at Tripoli Cabs just found a body across from my apartment building, in Ravenna Park. The guy's freaked out, says the body is still warm and it looks like it's been chewed on."

"Who the hell's calling to tell *you* th—" Morrison broke off mid-question and bared his teeth. "Muldoon. Walker, have you been spouting off about cases to your octogenarian boyfriend?"

"Septuagenarian," I said with a sniff. "Gary's only seventy-three." The *boyfriend* part didn't bear responding to. Half the people I knew were convinced I was dating a guy old enough to be my grandfather, and I'd given up arguing with them. On the other hand, being haughty about Gary's age gave me an excuse to not answer the bit about whether I'd been discussing cases with people who weren't members of the police force. Not that it mattered too much. As quiet as the department was trying to keep the killings, after six weeks of missing persons and murders, the media was starting to take notice. "Are we going, or what?"

The look Morrison gave me indicated I had in no way actually avoided the question of whether I'd been talking about the case off campus. Still, he made a sharp gesture toward the distant parking lot and got on his phone to invite the forensics team to join us. I slipped my way down the hill with Billy a few steps behind me. Five minutes later we were in his minivan, both of us hunched over the heater vents in hopes of thawing.

I caught a glimpse of Morrison's gold Avalon pulling out of the lot, and felt vaguely self-conscious that I'd had to ask Billy to pick me up. My classic Mustang, Petite, was in the shop, though even if she hadn't been, the increasingly snowy Seattle winters weren't good for her low-riding purple self.

It was a long drive back to our part of town. I watched out the window and Billy kept quiet, both of us stuck with what I bet were similar ruminations. Ravenna Park wasn't a real outdoors getaway place, not like some of the other areas we'd found bodies. It was also the first time a victim had turned up within the North Precinct boundaries. That meant we were moving back into our own jurisdiction, but it also meant any kind of pattern we might have established had been obliterated. I considered hoping it was a separate case, and then cringed at the thought. We really didn't need two cannibalistic killers.

We came down Brooklyn Avenue, a block to the west of my apartment building. Gary, leaning on the hood of his cab like a gargoyle protecting the crime scene, waved as we drove by. He was outside a police perimeter—the North Precinct building was only half a mile away, and Billy and I were far from the first cops to arrive—but didn't look like he minded at all. Billy pulled up and we got out, me shaking my head. "It's a quarter after five in the morning, Gary. You're not supposed to be hanging out at crime scenes looking like somebody gave you a Red Ryder BB gun for Christmas."

He put on a convincingly innocent expression and gestured to another cabbie, whose face looked green in the sallow amber lights as he talked with a couple of other cops. "Henley was all shook up. Thought it'd be only right to come down and give him some moral support."

"Uh-huh. Morrison's going to kill you, you know that, right?" I slipped up against the big old man and gave him a brief hug anyway. Gray-eyed, white-haired, and still sporting the linebacker build he'd had as a young man, Gary was essentially the kind of person I wanted to grow old to be. As far as I could tell, he'd never lost his sense of wonder. For a girl with shamanic potential lurking under her surface, I'd managed to thoroughly quench my own. Gary'd done his best to unquench it in the months we'd known each other, and I loved him for it.

He kissed my forehead. "Sure, darlin', but some things are worth getting killed for. Hugs from pretty girls, f'rex."

I grinned. "Did you really just say 'f'rex'? I didn't think people really said that."

"You don't think people call girls *doll,* either." He let me go with a vocally solemn, "Captain," that made no attempt at hiding the sparkle in his eyes. I turned to watch Morrison's approach and tried to judge the integrity behind his scowl. It looked pretty credible.

"Good morning, Mr. Muldoon," Morrison said with un-expected politeness. Possibly he didn't blame Gary for me telling tales about work. More likely there was some kind of strange male ritual of respect or tolerance that had been passed when they'd fought together against an army of zombies. Billy and I had been there, too, but apparently we hadn't earned the same free pass, as Morrison turned his scowl on us. "Walker, Holliday, quit screwing around and get to work."

I flicked a salute that my boss would no doubt take as sardonic, and ducked under the police tape. "Yes, sir."

Heather Fagan, the no-nonsense head of the North Precinct's forensics team, told me exactly where I was allowed to place my feet, forbade either of us to so much as breathe on the corpse, and walked away grousing about contaminated crime scenes. Billy and I exchanged rueful glances and tip-toed to the body, both teasing and completely serious in our attempts to not pollute her working area.

For once I didn't wait on Billy's conversation with a ghost, and just let the Sight filter over my normal vision. The world brightened again, night and streetlights fading to inconsequentiality. I could navigate mazes and mountain passes blindfolded, as long as I could call on the Sight: it poured its own brilliance all around me, and even its shadows were places of light.

Still-warm or not, the dead woman coiled on her side in the snow didn't have the slightest hint of color to her. Death wasn't black: it was empty, a space of nothingness surrounded by the living world. Even that was an illusion, as all the little bacteria that helped a body decompose had life of their own. But as long as I didn't look too deeply, I only saw a patch of cool gray nothing where she rested.

All around her, though, the earth was scoured with ridges of darkness. I called for a flashlight, tilting it down to illuminate the ground. Tall blades of dead grass stuck up and cast thin shadows, but there were no visible ripples in the snow to echo the lumps beneath it, nor any pressure from footsteps around her body. "Heather? How'd she get here?"

I could feel Heather's glare from fifteen feet away. "She lives in the building across the street."

Electricity shot down my spine and I jerked upward, staring first at Heather, then at the eight-story apartment building a couple hundred feet away. "*That* one?"

Heather turned to look at it. "Yeah. That's what her driver's license says, anyway. I don't think she wandered out here to die. There aren't any footprints, so somebody must have dumped her, but yeah, she died two hundred feet from her home. Her name was Karin Newcomb. University ID. I guess most of the tenants there are students."

"Most of them." My heartbeat rabbited hard enough I was surprised my voice didn't shake. "Heather, that's where *I* live."

"Jesus Christ. Did you know her?"

I shook my head even as I tried to draw some hint of recognition from her profile. "I don't remember ever seeing her, but there are forty apartments in that building. People are always moving in and out. God, how horrible." Her death hit me harder, all at once, than any of the others had. Not because I was afraid it could've been me, but because I might have known her. The fact that I hadn't was irrelevant. I found myself making a silent promise that we'd find her killer, like I'd been previously lacking motivation and only just now really meant it.

I said, "Shit," under my breath and tried to pull my thoughts back to what Heather'd been saying before ID'ing the girl to me. That was the only way I was going to keep the stupid little promise I'd just made. "How did they dump her? There's no skid marks, so she wasn't thrown out of a vehicle. She looks like she was placed here, but there aren't any footprints."

Heather stalked back to my side. With her winter hat and boots on, she came up to my eyebrow, which made her taller than most of the women I knew. "I know. It's been the same thing all over the city. No matter where we find the body, no matter how long we think it might've been there, there's no indication that anybody carried it there. She hasn't been dropped, either." A circling finger encompassed Karin Newcomb's form. "No spray of snow, and since neither rigor mortis nor the cold has set in, there should be some displacement of limbs if she had been. Instead she's nestled up perfectly. It's like—"

She bit her tongue on the last word: *magic*. "Yeah," I said, willing to go where she wasn't. "It is."

I crouched, flashlight bouncing a long oval off the snow as I examined the scene with the Sight again. Individual flakes, loosely packed, turned into a river of blue glitter under my gaze, but even then I didn't see footprints. Not in the snow, at least. The ridges beneath it, though, resolved into ten long narrow strips, five and five with a few inches of space between them. Roundish marks cupped the bases of both sets of ridges. I rocked forward in my crouch so I could feel the balls of my feet press into my insoles. Snow creaked under my boots, warning me of the impressions I was leaving behind.

Impressions that the killer hadn't left. Somehow his weight had been transferred through the delicate crystals and into the earth below. "Heather, I need to scrape away some of the snow."

To her credit, she only said, "Where?" instead of arguing with me. Up until very recently, if I'd been in her shoes, I'd have argued. Not for the first time, I gave thanks that the people around me weren't as obstreperous as I was, then gestured to the curve of the dead woman's back. There were other marks beneath the snow, but the crouched set had the most weight to them, as if they might last longer and give more information about what had left them.

Heather stepped forward, her aura a brilliant, efficient red. I put the flashlight in her hand with an apologetic grimace. "I know this is your job, but I'm afraid someone else's hands in there might contaminate what I'm seeing. If something comes up, there'll be plenty for you to examine."

Her aura leeched toward ice blue, a color that became audible in her tone, too. "*If* something comes up."

I sighed. "Yeah. I might be imagining things." It was a better answer than *it's magic*. Even if she'd heard the rumors about my predilections—and she had, or she wouldn't have bitten off her magic comment a minute ago—normal people didn't want their police work done by psychics and shamans. I suspected someone with a degree in Forensic Sciences really, truly and deeply didn't want *it's magic* as an answer for anything.

Heather exhaled sharply. I took it as permission and began brushing snow back from the frozen earth, trying not to disturb anything more than the narrow strips where I saw footprints in one level of my double vision. After a minute I scraped my way down to the ground, verifying that my eyes couldn't see what the Sight did. I breathed a curse and shook my head at Heather. "There's not going to be anything here that'll do you any good. I'm sorry."

"Then you can get out of my crime scene, Detective, and let my people get back to work."

"Yeah, in just…" I stripped my glove off and slid my hand into the hollow I'd dug. A hillock of snow collapsed over my fingers, sending cold shivering through me.

It had nothing on the black ice beneath my palm. It sucked away my body heat with a willful vengeance, like it wanted to drag me in and abandon me in the cold. I jerked back with an ingénue's gasp and coiled my other hand around my fingers. The ridges in the earth had flattened, like I'd put pressure on them. The notion that cold was all they were made of, and that my warmth had negated their chill, lingered in my thoughts.

Still cradling my hand, I pushed to my feet and turned in a slow circle, scanning the nearby earth for more of the narrow-toed footprints. Nothing: not on the ground, and not scored into any nearby trees. "It couldn't just disappear."

Morrison, a few feet away, said, *"It?"* and Heather drew herself up more stiffly.

I uncradled my hand and pinched the bridge of my nose with those fingers, half surprised they were willing to bend without shattering. "It. Him. Whatever. Billy, have you got…?"

God, how I'd changed. Billy and I usually retreated to The Missing O, a coffee and doughnut shop near the precinct building, to discuss the more unusual aspects of our cases. A few months earlier if anybody had told me I'd ask him straight out, in public, if he was getting a read on a ghost, I'd have sent some nice young men in clean white coats after them. I still wasn't quite bold enough to spell it out, but none of us—not me, not Billy, not Morrison, and probably not Heather, since Billy's fondness for the paranormal was legendary in the precinct—needed me to. We all knew what I was asking.

Billy came the long way around the body, his face tight. "Could be that she's clinging to the location she died in."

Heather made a disgruntled sound under her breath and walked away. Billy and I watched her, neither of us wanting to look at Morrison as I said, "But you don't think so."

"I don't know." My partner pulled his hand over his mouth. "I've never run into it before. Ghosts are usually tied to their physical forms, so even when the body is dumped they go with it. It could be there's some kind of trap in place to keep them where they're dying, though. Maybe…" He shot a guilty look at Morrison, who blew a breath from puffed cheeks.

"Go ahead, Holliday. Let's hear your supposition."

"That's all it is, sir. Conjecture. But this guy is eating, or at least tasting, these bodies. If it's something that feeds on human souls, then the physical desecration might be secondary to the spiritual one. It could be that chewing the bones is representative of…" He trailed off as Morrison got one of those looks that I recognized as something I usually triggered. It was one part disgust, one part disbelief and one part deliberate patience, all mixed well with resignation.

"Feeds on human souls."

I said, "We've encountered it before, Captain," in the smallest voice I possessed. Morrison turned his complicated expression on me, and it was all I could do to not dig a toe into the snow. "It's essentially what Barbara and Mark Bragg were doing, sir, under Begochidi's influence. Gathering strength by draining human lives. That's what was putting everyone to sleep in July."

Morrison looked to the sky, as if beseeching God to give him strength. I peeked at Billy, who shrugged his eyebrows, and we both came to attention as Morrison spoke again. "What I want to know," he said, "is how I've spent twenty years in the force without ever hearing a hypothesis that *it feeds on human souls* on a case before."

I didn't really get the idea he was talking to us. Besides, that wasn't what he wondered at all. What he really meant was, why was he *now* hearing that kind of hypothesis, when the world had been a sensible and straightforward place up until about a year ago.

The answer to that, of course, was me. One Joanne Walker, reluctant shaman thrust into a life that walked half a step out of pace with the normal world. Billy's talents had always helped him solve cases. They hadn't brought the truly bizarre to the fore. I was the one who fought gods and tangled with demons on the department's time. I was coming to believe that all of those things—gods, demons, witches, spirits—had always been there, slipping alongside the real world and going more or less unnoticed. Sometimes cases went unsolved, or inexplicably strange things happened in them, but it took a mirror to show most people the explanation for those incomprehensible events.

I was that mirror. Without me, last winter's ritual murders would have been just that, with no banshee's head to show as a prize. Without me, no one would have seen a thunderbird battle a serpent over Lake Washington, or gone traipsing through dream worlds to share secret moments in each other's souls. I'd come around to believing in magic, but forcing those around me to believe, too, wasn't something I liked at all.

I said, "I'm sorry," very, very quietly.

"You're saying that too often lately, Walker." Morrison shoved his hands into the pockets of his seaman's coat and hunched his shoulders before letting them fall in a show of having given up the fight. "I called you two in for a reason. I shouldn't bitch when you do what I brought you in to do. This hypothesis. Tell me how it would work."

To my dismay, Billy lifted his eyebrows at me. I was the slow kid in class, the one scrambling through years of make-up work. If either of us had an answer, it should be him.

Well, really, I *should* have one, too. I pushed my hat off and scruffed my fingers through my hair, staring at the dead woman. "If it's murder by magic, if somebody's trying to capture souls, then there's probably some kind of power circle involved." I shot a quick glance at Billy, who looked approving, and a second one at Morrison, who looked dangerously uncomprehending. "Like people would use in a horror movie," I said lamely. "A pentagram, for example, but it doesn't have to be a pentagram. You can use—"

I fumbled at my throat, flipping the thumbnail-sized pendant of my necklace above the collar of my shirt. It was a quartered cross wrapped in a circle, a symbol used by both sides of my heritage. In Ireland, it was the Celtic cross, older than Christianity's, and for the Cherokee it was the power circle, all the directions encompassed by the universe. "You can use something like this, or probably anything else that's meaningful to you. A peace symbol, maybe." My attempt at a smile was met by Morrison's steely gaze. "Anyway, you create your circle and invoke your patrons and when you're done you have a sealed area that can either keep things in or out, depending on which you set it up for." I'd participated in one fairly recently, or I'd have had no idea how to catch a wayward soul.

Morrison stared at me, or possibly at my necklace, for a long moment, then made his voice very steady. "All right. This power circle. Would it leave a mark?"

This time I got my expect-an-answer glance off first, planting it on Billy. His mouth pursed and he shook his head. "It might, but I wouldn't be able to see it. Jo—"

"I don't know if I can see residue, but I can check by

looking for Mel's. But if we have murder by magic—" I liked that phrase "—going on, then whatever mark it leaves isn't going to be anything like Melinda's. If I *can* see a shadow cast by hers, maybe I can figure out how to look for its opposite, but I can't guarantee anything."

"You have to," Morrison said. "I've got nobody else."

I breathed a laugh that wasn't. "So no pressure, then. All right. Okay. I'll try, Captain. I'll do my best."

He gave me a short nod, and I took a few steps back from the dead woman's body. Police tape rustled against my hips and I turned to duck under it.

Blinding light erupted in my vision, and from out of it came a microphone and a woman's voice: "Detective Walker. Laurie Corvallis from Channel Two News. I'm sure you remember me. What a delight to find you at the heart of another grotesque crime scene. What would you like to say to our viewers?"

CHAPTER THREE

The first eight or twelve things that sprang to mind were not answers Morrison would approve of. I squinted into the light and managed to pull up a terse smile in lieu of what I wanted to say. By the time I made out Corvallis's silhouette against the brilliance, I'd come up with something other than *chuck you, farley,* and kept my voice as pleasant as I could. "Ms. Corvallis, I don't find it at all delightful to be in the midst of a murder scene, and I think it's dismaying that you do. Beyond that, no comment. Sorry."

Truth was, I probably shouldn't have indulged in that much commentary, but at least I got the satisfaction of seeing Corvallis's lip curl like I'd made a palpable hit. I ducked out of the camera light, blinking furiously to readjust to the dark, and heard Morrison's grim, "Ms. Corvallis. What do you think you're doing here?" behind me. I turned back to watch them, glad to be out of the spotlight.

Corvallis was just a little over five feet tall and had some kind of truly American ethnic background that had graced her with epicanthic blue eyes and café latte skin to go with very straight black hair. On TV, I thought she was gorgeous. In real life, I thought she was a pain in the ass. Even so, I had to admire how she stood up to Morrison, whose ten inches in height advantage didn't seem to faze her at all. "I'm trying to report a news story, Captain. You wouldn't want the story to be about the police obstructing the media, would you?"

"I *want* to be able to notify the family before they see their daughter's death as the lead story on the morning news," Morrison snapped. "And I want you to heed the decision that came from over your head to leave this story alone until we get some kind of break on it. I understand that investigative reporting is your job," he said over her protest, and to my surprise his voice softened. "But you know enough details on this case to understand how frightened people are going to be, and that it's dangerous and disturbed enough without adding the possibility of copycat murderers."

"So you admit this morning's victim is the last in a long line of murders by the Seattle Cannibal?"

My mouth bypassed my brain and said, "You're kidding. Seattle Cannibal? There's nothing euphonious or catchy about that at all. Maybe the Seattle Slaughterer. At least that's alliterative." About halfway through the last word I tried stuffing my fist in my mouth to shut myself up, but it was far too late. Morrison and Corvallis both turned to me, and from Morrison's expression I figured I could count what was left of my detecting career in a matter of hours. Possibly minutes.

Corvallis, on the other hand, was smiling. For a pretty woman, she looked remarkably like a barracuda. "The Seattle

claw marks as anything else. I looked over my shoulder toward my apartment building, where my bed lay cold and abandoned. "It's Tuesday. I'm not even supposed to be at work today, but somehow I'm out chasing yeti at seven in the morning."

"It's a great life, innit?" Gary split a broad grin full of white teeth and I laughed despite myself.

"You have a demented sense of great. Hey! Billy!" I lifted my voice and waved as my partner ducked under the police tape. He crunched through snow turning to slush and joined us, rubbing his gloved hands together for warmth. "Morrison just gave us orders to go study Melinda's power circle, right?"

"What you really want to know is if you can use that as an excuse to get out of here before Corvallis finishes with him and he comes to tear you a new—"

"Yes," I admitted hastily. "Please. I'm trying not to think about my impending doom. Can we go?"

"You think he's going to be any less pissed if he has to wait to yell at you?"

"I think if I'm really lucky we'll come up with something and distract him from yelling." I pushed away from Gary's cab, looking between it and him. "I'd invite you along, but you're covering Mickey's shift."

"Think you can handle it without me?"

That was actually a surprisingly good question. I glanced at Billy, who shrugged his eyebrows. "Mel can pull up that power circle by herself, if that's what you need."

I turned back to Gary, knocking my shoulder against his. "Okay, so probably, if I'm just looking for residue." I sounded confident. I wished I felt half as certain. "I'll call if something comes up, okay?"

"Arright, doll." Gary lumbered into his cab and I leaned over the open door as he buckled in.

"Look, Gary, in case nobody else says it. Thank you. You caught us a break here this morning."

He gave a dismissive snort, but his eyes were bright with pleasure as he pulled the door closed and drove off. I waved after him and turned to Billy with a smile still on my face.

My partner had his own smile, smirkier than mine, though there wasn't any meanness in it. I puffed up, indignant without knowing why. "What?"

"Nothing." Billy's amusement expanded as I huffed. "I swear, nothing! You've changed a lot in the last year, that's all. Gary's good for you."

"Oh, don't you start that, too."

"Nah, that's not what I meant."

"Then what did you mean?"

"Nothing. Get in the car." Billy, grinning unrepentantly, herded me toward the minivan, and I went, muttering dire but unmeant imprecations on the way.

Tuesday, December 20, 7:42 A.M.

My pique at Billy couldn't withstand the warm fuzzy feeling I always got at seeing his sprawling house, which said *home* to me in a way nowhere I'd lived ever had. A new front porch boasted Christmas decorations and colored lights, and a plastic snowman dominated the front yard. Two much smaller actual snowmen flanked him, the larger wearing a winter hat I recognized as belonging to Billy's oldest son, Robert. He was pushing twelve, old enough to start thinking about looking cool over being cold, and I doubted the hat would be rescued before spring.

Billy's wife, Melinda, appeared on the porch in the midst of a rush of children. Most of them converged on the van, yanking the doors open hard enough to rock the whole vehicle as they spilled in with a cacophony worthy of a marching band. I picked out a demand from Clara to be brought to school and squeals of delight that I'd come to visit, followed by howls of dismay as six-year-old Jacquie realized she couldn't both visit me and go to school. It made me feel loved, and somehow made up for the ear full of jam-slathered toast courtesy of Erik, the three-year-old.

Billy did an excellent impression of a roaring bull elephant, and ten seconds later the older kids were buckled in and I was standing in the driveway with Erik on my hip and strawberry jam in my hair. Melinda minced down the steps to join me, and we all waved goodbye, though baby Caroline—not quite two months old—required her mother's assistance to do so. Billy pulled out of the driveway and I turned to Melinda, sagging in astonishment. "I honestly don't know how you do it."

Erik caroled, "With meeee!" and smeared some more jam across my face. I wrinkled my nose, trying to get the itchy, sticky stuff to retreat, and Melinda laughed aloud.

"Yes, with you. You're mama's helper, aren't you? How about Joanne puts you down and you run inside to get us all a washcloth? Look how messy Joanne is! Silly Joanie!"

"Siwwy Joanie!" Erik squirmed down my side, depositing crumbs, butter and jam as he went, and ran for the house.

Melinda looked me up and down. "I'd lend you something clean to wear while I threw those in the wash, but all of my clothes would be too small and all of Bill's would be too big."

I rubbed a bit of jam off my cheek. "It's okay. I just expect you to peel me off the walls if I get stuck to them."

"Fair enough." Melinda herded me inside the house as if I were one of her children, and I went without complaint. Erik met us in the front hall bearing a soaking wet washcloth, which his mother wrung out and applied to me with the same brutal efficiency she turned on her son a moment later. I stood there trying not to laugh, and a moment before Erik's cherubic smile came clean, she realized what she'd done and turned to me with cheeks pink from mortification.

I held on to solemnity with every ounce of my being and thrust my jam-sticky hands out for her to scrub. Melinda hit me with the washcloth, and I threw my head back and laughed. "You're the best mom ever, Mel. Woe betide any mess that gets in your way." I went to wash my hands, still laughing, and Melinda turned her ruthless washing back on her son. Half an hour later he was involved with a complex game of "pile up blocks and knock them over" in the playroom, and Melinda and I slipped into the room off it that was hers alone.

The only time I'd been in there previously, it had been a place of ritual lit by candles. It was dramatically less mystical with floor lamps turned on and light pouring in from the playroom, but the wide power circle painted on the concrete floor remained the same. A sister circle marked the ceiling, and I'd seen how power could flood between the two of them, making a column of living magic. Caroline unfolded a hand from within her sling and grasped for the upper circle, burbling with dismay when it didn't come closer. I found myself eyeing the baby, then her mother, who lifted a hand, palm out, to deny me. "She can't talk. I'm not even sure she can see as far as the circle."

"They all saw the Thing in the kitchen." "They" were Melinda's kids, and the Thing had been a terrible, enormous serpent: a monster made manifest in the Hollidays' home. It, in fact, was the reason there was a new front porch; half the house had been stretched and torn in getting the serpent out of there.

Melinda gave me a flat look. "The Thing in the kitchen was real. Anybody would've seen it."

"Robert knows when magic's being done. He says the dead make hospitals cold. And he says Clara senses things, too."

"Does that really surprise you? Given Billy? Given me?"

"Mel, the day this all stops surprising me is probably the day I wake up dead. I know Billy's a medium, and I know you see auras and know how to run a coven, but I don't know anything *about* your talent. Do you have a name for what you are?" I'd been wanting to ask for months. It'd just never seemed like the right time.

I wasn't sure now was right, either, but Melinda considered me briefly before shrugging. "Only a wise woman, maybe. A witch, a midwife. I would have been the one people came to for potions and cures in Mexico, but only because my grandmother was truly a *bruja*. She had the Sight, she had power, and she was the one who taught me to honor *la diosa,* the goddess. My mother," she added, eyebrows elevating, "was very Catholic, and hated that I was drawn from the church to follow Nana's path. My own children will not have to face that fight."

A smile crooked my lips. "What if they go back to the church?"

"That's their decision. They will not face that fight," she said again. "Not from me." She gave Caroline a finger to hold on to and waggled the baby's hand for a moment before speaking again. "I grew up watching Nana communicate with and see into a world beyond ours. She called me sensitive and taught me what she could, but that's all I am, Joanie. Sensitive. I see auras, but not to the depth you do. I can gather my energy and waken a power circle, but I can't heal. I've been part of a coven, and found it didn't suit me. My grandmother had seven children, but she lived alone after my grandfather died. Wise women in the tales often do, and let those who need them come to them. Not many people come looking, but I'm here when they do."

"I'm grateful." I cleared my throat on the words, discomfited at how they'd burst out. I was more grateful than I could say. Without people like Billy and Melinda, the past year of adapting to my burgeoning powers would have been impossible, rather than merely extraordinarily difficult. I still thought I didn't deserve them, but I was trying hard to step up so I did.

Melinda smiled, then tipped her head toward the power circle. "I awakened it after Billy called so there would be residue for you to investigate. At least, if it works that way."

"I hope it does, because I doubt whoever's out there—" I broke off, glancing out of the room toward Erik, and breathed, "eating people" before continuing in a normal voice, "I doubt they're going to light up any kind of power circle just for my benefit in finding them."

"Caroline and I will get out of your way. I'll be in the playroom with the babies if you need anything."

A smile didn't seem sufficient. I stepped over to her and squooshed both friend and baby into a hug. "I don't think it'll take long. Thanks, Mel."

"My pleasure," she said, and from the light in her aura, I knew she meant it. Inexplicably happy despite having been awakened at two in the morning to hunt cannibalistic killers, I turned my attention and the Sight on the remnants of the power circle, eager to see what could be seen.

CHAPTER FOUR

A whisper of power danced in the room, so faint with sunshine yellow and streaked orange that I wouldn't have been able to name the colors if I hadn't already associated them with Mel. They glimmered up and down like a fine sheen of waterfall mist caught between the wheels inscribed on the floor and ceiling.

More, there was a lingering sense of what she'd done to awaken the circle. The one time I'd seen her use magic, she'd been calling on a goddess in hopes of getting some questions answered. As it happened, talking with a goddess had been trumped by other events, but I could feel a hint of similar intent in the circle now. It wasn't quite the same: then, we'd come as supplicants, and what was left now was more a greeting, offering honor and admiration, and taking nothing in return.

It reminded me that I'd promised my black-winged spirit

guide that I'd do a better job of honoring and listening to it, and that I hadn't made any effort to lately. "Hey, Melinda?"

Her answering, "Yeah?" came from the playroom, followed by Erik's cheery shriek as he knocked over another pile of blocks. I smiled and put my hand up, not quite touching the shimmering curve of fading magic. "Was this a keep-things-in or a keep-things-out circle?"

"Figure it out yourself, Joanne!" She sounded rather like Erik, quite cheerful and maybe a little teasing. I raspberried her without rancor and focused on the circle again. She was right. If I was a slightly more clever shaman I'd have known it without asking. Nobody'd ever accused me of brilliance, though.

Emboldened, I touched the faint residue, trying to keep an open mind to learn what it could tell me. The open mind bit was the hard part: on one level I wanted to snort at myself for imagining thin air would give me any information at all.

The circle had been for keeping things in. Certainty exploded in me, then tumbled into bits of information that seemed to rise up rather than be the product of any conscious thought. For a few heartbeats I was Melinda, greeting my goddess with gladness and an open heart. The circle's walls were protection both for the being within and for the world without: neither was entirely meant to interact with the other in this plane. Here, in the confines of Melinda's sanctuary, there was very little chance of outside elements attacking, and so the power circle's purpose was to constrain the goddess so she wouldn't warp the world around her with her presence.

Constrain was an awkward word there, implying control. But it was the constraint of a thousand-acre wildlife preserve: the creatures inside it were free to do as they pleased, with no outside interference. Melissa didn't control her goddess, and indeed, standing there with the awareness of her power circle thrumming through me, I knew that whomever she worshipped had barely been present at all. It was, again, like the sun: it would come up and warm the earth whether someone stood to greet it or not. I was half glad and half disappointed that she hadn't had time to answer our call at Halloween. The gods I'd met had been awe-inspiring, but they'd both been men. Meeting the female of the species would've been interesting. Probably in the apocryphal Chinese curse sense of the word, but interesting.

I put a little pressure against the remaining magic, then stepped over the painted lines to enter the power circle. There was no resistance; wouldn't have been even if Melinda had been pouring strength into it. It was meant to keep things in, after all. If it was active I might not be able to get out without Mel's help, but with nothing more than a biding memory of magic in place, I thought I could come and go as I pleased. If not, Melinda would presumably rescue me as soon as I promised to babysit her horde of children so she and Billy could have a date night.

Amused, I turned to each of the four cardinal points of the circle and offered awkward bows in each direction before kneeling in its center. "I didn't bring any gifts," I said aloud, trusting that Melinda either wouldn't hear or—more likely— wouldn't think I was batshit insane for talking to an empty room. "I wasn't really planning on dropping in, but I remembered that I promised I'd do better, so I thought I should strike while the iron was hot."

I wet my lips, wondering if spirit guides worked in metaphor, then wondered what the hell else they could possibly work in. "I could use some help, if you're in the mood to provide it." It wasn't graceful, but at least it acknowledged that my guide was autonomous, which was a lot smarter than trying to make demands.

Once upon a time, not all that long ago, I'd have been deep inside the spirit realm talking to my mentor, Coyote, when I asked for help. Chances were he'd have been six kinds of useless, offering up little more than cryptic advice for me to sort out on my own. That was one of several million problems with being a shaman: they dealt with, and often were, tricksters who never gave straight answers to anything. But Coyote had died months ago, leaving me with achingly little wisdom and even less surety as to the path I was on. The closest thing I had to a saving grace—aside from Billy and Melinda and Gary, who were angels from on high as far as I was concerned—was somewhere in the heart of the spirit world, a raven had befriended me and become my guide. Billy was alive because of that bird, and I wondered if I'd ever really said thank you.

Stung by the thought, I closed my eyes and dropped my chin to my chest. The circle's power lines glowed against the back of my eyelids, much more strongly than before. Sometimes the Other was like that, easier to see when I wasn't looking in the real world. "Actually, nevermind. I can probably get through what's going on now on my own. Let me just say thanks for last time, instead. I wish I knew how to do this properly. Do spirit ravens like shiny things as much as real ones do?" I closed my fingers around my silver necklace, smiling at the idea of a raven trying to steal it. "Maybe I'll find you something else."

An approving *klok!* echoed, the big popping noise ravens made when they were interested in or scolding something. It sounded real, like it had happened in the room instead of in my head. I opened my eyes, bemused, to find a raven standing in front of me. He tilted his head and I tilted mine the same way, mirror image to a curious bird.

He was white outlines, like he'd grown up from the power lines of Melinda's circle. I could see individual feathers etched in shining light, and I could also see right through him, to the concrete and paint beneath us. He'd looked that way before, in the darkness of a spirit animal quest, but mostly when I'd seen him he'd looked like a proper raven, glossy black-blue and startlingly large with a ruff of sharp feathers at his throat. He preened, stretching one translucent wing out to its full length, then tucked it back in and peered at me.

At a loss for what else to do, I extended a hand and said, "Hello, Mister Raven," and only afterward considered the possibility that not everyone called animals "mister," or worse, that my guide might somehow be offended by the human appellation. I frequently greeted animals that way, though, and evidently he didn't mind, because he hopped forward, said *klok!* again, and nipped the sleeve of my sweater until the copper bracelet I wore was exposed.

He bit that even harder, hooked beak bouncing off beaten metal and scraping into the etched animals that encircled it. I pulled back, squelching the urge to thwap his beak. "Hey. That's mine. No eating it, even if it is shiny. I'll bring you tinsel or something, next time." What possible use a spirit raven could have for tinsel or, in fact, any tangible object, I didn't know, but at least I now had it confirmed that he liked shiny things. He went *quaarrk* and settled back, tilting his head again, so I tentatively scratched him under the beak, like he was a cat. His *quark* was softer this time and I smiled before mumbling, "So, thank you, anyway. For helping me with Billy. I couldn't have done it without you."

For a bird, he looked remarkably self-satisfied. I chuckled and rubbed his jaw harder, and he leaned into it, making little raveny sounds of contentment. I felt my own shoulders relax and only just then realized how tired I was. 2:30 A.M. wake-up calls were not my friend. I exhaled a long breath, and half-consciously watched it bead on the air like frost.

It wafted over my raven, making him sparkle briefly, and when it passed, he looked like a normal raven, gleaming black with bright eyes. He hopped into my lap and we both watched the remnants of my breath extend over the lines of Melinda's power circle. Shadows made of light shifted in the paint, then drifted up, reaching for the matching circle above me. When they touched, brilliance flared, then faded again, leaving me feeling rather safe and warm and cozy in a wreath of active power.

"Ah," I said a bit distantly. "Reached one of those altered states of being, have I? This is nicer than being hit on the head." There were dozens of ways to reach power and other worlds: sleep deprivation, drugs, unconsciousness, drumming and simple practice were among them, and so far the only one I hadn't tried was drugs. Drinking myself into oblivion and waking up with a god-infested mortal didn't count. I tipped my head to peer at my raven. "Can you talk now?"

He said, "Nevermore," then looked incredibly annoyed.

I couldn't help it: I laughed, then more carefully rubbed the top of his feathery head. "Sorry. My subconscious probably made you say that, if it's possible. What's going on?"

He made a popping sound, his own breath steaming, and all around me Melinda's sanctuary fell away.

Desolate snow and ice rose up in its place. A howling came with it, so high and sweet and sad it took a long time to under-stand it was the wind shrieking over frozen wastelands. Once

I understood, I felt it, cutting through my sweater and into my bones, making them as cold as the spaces between stars. The Bigfoot print I'd seen under the snow had felt that way when I'd touched it, so icy it was almost beyond words.

A figure appeared in the blowing wind and snow, gray in the brightness. It walked erratically, pushed by the elements, and stumbled often, as if it had very little strength to carry on. I jumped to my feet and saw a blur of wings, the raven a singular midnight-colored spot in all the white. He latched on to my shoulder, digging in with powerful talons, but the pain was a comfortable thing compared to the cold bisecting me.

A second figure, then a third, joined the first. Other shadows made silver spots in the snowstorm, too indistinct for me to be certain they weren't mere mirages. They all moved in different directions, though if I was close enough to see all of them, they had to be able to see each other. I waved a hand, shouting, and heard my own voice swallowed up by the wind. Anger burgeoned in me and I braced myself, drawing a deep breath and shouting from my diaphragm.

One of the figures hesitated, then turned a shadowy face toward me. I yelled in relief, waving madly, and it stopped where it was, then looked around as I bellowed, "Over here! Come on, over here!"

Instead, it swung around, suddenly purposeful, and strode away through the storm. I let out another yell, this time of frustration, and flung myself after it. Snow reached up and grabbed my thighs, my hips, and then gobbled me whole, ice and snow collapsing over my head.

I screamed, clawing for the surface, and the raven tightened his claws in my shoulder again. Inside a breath I was on top of the snow again, bullied by the wind and floundering with exhaustion. My compatriots were gone, leaving me alone on the ice field with only a raven as company. I ran a few feet, then fell to my knees, panting for air that was too wild to run smoothly into my lungs. "Where are we? Who are they?"

Quoth the raven, Nevermore, and this time he didn't sound irritated by it. I craned my neck, trying to see the bird on my shoulder clearly. "They're dead? This isn't the Dead Zone. And I can't see ghosts."

As soon as I said it I knew I was wrong. I *could* see ghosts, when the raven was on my shoulder. I thought it was something to do with a raven's transitory state between life and death, with its history as a beast found feasting after battles and its mythology of riding the shoulders of those who ushered the living into another world. "They're ghosts?"

Ravens didn't have lips to curl, but he did a fine job of curling his lip anyway, thereby relegating me to my usual position of being a day late and a dollar short in terms of esoteric knowledge. "If they're not ghosts and this isn't the Dead Zone—" Which it wasn't; that much, at least, I was sure of. What I referred to as the Dead Zone was a bleak nothingness about half a meter smaller than eternity. This frozen landscape had bleak written all over it, but it also had the personality of a storm. The Dead Zone had no such thing. "—then where are we?"

The raven dumped me unceremoniously back into Melinda's power circle.

I had not been lying on my back when I went under. I was now, and out of the corner of my eye I could see Melinda in the doorway, Caroline in her arms and a curious expression on both faces. With Caroline, it probably meant gas. With Mel, it probably meant she was trying really hard not to ask why I was flat on my back in the middle of her sanctuary. "Do you have any spirit animals, Mel?"

She, after a moment's hesitation, said, "Yes…."

I fluttered a hand in reassurance. "Don't worry, I'm not rude enough to ask what they are. Just, do they ever effectively coldcock you and leave you sprawled on the floor?"

The corner of her mouth quirked. "I'm afraid not."

"I didn't think so. I don't get no respect." The raven was no longer visible, though I could feel his weight on my chest, like he was staring at me. Waiting for me to get my act together, presumably. "I think I jump-started your power circle. Sorry."

"It's okay. You shouldn't have been able to, but it's okay."

"Really?" I pushed up on my elbows. Light still glimmered around the edges of the circle, stronger than the residuals Melinda'd left for me to study. I suddenly got the idea she was outside it because she wasn't allowed in, which wasn't good on two levels. One, it was her circle, so it seemed like she should be able to breeze right through anything I did. Two, and possibly more important, I didn't know how to take it down. It felt nothing like the healing power I'd become reasonably competent at drawing on; that came from within, and the circle's power seemed to be outside of me. Its strength had come from somewhere else. The raven, maybe. I squinted the Sight on to give him a hard look, but the little bastard disappeared and left me to deal with my own problems. "Really on both counts? It's really okay, and I shouldn't have been able to?"

"Really on both counts. If I didn't like you, it wouldn't be okay at all, but if I didn't like you, I think you probably wouldn't have been able to. I hope." Melinda frowned, giving me the uncomfortable sensation that I was out of her league, magically speaking. I mean, I knew I was, according to what she and Billy kept telling me, but knowing it and feeling it were two different things.

"We'll go with me not being able to. I'm not even sure I opened this one. Did you see a, um, bird on my chest?" I didn't want to define my spirit guide as a raven any more than Mel wanted to confess to her own totem animals. It was irrational, but I felt strongly about it, and Mel didn't look surprised as she shook her head.

I whooshed air out and put my head on my knees for a moment. Memory crept over me and I peeked up again, the Sight in place once more.

Breath only showed up in cold air, and Melinda's sanctuary was nice and warm. But I still saw the particles of my exhalation dance across the power lines, shaking down the magic that had grown up. I stared at it, flabbergasted. The only other time I'd opened a power circle, it'd been with a blood sacrifice— not, in the grand scheme of things, the best way to go. It struck me that the breath in my lungs was just as important a component of what kept me alive, and, as far as offerings went, seemed pretty profound. "I think you've got to teach me how to deliberately awaken a power circle, Mel." Before I did something critically stupid and woke up dead from attempting it someday. My raven guide probably wouldn't have let that happen just now, but I didn't like to think what could've happened if I hadn't already entreated him.

It also struck me that breath was, in its way, incidental. Once it left the body, it became part of the air again, always in transition. That might have accounted for the disconnect I felt with the magic powering the circle.

I suspected that on a fundamental level, what I'd just accidentally done was extremely dangerous. I scrambled up out of the circle and did my best to hide behind Melinda, who was at least seven inches shorter than I was. "Soon," I added. "Maybe now would be good."

"Not unless you've got a babysitter in your pocket. The kids would be too much distraction."

I felt my pocket. "I have a cell phone. That's almost as good."

Melinda laughed. "Cell phones are notoriously bad at watching three-year-olds. They have no defense system."

"But Gary does! Maybe I can get him to come over when he gets off shift." I pulled the phone out and it rang, surprising me enough that I nearly dropped it. Caroline giggled and waved her hands, apparently delighted by my antics. I gave her a finger to hold and, charmed by her smile, picked up the call without looking to see who it was.

"Walker," Morrison said tightly. "Get to the morgue as fast as you can. Something's happening to the bodies."

CHAPTER FIVE

Charlie Groleski had shriveled into a husk.

If I hadn't known better, I'd have thought he was an ice-age corpse, the kind that occasionally turns up in glaciers. His skin had that same dried brown leathery look to it, with his hair matted and stringy by turns, and his fingers clawed as if great age had withered them to nubs. He had a faint odor of decay, the smell of something so long dead that it's given up stinking and is just a few hours away from collapsing into nothing. Part of me wanted to give him a prod and see if he would fall in on himself and become nothing more than a dust shadow on the cold morgue slab.

I resisted, based on the certainty that it wouldn't win me any friends, but I really wanted to. Billy, as if suspecting the direction of my thoughts, edged between me and Groleski's body, and pointed toward Karin Newcomb's.

I'd been avoiding looking at her, a little afraid I might recognize her after all. I didn't; either we'd never crossed paths in the months we'd lived in the same apartment building, or she'd become one of a blur of college-aged brunettes who'd lived there in the seven years I had. Either way, she deserved better. Whether she deserved better of the world at large, or me in specific, though, I wasn't sure.

Unlike Groleski, she hadn't had time to freeze, but like him, she was falling in on herself. Taken together, they looked like separate stages of a horror film special effect, with Groleski the advanced decomposition. "Know what it reminds me of?"

Billy gave me a pained look. "If you make a joke, Walker…"

"No, I'm being serious." I crouched, studying Karin Newcomb's deteriorating form. "They're falling apart the same way Ida and the girls did, but more slowly. Like they weren't just frozen, but they were being held together with magic, too."

"Huh." Billy put his arms akimbo and stared down at the dead people like he was trying to find fault in my comparison. Apparently he didn't find any, because after a moment he said, "Think we've got another banshee on our hands?"

"I love how you say that like it's normal." I glanced up, looking for rubber gloves, and waved at the box when I found it. Billy handed me one and I did my best proctologist's snap putting it on, then risked poking a finger into the dead woman's ribs. The flesh dented like an ancient Peeps, with a soft rain of marshmallow cascading over my fingertip. Only it wasn't marshmallow. I withdrew my hand and stared into the hole I'd made. It didn't look like something that could happen to a human body. "Billy, those women who died back in March…did anybody notice anything like this happening to their bodies?"

I stood up, not wanting to look into the dried-marshmallow effect in Karin's ribs any longer, and caught Billy's quick shake of his head. "They'd all been eviscerated. Cause of death was pretty obvious. And they all had ID on them, so I think the bodies were released to the families pretty fast. I don't remember anything like this. I guess we could get a court order to have them exhumed, if you think we need to."

A shudder made hairs rise on my arms. "Let's not unless we're sure we have to. How about our other victims, has this been happening to them?"

He shook his head again. I stripped the rubber glove off and pushed my fingers through my hair. "What's the date?"

"December twentieth, why?"

I'd known that. I'd known it very clearly, because tomorrow was the first anniversary of my mother's death. I'd only asked in order to buy time. Sadly, the second and a half it took Billy to answer wasn't nearly as much as I'd hoped to buy, and it didn't give me any way out of proposing a supernatural hypothesis. "Tomorrow's the solstice. These things tend to get stronger around the pagan high holy days."

Pagan high holy days. Like half of them—more than half—weren't marked in some way by the modern world and practitioners of most modern religions. Easter fell suspiciously close to the spring fertility festival of Beltane, midsummer meant a weekend of partying while the sun didn't go down, and I didn't think there was much of anybody fooling themselves about Christmas lying cheek-by-jowl with the midwinter solstice. Mardi Gras, Halloween—they were all tied in with ancient holy days, even if we didn't always consciously draw the lines between them. I snorted at myself and shook it off; it didn't really matter who celebrated them or what they were called. The point was, certain times of the year had natural mystic punch, and we were on the edge of one of those days today. That didn't exactly comfort me.

Neither did the fact that banshees seemed inclined to swarm during the holy days. Twice this year I'd faced them, and I was in no particular hurry to go up against one again. They worked for a much bigger bad, a thing they called the Master. I only knew a handful of things about him, but none of them was good.

No, that wasn't true. One of them was good: as far as I could tell, he wasn't corporeal. No killer demon walking the earth. That was a win, and I'd learned to be grateful for small favors.

Everything else about him, though, scared the crap out of me. I knew he found me amusing, and it was my general opinion that being found amusing by alarmingly powerful entities was not something to be sought. I also knew that ritual murders, carried out by his banshee minions, fed him enough strength to keep an eye on the world. I knew he could come a hair's breadth from killing a god, and I knew the only reason I wasn't already dead was my mother had sacrificed herself to keep me alive.

I very much didn't want Charlie Groleski's and Karin Newcomb's shriveling forms to be the work of banshees, because that meant the Master was stirring, and I'd already pissed him off twice this year. Unfortunately for me, that's what experience suggested we were looking at.

"Joanne?" Billy put his hand on my shoulder, startling me out of my grim examination of the bodies. "You okay, Walker?"

"Are the bodies exsanguinated?"

My partner gave me a look usually reserved for his kids mouthing off. "You know they aren't. You just wanted an excuse to use 'exsanguinate' in conversation."

I flashed him a guilty little smile that turned back into a frown. "Yeah, but maybe it's good that they're not, since the winter moon murders were all pretty much drained of blood. Even if it's banshees again, this is different."

"If it's banshees again I'd rather it was the same, so we'd have a pattern to follow. Holy shit!" Billy levitated about four feet back, with me right beside him, as Groleski's body *fwoomped* into a much smaller mass. Dust rose up, lingering in the air, and Billy all but vaulted another slab to snatch up medical masks. He tossed one to me and put one on, eyes bugged above its white line. "What the hell was that? Where's the doctor?"

"Here, Detective." A red-haired woman wearing medical glasses over her own mask swept in, hurrying but not alarmed. "You did ask me to step outside."

We had, because although Sandra Reynolds had been the coroner on this case for the past six weeks, neither Billy nor I had wanted to stand around discussing things like banshees in front of her. She'd been watching through the window of the observer's room, the place where families were most often taken to identify the bodies of their loved ones. It wasn't soundproofed, but with the door closed it was unlikely she'd have overheard us running through mystical answers to our murders. Magic didn't seem like her thing. She picked up a slim metal rod and bent over Groleski's deflating body, dust poofing up to mar her safety glasses. I felt a shock of relief she was wearing them. I had no reason to think the particles were dangerous, but then, I didn't have a reason not to think so, either.

Groleski flattened a little more as she edged the rod through his remains. I was glad I hadn't poked him after all. The guilt of making him collapse like that would've kept me awake for days. Reynolds muttered, "This is fascinating," in a tone that suggested that it was genuinely fascinating, and also a pain in the ass. "None of the other bodies have shown this kind of exsanguination."

I shot a triumphant look at Billy, who rolled his eyes as the doctor continued, "It's not just blood loss. A thawing body should be—" she glanced at us and clearly decided to go for a non-technical term "—squishy. I have no explanation for the rapid decay into dust." Apparently quite happy, she scraped a pile of Charlie's remains into a test tube and stoppered it. "I'm going to have to take a look at this."

"So," I said much more quietly, "am I."

I hadn't been using the Sight, mostly because it'd shown me nothing useful when we'd come across the bodies in the first place. I let it slip over my vision now, and watched a trail of red and yellow sparks follow Dr. Reynolds out of the morgue. I'd heard guys on the force call her a spitfire, and thought her aura colors reinforced that.

To my dismay, hers was the only aura I got a read on. There were no hints of dark magic clinging to the disintegrating bodies. They just looked dead. I glanced at Billy just to make sure my mojo was working, and got a reassuring flare of his orange and fuchsia colors. Well, reassuring in that I wasn't defective. Less reassuring in that I was still batting zero in the paranormal detecting ballpark. "Morrison's not going to like this."

Worry sharpened Billy's voice: "Not going to like *what*? What do you see?"

"Nothing." I leaned against the nearest non-body-carrying slab and pulled my mask down. "You don't need that thing. There's nothing more dangerous there than any long-dead body might be carrying."

Billy tugged his own mask down. "Like bubonic plague, you mean?"

I snorted, waving him off. "They're not that long dead. And besides, aren't most of the annual cases of plague in this country in, like, Arizona? No, what Morrison's not going to like is I'm still not getting anything. If they weren't falling apart like rotting…" I couldn't think of anything that fell apart like they were doing, and finished, "…corpses," lamely. "Anyway, I'd just think it was natural if it wasn't happening so fast. I don't like to go back to the captain with nothing."

"None of us do."

"Yeah, but…" There was nothing to say after that, because the sentence would end "but you don't have a crush on him," if I was being flippant, and with the same sentiment expressed in weightier terms if I was being brave. I wasn't brave. Or flippant, for that matter, because even though it was an embarrassingly open secret, I wasn't actually in the habit of going around admitting I'd sort of fallen for my captain. I didn't even like admitting it to myself.

Billy, who was a better man than I, said, "So how do we find something to go to him with?" instead of taking the opportunity to razz me.

"I have two ideas. Do you want to hear the one you'll be okay with or the one you'll hate first?"

He stared at me. "If I say the one I'm okay with, is there any chance I won't have to hear the one I'll hate?"

I held my fingers an inch apart. "A little one."

"Let's go with that, then." He folded his arms across his chest and glowered at me, which would have been thoroughly intimidating if I was one of his children.

"Okay. We go talk to your friend Sonata and see if she's in

tune enough with the dead to get a rise out of any of our murder victims. We also find out if she knows anybody who can diagnose a decomposition like this one, because it's obviously not natural. Then we go to Morrison with whatever we've learned."

"This is the better idea? Share case details with someone outside the force? How much will I not like the other one?"

"A lot." I tilted my head toward the door. "So shall we go talk to Sonny?"

Sonata Smith outclassed Billy by a mile in the rank of speaks-with-the-dead. She was in her sixties and lived in a gorgeous old Victorian up on Capitol Hill, exactly the kind of house I'd imagine a medium lived in. That, though, was the end of where she conceded to meet my expectations. Her séance partner was a surfer-boy-looking former theology student in his early thirties, and she liked wearing violent comic book T-shirts, neither of which seemed very peaceable and medium-like to me. On the other hand, Billy was a six-foot-two police detective with a fondness for yellow sundresses, so I should've known better than to try to lay expectations on what constituted typical behavior for a medium. Or anybody else, probably.

Either way, Sonny was one of the relatively few Magic Seattle people I knew, and pretty much the only one I trusted besides Billy and Melinda. Left to my own devices, I'd managed to meet up with entirely the wrong crowd, so I was happy to lean on Billy's expertise instead of my own shaky judgment.

We'd called ahead, but Sonny still pursed her lips as if we were unexpected when she answered the door. After a moment she rearranged the expression into a smile and said, "William,

Joanne, come in," and stepped aside. We got about two steps past the threshold before she said, "I take it this is about the murders. Can I get you some tea?"

Billy and I exchanged looks, and I put on a patently fakey smile. "At least Morrison can't be pissed if everybody's already talking about them, right?"

"Not everyone," Sonata said. "Just that awful woman on Channel Two. She broke the story this morning. The Seattle Slaughterer, they're calling him."

I winced from the bottom of my soul all the way out. Billy groaned. "Tea would be great, Sonny. Green tea is supposed to be good for you, right? Would enough of it make somebody invulnerable? Because Joanie's going to need it." He followed Sonata into the kitchen, and I trailed along behind, wondering how many different ways Morrison was going to kill me. I'd gotten up to four highly creative ways to die before Sonata got us seated at the table and put a kettle on to boil.

"I'm afraid not," she said. "I don't know of anything that's that good for you."

Billy, more cheerfully than I thought was appropriate, said, "You're dead," to me.

I dropped my forehead to the table and said, "Maybe not," words muffled by the shining wood. It smelled faintly of lemon Pledge, old and familiar. "Neither of us can pick up anything at all from the bodies we're finding, Sonny. Even the one this morning didn't have a ghost lingering, and she was freshly dead. I was thinking maybe if you gave it a shot, or if you knew somebody who could…" I peeked up, trying for convincing puppy-dog eyes.

Sonata looked unmoved, not even blinking when the kettle

suddenly whistled. She let it go on, piercing the air, and finally shook her head. "I know who should be able to help."

I sat up, hope surging in my chest as Sonata went to take the kettle off. "Who?"

She turned her profile to me, concern thinning her lips. "Joanne, it should be you."

CHAPTER SIX

The kettle's whistle faded into a rush of staticky background noise that lingered underneath, then swallowed, Sonata's words. I was vaguely aware of Billy's grimace, but mostly I was paying attention to the hiss between my ears and the abiding feeling that I should have expected Sonata to say something like that.

Three or four thousand self-directed recriminations lined up to pile themselves on me. If I hadn't done this, if I'd only done that—I had a list of mistakes longer than my arm. It was all too easy to believe that by foundering around as I'd done the past year, I'd missed the mark on where I was supposed to be standing. Back in January, when everything had started and I'd been burning with power released after years of imprisonment, there'd been one brief and kind of glorious moment when I'd believed I could save, or heal or protect the whole city of Seattle. I'd lost most of that confidence while struggling to learn about my talents, but apparently I hadn't lost the sensation that I *should* be able to do something like that. That I should, in essence, be so much better than I was.

Memory caught me in the gut, a visceral recollection of an alternate timeline I'd briefly been given viewing access to. There'd been a woman a lot like me in that other world, only she had her shit together. She had a life, a family, friends and she would have known how to hunt down whoever was killing and snacking on Seattleites. For a moment I ached with the regret of not being her.

But—and this was the crux, and always would be—she had never chosen to come live in Seattle. Whatever battles she had to fight, they were somewhere else, with someone else. This was the path I was on, and if I'd screwed up, well, that was life. I was finally starting to wrap my mind around the idea of making things better in the future instead of beating myself up for things that had gone wrong in the past. Maybe it wasn't much, but it had to be enough.

I spread my fingers wide on the shining kitchen table, and made my voice louder than the blood rushing in my ears. The moment of believing I could protect Seattle came back to me, but like through a fun-house mirror: it was a little too far away, a little too distant to feel real. "You're probably right. It probably should be me. Here's the thing, though, Sonny. I hardly even know what that means. Can you..." I got up, suddenly unable to hold still, and stalked across the kitchen, trying not to look at either Billy or Sonata.

"Can you tell me what's missing? What...what I should be? God, what a stupid question. It's just that I'm so far behind the curve I can't even see it. I don't know what's *wrong,* much less how to fix it. If I can understand..." I spread my hands again, this time against the air, and made myself meet the others' eyes. "Some hero I am, but right now I don't have any idea where to start."

Tension turned to uncomfortable sympathy in Sonata's gaze. "For what it's worth, Joanne, it wasn't until I met you that I began to understand, myself. William...?"

Billy shook his head. "I'm not part of the scene like you are, Sonny, you know that. For me it's mostly what I can do through the job. You're my one real contact with the world."

"Why is that?" I interrupted, genuinely surprised. "You're like a true believer, Billy. Why aren't you neck-deep in it?"

"Mostly because of Brad."

"Oh." I wished I hadn't asked. Doctor Bradley Holliday was Billy's older brother. They'd had a sister, too, Caroline, who'd been between them in age, but she'd drowned in an accident when she was eleven. Her bond with Billy had kept her ghost at his side for thirty years, and that had driven a wedge between the brothers. I wasn't certain whether it was envy or anger or some combination thereof, but Brad had never taken to the paranormal the way Billy had. It'd never occurred to me that maybe Billy hadn't embraced it as much as he'd have liked, in order to keep a degree of peace in the family.

Or maybe he'd embraced it just as much as he needed to. I knew he and Melinda had met at a conference about the paranormal. Fifteen years and five kids later it didn't look, from the outside, like he was missing too much.

"We had a disaster last year," Sonata said quietly. "Within the community, at least, it was a disaster. This city had a number of genuinely powerful protectors, Joanne. Shamans, mostly. People who mitigated the world's effects, both meteorological and anthropological." A brief sad smile turned one corner of her mouth. "They were one of the reasons Seattle had a reputation as a good place to live."

A space in my belly turned hollow and worried. "They all died, right? Hester and Jackson and…"

Pure surprise wiped Sonata's sorrow away. "That's right. You knew them? Roger and Adina and Sam?"

I sat again, suddenly weary. "I met them. I met them after they died." They, as much as Coyote, had set me on a shaman's path.

Sonata, who communed with the dead, didn't even blink at that confession. Instead she said, "A few others left, after the murders. They were afraid, and that fear poisoned their ability to help the city, so maybe it was the right choice. But it left Seattle vulnerable. I thought we would have to simply work it out, that we'd eventually draw new talent back to us. But then I met you."

"And you realized the new talent was here in a shiny incompetent package."

Sonata pursed her lips. "I wouldn't have put it that way. You're not incompetent, merely…"

"Uneducated." Really, not even I thought I was genuinely incompetent, not anymore. When push came to shove I had so far managed to get the job done, so I probably wasn't actually incompetent. Inept, inexperienced, ill-equipped, yes, but those all had a little less sting than incompetency. "How can you tell I'm supposed to be the one who steps up? How can you tell I'm worth half a dozen other shamans?"

"You single-handedly destroyed the black cauldron."

I wet my lips and caught Billy's gaze. "That wasn't technically me."

To my surprise, he shook his head. "Sonata's right, Joanie.

That was pretty close to impossible. The cauldron was hundreds, maybe thousands, of years old, and imbued with enough magic that it essentially had a life of its own. You know what getting near it felt like."

I did. It was seductive, calling me home to a promise of rest and peace. Not even gods were immune to its song. But I clung to a stubborn thread of denial. "Billy, I didn't destroy it. You know that."

"I know that over the cauldron's whole history there are stories of people trying to break it. In all that time, you were the only one who pulled all the right elements to her so that it could be shattered. It wasn't your sacrifice, but I think it was your presence as a nexus that made it possible."

I wailed, "But what if I'd moved to Chattanooga?" and they both looked at me before Sonata laughed.

"Then perhaps the cauldron would have gone to Chattanooga. You'll drive yourself crazy if you start wondering down those lines, Joanne. We can't know what might have been."

I thought of the alternate self whose life I'd seen glimpses of, and clamped my mouth shut on an *I can*. It hadn't, after all, been my talent that let me see a dozen different timelines. "Okay. One more stupid question, and then I promise to go…" *Save the world* seemed a little melodramatic, so I went with "stop the killer," and added, "somehow," under my breath.

Out loud, I said, "Does every city have a group of shamans like Seattle did? People who try to protect the place?"

"Many do. There are…" Sonata sighed and went back to the counter, brewing the tea that had been abandoned. "There are both more and fewer shamans, or adepts of any kind, than there have ever been, Joanne. More, because there are more people than ever before. Fewer, because…"

"Because there are more people than ever before." I mooshed a hand over my face. "Five hundred years ago there'd have been a shaman in every tribe, maybe. One person for a few hundred, maybe a few thousand, individuals. Now there're billions of people, and any given shaman has tens of thousands to tend to. Right?"

"In essence."

I blew a raspberry. "Why aren't there more...adepts?" I liked that word better than "magic users", probably because people could be adept at lots of things and I could at least pretend I wasn't talking about the impossible as if it were ordinary. The whole train of thought led me to snort at my own question before anyone had time to answer. "Like Joanne the Unbeliever has to ask."

"It's partly an artifact of the era," Sonata agreed, then glanced at Billy, who looked uncomfortable. I sat up straighter, ping-ponging my gaze between them, and Sonata sighed again. "The last twelve months have been hard on the magic world, Joanne. More of us have died than usual. It's like a catalyst was set."

Oh, God. I said, "Was that catalyst me?" in a small voice, and to my undying relief, Sonata's frown turned into a quick shake of her head.

"I don't think so. I could be wrong," she amended hastily, "but you strike me as the response, Joanne. When I look at you I see the answer to, not the start of, the troubles."

The hollow place in my belly came back. My brain disengaged from my mouth and went distant, surprised to hear the question I voiced: "Do you know an Irish woman called Sheila MacNamarra?"

Sonata's eyebrows went up. "Should I?"

"I don't know. She was an…adept. As far as I can tell, she spent her whole life fighting—" I broke off, looking for a less dramatic phrase than what leaped to mind, then shrugged and used it anyway. "Fighting the forces of darkness. She went up against the Master, the one who created the cauldron. More than once, even. I think that was sort of what she…did."

Recognition woke in Sonata's eyes. "The Irish mage. I know of her. I didn't know her name."

My heart leaped and a fist closed around it all at once, sending a painful jolt through my chest. "You've heard of her? What do you know about her?"

Because what I knew about Sheila MacNamarra was embarrassingly limited. She liked Altoids; that was almost the sum total of what I'd learned about her in four months of traveling at her side. It was only after she died that I discovered she was an adept of no small talent, and that she'd spent her life fighting against—to put it extravagantly but accurately—the forces of darkness.

It was only after she died that I learned how far she'd gone to protect me.

Sonata was nodding. "I know of her as a power, yes. We don't use names often, Joanne. You should know that by now. And mages are by their nature reclusive. As far as I know, no one's seen the Irish mage outside of her homeland in decades. I've never even heard of anyone going to study with her, which is a little unusual. I don't know if she has any protégés."

"One," I said. "In a manner of speaking."

It would have taken a dolt to miss the implications, and while Sonata was a bit of a long-haired hippy freak, she was by no means stupid. She sharpened her gaze on me, eyebrows shooting up again, this time making a question all of their own.

"She was my mother," I said tiredly, "and she died a year ago tomorrow."

I didn't typically think of myself as an emotional lightweight. I didn't tear up at Hallmark commercials, although extreme vehicle makeover shows could get me. I had a secret stash of romance novels that didn't fit my girl-mechanic image, but even when they got angsty I didn't sniffle over them. I had not, in fact, cried when my mother died. I'd barely known her, and I hadn't liked her very much. But for some reason my throat got painfully tight and my nose stuffed up as I made my announcement.

Billy and Sonata were conspicuously silent, for which I was grateful. After a couple deep breaths I regained enough equilibrium to say, "She gave me to my dad when I was just a baby, because she had to keep fighting the Master." That was so inaccurate as to be an outright lie, but I didn't feel like getting into the complex time-slip that had happened both nine months and almost thirty years ago in my personal timeline. "Would her death be enough to start messing up the balance? Was she that big a gun?"

Sonata's eyes were dark. "What's your calling, Joanne? What are you, in adept terms? What are we?"

"Me? I'm a shaman. You two are mediums. Melinda's, I don't know, a witch or something. Why?"

"And what do you suppose a mage is?"

"I don't know. It's a wizard. A sorc…" Except *sorcerer,* in my experience, connoted *bad guy,* and I was pretty damned sure Sheila MacNamarra hadn't been a bad guy. I fell silent, staring at Sonata and working through the rankings I was aware of.

Mage didn't fit anywhere on the scale. It suggested major mojo, skills on a level that beggared the rest of us. Which, from what little I'd seen, summed up my mother nicely. I said, "Phenomenal cosmic powers?" in a small voice.

Sonata nodded. "If she's dead, then our side has lost a great warrior."

I snorted loudly enough to make my ears pop. "Our side? So far I haven't seen a lot of us versus them, Sonata. I've mostly seen badly screwed-up people in need of help." Where "people" sometimes meant "gods of unimaginable power," but who was counting?

"And yet you just said your mother spent her life engaged in battle against this 'Master.' Is he not the other side?"

Anybody who commanded banshees—or anything else—to ritual murder in order to feed on the blood and souls of the dead was, I had to admit, pretty much inherently on the other side of where I stood. "All right, point taken. So her death could've been the catalyst. Or a catalyst." I didn't like the idea of that much hanging on my mother's life.

She probably hadn't liked the idea, either.

I put my face in my hands. "Basically what you're telling me is that never mind the cannibal, I have much larger problems looming. Only I can't never mind the cannibal, so I'm just going to have to figure out a way to make it all work. Which is what I've been doing all along."

God, I missed Coyote. He was only moderately helpful, mostly by way of kicking me in the ass until I did, in fact, figure it out myself, but having him there to kick my ass would have made me feel a lot better. I exhaled into my palms, then looked up at Billy. "Okay. Sonata was the likable idea. Now for the one you're going to hate."

He sighed. "All right. What do I hate?"

I put on what I hoped was a convincing, cheerful smile. "I'm going to use myself as bait."

CHAPTER SEVEN

Billy said, "Excuse us," and hustled me out of Sonata's house so fast it could have been magic. I warded off his outrage with raised palms, or tried to, and opted to explain rather than wait for him to stop telling me what a bad idea it was.

It wasn't that I thought it was a particularly great idea myself. It was just better than setting somebody else out as bait, which argument didn't slow Billy down at all. "Look, I'm going to head up to the Space Needle and have a look around the city first," I said in my best reasonable tone. "I'll see if I can pull up any residue like I saw from Melinda's circle—"

That, at least, got his attention. "You saw something? Why the hell didn't you say so earlier?"

"Because I took a cab from your house to the coroner's instead of you picking me up, and I forgot while we were examining decomposing bodies and talking to mediums, okay?

I'm sorry." Billy had the grace to look apologetic, and I charged onward. "Anyway, yes, I saw residue from Mel's circle, so I thought I could at least try picking up someone else's. If we're lucky it'll turn out there's some lunatic controlling a…" I had no idea what, really. A cannibal, clearly, but beyond that I didn't know. "A flesh-eating monster. And then we can bag the guy and be done."

Billy gave me a look that said *when have we ever been lucky?* and I shrugged it off. "And if that doesn't work, then I'll try the bait thing."

"Need I point out that this thing is going after outdoorsy types, which you're not?"

It was true. I was more the grease monkey type. I said, "Still," like I'd presented that comment aloud, then leaned heavily on the hood of his minivan. "Ravenna Park isn't exactly a great outdoors kind of landscape, either, Billy."

"You know, I'm pretty sure I hate where this is going, too."

"She was found in Ravenna Park. She lived in my apartment building. What if—"

"I seriously doubt it."

A tiny rush of relieved laughter escaped me. "You didn't let me finish."

"You were going to say, what if this thing that eats souls was after you. What if it's circling around to you, and Karin Newcomb just got in the way. Joanne, do you know any of the others who died? Is there any kind of connection at all?"

"No…." Even I knew the apartment building connection was tenuous, but my life had been one unpleasant coincidence after another all year long. Stranger things could, and had, happened.

"Then don't do that to yourself. This is bad enough as it is."

"On the other hand, if it's not coincidence," which I really wanted it to be, "I'd make good bait. So unless you've got a better idea, let's try scoping out the city from the Needle, and then…" I shrugged. "Then we'll see."

Billy ground his teeth, got in the minivan, and drove us to the Space Needle. Normally he might've proposed we do something crazy like actual detective work, but there were about a hundred cops on the cannibal case and so far no one had gotten a break. Every crime scene had been utterly bereft of DNA evidence. We hadn't been able to pinpoint an area the killer might be in, because the victims were from all over the city. In my grumpier moments I suspected our cannibal had watched too many crime shows and knew better than to hunt in a six-block radius around his home. Or a six-mile radius, for that matter.

The total lack of DNA was part of why Morrison had called Billy and me in. It wasn't like chewed meat could be licked clean, and there were streaks of blood *on* the bodies, if not puddles under them, which suggested they hadn't been thoroughly washed before being dumped. But even if they had been washed, even in the unlikely event that someone could scrub every last bit of their own genetic markers out of the body they'd just snacked on, that would've left residue, too. The absolute nothing was impossible, and impossible was supposed to be our department.

Billy, who would've scolded me for doing the same thing, came down Broad Street, parked the van in a taxi zone about a hundred feet from the Needle's foot and hung a police vehicle tag in it. We waved our badges at security and hopped the "only going to the restaurant, don't need the tour guide" elevator to the fiftieth floor. It wasn't as much fun, but it was faster.

The police badges also meant we didn't have to buy the

restaurant's overpriced lunch, although my stomach rumbled when the scent of food hit my nostrils. "Think we can expense it to the department?"

"I'm writing off filling up the minivan's tank. Might as well try expensing filling up mine." We got a table at the room's outer edge and ordered lunch while I turned the Sight on the city.

It looked healthier than it had the last time I'd done this. Then there'd been a malaise spreading over Seattle, one that eventually awakened the dead. Today there was nothing so appalling, and, as the room turned and I drifted through the surreal, brilliant colors of the shamanic world, I thought there were worse ways to spend a lunch hour. Maybe I could come up here once a week to make sure all was well, though the pragmatic part of me suggested I'd better get an annual pass if I wanted to do that. They'd probably notice if I kept dropping by and cheating my way in with a police badge.

Billy, diffidently, asked, "Getting anything?"

I shook off my musings enough to answer. Our seats had rotated far enough to the north that I could now see down Aurora Avenue. Billy's house, off to the west, lit up with the remains of the circle Melinda'd drawn for me. I glanced farther east, toward Lake Washington, and caught a glimmer of brightness at the corner of my eye. "Nothing I don't recognize. I can see your house, but it's almost straight on to us now. I might need line of sight to really pick things up."

"You didn't with the cauldron."

"The cauldron was spilling gook all over the city," I said irritably. "I've never tried looking for the remnants of somebody's power before. I can see a glimmer over at Matthews Beach, but I—oh. I guess I don't have to wait for the restaurant to turn that far before I get a straight look at it, huh?" Embarrassed, I got up and walked around the restaurant until I could see the lake.

Matthews Beach was where the thunderbird had fallen six months ago, and where my prize idiocy had torn the landscape into a new shape. There was a waterfall there now, and almost no one in Seattle remembered how it got its name. Some of those who did, though—people who belonged, like it or not, to Magic Seattle, like me and Billy—came together there daily, greeting the sunrise, waking the world and generally pouring goodwill and power into a place they saw as mystically significant.

The result was a glow that beggared the light from the Holliday's home. It was like a miniature nuclear warhead had gone off, that much purity of white. I rubbed one eye and went back to the table. "I can definitely see power spots if I'm looking for them. Thunderbird Falls is brimming over. It kind of makes me wonder how things can get out of kilter here, if there's that much basically positive energy being poured out."

"Watched the news lately?"

I sagged and didn't even perk up when the waitress brought my onion-and-cheese-tart appetizer. Hey, if I was expensing the meal, I figured I should enjoy it. And if I wasn't able to expense it, I'd *definitely* better enjoy it. "Yeah. It's all Laurie Corvallis, Talking Head, Spreading the Bad Word. Why doesn't anybody ever report on the good stuff?"

"Disaster's good for the oligarchy. Ha," Billy said to my goggle-eyes. "Fair's fair. You pull out 'exsanguinate,' I pull out 'oligarchy.'"

"I'm in awe. There's nothing sexier than a guy with a big vocabulary. Don't tell your wife I said that." I glanced back at the view, searching for telltale shimmers of power. There were flashes here and there, tiny bright spots that didn't have enough strength to hold my attention, much less to represent a power circle. "I wonder…"

My gaze drifted back to the Hollidays' distant house. The power emanating there was the good kind, full of life, rather than anything that would harness a killer and send it to do its bidding. I'd never looked for something darker. "Ritual murder probably leaves a different kind of mark than happy fluffy-bunny magic, huh?" I held my breath a moment, working myself up to it, then reached for the magic inside me.

I'd been depending on auras, and on the brilliant light and dark of a world viewed through shamanistic eyes. There was no healing component to that, nothing that required a wakening of the particular magic I commanded. But that magic was life-magic, so attuned to preservation and healing that the one time I'd used it as a weapon against a living thing, it had nearly wiped me out. It rebelled against death, and in so doing, might help me See places in Seattle where darkness had prevailed.

After one glance, I wished I'd never thought of it.

A couple hundred people died every year in Seattle through homicide or suicide. I knew the statistics; I'd worked some of the cases. But I'd never thought about what kind of mark that might leave on the psychic landscape, or how long it might last. There were jagged spots all over the place, far more than could be accounted for over the course of a single year. Dizziness caught me and I widened my eyes, trying to See more clearly. Trying, mostly, to See when the world itself started to heal from the wounds cut in it by violent deaths. There were places where healing was obviously happening, the mark of murder fading but not yet gone, but from the sheer number of still-vicious slashes, recovery time looked to be in the decades or even centuries, rather than months or years. My stomach seized up, making me regret the onion tart appetizer, and I put my hand on the curved window in front of me, ostensibly for balance.

Really, though, the greater part of me was trying to reach through the glass into the city. I wanted to soothe the damage it had taken; the damage the dead themselves felt, though it was much too late for that. Billy said, "Joanie?" worriedly, and I dredged up a wan smile to accompany a whispered, "It's so sad."

Murders looked different from suicides. I stared across the city, both fascinated and horrified that I could tell the difference. They all bled black and red and spilled out to leave dark gashes in the lives around them, but murders had an external violence to them, leaving behind a spray that reminded me of a blood spatter. Suicides were more internal, wrapped up tight with sharp edges pointing inward. Nauseated, I jerked toward the north, searching for the Quinleys' home.

Its mark was no worse than any of the other murders I'd just studied. Incomprehension swam between my ears, then cleared up as I struggled to link thoughts through the bleak chaos of the dead's world.

Rachel and David Quinley hadn't died in ritual murder. They'd just been slaughtered by a madman who wanted to steal their daughter. A warning had been left written in their blood, but sick as that was, it wasn't ritualized. My hand turned to a fist against the glass, then dropped to my side. I could think— dismayingly—of at least three places where actual ritual murder had been attempted or achieved, and one of them was still in my line of sight: Billy's home.

I badly did *not* want to see what Faye Kirkland's death looked like, splashed across Billy's lawn. On the other hand, maybe recognizing it would give me a hint as to how to heal that space a little faster, so there were no malingering effects to distress his family. I actually held my breath, trying to pull the bright shamanistic world into conjunction with the darker, murderous version I was looking at now. A headache spiked in my right eye as two opposing world views fought for domination, then finally settled down like a cat and dog determined to ignore each other. The Hollidays' home came into focus, a beacon in the dark.

For long seconds I wasn't at all sure I was actually seeing their house, because all I really Saw was the brightness, same as I'd seen earlier. Faye's death came into slow focus, but it was a shadow, with nothing of the strength or horror I expected it to have. I felt Melinda there, full of love and confidence and determination. Full of serenity, greater by a considerable margin than the terrible things that had happened that summer.

Relief and delight bubbled in my chest and made my eyes sting enough to threaten the Sight. Apparently a deliberate application of positive energy could make a difference, which gave me an uplifting spark of hope for the whole wide world. "Your wife is something else, you know that, Billy?"

"Yeah," he said with a note of pride that fell just short of smug. "Yeah, I do."

Buoyed by the knowledge that it was possible to fight back against marks left by abominations, I turned toward the next-nearest site of ritual murder that I knew about: Woodland Park.

Dark power sledgehammered me alongside the skull.

I dropped into my chair like I'd had my strings cut. Nausea rose up, hurrying to find an escape route, and I ducked my head between my knees, classic crash position as I gasped for air.

Billy's worried "Joanie?" was louder this time, and I barely managed to get fingertips above the table's edge to give him a semi-reassuring wave.

"I'm okay. I'm…" I fumbled for my glass of water and took a few tiny sips while still in crash position, which wasn't the easiest of tasks. "Oogh. Okay. I'm…" I'd said that once already. I got my elbow onto the table and cranked myself up inch by inch, neck stiff as I made myself peek outside again.

Three points of a diamond raged with malevolence, pouring sick purple-gray power into the sky. I couldn't imagine what kind of whammy that field would've had if the last murder, the last point on the diamond, had been completed. As it was, if I hadn't been heartened by what the Hollidays had accomplished just before looking at the diamond, I would've been down for the count. It was so astonishingly strong and so utterly desolate that I had no idea how I'd failed to notice it earlier.

Two answers came to mind: one, I hadn't been looking for it, and two, on a subconscious level I suspected I'd been trying hard to ignore it. Seeing the world in shades of sick and well was supposed to be my purview, but right here, right now, I was just barely able to handle it. Six months ago it would've sent me running for the hills.

Billy came around the table and caught my hand. His fingers felt scalding, which slowly resolved itself into an awareness that mine were icy. "You all right, Joanie?"

"All right" covered a host of sins. I nodded, pressed my eyes closed and nodded again. "Yeah. I just got…an idea of what I should be looking for."

"That bad?"

"Worse."

An uncomfortable shuffle behind us made us both turn to find our waitress, plates in hand, looking concerned. "Is everything okay? Did the tart not agree with you?"

Visions of consorting with saucily-dressed women over lunch rose unbidden. I fought back the urge to admit that they weren't really my type, instead mumbling, "No, no, it was fine, sorry, I…"

Billy stood up with a smile. "Banged her knee on the table, you know that nervy place doctors hit with the hammer? Only worse. She's fine. Lunch looks great."

Relieved, the waitress put our food on the table and scurried off. I worked my way to sitting and looked sadly at my food. "I probably shouldn't eat if I'm doing all this vision stuff. You're a good liar."

"I'm a very good liar," Billy corrected, "and you're not doing quest work here. Even if you were, you should see yourself, Walker. You look like a ghost. Eat. If we have to wait a couple hours to look at the city again, so be it." He nodded at my plate and repeated, "Eat."

He was the senior partner in this relationship. Who was I to argue? Besides, I felt like I'd been run over, and food sounded like the first step to recovering. I bent over my lunch and shoveled it in like a prisoner.

Twenty minutes of intense eating and the savoring of an incredible chocolate concoction that should have been called "I'll do anything the chef says as long as he lets me have another one of these things" later, I nerved myself up to take another look at the city. The double vision of life and death settled more easily this time, suggesting that I was probably supposed to be able to do something like this. Still, I avoided looking toward the Woodland baseball park. It would've been a shame to lose that lunch.

We'd rotated around so we were looking over the south of the city. There were all the marks of homicide and suicide and car wrecks—those several hundred deaths a year on Seattle roads made a real mess of the streets—but nothing like the hideous power of the banshee's murder site. I knew where another one should be, and got up to walk widdershins around the restaurant, watching for the black spike that should be the Museum of Cultural Arts.

It was nothing like as nasty as Woodland Park, though Jason Chan's death throbbed in the air. He'd died to set the black cauldron free, his blood smeared around it to break binding spells, but it was less ritualized than the banshee's work had been. That, and there was only one of him, to the three dead girls in the park.

I was just starting to think there was nothing to find, no power circle or controlling factor, when black light flared at the Troll Bridge.

CHAPTER EIGHT

Tuesday, December 20, 12:13 P.M.

I forgot about the bill and ran for the elevator, struggling to get my cell phone out of my pocket as I went. Billy shouted after me, then swore and hurried to pay the bill as I hopped around, waiting impatiently on both the elevator and the phone.

The phone came through first, Morrison sounding unusually gruff, which was saying something. "What do you want, Walker?"

"Get somebody over to the Fremont Troll right now. I don't know what I just saw, but it was something. Something bad. Billy and I are on our way, but we're at the Seattle Center and traffic's going to be impossible."

Morrison went silent and the elevator dinged. I rushed in the instant the doors were open wide enough to let me. Billy finished dealing with the check and hurried after me, but not fast enough. By the time he joined me in the elevator I was jittering around like a wind-up toy. Morrison came back to the phone, gruffer yet. "I've got a car on the way. Call me the minute you know something, Walker."

"You're a good man, Charlie Brown." I hung up before I heard Morrison's response to that, and Billy folded his arms and gave me a look that said "Well?" as the elevator made its way down six hundred feet.

"I don't know. I saw something. It looked bad." I had the gut-deep feeling I'd just witnessed a murder, and I was weirdly excited about it. I mean, not that I wanted to be seeing murder done at a distance, but it was a brand-new and interesting aspect to my powers. It seemed like it could do some good if I could figure out how to harness it.

"Is it our guy?"

"I don't know. The troll's even less rustic than Ravenna Park. We're just going to have to go find out. Do you have a siren for the minivan?"

"Yeah, but if you tell my kids, no one will ever find the body."

I made a vague attempt at a Scout's oath salute, and we ran for the car the moment the elevator disgorged us.

It took eight minutes to get to the troll. Short of teleporting we couldn't have gotten there faster, but I still leaned into the seat belt like I was at the races and my willpower alone could get my horse across the finish line first. Well, except any races I'd go to would be NASCAR rather than Kentucky Derby, but the sentiment was solid.

The Fremont Troll was one of Seattle's more charming landmarks, as far as I was concerned. He was a concrete monster beneath the Aurora Avenue North bridge—they'd even renamed the road Troll Avenue in his honor—and he had a real Volkswagen Bug in one hand, like he'd just grabbed it from the bridge above. People came to climb and play on him regularly, and every Halloween the locals threw a party at him. I'd never gotten around to going, and now with my exciting new power set, I was sort of afraid to. He was only concrete and rebar, but that was in the Middle World, the one we lived in day-to-day. I wasn't quite sure what would happen if somebody with shamanic gifts came by on a night when the world walls were thin.

Two patrol cars and a paramedic ambulance had gotten to the scene before us. I knew one of the cops—Ray Campbell, a six-foot-tall bodybuilder squished into a five-foot-five body. He'd been a patrol cop for years, never interested in moving up to detective or even to a command position. "No chance to bust balls," he'd explained to me once. Busting balls was Ray's favorite expression and possibly his favorite pastime, and I was hardly going to argue with him about when and where the most opportune moments to do so came along.

He turned toward us with a determined expression that said "I'm sorry but you'll have to leave now" before it faded into a grimaced greeting. "Hey, Walker, Holliday. Don't know why the captain sent us down here, but it was a good call. She's not dead yet."

Billy and I said, "Yet?" together, then traded off on other questions like, "Is she going to be?" and "What happened?" and "Can I help?"

That last was me, edging toward the ambulance. The paramedics no doubt had it under control, but healing magic made my palms itch with the desire to do something.

Ray looked back and forth between us, then folded his arms over his broad chest. "You know how bums hole up down here. Looks like a fight over some booze got out of hand, and she got stabbed with a broken bottle. She oughta be dead. If we hadn't gotten here she would be. Stay out of it, Walker. You don't want to give the Captain anything else to explain."

I did a fine job of freezing like a nervous rodent before my shoulders slumped and I shifted back toward Billy. Ray looked like he'd gone up against a wrecking ball and lost, but he was plenty smart. He nodded firmly once I got back to where I'd started, and cheer crept across his face. "Somebody'll have blood on their hands, or know who does. Just gotta bust a few balls to find out who. Probably don't need you two down here, if you want to head back up to the station."

"Okay. Good. That's great. I mean, it is. It's great. I'm glad she's not dead." And I was. I'd just been hoping we'd gotten a lucky break, and happened on our cannibal in the middle of chewing on someone. I got on my phone and called Morrison, feeling like quite the sad sack as I offered, "All it was was a mugging over some booze. A woman got stabbed, but the paramedics got here in time, so it looks like she's going to be all right."

"All?" Morrison said incredulously. "You just saw an aggravated assault from halfway across the city and saved somebody's life, and all it rates is an *all?*"

When he put it that way it seemed like more of an accomplishment. I cleared my throat uncomfortably, and Morrison said, "Good job, Walker," and hung up the phone to leave me standing next to a giant concrete troll. I stared up at his hubcap eye, and thought if he winked it wouldn't be any more startling than my boss telling me I'd done well.

He didn't wink, and after a minute I reeled back toward the minivan. Ray and the others had this one under control; no need for the Paranormal Pair to hang around getting in the way of a perfectly ordinary assault investigation. "I think this puts us back at Joanne Walker as bait. Unless you've come up with something better."

Billy said, "I think I have," and a Channel Two news van came whipping down the road and screeched to a halt in front of the ambulance.

Laurie Corvallis jumped out of the van like she was on the verge of a huge news story. To the driver's credit, he pulled the van back out of the paramedics' drive path before dragging a camera out and following Laurie. She was already halfway to where I was struggling to yank the minivan's door open. Billy had locked it. Very safe of him. Annoying, but safe. I jerked at the handle, then put my back against the vehicle like I had enemies approaching from all sides. "What in God's na—"

Wrong approach. I thrust my jaw out, trying to rewrite my internal dialogue, and tried a second time. "Can I help you with something, Ms. Corvallis?"

"Just going where the stories are, Detective Walker. Do we have another cannibal victim here?" Her blue eyes were eager in much the same way a piranha's were. I wondered why I kept comparing her to carnivorous fish.

"We have a completely unrelated incident here. Go away." I winced. "I mean, sorry you came out for nothing."

"Now, Detective." Corvallis's voice went from eager to warm, even condescending, like we were old friends and I was being silly over something unimportant. "I saw how you went tearing out of the Seattle Center. Do you really expect me to believe it's over nothing?"

"You were following me?"

Her cameraman got the camera up and running as I asked, and I found myself suddenly blinking into its brilliant light. It was a gray Seattle day already, and under the bridge it bordered on dark, but the floodlight seemed like overkill. I shielded my eyes with one hand and squinted toward the camera guy. "I fed you a burger and fries this summer. Is that enough of a bribe to get you to turn that thing off if I ask you to?"

He gave me a bright smile. "Maybe once."

"Right." I didn't ask, and his grin broadened. Corvallis gave him a dirty look and he wiped the smile away, but he winked when she turned back to me.

"To answer your question, yes, I was following you. I think you're where the action is, Detective."

Billy, on the far side of the minivan, snorted over the *clunk* of the doors finally unlocking. "You've obviously never checked her social calendar, then."

"You're not helping."

"Want me to?" Ray stumped over to us, looking Corvallis up and down with an expression that lay between lascivious and threatening. I had a sudden vision of him asking me if she needed her balls busted while the cameraman was filming, and blurted, "This is Ray Campbell, the officer on this case. He's the man you'll want to talk to, Ms. Corvallis. Thanks for your interest. I'm sure your superiors are eager for an in-depth report on the plight of the homeless in Seattle. We all need our social awareness raised."

I pulled the door open and fell into the seat, hauling my legs up in my haste to escape. Ray planted himself front and center between the minivan and Corvallis, and she gave me a daggered glare over his shoulder before putting on a reporter-playing-nice smile and stuck her microphone in Ray's face. Billy hopped into his side and closed the door behind him. "That woman's going to get you in trouble someday."

"You mean more trouble than the Seattle Slaughterer thing this morning?" I put my seat belt on and tried not to look over my shoulder as we left the scene a few seconds behind the ambulance. "I know. Worse, though, she's going to get herself in trouble. Look, this whole Magic Seattle thing, the whole world of the other and all that. How do you keep people from getting in over their heads and getting hurt?"

"Lobotomization." Billy grinned at my expression. "You can't keep people from getting hurt, Joanie. You can warn them, but somebody like Corvallis isn't likely to leave the hunt unless something throws her off the scent. You're doing a good job of leaving a scent." He thumped his hand against the steering wheel and muttered, "That analogy might've gotten out of control."

I laughed. "You think?" My humor slipped away. "I just don't want people getting hurt on my account."

"Laurie Corvallis won't get hurt on your account. She'll get hurt on the story's account, but never on yours." He shook his head. "We do the best we can. You did good today. You just saved somebody's life. That's about all we can ask for."

"That and a break on the cannibal case."

Billy eyed me. "Don't break your arm patting yourself on the back, there, Joanne. You just pulled off a miracle. What's the problem?"

I rubbed my thumb over my palm, then cracked my knuckles, feeling like I was trying to discharge the healing power that had sprung to life. "I don't know. I wanted that to be our cannibal."

"So did I, but come on, Walker. What's it take to make you

happy? First you don't want to be a shaman, now you're hitting it out of the park and you're not satisfied because it's a different ball than the one you were watching? Give yourself a little credit."

"Okay, okay, I'm happy, I'm happy!" I wrinkled my nose at the traffic and said, more quietly, "I'm glad she's alive, Billy, and maybe you're right. Maybe I should be elated. It just feels like in the grand scheme of things this is what I should be doing all the time, so it doesn't feel like…enough." By the time I got to the end of that, I was smiling again, ruefully. "I need some serious work on my perspective, don't I?"

"You sure as hell do."

"Arright." A little bubble of delight burst inside me, like that healing power had figured out what to do with itself after all. I'd saved somebody. That was, in fact, pretty cool. Good thing I had people like Morrison and Billy around to beat that into my head. "Okay. Can we head back up to the Needle? We kind of bolted out of there, and I can't think of anywhere better for a perspective adjustment."

It wasn't perspective I was after so much as trying to map out Seattle's hot and cold spots, magically speaking. The good news was, our brief dash to the Troll had given me enough time to digest lunch. Turning the in-depth Sight back on didn't upset my tummy again. Triumphant, I ordered us each another one of the amazing chocolate desserts. Billy pulled his cell phone out and sat down to wait for them while I took a slow meander around the restaurant.

I wanted my city to be a bastion of light and happiness. What I could See, with the initial shock of looking into darkness reduced, was that it looked pretty well-balanced. It was no shining city upon a hill, but neither was it one drawn into despair. Pockets of brilliance matched patches of darkness closely enough that I actually let go a sigh of relief. Sonata's concern about the city, maybe the world, being pulled out of whack was very likely a valid one, but at least it wasn't going to all come tumbling down tomorrow. Reassured, I turned my focus on Ravenna Park, where Karin Newcomb had been found that morning.

Someone or something mystical had dumped her there. It had left ice-cold marks on the earth. It *had* to have left some kind of trail. If I thought it with enough determination, maybe it would be true.

Apparently I wasn't thinking hard enough. Either that or I'd wiped away any trace when I'd pressed my hand into the cold tracks the thing had left, because there was barely even a streak of darkness where Newcomb's body had been found. She hadn't died there, and dead bodies evidently didn't carry bleak marks of their own; only violent deaths did.

Good to know, but not at all helpful to me at the moment. I stood there a long time, gaze unfocused as I studied the highs and lows of passion and power within the city, but there were no trails leading in or out of anywhere we'd found a body. Our cannibal was a lot better at hiding his tracks than I was at following them. I felt like I was just a step too far behind, like I could track him if I could only catch up just a little more. I wished to hell I hadn't flattened out the cold marks he'd left beside Karin Newcomb.

Next time. Next time I'd know better, but next time meant somebody else would already be dead.

Billy said, "Anything?" quietly from just behind me. I startled out of my reverie and blinked over my shoulder at him before shaking my head. He put his phone away and pointed a thumb at our table. "In that case, you might as well eat dessert before it melts. And then we'll try my idea."

"Your idea is to consign me to consumer hell?"

I balked in the doorway of an outdoors store, which was to say it sold outdoors equipment, not that it was outside. If it had actually been outside it might've been less overwhelming; there wouldn't be three visible stories of canoes, bicycles, skis, winter gear, tents, campfire utensils, hiking boots and back-packs. And those were just the things I could recognize. There were hundreds of items within eyeshot that I simply had no name for, and no earthly idea what their use might be.

The whole place made my heart beat too fast, like it was actively dangerous. Grumpiness didn't so much creep over me as bludgeon me, and I tried to back up, trusting the door was an escape route. "I don't like shopping, Billy. Especially in giant warehouses filled with a million things I can't possibly need."

Sadly, the door was blocked by my partner, and made a lousy escape route after all. He prodded my spine to drive me forward, and I dragged my feet as I went. "What are we doing here? I guess if I'm going to go play bait I need equipment, but the department must have some." That didn't really seem very likely, now that I thought about it. "Or they could borrow it from Fish and Game, or something. I'm not spending eleven thousand dollars on setting a trap."

"I just want you to meet someone."

"Who, a psychiatrist?" Not that an outdoors store struck me as the most likely place to find a head doctor. A guru, maybe, but not a shrink. "Look, I know it's not a great idea, but we have to do something."

"Hey, Billy!" A tall, athletic brunette woman in the store uniform of a polo shirt and khakis leaned over the second floor wood railing and waved. Billy waved back, and she swung herself around the railing corner and took the stairs down two at a time, like a kid. I was torn between liking her instantly and utterly distrusting her, though the latter impulse came from the suspicion that she was the shape of my doom. She was close to my height, and her hands, one of which she offered me to shake, were bigger than mine. "Hey, I'm Mandy Tiller. You must be Joanne. Billy called a while ago to say you were coming by."

She turned and socked Billy's shoulder hard enough to make a meaty *thump*. "Good to see you, Holliday. How's Mel? How're the kids?"

"They're all good. Mel says hi." Billy rubbed his shoulder, smile a little pained as he explained to me, "Mandy's oldest son is in Robert's class. We've been doing field trips and class picnics together for years."

A tiny spark of recognition shocked me. "Jake Tiller? I met him one time over at Billy's house. He looks like you." They both had long jaws and sandy-gold skin that offset light eyes, though Mandy's hair was darker than her son's.

Mandy's smile lit up. She wasn't quite pretty, but the smile was terrific. "That's him. He's a good kid." The smile went away as fast as it'd come, worry pinching the space between her eyebrows. "Billy says you guys are on that cannibal case. He says you need a wilderness guide to try and flush the guy out."

I opened my mouth, shut it again, glanced at Billy, then looked back at Mandy with my own eyebrows elevated. "Yeah, I guess I kind of do."

She nodded once, somehow making it a stern expression.

"I can take a quick break if you want to go over to the coffee shop with me and talk about it."

"I'll never say no to coffee." The three of us trundled out of the store, and I felt my stress level drop. It probably said something about me that I would prefer to discuss trapping a killer than face the prospect of shopping in a big box store.

We ordered what turned out to be more-than-passable coffee and sat around a table as far away from the other patrons as possible. Mandy said, "Sorry, I don't have much time, so let me tell you like it is. I know the news story only broke this morning, but for a big city with a lot of people, the real wilderness types are pretty close-knit. We don't all know each other, but it's like two degrees of separation, not six?" She nodded when we did and kept going. "So it's not like we haven't been talking about this among ourselves for weeks. It's gotten bad enough that the last week or so almost nobody's going out, or if they are they're going up to Canada to do their hiking and weekend camping. We're talking about a lot of green freaks here, people who avoid driving when they can, so that should give you an idea of how uncomfortable we are."

I said, "Maybe that's why this morning's body was found in Ravenna Park. The hunting in the wilder areas is getting scarce," to Billy, who nodded. I liked that idea better than the one about the killer looking for me.

"I haven't gone out since the second body was found," Mandy said. "Jake's dad and I are divorced, and there's no way I'm risking leaving him alone. That said, Billy wouldn't have called if he didn't need help, or if he didn't think you could make a difference. Do you think you can catch this guy?"

Truth, rather than reassurance, popped out: "I hope so. What I *can* do is make sure you're not going to get hurt out there." Mandy looked unhappy. I couldn't blame her. "Maybe there's somebody else, somebody without kids—?"

"Plenty of people. The problem is they're mostly guys."

I said, "Ah," after a moment, while Billy looked between us in bewilderment and demanded, "What's that supposed to mean?"

"It means guys are a lot more likely to get overprotective if something bad goes down," I said when it was clear Mandy wasn't going to explain. Billy started to look offended and I raised my coffee cup to stop him, then took a sip. It really was pretty decent coffee. "Say you're Generic Joe the Hiker. You're bringing a woman, somebody who hasn't done much hiking before, out on a trail for the first time. You happen to know she's a fourth dan in kung fu, but while you're out there a nutjob appears out of nowhere and attacks her. What do you do?"

Billy, just like I had earlier, opened his mouth and shut it again. I said, "That's what I thought."

"*I* would just let her kick his ass," Billy muttered sullenly. I laughed and reached over to pat his shoulder.

"I know *you* would, but you're a member of a specially trained elite force, and you're more likely to remember that your girl Friday there has a black belt. But most guys with an ounce of decency would act to protect the girl. In this particular case, working with somebody whose first instinct is to duck is going to be safer for all of us."

"So it's a date." Mandy still didn't look happy, but she sounded determined. "I don't work tomorrow, Detective Walker, so if you're free then, I'd like to get this over with?"

"Just tell me where to meet you."

We made arrangements, and I, heroically, went home and went to bed.

CHAPTER NINE

I dreamed of a funeral on Christmas day. Dozens of mourners were in attendance, washed out in the gray winter light. I was among them, taller than most, grim in the black slacks and sweater I'd bought for the service. I'd worn the only shoes I had with me, stompy black boots that didn't match the outfit. I'd secretly liked the fact that they set me apart, that they weren't appropriate. They played to an already-present sense of alienation from the people around me. I thought of myself as fish-belly pale, but looking at my distant family, I saw a golden cast to my skin that none of them had. I looked better in black than most of them did.

Growing up, I'd never thought about my mother's family. She was persona non grata to me, the bitch who'd abandoned me with a father who didn't know what to do with me. I'd never indulged in the luxury of imagining my life would've been better with her, and it had flat-out never occurred to me that I might've had aunts and uncles, or cousins, much less siblings and nieces and nephews.

By the time she finally called, I was twenty-six and she was dying. She wanted to get to know me in the time she had left, but she never did. We spent four months traveling around Europe on the basis of a relationship that meant nothing to me, and, as far as I could tell, meant very little to her. We never broke down the barriers of silence, and saw Rome and Barcelona and Prague as two strangers standing side by side. When I met her family at the funeral—aunts and uncles and cousins, yes, but no half siblings, for which I was grateful—they were too caught up in their own sorrow to know what to do with me. I didn't exactly blame them, but I was bitter anyway.

Three months later, when my dead mother rescued me from a banshee, I learned that every one of her choices had been based on trying to keep me safe. I learned, way too late, that she'd loved me. But in the immediacy of the dream, all I knew was I stood amongst strangers who had lost someone much more important to them than she'd been to me.

They had offered—or asked, I wasn't sure which—to let me help shoulder the weight of her casket. I'd wanted to say yes, and had declined because I was so much taller than the others. It was a stupid, pathetic logic, and I'd regretted it immediately, not just for my sake or my mother's, but because of how her family's faces had shut down. In instantaneous hindsight I'd understood they were trying to reach out to me, but my talent had always been in pushing people away.

The priest spoke, as unmemorable in dreams as he'd been in life. Others nodded, wiped tears away; I stared at my stompy boots and waited for it all to be over. Voices murmured around me, whispered remembrances that the priest's words brought to the fore, and all I could offer was *she liked Altoids.* A bark of laughter filled my throat, inappropriate to release, and so I jolted guiltily when I heard that sound outside my own head.

It wasn't laughter. It was a raven, sitting on Sheila MacNamarra's headstone. The grave was still open, shining casket a black gleam under the dull sky. The raven tipped forward, peering into the hole, and gave another one of its laughlike caws.

That had *not* happened at the funeral. I edged forward, somewhere between relieved that this wasn't just a miserable dream and worried that it was a portent of some kind. The raven cawed again, then sprang into the air, wings whispering as he flew away into the winter sky.

Wailing followed him, a screech of metal tearing, and it rendered the clouds bloody and red.

I woke up far more weary than I'd been when I went to bed.

Wednesday, December 21, 5:19 A.M.

I couldn't shake the dream, so I just got up. I was meeting Mandy early anyway, although not quite five-thirty-in-the-morning early. Still, finding breakfast and taking a shower seemed better than lying wide-eyed in bed trying to read meaning into haunted dreams.

Truth was, I didn't think it needed that much interpretation. No banshee had cried at my mother's funeral, but with the murders a few months later, and everything I'd learned about her then, I wasn't surprised there was an association. The raven's appearance seemed even less peculiar, especially with my power circle encounter the day before.

Reminded, and feeling a little foolish, I took a foil bag of Pop-Tarts up to the roof of my building and put it on one of the heating vents. "Here you go, Raven. Shiny food. Thank you for getting me out of that psychic snowstorm yesterday." I patted the bag and, feeling even more foolish, retreated to my apartment.

Mandy Tiller swung by to pick me up about a quarter after six, which really meant she lugged a backpack up to my apartment and examined my winter gear. My boots, which were police-issue for winter wear, passed muster, but she looked dismayed at the rest of what I thought qualified as outdoor gear.

"Jeans are out. Cotton's no good for keeping warm. I thought that might be the case, so I brought extras. They should fit pretty well, you're a little taller but I think I'm bulkier?"

I said, "In the thigh, anyway," before realizing that might be insulting. Mandy only nodded, though, and unzipped the backpack to reveal what looked like two-thirds of the stock from the store she worked in. She peeled a pair of leggings out and tossed them to me, grinning at my expression.

"They expand. Really. I know they look like they won't fit a skinny thirteen-year-old, but I wear them all the time." Disconcertingly, she peeled her waistband down to show me the pair of leggings she wore under her pants, then let the pants slide back up. "They wick sweat away. I've got a long-sleeved shirt for you, too. Do you have any sweaters? Wool sweaters?"

Half an hour later I was securely bundled in more layers than I knew could fit on a single human being, and was somehow still only carrying only slightly more bulk than I typically did. I wriggled my toes inside liner socks inside wool socks inside my boots and chortled. "This is kind of cool."

Mandy got a sly look. "If you think it's cool already, you've got the heart of an outdoorsman. We're going to have fun today. Ever been snowshoeing?"

I said, "No," fascinated, and her sly look got even craftier.

"Yeah," she said again. "This'll be fun."

Except for the part where we're trying to lure a killer to us, I didn't say and tromped outside after her.

We took a ferry across Puget Sound, both of us getting out of Mandy's SUV to lean into what was, with all the cold weather gear we were wearing, merely a bracing wind. I'd had my filling breakfast of pastries, but she threw me a ham sandwich and a protein bar, which I ate obediently, figuring there was no point in tagging along after an expert if I didn't take her advice. "You do a lot of walking, right?" she asked as we got back into her car. "A five-mile trail isn't going to kill you?"

"I did more when I was a patrol cop, but I should be okay as long as you don't expect me to climb mountains."

"Only a little one," she promised cheerfully. "If you were really outdoorsy I'd bring you on a much harder hike, farther out. From what I know about the people who've died, most of them would be found on the tough stuff, not on Hurricane Hill. I'm hoping it's enough to draw him out." She gave me a sideways glance and asked the question I'd been expecting all along: "So *are* you like a black belt? I've never heard of cops going out alone to set themselves up as bait. Don't they usually at least have backup?"

"You're my backup." And I hadn't exactly cleared this stunt with Morrison. "I'm not a black belt, but I have a kind of…profiling thing with people like this. A way to fight that most people don't."

"And you can be sure he'll go after you and not me?"

I found myself studying her awhile before answering. "You're very brave," I said eventually. "You must be, or you wouldn't be out here offering to help me with only the bare bones of the situation explained to you."

She went quiet awhile, too, as we drove up into the park. "Maybe. Maybe I'm a little stir-crazy, too. I haven't been out hiking in weeks, and I promised Jake we could go out during Christmas break? That's not happening if there's still a psychotic cannibal out there. So that's some of it. And some of it is that the Hollidays never ask for anything. Melinda's incredible, with all those kids and the volunteer time she puts in at the school and the extra-curricular activities she helps chaperone…so I thought if I could do this, it would be a good thing?" She made a lot of should-be statements into questions, like she was seeking reassurance about her opinions and commentary, and I wondered if she was even aware of it. I figured it wouldn't go over well if I called her out on it, though, and she went on breathlessly. "Besides, you're cops. Decent people help the police when they can."

"I take it back," I said. "You're not just brave. You're also awesome." Mandy flashed a smile, and I went back to her original question, figuring she'd earned an answer. "I can't promise he'll go after me instead of you, but I *can* promise he's not going to get his teeth into you, and I'm ninety-nine percent certain he'll lose interest in you once I start my thing."

"Which you're not going to explain?"

"I'd rather not until it's over." And only then if I had to. I didn't want to detail how I could build a shield of my willpower and surround someone else with it, or how in psychic terms I was a much tastier morsel than your average bear. Mandy gave me a careful look, but nodded, and I turned my attention to the park's winter-wonderland cascade of snow and trees. "You know I've never been out here?"

"Too many people haven't. We're going up to the Hurricane Ridge visitor's center and we'll head out from there. Hurricane Hill's all paved, not that you can tell right now? So it shouldn't be too bad a walk. Besides, families will have probably broken the trail already. The parks aren't advertising that outdoorsmen are being slaughtered." The SUV gave a sigh when we reached the visitor's center and settled down into the new snow covering the parking lot. We got out into a wind brisk enough to make my eyes water, and I laughed.

"Can I change my mind now?"

"You'll be fine. You're dressed for it." Mandy took snowshoes from the vehicle's back end and got me into them, then made me stomp around the parking lot like Bigfoot. I felt like a kid borrowing her dad's shoes, and caught myself making crunching noises to accompany the squeak of snow compressing under my feet. In almost no time we were on our way up the hill toward the distant ridge.

The sky had turned gray, then gradually clearer as we'd driven, and some minutes into our hike Mandy turned abruptly and said, "Look."

I spun around in time to watch the sun break over the horizon, a bright ball of white fire in a pale sky. There weren't enough clouds to turn pink; it was just pure light spreading above and below us. A chime rang out behind me, and I looked back in astonishment to see Mandy swinging a tiny silver-capped bell. "You should always greet the sun with music on the winter solstice," she explained. "It gives it a reason to come back."

"You didn't tell me to bring a bell!" To my utter surprise, I kind of wished she had. Greeting the sunrise hardly seemed like a me thing to do, but with the clean light spilling toward us and the music of Mandy's bell shimmering in the air, I wanted to take part. Not to be outdone, I reached for a Christmas carol, skipping straight to the chorus: "Star of wonder, star of night, star with royal beauty bright!"

Mandy, sounding as happy as I felt, picked up the tune, and we stood there on the mountainside, singing in the solstice.

When the sun had reached a hand's breadth above the horizon, we tore ourselves away from watching it, and Mandy tucked her bell back into a pocket. I was in too high spirits to let the feeling go and threw the opening line from my favorite carol toward Mandy: "Said the night wind to the little lamb."

She gave, "Do you see what I see?" back, and we traded off lines increasingly breathlessly as we tromped up the hill. I fell over laughing and winded when we were finished, and she stood above me with a grin. "You've got a really nice voice."

"So do you. We should start a choir." I let her pull me back to my feet and accepted the ski poles she'd packed across her back. "I didn't know snowshoeing was this hard!"

"This is nothing. If you're not wiped out when we get to the top I'll take you out on the ridge and make you wish you'd never been born."

"You might want to work on your sales pitch." We scrambled farther up the hill, exchanging mutters and jokes until Mandy said, "Almost there," and ran a few steps ahead of me so she could turn back and offer her hand. I took it and she pulled me up over the top of the ridge.

Half the world spread out below us, sunlight bouncing hard off snow and sending blue-white flares through my vision. I turned in a slow circle, delight and awe spreading through me.

It turned to laughter as I caught Mandy's smug expression, and I put it into words sheerly for her benefit: "This is incredible."

"Yeah, I know." She grinned back, broadly, and a shapeless blur of nothing came out of the snow to knock her off the top of the mountain.

CHAPTER TEN

The world filled up with sound: Mandy's scream, my shout, and below those, a bone-rattling roar that came from everywhere and nowhere at once. Its depth made my heartbeat do funny things and upset my stomach, like I'd swallowed a stone. My first reaction was to drop to my hands and knees and breathe carefully so I wouldn't throw up, but once there I had a vividly clear thought: this was a hell of a defense mechanism on the monster's part. If its voice could make people sick and rubber-kneed, it would rarely have to fight more than one opponent at a time.

Pity for it that I was uniquely well-equipped to fight off sickness. I buried my mittened fingers in the snow and reached past a wobbly heart and sloshing stomach for the healing power that imbued me.

Nausea burned away as cool, welcome magic rose up in me. The world went dark with winter, snow rendered invisible through the Sight, which looked into the mountain sleeping beneath it. Sleeping, not dead; winter was a time of rest and renewal up here on the mountain, a time of hibernation. Even the pale blue sky had that same sense of waiting: waiting for spring and warmth that would return birds and insects to it. It was comforting in its quiet way, and I thought that someday I would like to come here to sit at the top of the world when there was nothing more pressing to do than admire it. Fleeting observations, filling my mind and replacing the beast's roar.

Peculiarly serene, I sat back on my heels—more of a trick than usual, since I was wearing snowshoes—and reached down the mountain with my power. The real world came back into focus, underlying what I saw with the Sight. The morning sun made pockets of gold in the snow, overruling blue shadows, rich colors tangling with the winter calm of the earth.

Mandy was fiery against that calm, both in real vision and with the Sight. Half buried in snow, she poured off heat and life and fury and fear, her aura as vivid as the red coat and black snowpants she wore. Everything she had was being poured into fighting, but the way she flailed told me she couldn't see her opponent.

I could barely see it, even with the Sight. It was a massive blur, hardly even a shape. It had tooth and claw, but even those were translucent, like someone was shining light through packed snow. There were no eyes, no visible edges to its body, although it had a sense of weight to it. It had to: it kept pressing Mandy farther into the snow, and I caught an impression of talons lifting to strike.

When they fell, it was to reverberate off the glittering hard shell of my magic.

I had gotten pretty good at shielding both myself and others over the past year. It was easier, in fact, to protect someone else.

My own demons tended to get inside the deepest part of me and work their way out from there, making shields less useful than they might have been. But my friends tended to just face external threats when I was around, and that I could handle.

The picture before me could've been an expensive special effect, a give-and-take of power flowing from me to the pair thirty feet down the mountain. Mandy looked like a superhero, wrapped in silver-blue shielding that glowed even in the sunlight. Her scream became a squeak of astonishment, and the creature's dull roar ricocheted into a pained howl.

For just a second I felt proud of myself.

Mandy won my admiration forever by slamming the mittened heel of her hand upward, straight-arming her invisible assailant. Its head, for lack of a better term—that's where the teeth seemed to be, anyway—cracked backward, briefly illuminated by the power wrapping Mandy. I had a glimpse, nothing more, of a human face badly distorted, and tried frantically to rewind my memory and remember if its teeth had been manlike or more predatory. The idea they'd been both popped up, then retreated again as the infuriated blur of nothing tumbled ass over teakettle down the mountain.

Trying to see it—or See it—was giving me a headache. It changed shape and size like it was struggling to figure out what it was. It landed on all fours, facing me, and slid yards before coming to a stop. Claw marks marred the snow, five surprisingly delicate lines from barely-visible paws. Ten seconds earlier it'd had enough weight to drive Mandy into the snow. Now it barely broke the crusted surface, and the gut-clenching low rumble of its roar rolled over me again. I let go a shout of my own, feeble in comparison.

The snow under my feet compacted alarmingly, like it was

suddenly bored with its current location. I had a vivid realization that I was standing on top of a mountain, and that deep noises could start avalanches. There was a tree line that might help mitigate disaster, but if a good snow slide started, the trees would break like twigs. And so would I.

Mandy flinched upward, escaping the worst of the snow's grasp in a sudden poof of color. Snow crunched and cracked beneath her, but she rolled carefully, edging her way toward the ridge at an oblique angle, away from the divots she and the monster had made as they'd rolled down the mountainside. She still shone with the protective glitter of my shielding, but I had no way to reduce gravity within that shield.

Maybe I didn't have to. The idea hit me with the same dazzling clarity as sun on snow. I'd made all kinds of shapes with my shields in the past, and it didn't seem impossible that a flattened oval could help spread her body weight over a greater distance. Trusting that the formless monster couldn't move fast enough to eviscerate me in the time it took to rearrange my concept of the shield and Mandy's weight within it, I turned my attention to her alone.

I'd never thought about the mass I was protecting when I'd created a shield before. Now I could feel her weight like the shielding was a hammock, drawing down toward the buried earth where her body touched it. But that drop-point could be eliminated by increasing the hammock's tension, pulling its corners farther apart until it was a smooth, stretched-out expanse still capable of bearing the same weight. All the change was in the hammock, rendering its burden unchanged, yet perfectly safe on a taut surface.

Mandy's shield popped out wide and thin, just like my image of the hammock. The wind carried her gasp of relieved bewilderment to me as she got free of breaking snow and lay atop it. She went preternaturally still, lying with her arms and legs spread out like she was on thin ice and, intentionally or not, reducing my need to pay attention to her shielding's form.

I had exactly enough time to look back toward the feature-less monster before it bashed into me.

Up close it smelled like carrion. I gagged, choking for breath, and aspirated snow. I coughed it out, vision blurring, though I couldn't tell if it was tears or just that the world itself had gone white and cold, with no sense of up or down. I wasn't hurt—the shielding I'd wrapped around Mandy surrounded me, too—but the thing rolled me in the snow, disorienting me further. I grabbed at it, fingers clawed uselessly inside my mittens, and it pulled away without effort.

I got a glimpse of it, an outline against the pale blue sky. Its eyes were white, or transparency's closest brother to white, and its mouth was a tear across its head. The teeth, more visible than anything but the claws, were a skull's grin, but the head stretched wider than a human head should have. There was no way this thing had eaten the people we'd found so far.

Or, if it had, it was becoming more and more wild, losing any vestiges of humanity that it had once had. I caught a downward strike with my mittened hand, and felt myself sink deeper into the snow. I didn't want to think too hard about how far it might be to the mountain rock below; the idea made me feel like I was drowning in snow, just as I had in my vision the day before.

Snow collapsed on my head, which didn't help at all. I gasped for air and got a lungful of rotted meat stench. For something that had landed on the snow crust light as a feather, it certainly was strong and stinky. I tried Mandy's trick, straight-arming it, and caught it solidly in the chest to no dramatic effect except fueling another roar.

That time I felt it in the ground, the way it shivered and dis-lodged a bit of the packed snow it held in place. One more howl like that and the whole mountainside was going to go, which might be okay from my monster buddy's point of view, but which would be a world of hurts for me and Mandy. I reached for a psychic net, an idea that had worked for me in the past. A blue-white mesh burst out of my fingertips and stuck against the monster's mutating form.

It reared back, clawing at the net, then simply dissipated like it had never existed. My net collapsed, partly because it had nothing to hold and partly because I was too surprised to keep its idea in mind.

Barely a heartbeat later the creature reappeared and clob-bered me with a mallet-sized fist. Stars burst in my vision, and right about then I started wondering why I'd been trying to capture instead of kill it. I slammed a hand out to the side, grabbing a fistful of snow and willing it to become my weapon of choice, the silver rapier I'd taken from a god.

Power surged, and I held the blade like it had always been there. In a way it had been: it made up part of psychic armor and weaponry grown from gifts I'd been given and tokens I'd won. The first time I'd drawn it had been in a dreamscape plane, but since then I'd learned I could pull it across the real world from its usual hiding place under my bed into my hand when I needed it. It was more convenient than carrying a rapier around in day-to-day life, though its lack of physical presence tended to make me forget about it until I really, really needed it.

Like now.

Technically it was a stabbing weapon, not a slashing one, but it had an edge and that that was enough for me. I swung wildly, pouring power into the blade. I'd overloaded monsters before, essentially exploding them with magic, but the invisible snowman only squealed and scampered backward. I lurched forward, trying to follow the path it broke in the snow, but a sword in one hand and snowshoes on the feet did not make for easy movement.

I burst out of the snow like a bit of a fool, powder spraying everywhere. The critter was out of reach and in arrest, making it almost impossible to see. It shimmered slightly, a miragelike distortion of light, and I couldn't take my eyes off it for fear I'd never locate it again. It was on top of the snow now, no longer breaking it, but the path it had made while escaping me gave me an angle to run up, in so far as I could run while wearing snowshoes. Nothing about the carnivorous beast had suggested it had a sense of humor, or I might've slain it with laughter at my blundering.

It crouched, visible only because the distortion in the air lowered: its only two easy markers, tooth and claw, were hidden in mouth and snow respectively. I did a *c'mere* gesture with my free hand, hoping it'd jump me again, since I already knew which of us was faster. Being on the defensive was just fine with me, when my opponent could cover twenty yards while I blinked.

I still wasn't ready when it sprang at me. It came from up high, which I expected, but it was smarter than I hoped: instead of skewering itself on my raised sword, it twisted at the last second, coiling toward my undefended left side. Well, my semi-defended left side; I snapped the blade around, scoring a point-tip slash across what I thought of as the thing's ribs.

It didn't so much as flinch, though its howl turned aggravated, like it was smart enough to change its line of attack but not smart enough to imagine I might change mine. This time when it hit the snow beyond me it turned with a snarl, but backed away. I swore and tromped after it, earning another one of its low-bellied rumbles.

A crack opened up between me and the thing, and a heavy block of snow slid several yards down the mountain, then edged to a stop. I froze, arms spread wide and eyes even wider, and although I couldn't see the damned critter's face, I got an overwhelming sense of smugness from it. It emitted another low roar, then another, and when the snow began to slide that time, I knew it wasn't going to stop.

I'd been in earthquakes, but they had nothing on the sensation of watching the snow before me collapse and surge as it started an irreversible downward trend. Time dropped into a zone that only happened in emergencies, and I watched chunks of snow break loose and surge forward in slow motion as the packed material in front of it gave way. It was utterly beautiful in a purely chaotic way.

The half-embodied monster was clearly able to stay on top of the havoc it was wreaking, the impressions its claws made gobbled up by rolling snow. I doubted I could manage the same trick, but even if I could, the nasty beast had put me between a metaphorical rock and a hard place. I could try to go after it.

Or I could keep Mandy Tiller from getting killed.

I sucked my gut in, made an apology to my sword, and threw it away so that when the snow fell out from under my feet, I could fling myself forward with it. All I had to do was get to Mandy before her part of the shelf turned to icy dust. The slow-time of heightened awareness helped: even though I knew everything was happening impossibly fast, I could see giant snowballs breaking free, big enough for me to throw my weight onto them as I dashed across a shattering snowfield. The avalanche's momentum helped, driving me forward faster than humanly possible. I belly flopped on Mandy, my arms spread wide, just as the snow beneath her collapsed.

I snapped a quicksilver shield up around us as the snowslide threw us down the mountain. Mandy rolled over beneath me and wrapped her arms and legs around me, face buried in my shoulder. I knotted my arms around her shoulders and drew my legs up as far as I could with her in my lap, so we made a ball that bounced smoothly—for some value of smoothly—down the thundering wash of snow. I felt like a giant bruise inside about six seconds, and caught myself muttering, "Shock absorbers, shock absorbers," into Mandy's ear as the world spun by in a roar of white and rock and trees.

I'd always worked best with car metaphors, and after another couple of bounces the shielding seemed to soften, taking some of our impact against hard snow and harder debris. Mandy made the first sound I'd heard since her earlier screams: a tiny whimper that sounded like relief. I squeezed her a little harder, then closed my eyes against the cyclone of white around us and waited for it to be over.

We thumped and rolled and bumped to a stop about a million years later, still utterly buried in white. There was room around us, enough to breath, but not enough to untangle from each other. I lifted my head a few inches and Mandy loosened her grip to say, "We're never going to be able to tell which way is up. People die digging the wrong direction."

I whispered, "Actually, not a problem," and, perhaps genuinely grateful for it for the first time, turned the Sight onto the world around me.

The torn-up mountain lay at an oblique angle to us, off to my left. It was no longer sleeping, but half awakened through shock and wounds. I could feel fresh gashes in its face all the way down the path the avalanche had taken, and sent out a pulse of sympathetic healing magic, the same way I'd done with Gary after his heart attack, toward the earth's surface. My, "Sorry," was murmured aloud, the confines of my mind seeming too small for an apology to an entire mountain I'd disrupted.

Mandy let out a moan, clearly interpreting the apology as meaning I couldn't find our way out of there, but the mountain itself gave a shuddering groan, like I'd soothed an injury. I said, "No, it's okay," to Mandy, and turned my head the other way, nearly bumping noses with her as I did. I hadn't been this intimate with someone in weeks.

The calm sky was up there, waiting for us to emerge. I gave a tentative push with the shield, wondering if it would move packed snow, then shoved harder and was rewarded with a sudden increase in breathing room. Heartened, I leaned into it, and seconds later snow burst upward and sunlight rained down on us. Mandy shouted in disbelief and scrambled up the ridged snow with me a few crawling steps behind her.

When I got to the top she was lying on her back, arms spread as she gasped at the sky. Not from a lack of air, I thought, but just sheer gladness at being alive. Somehow our snowshoes had survived the tumble, so their narrow backs were poked into the snow, making her legs arc peculiarly as they rose to her bound feet. I smiled and looked up the mountain, at the hideous score of broken trees and boulder-sized snowballs littering the path we'd taken.

My sword was somewhere in there. It was an incongruous

thought in face of wonder at being alive, but surviving certain death was familiar, and the rapier was important. I put out my hand and whispered a welcome to the blade, inviting it back to me without the strength of panic behind the offer.

I was a little surprised when it materialized, bright and un-damaged. Mandy, behind me, said, "What the hell?" I turned to face her, twisting the sword behind my back guiltily, like I could pretend it wasn't there. She demanded, "Where did that come from?" anyway.

"Um. You ever see those movies with the sword-fighting immortals?" At Mandy's slow nod, I perked up a little. "My sword comes from the same places theirs do."

"In other words," she said after a moment, "don't ask." She was still lying on her back with her snowshod feet in the air. "Just like I probably shouldn't ask how we survived that?"

"Pretty much." I waited a long moment, wondering if she would accept that. Eventually she gave one tight nod and put a hand into the air. I caught it and pulled her to her feet. "Come on. Let's see if we can get out of here."

Because there was no one to tell us nay, I told the park of-ficials that we'd been on our way back down when the ava-lanche struck, and that it had passed behind us offering no more than a thrill. Mandy nodded silent agreement to my version of events, and we both agreed we'd been very lucky when the rangers said, repeatedly, how fortunate we'd been. One of their paramedics even looked us over before they were willing to send us back to Seattle while daylight lasted.

My phone, buried deep in a pocket, buzzed a voice mail warning as we came back into full satellite coverage. Mandy glanced at me as I dug the phone out. "If you answer that, is it going to throw you back into something like what just happened?"

"There probably won't be an avalanche involved, but…" The missed call was from Billy. "But yeah, it's likely."

"Then do me a favor," Mandy said. "Don't answer until you're out of my car."

I closed my phone and leaned my head against the window, feeling the rift between myself and the rest of the world all the way back into town.

CHAPTER ELEVEN

Wednesday, December 21, 4:55 P.M.

I didn't even bother to listen to Billy's message, just went straight to the station after returning Mandy's hiking gear to her. Billy wasn't technically at work today, not any more than I was, but if something new and horrible had gone wrong, he'd almost certainly be at the precinct building to tell me.

I ran into Ray just inside the doors, more literally than I would've liked. He stayed planted where he was, like a fireplug, and I bounced off with a grunt. "Ow. What do you do, eat hubcaps for breakfast?"

"Plate mail," he said unexpectedly, and looked pleased when I laughed. "That woman yesterday, she's okay. Even agreed to go into a sponsored dry-out program. Guess getting her balls busted with a busted bottle showed her the light."

I spent way too long working out the busted bottle balls, then shook myself all over and smiled. "That's great. Sorry for siccing Corvallis on you. How'd that go? I swear, that woman's a betta." I was doing it again, comparing her to vicious fish. At least bettas, like Corvallis, were pretty. Cold and scaly, but pretty.

Surprise dug deep wrinkles into Ray's forehead. "You think? I always liked her on the television, the way she doesn't take crap from anybody. A real reporter, not like most of 'em on TV now. Anyway, it went great. We're going out to dinner tonight."

I scraped my jaw off the floor soon enough to stutter, "Have fun," before he stumped out the doors, and stood there in the blast of cold air marveling at philosophies undreamed of.

A cynical worm crept into my thoughts, wondering if Corvallis had only agreed to go out with Ray as a way to gain inside information into the department and, by proxy, me. Then the worm began eating its own tail until it disappeared into a *plonk* of nothingness inside my brain, because Ray could most certainly handle himself. I didn't envy Corvallis trying to pump him for information he didn't plan to share.

That brought an unfortunately suggestive image to mind. I clutched my head, trying to shake it—both head and image—loose, and went upstairs to see if Billy was around, or if anybody had details on what else had gone wrong.

To my dismay, Billy was there, which meant something *had* gone wrong. I sat on the edge of his desk and waited silently for him to look up, but I wasn't expecting the haggardness in his face when he did. I slid off the edge of the desk into the chair beside it, ice forming inside my stomach. "What happened?"

"What *happened?* My partner disappeared all day and I've been sitting here with my gut turning to acid waiting for her to get back. And to keep my mind off it I've been going over the files of a dozen people eaten alive over the past six weeks, and coming up dry. What the hell do you mean, what happened?"

I slumped in the chair, relief turning to a burp that I inexpertly hid behind one hand. "Sorry. From your expression I thought maybe somebody else was dead. Our gambit kind of worked. We flushed the thing out, but it started an avalanche and got away." I related the relevant parts of the day, ending with, "I don't know what it was, Billy. I know what it wasn't. It's not a god. It didn't have that kind of power. It's not even a sorcerer, but it's not exactly human, either."

Billy was taking notes and muttering, "Not quite human, eats human flesh, invisible but physical spirit form…you do that."

"What?" I cranked my jaw up for the second time, a guilty blush burning my ears. "Oh. God. Yeah, I guess I do." There was no *guess* about it. Very early on I'd learned to bend light around myself to make a mirage, to suggest I wasn't there. It was a matter of changing perceptions, which was one of the basic precepts of shamanism, and nobody had to know I'd gotten the idea from a comic book.

I'd looked at my reflection once when I'd pulled that cloak around me, and I had the sudden disturbing realization that Billy was right: what my opponent had done that morning had looked a lot like my trick. "It's another *shaman?*"

That was disturbing on a lot of levels. One, and rather obviously, shamans weren't supposed to go around eating people, except maybe symbolically. A shaman who went bad wasn't a shaman anymore, but a sorcerer, at least in a lot of Native

American myths. But my admittedly limited experience with sorcery had a different feel to it: seductive, rational, sacrificial....

I was starting to notice a lot of nasty things came across as seductive. Not blatantly so—no women in red dresses, no rain of wealth from the sky—but seductive nonetheless. Good didn't seem to be quite so charming, which I kind of thought was a mistake on the home team's part. Enlightenment and altruism weren't actually that common, as far as I could tell. People tended to want things, and evil tended to offer those things.

"Is that even possible?"

I rattled myself out of considering good's ineptitudes and frowned at Billy. "I don't know. I mean, it wouldn't be a shaman anymore, but I don't know if a sorcerer still has the same bag of tricks. Virissong was never trained as a shaman, and he's the only sorcerer I've ever met."

"Okay, how about other shamans you've met?"

"They've all been dead." I sounded pretty lost and miserable when I said that, and cleared my throat like it would make me bigger and stronger. "Really. The only other living shaman I've ever spoken with was Coyote, and..."

"Yeah." Billy sighed. "I'm sorry, Joanie."

"Me too." I scrubbed my hands through my hair, itching my scalp and hoping invigorated blood flow would awaken some kind of deep understanding in my soul. "Okay. This is what I know. That thing—" I straightened up suddenly. "Billy, I want to try something. Can astral projections have physical manifestations?"

To my chagrin, Billy threw his head back, laughed aloud, then settled back in his chair with a broad grin. "I can't believe I just heard you say that. A year ago you'd have been snorting in your sleeve and rolling your eyes if you'd heard me say something like that. And here you are, full of confidence and completely serious when you ask about physical manifestations of astral projections."

A little blossom of embarrassed pleasure burst in my chest. I hunched my shoulders and looked down, but shot Billy a glance through my eyebrows. "You know I think that's the first time you've given me even a little bit of shit about any of this?"

His grin got even wider. "I guess I figured you could take it by now." Some of the teasing slipped away, though the smile stayed just as big. "Don't get me wrong, there were times I wanted to say I told you so, but…"

"But you're a much better person than that, and you thought sending me off in a sulk would be counterproductive?"

"Something like that, yeah." Billy grunted as I scooted my chair forward to lean over and give him a hug. Normally I reserved that kind of soppy behavior for Gary, but just this once I thought we both deserved it.

"Thanks, Billy. Seriously. For putting up with all the crap I ever gave you, and for not rubbing my nose in it when I got hit in the teeth with your world. I owe you a lot."

"You can fix my car for free for the rest of your life in repayment."

"I do anyway."

Billy shrugged, still smiling. "Guess that works out, then. All right, Walker. What was that about physical manifestations of astral projections?" He started laughing again, and I couldn't blame him.

"Can it be done? Because if it can—" I hadn't often left my body behind. A handful of times, maybe, and always in a crisis. I relaxed into my chair—a task in itself, as it was hard plastic—

and thought about the peculiar sensation of standing over *there* when I could see my body sitting over *here*. An underlying part of me considered leaving my body behind to be joining the world of the Sight wholesale. I wasn't comfortable with that. I liked my body, and the world the Sight showed me was detached and gorgeous. I was afraid to become too attached to it, for fear I'd become detached myself.

The middling detail that I'd spent a significant chunk of my life deliberately detached was not to be considered. Vaguely grumpy at the thought, I got up and walked across the room, arms folded under my breasts and gaze locked downward. "All I need is a—"

My voice wasn't. I put my hand on my throat, then turned back to see myself lolling in the plastic chair beside Billy's desk. Billy grabbed my wrist, and I felt the distant pressure of his fingers checking my pulse before he looked around the room, eyebrows drawn down. "Joanie?"

It was a few minutes after five, and Homicide was mostly cleared out. Even so, everybody who was left glanced up, then exchanged looks that said they were suddenly in a hurry to go out for coffee and gossip about the Paranormal Pair.

Me, I walked back to Billy, silent on weightless feet, and gave his paperwork a push with one finger.

My finger slid through it with the sensation of paper cuts. I yelped and drew back, shaking my hand, then glanced at my body. A sliver of red awakened on one fingertip, and I grimaced. A little more determined, I reached for the papers, picked them up, and tapped them into a tidy stack before setting them back down on his desk and snapping back into my body, where I stuck my bleeding finger in my mouth. "Ow."

Billy did a fine impression of a goldfish, his eyes bulging and mouth popping. "Did you just—?"

I said, "I did," around my finger. "Never tried that before. See what I did?" I stuck my finger out at him and he eyed it.

"Aren't you a healer?"

"Oh. Right." Something like a paper cut didn't even require a car metaphor anymore. I just wanted the injury sealed, and voilà, it was. In theory I should be able to do that with much graver damage, but I hadn't leveled up that high yet. "So I can affect the physical world even out-of-body. I have this…nasty theory. We keep finding bodies with no signs of foul play in the immediate vicinity. Maybe they're being killed where we're finding the bodies, but the attack is coming on an astral level. The blood and viscera could be feeding back through the spirit into the separate body. No physical mess to clean up."

Billy, whom I thought of as being fairly tough, turned a little green around the gills. "Is that possible?"

I faced my palms upward. "The murders in Woodland were ugly, but their point was to channel souls to something separate that hungered for them. Same thing with the mess at Halloween. This is a little different, so I don't know that it's possible, but I'm not ruling it out."

"Wouldn't it leave a mark? Like Mel's power circle?"

I'd never seen Billy seem out of his depth before. Maybe it meant I was finally catching up to the rest of the class. I wasn't sure if it felt good or profoundly alarming. "I just rearranged your desk with almost no effort, much less a power circle, so not necessarily. If you're talking about somebody with a lot of rage or fear, and I'd think we kind of have to be, it's…" My brain caught up with where my mouth was going, and stopped my chatter with a sound of dismay. "Somebody could be doing this without knowing it."

"They could be eating bodies, stripping them of their souls, and leaving the corpses on unmarked territory without *knowing* it?" Billy's voice rose sharply enough that the handful of remaining detectives looked around at each other again, then, to a man, started mumbling about coffee breaks. In a rustle of coats, heavy boots and slamming doors, we were alone. Billy glowered after them. "Nobody offered to bring us a cup back."

"I wouldn't have, either. Look, I'm just saying it's possible. Maybe not probable, but the human psyche is messed-up territory. So we need to pursue this, but for the first time I'm thinking maybe we shouldn't go in with all guns blazing."

My cell phone gave its six-note warning that a text message was coming in as I finished speaking. So did Billy's. We both went still, my tense expression mirrored on his face, and I silently put a fist on one palm. He echoed the motion and we beat our fists against our palms in tandem, one two three.

I came up scissors. He came up rock. I swore and stood up to pull my phone out of my pocket, reading the message out loud: "Possible new victim. Positive identification, oh, *shit*."

"What?" Billy was on his feet, leaning toward me like the tension in his body would negate whatever I had to say. "Who?"

I pressed my hand over my mouth, fingers icy, belly cramping. "I'm sorry, Billy. I'm so sorry. It's Mandy Tiller."

And it was unquestionably my fault.

CHAPTER TWELVE

Mandy was still breathing when we got there.

We were fast: the paramedics were only just pulling into the driveway when we reached the Tillers' home, a few blocks away from Billy's. The fact that there were paramedics at all pushed some of the churning terror in my stomach aside and made room for something almost worse: hope. No one else had needed a paramedic. I fell out of Billy's van and ran across the Tillers' lawn, skidding across snow to reach Mandy's side.

Unlike the other victims, she had only one bite mark. A stretched-out wound had torn her coat and shirt and left a broad toothy gash in her forearm. A pool of blood stained the stairs under her head, which was both horrible and wonderful. All the others had been found in clean sites, and I knew for certain Mandy hadn't been attacked miles away and been dumped on her own front steps. I'd been with her barely an hour earlier.

A paramedic put a hand on my shoulder. "Excuse me, ma'am."

I whispered, "Ten seconds. Just give me ten seconds. Please," and let the Sight wash over everything.

Blood seeped from her skull, a simple but significant wound that cried out for healing. I clenched my hands, wishing I had time, wishing I didn't have an audience. But the paramedics could care for the head wound; what I was more worried about was the utter nothingness which had surrounded all the other victims. And though unlike them, Mandy still breathed, she also had no spark of life. Her aura didn't even lie flat against her skin, giving me some hint of her well-being. It was just gone.

What I *could* See were vestiges of my own power, familiar silver-blue tendrils still lingering from our adventure earlier in the day. I jerked around to look at Billy with the Sight, searching for similar remnants around him, and found nothing. But it had been weeks since I'd used my power on him, and even then it hadn't been the kind of physical shield I'd used on Mandy. I didn't know if the residue had protected her in some way or not, but even if it had, that didn't exactly balance out setting her up as a potential victim in the first place.

While I was looking at Billy, the paramedics swooped in and got Mandy onto a stretcher. Jake Tiller sat on top of the porch steps, wrapped in a huge winter jacket and blank-gazed with fear. One of the paramedics offered his hand. Jake took it blindly, letting the man guide him down the stairs toward the ambulance. The poor boy's aura was static white, shock too great for his true colors to wash through. Billy, a few yards away, was talking to the cop who'd texted us, and I heard the guy say, "The kid came home from ball practice and found his mom lying on the steps. He called 911. Probably saved her life."

"He's smart," Billy agreed. "Friends with my son." I let the rest of their conversation fade away as I turned my gaze to the snow-littered steps and yard.

Anybody else and I might've thought she'd slipped on the stairs and cracked her head, but I *knew* Mandy Tiller hadn't received a gash-toothed bite on her arm that morning. I'd have healed it if she had. So the thing had come after her, and somehow, it had failed to walk away with her life. I was less certain about the safety of her soul.

There were imprints in the snow on the uncovered porch, just like the ones I'd seen yesterday morning. I didn't touch them this time, afraid I'd flatten them into nothing and destroy any chance of a lead. I'd seen, that morning, how far this thing could jump in a single bound. And it did jump, traversing space like it was real. But then, so did I, when I separated from my body. I didn't float through walls or fly up to rooftops. I walked through the doors and climbed stairs, treating the astral world essentially like the real one.

It was a paltry thing to go on, but at least it was something. I stood up and followed their imprints' potential trajectory, scanning the yard and sidewalk and street without finding a hint of where the thing might have landed. Neighbor's yard, across the street, empty. No trees bigger than bushes to ricochet off anywhere in easy sight.

A quick wash of snow, unsettled by the rumble of ambulance engines, slid off the roof and poofed into the yard, narrowly missing the porch. I flinched, reminded of the avalanche.

More snow flopped down, less vigorously than if someone had shoveled it, but with a certain amount of enthusiasm. A ghost of forensics training came back to me and I crouched again. There was no kickback in the imprint, no spray that suggested the beast had jumped forward. The indentations looked like it had squatted, just as I was doing now. My gaze strayed to the roof.

Well. Just because I'd never tried floating up to a rooftop didn't mean I couldn't do it. I pressed my spine against the house, propping myself against it, and for the second time in an hour, slipped the surly bonds of earth.

My subconscious had a mean sense of humor. It had let me float through a closed door, but not a wall, because one was meant for walking through and the other wasn't. But that had been nearly a year ago, and I had more control now. Gravity was permitted, I decided, to exert the smallest influence over me, just enough to keep me from floating into the stratosphere and beyond. I weighed in at a little over one-sixty, but there was no reason my astral form couldn't be light as a thought.

I stayed firmly stuck to the ground in both body and spirit. I bared my teeth at the sky, willing to admit that thoughts could be depressingly weighty. Better to be light as a bird, with hollow bones and an ability to fly. I could break free from gravity's pull and soar up to the roof on an impulse of will.

My astral self, it seemed, was absolutely unimpressed with my puny logic. Eventually, swearing silently, my astral form crawled up a drainpipe and swung onto the roof. There was no way I could've done that physically. Neither the pipe nor my dignity nor my hand strength—which was pretty good, but not *that* good—would have let me. Astrally, though? No problem. It made no sense at all. On the positive side, it didn't have to make sense. It just had to work.

And up there on the rooftop, the monster was waiting for me.

★ ★ ★

By all rights I should've woken up dead. I'd thought the thing would've been scared off. It was only once I was up there on the roof, nose to nose with a stinking beast, that I wondered why I thought an invisible ravening magic cannibal would be frightened by a kid with a cell phone or a few police sirens.

While I was standing there stupefied, it raised a lazy paw and backhanded me so hard I flew off the roof and slid across Mandy's front yard to smash up against her white picket fence. Little peaks of snow fell off the fence and right through me, making tiny lumps on the frozen lawn.

I couldn't remember anything ever doing that before. I tended to think of my astral form as a pretty safe place for me to be. Sure, a god had stuffed a sword through me once when I'd been incorporeal, but we'd been traveling through time and space, too, so under those circumstances it seemed fair that I could be hit. I'd fought another god in a kind of dreamscape, but dreams were a little different. I didn't remember anything ever flat-out belting my astral self while it was just standing around in the Middle World. But this thing had, and I didn't like that at all.

It hadn't come after me. I pushed onto my elbows and scowled at the roof, where its form was barely more than a glimmer against white snow and gray skies. It stood on two legs, but its shoulders were hunched forward, like it was de-volving toward four legs. It hadn't moved beyond hitting me.

A clear, unpleasant thought unfurled itself. Maybe it hadn't come after Mandy. Maybe it had just used her to draw the more powerful agent to it, so it could get another look at me. Size me up, study me. Decide if I was a threat or a tasty morsel.

I figured lying on my back in the snow wasn't at all threatening, and got to my feet. The thing watched. Warily, I thought. Hoped. I wanted to be scary enough to set it on edge. That would be a definite score for my side.

It had hit my astral form. That suggested maybe my astral form could hit it. All I had to do was get close enough, but I was pretty sure it wasn't going to give me another chance to climb the drainpipe.

Which meant I had one chance to convince my recalcitrant brain that the laws of gravity and physics didn't apply to a soul set loose to wander away from its body. I'd crossed great leaps and bounds effortlessly in other planes of reality. I could do it in this one, if I had to.

And I had to. The monster on the rooftop was still watching me, and I didn't want its attention to land on anyone else. I muttered, "There is no spoon," took three running steps, and jumped.

The creature vanished, I smashed into Mandy's house, and warm fingers touched my face as Morrison said, "Walker," drawing me back into my body.

I opened my eyes disoriented and confused. The world had tipped over sideways, and a puddle of slush had crept up to envelop my left cheek. Rather a lot of weight seemed to be pressing the slush into my jaw and shoulder, and enough blood rushed to my head to make my nose itch.

Morrison was perpendicular to me, feet planted in the same icy water that was crawling over my face, and his forehead was wrinkled with concern. "You fell over, Walker."

That explained a lot. The pressure, for example, was my own body weight resting on my head and shoulder, which were at the foot of the stairs, while the rest of me was angled down them. It was profoundly uncomfortable, and I was beginning to fear it might be embarrassing, too. On the other hand, it distracted from the dull ache running from head to toe, which I suspected was the physical response to psychically smacking myself into Mandy's house. I'd been so sure I could make it, too.

Morrison offered me a hand up, which proved to be more like putting his hands under my armpits and bodily hauling me to my feet. "You okay?"

"Yeah. Sorry, I thought I'd propped myself up well enough that I wouldn't fall. I was…" I made a feeble gesture, which was apparently enough to remind Morrison he was holding me up. He let go and stepped back. I was kind of disappointed.

No, not disappointed. A little sad, maybe. I liked being close to my boss; he smelled good. But I'd blown it on that front, and was working on living with the consequences. "I was trying to follow the killer. Hang on a second, okay?"

Dismay and confusion spasmed across Morrison's face, leaving his blue eyes darker than usual. The color he'd put in it at Halloween had grown out of his hair, leaving it short and silvering, the way I liked it, and the whole package made for a handsome man in need of some reassurance. Or at least explanation, if I couldn't offer the other. The best I could do was step away and look up at the roof.

No monsters. There were tracks, cold trails through the air visible with the Sight, but my prey had run away. I whispered, "Maybe it decided I was tougher than it was," without much hope, and glanced toward the ambulance.

Two paramedics were still checking Mandy over. A third stood with Jake at the vehicle's tail end. They had her on an IV already, and I figured it wouldn't be more than another minute before they brought her to the hospital. I wondered if they'd let me in to see her, and if I could be any help if they did, or if I'd be better off trying to track the thing that had attacked her. But I hadn't spoiled the marks this time, so its trail wasn't going to get any colder, and there was something I really had to do before trying to either follow it or help Mandy.

It took everything I had to look back at Morrison and say, "This is my fault, boss."

Every shred of warmth fled the captain's face, turning him back into the nemesis he'd been for years. A short jerk of his chin said "Keep talking."

I did, through knots of anger and guilt. "She volunteered," wasn't much of an excuse, and I knew it as I told him what Mandy Tiller and I had done that morning. "I never imagined it might come after her once we were off the mountain. I should have," I said before he could. "I should have, and I didn't. I completely fucked up. I'm sorry." Sorry didn't begin to cover it, but language was badly suited to expressing hand-shaking chills of misery and a hollow feeling burning my eyes in a single word. "Sorry," inadequate as it was, had to do the job.

"You got a civilian involved in a dangerous case that the media is all over, and now she's hospitalized and you're *sorry?*"

"This one's on me, Captain." Billy put himself between me and Morrison. "I asked Mandy to give us a hand."

"Why?" Morrison erupted like a bull seal, and Billy, who was bigger than either of us, somehow seemed to absorb the captain's rage and expand a little with it. "There are dozens of *officers* who could have—"

"Two reasons, sir," Billy said very steadily. "One is that Walker's original plan was to use herself as bait—"

"Which she would have needed permission for!"

"Not," I mumbled, "if I did it off duty. Which I did." I was sure I wasn't actually helping the situation, but sometimes I talked when I knew I should shut up. It was a character flaw.

"And the other," Billy went on as though neither of us had spoken, "is that this is getting worse fast, sir, and even under the best of circumstances, going through the department on this would have added another twenty-four hours to the search. Getting permission from you, possibly having to wait for a green light from your superiors, getting volunteers, getting equipment...this was faster."

"That wasn't your decision to make!"

"No, sir, it wasn't, and I regret my error in judgment." Billy, stiffly, reached into his coat, withdrew his badge and gun, and offered them to Morrison.

Who stared at them, then at Billy and me, and then said, *"Shit,"* more violently than I'd ever heard him speak before.

All three of us knew he had to take them. Involving civilians in police business, even surreal police business like the stuff Billy and I handled, was bad enough. Getting a civilian hospitalized, maybe killed, was at the very least a suspension offense, and would likely have both of us up on charges. I fumbled for my own badge and gun, because I couldn't let Billy take the fall for me even if he was technically right. I was still the one who'd gotten Mandy Tiller hurt.

Morrison saw what I was doing and made a very sharp, short gesture and pitched his voice bone-scrapingly low: "You have until the nine o'clock news to find a way to make this right. If I get called before then, if I have to make a statement, I'll do it with your badges in my hand. Do I make myself clear?"

My knees went weak and I nodded feebly. "At least Corvallis is at dinner with Ray right now, so she's probably not going to be breathing down our necks for a couple hours."

Despite his fury, Morrison got an expression very much like the one I'd had when Ray had announced his date for the evening. He eventually said, "Ray *Campbell?*" like the department might have sprouted another Ray recently that he didn't know about.

I nodded, and Billy whistled. "Takes all kinds, I guess." He put his badge and gun away very carefully, offering a quiet, "Thanks, Captain."

"Don't thank me. If we get away with this I'm stringing you both up by your toes. If we don't, I'm crucifying you."

I'd been skewered more times than I cared to think about, which gave me an uncomfortably visceral idea of what cruci-fixion might feel like. I looked over Morrison's shoulder, not wanting to read any truth in his eyes. The ambulance crawled out of the Tillers' driveway and stopped a few yards down the street, blocked by a black-haired man standing in its path. The driver leaned on the horn, then rolled down the window to shout at the man, who smiled apologetically and shrugged, but didn't move.

A tiny smile of my own was born somewhere around the fine muscles of my eyes, not even getting close to my mouth as it spilled golden happiness, rich and sweet as warm honey, all the way through me. It neutralized the worry bubbling in my belly and revitalized the tiny shred of hope I'd felt at seeing Mandy was alive. I thought my heart was likely to burst, and my chest filled with breathless giggles that I didn't dare let out. Even my hands felt wrong, but in a good way, as they alter-nated between thrums of thick aching heat and icy coldness with every pulse-beat. For the first time in six months, in a year, maybe for the first time in my whole life, the overwhelming confidence that everything was going to be all right filled me.

The ambulance driver swung his door open, angry words a wash of meaningless noise to my ears. The self-imposed obstruction raised his hands placatingly, then shot me a direct look, one eyebrow elevated in amusement. My itty-bitty smile crinkled my eyes enough to turn my vision all blurry with tears, and finally made it to my mouth. I couldn't breathe, not at all, but I felt so light I thought I might be able to fly.

"Walker, crucifixion isn't a threat that should make you smile." Morrison sounded justifiably annoyed, like I'd taken the wind out of his melodramatic sails. I wanted to promise that I had no doubt at all he meant he'd crucify us, professionally if not physically, but the little smile he was complaining about blossomed into this huge, foolish, jubilant thing that I laid on him like a blessing.

Then I was running just like an ingenue in a bad movie. Running across a snow-covered yard, vaulting the Tillers' low fence, and sliding across the slush-slick asphalt street to crash, joyfully, impossibly, wonderfully, into Coyote's arms.

CHAPTER THIRTEEN

Coyote caught me with a grunt that sounded like a laugh and squeezed hard enough to take my breath as he swung me around and around in a slushy circle. I squeaked and buried my nose in his neck, and he didn't let me hang on nearly long enough before he set me back, hands on my shoulders.

His smile was the most beautiful thing I'd ever seen, bright and gentle in a face that wasn't nearly as red-brick colored as he was in my dreams. Nor were his eyes golden, but the rest was as I remembered: straight nose, high cheekbones, hip-length black hair. He was a little shorter than me and smelled like the outdoors, and he wiped happy tears away from my cheeks. "We don't have a lot of time. How is she?"

I didn't care about the tears, didn't care that they tickled the creases around my mouth where my face was already getting tired from such a big smile, and somehow didn't care that I had a hundred thousand questions that were all going to have to wait. "She's all right physically. Banged up. But her aura, Coyote, it's gone. Like nobody's home."

He nodded, and though his joy didn't dissipate, the smile became something more serious. Something trustworthy and confident, something that I suddenly wished I could command myself. He took my hand and said, both apologetically and in a tone that brooked no nonsense, "We need to see your patient. Go ahead and drive us to the hospital, if you want, but I hope it won't be necessary," to the incensed ambulance driver.

We let ourselves in while the guy spluttered.

Both paramedics in the back gave guttural sounds of protest that faded into uncertainty when Coyote said, "It's all right. We're healers. Excuse us, please."

They both moved, and neither of them looked like they had the foggiest idea why. I didn't either, but I wished to hell I could do that. Jake Tiller, his face tear-stained, stared between us like we were aliens, and Coyote gripped the boy's shoulder a moment. "My name's Cyrano. This is my friend Joanne. You're…?"

"Jake," he whispered. The ambulance driver threw the back doors shut again as the kid spoke, and a few seconds later we were in motion. "Jake Tiller. This's my mom."

Coyote nodded solemnly. "I think Joanne and I can do something for your mom that the paramedics can't, Jake. Will you let us try?"

"Will it make her wake up?"

"I hope so."

The kid nodded. "Then okay."

One of the paramedics made another strangled noise, surging forward. "We can't let you—"

Trying to sound as calm and reassuring as Coyote, I said, "She's stabilized, right?" At the medic's reluctant nod, I offered a brief smile. "Then if we're right and we can help, you won't have anything to worry about. If we can't, well, this won't take more than a few minutes and we're already on the way to the hospital, so no time will be lost. Okay?"

"We could get sued—"

"You won't," Coyote said with serene confidence, then reached across Mandy's still form and said, "Have you done a soul retrieval yet? Besides me, I mean?"

"Besss—" I bit my tongue on the *s* and tried to claw shocked thoughts back under control. There would be time later. There *had* to be time later. "Billy, a few weeks ago. But I know him, Coyote. I know him really well."

"I'm here now. You'll be fine. We don't have a drum, Joanne, so I'm going to need you to—"

"I can do it." For once I felt as confident as I sounded. "Where are we going?"

"The Lower World."

I nodded, closed my eyes, and let the rattle of the ambulance over rough roads drop me into a world not my own.

Red skies and yellow earth, a flat sun and a world more two-dimensional than my own: that was the Lower World, in my rare experiences with it. I was certain there were other ways it could be viewed—roots of a mighty tree, burrows and hollows beneath the earth—but I saw it as one of the strange, not-quite-real worlds-that-had-come-before in terms of Native American mythology. It was beautiful and intimidating, and I knew almost nothing about navigating it safely. I said, "Raven?" into the empty air, hopefully.

My raven fell out of the sky, something glittering in his beak. He landed on the ground and dropped it, cocking his head first at me, then it, then back again before he pounced on it with both feet and tore it apart.

It was the shiny food I'd left him, Pop-Tarts wrapped in foil. He made delighted burbling sounds in the back of his birdy throat as he stabbed pieces of frosted raspberry tart and shredded the wrapper with his claws. I sat down, laughing, and stole a piece of pastry that had been flung away so I could offer it to him directly. He hopped over, snatched it from my fingers, and scurried back to his feast.

Coyote said, "This is a good sign," and licked my ear with a very long wet tongue. I squawked and reached out to grab him around the neck without even looking. I had thousands of questions, and none of them mattered as long as I could hide my face in his neck and hold on.

He leaned against me hard, until fur tickled my nose and I sneezed into his shoulder. I sat up to rub my nose, then grabbed him again, scruffing the top of his bony head and pulling on pointed ears. "Where've you been, you dumb dog? I missed you. I missed you so much." I could barely control my voice, even my whispers all shaky, and I tried to push relief so big it exhausted me away so I could ask, "How do we help Mandy?"

He rolled over on his back, legs waving in the air and neck stretched to try to nab a piece of my raven's treat. It quarked in agitation, wings spread as it hopped toward him, and he gave a coyote laugh and rolled away to sit up, prim and proper as a cat with his feet all in alignment. "I'm not a dog."

"You look like a dog." I never thought I'd be so happy to have that same stupid conversation again. Bewilderment and relief and joy knocked me flat again, and I toppled against him, hanging on to his skinny coyote form. He pressed a surprising amount of weight back into me, and we sat together for a moment, watching the raven stuff himself.

When the bird was finished, Coyote stood up and shook himself all over, then cocked an ear at me. "You arrived first, and your spirit animal came to join us. You lead the retrieval."

"But I don't know how!" It struck me that I'd spent six months fumbling through even when I didn't know how, and that probably relying on Coyote for all the answers was a crutch I couldn't afford, even if he was back. Lips pursed at the idea, I stood up and offered an arm to my raven. "A woman who greets the sunrise with music is lost, Raven. Will you help me find her?"

He bounced from the earth to my shoulder with a half-assed flurry of wings, like he could've made the jump without them but instinct forced them to spread anyway. Then he opened them farther, the better, I thought, to smack me in the head with one, and urged me into a run with strides so enormous it was almost like flying.

Coyote chased along behind in a long-legged lope. We tore across the landscape, leaving yellow fields and purpley forests for low hills that became rolling blue mountains. There was an odd flatness to them, as though, if we crested a peak too suddenly, we'd find ourselves looking down on plywood and two-by-fours propping up stage scenery rather than the back side of a proper mountain, but it never happened. Instead a storm came up, white howling blurs of snow that blocked out the mountains entirely. The raven leaped off my shoulder and flew ahead, cawing excitedly.

He was good at blizzards, was my raven. I wondered why he hadn't been on hand to help in the avalanche, though to be fair, one little bird against all that rolling chaos didn't seem like an equal fight. The fact that I'd have put money on the raven was beside the point.

I heard a woman's voice crying through the storm and followed it, aware that other cries were gaining in strength as I came closer. They weren't like hers: she was asking for help, and the others were shrieking for blood. They had a terrible hunger, and Mandy, it seemed, could feed it.

We found her huddled in a snow-scoured igloo, though its protective curve seemed to have been born of her body providing something for drifts to lodge against, rather than from deliberate construction. A *thing* danced in the snow, no more than a formless blur in the white. It plucked at Mandy's hair, at her hunched back, at her exposed arms, and where it did, welts and blood rose up.

There was probably some kind of formal ritual phrasing to gain the attention of demons chewing up living souls. I yelled, "Hey, knock it off, you bastard!"

Even I knew it lacked elegance, but it got the thing's attention. It swung to face me in a disjointed ugly way that somehow suggested it had once been human, but that too many ligaments and tendons had slipped loose, and nothing could be counted on anymore. I repressed a shudder and stood my ground, hoping like hell Coyote would back me up when I got in over my head. "This woman isn't yours to torment."

"She is marked for me," it said unexpectedly. Its voice was a scream around too many teeth, words slurred but comprehensible. "She has the scent, the taste, the blood, of the wild world in her."

Outrage turned the snowstorm red, and I fought it down, pretty certain that fury in the Lower World did other things more good than it did me. "She's not marked for anybody. I'm bringing her home safe and sound."

"But she lives. She knows her path. She walks it. She shows me. I follow. I hunger. I eat. She is mine." There was a gleam of ruthless greed in its half-visible eyes. Like the creature on Hurricane Hill, on the rooftop—and I was sure this was the same thing—all I could really see were claws and teeth, like they were the only thing tied to any level of reality at all.

"She isn't yours." A flicker of an idea came to me. "She's an outdoorsman. Is that what you mean? Is that why she's yours?"

It swung its head heavily, whole body shifting with the motion. "They are all mine."

Man, if it had marked all the outdoorsy types in Seattle as its own personal smorgasbord, I needed to get this thing six feet under a whole lot sooner than later. The eight or so deaths we'd seen were nothing in the face of how many people were going to die if it kept hunting. I swallowed and shook the thought off. I had to save Mandy first. "But she's not really what you want. She's weak. I see how you're looking at me. You can tell how much stronger I am, can't you? You know it from when we fought. That's why you didn't kill her straight out. You wanted me to come, so you could test me."

A certain animal cunning came into the creature's eyes, and I wasn't sure if I was right, or if it was a new and enticing thought to the monster. "You couldn't find me on your own, could you? Even with all my power, you hunt the ones that go into the woods, and I don't. So you needed her. But you don't need her anymore. You can have me."

Raven, I whispered deep enough inside that I hoped no one beyond me could hear. *Raven, will you play in the snow?* I showed it a picture of what I wanted, and heard Coyote's teeth snap, the sound audible above the sobbing wind. Emboldened, I took a half step back, beckoning the beast. "All you have to do is come and get me."

It pounced, slower in this world than it was in mine, or I was faster. I flung myself to the side, hitting a snowbank in a spray of cold and ice, and lurched to my feet barely in time to duck another attack. Coyote and the raven zipped around each other a few yards away, gamboling in the storm, and I did my best to watch them while avoiding being eaten.

A figure grew up between them, a snowman in jeans and a sweater and with my short-cropped hair. The raven alighted on its head and shook itself, and color fell into the snowman: black hair, black coat, black pants, black boots. Coyote leaped up and slurped his tongue across its face, and a blush of flesh tones filled its rounded features and its blunt snowman hands.

The final time the monster jumped for me, I ducked, and it knocked my simulacrum to the earth with a howl of triumph, rending it with tooth and claw.

I surged forward and snatched Mandy's cowering soul in my arms, lifting her with no trouble at all. It was tiny, almost weightless, like a very young child, and I hoped that didn't mean it was dying.

Coyote said, "Quick, come on," and I turned and ran after him out of the snowstorm, a raven winging above us.

I woke up still cuddling Mandy's spirit. The woman on the paramedic's stretcher looked thin and wan, while the ephemeral thing in my arms was bright but fading fast. I leaned forward without thinking, hugging her body close, and felt her soul slip away, settling back into the form meant to hold it.

Color sprang up around her, flat against her skin but visible: her aura returning a little worse for the wear, but indicative that all would be well. Coyote murmured, "Well done," and when I glanced up at him, his eyes were gold and his smile wide. "The rest is easy. Finish it."

The blow to her head was nasty blunt trauma, a radial fracture like what happened when a rock hit a windshield. There was no blood below it, no sign of deeper trouble, and I tended the fracture with the images I was most comfortable with: new bone filling the cracks like it was heated glass melding a window together. Reluctantly, I left some of the bruising in place so she still had a goose-egg lump on her head. I'd offer to fix it later, but utterly obliterating the signs of injury when there were paramedics standing by seemed excessively complicated.

The bite on her arm, unexpectedly, was harder. It had a cold core to it, like winter had lodged in the bone and seeded there, difficult to root out. I looked at Coyote, but he only raised an eyebrow, a none-too-subtle hint that this was a test, and that it'd be better if I passed.

Vehicle analogies didn't work so well with cold spots, though the idea of a faulty heater crept in. It gave me a place to start, at least: from inside, like the wiring had gone bad, rather than from the outside where all I'd be doing was poking around at an external symptom of an internal problem.

I put my palm over the bite and let magic sink all the way through, until I could see through her arm the same way I'd seen through mine a handful of times. Skin and sinew and blood and muscle and bone all lit up in shades of life, Mandy's colors gaining strength now that the greater physical damage was healed. But there were dark spots inside the wound, those seeds of cold, and delicate trails danced out of them and led into the world.

Marking her. Marking her more literally than I'd thought. It wasn't just that she was outdoorsy, not anymore. The bite connected her to the monster, so if I didn't get those tendrils cleaned out, it would come for her again. I gathered them up and tugged gently, just to see if they would loosen. They didn't. I hadn't thought it would be that easy.

The trick—the real trick, the most effective expulsion—would be to convince her body to reject the seeds itself. Thoughtful, cautious, I murmured, "Mandy? Can I come in?"

After a brief hesitation, I felt—not agreement, exactly, but a lack of resistance, and with that invitation, stepped inside the garden of Mandy Tiller's soul.

I wasn't in the least bit startled to find myself in the mountains of the Pacific Northwest for the second time that day. This time, though, it was summertime, the sky a blaze of blue glory and the mountainside green and ripe with life. Mandy, lithe and athletic in hiking shorts and a tank-top, was climbing toward a host of pine trees. A backpack was slung over her shoulders and a hiking staff was in one hand, making her the epitome, in my opinion, of wilderness chic.

She waved when she noticed me. "Come on over here, take a look at this? See that clinging moss? These trees are going to be dead by the end of the year if we don't give them a hand."

I almost said, "Isn't that the natural cycle?" but bit my tongue before the words escaped. There was sickness in her garden, and she had the wherewithal to be rooting it out on her own. I hurried after her.

"It spreads," she told me with a sort of resigned dismay. "One tree to another, blocking their ability to draw down sunlight. The hard part's getting it off the tree without damaging the bark, but if you can they'll survive? Here's a knife." She tossed me a relatively blunt blade and showed me how to work it under the moss, how to loosen its clinging runners, and ultimately handed me the backpack so I could stuff the moss we'd cleared away into it. "I take it home and burn it."

On a whole different level, I felt one of the seeds of cold in her arm loosen, then shrivel and die.

It was good hard honest work, both of us sweating and swearing cheerfully as we scrambled up thin-trunked trees to find far-spreading gobs of moss. Every time a tree came clean, another seed fell away, until suddenly the whole grove brightened, fresh green needles sprouting instantly on all the afflicted spruce. Mandy stood back, brushing her hands with satisfaction, and gave me a sharp, pleased nod. "Thanks!"

The great Northwest faded out, leaving me in the back of an ambulance with Mandy Tiller blinking up at me.

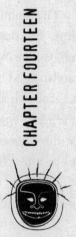

CHAPTER FOURTEEN

Jake Tiller squeaked, "Mom?" and threw himself forward. I lurched back, getting free of paramedics and kid alike. The latter didn't care what had happened, but the former rushed in to check Mandy's vitals, then turned to Coyote and me with expressions raging between incomprehension, anger and relief.

"What are you?" one of them said. "Some kind of faith healers?"

Coyote shrugged a shoulder, graceful smooth movement. The truth was he probably could've picked his nose and I'd have thought it was gorgeous because I was just so glad he was alive. My heart sped up again like it was going to burst, then kind of exploded with messy joy inside me like it *had* burst. It was the happiest thing I'd ever felt, and it made the corners of my mouth turn up in an idiot smile. Again. Coyote said, "Something like that, without the religious overtones," and the medic who'd asked crossed himself anyway.

The ambulance thumped over speed bumps and came to a stop. The doors flew open, two new paramedics ready to help unload the injured person, and were greeted by six fully awake, undamaged human beings. Mandy'd gotten half her restraints off and was alternating between hugging Jake and prodding at the goose egg on her head. She looked at the new medics, then at the ones on either side of her. "I'm not sure I really need to be checked into the hospital?"

"You do," the one who hadn't spoken said, firmly. "I want to get those injuries X-rayed, maybe do a CAT scan. Or an MRI."

What he wanted, really, was an explanation for her recovery. He wanted something to tell him he'd been wrong, that she'd never been hurt as badly as it had seemed, even though he'd seen it with his own eyes. He didn't want a miracle. He wanted something comprehensible.

"I want Mom to come home!"

Mandy put her hand on Jake's head. "It's okay, Jake." She fingered the torn sleeve of her shirt and the still-raw wound beneath it. I hadn't healed that all the way, either, though it was neither as deep nor as dangerous as it had been. "I had a bad fall on the stairs," she said to no one in particular. "Maybe a neighborhood dog bit me while I was out, I don't remember? But with that cannibal everybody's talking about, and me being an outdoors type, it got a little out of hand?"

Tight-mouthed and unhappy, the second paramedic muttered, "Please stay on the stretcher, ma'am. We'll wheel you into the hospital for your examination."

"If you have to." She lay back down and the paramedics

lifted her out. Jake jumped after them and grabbed her hand as they abandoned Coyote and me to the ambulance.

We sat in the vehicle's back end, watching with an air of detached interest. The part of me that wasn't bubbling with glee said, sensibly, "Her insurance is going to have a field day with this. I didn't heal everything all the way, but it's going to look pretty lame in light of ambulance rides and MRIs."

I heard the smile in Coyote's answer: "Yeah. Sorry I didn't get there before the ambulance did."

"Oh," I said lightly, "it's okay. I didn't, either. Our timing was off."

Just like that, with a handful of frothy words, all the composure I'd been holding in place shattered. Every emotion the paramedics had shown, anger and bewilderment and relief and fear, erupted through me. My hands turned into a shaking mess and tears wiped my vision out entirely. I turned on Coyote in the worst display of Girl Behavior I'd ever manifested, sloppy fists slapping at his shoulders and chest as my voice shot into a squeaky register. "Where have you been? What happened? I thought you were dead! It's been six months, Coyote! You disappeared, you saved my life and you disappeared and I thought you were *dead!*"

I couldn't have hurt a bug with the power behind my smacks, but he grabbed my wrists, then hauled me against his chest, capturing my flailing hands between us. "Shh, shh, hey hey hey. It's all right, Jo. I was only mostly dead, hey? Hush, hush, shh. It's okay."

Wracking sobs stole my ability to flail at him anymore, even if I'd wanted to. Coyote put his chin on top of my head and held on while I ran through the stages of a crying jag, ending with exhaustion so profound it left me nauseated. It was quick, as that kind of thing went, and no one bothered us. I figured people sobbing in the back of ambulances wasn't that uncommon a sight, and that paramedics would rouse us if they needed to go on a run. I finished crying before that happened, and looked up at Coyote feeling all red-nosed and swollen-eyed and hideous.

He smiled, a sort of rueful, fond expression, which was as much as any woman could possibly ask from a man when she's just cried all over him. In relationship terms, in fact, it probably meant the guy was a keeper. This particular guy got up and rooted around in the ambulance until he found paper towel that could double as a tissue, and brought it back to me. Definitely keeper material. I honked my nose clear and hiccuped an, "I'm okay now," that made him smile again.

"Why don't we go get some takeaway and go back to your place to talk?"

That sounded like the best idea in the entire universe, ever. I nodded and snuffled and said, "There's a great Chinese place on University. I'll call Gary and he can…" pick us up, then join us for dinner, was how that scenario would realistically end, although it wasn't what I'd had in mind. I stared blankly at the distance, trying to think of another cab company I could call. It wasn't that I didn't want to share Coyote with Gary. I just wanted to find out what had happened on my own, first. I was in no fit state to juggle more than one man in my life.

Right on cue, Morrison pulled into the parking lot with Billy in the car.

I got out of the ambulance and tried to make myself look presentable. There was no chance of that, not with my face puffy and red from crying, but I tried. The captain had on his

Dread Morrison face as he got out of his car, and Billy just looked worried. I said, "We managed the hat trick, boss," before either of them got close enough to start yelling.

"Hat trick?" Whatever Morrison had expected me to say, that wasn't it. I was deeply grateful. Any chance to derail a lecture was a win.

"Mandy Tiller's okay."

Billy let out a sigh that came from the bottom of his soul, and dropped his chin to his chest. I wanted to hug him, but Morrison was still glowering at me. "She had a bad slip on the stairs, that's all."

That's what she'd said in the ambulance, and I had absolutely no doubt it was the party line she was going to feed anybody who tried bleeding her for information. I thought she'd offered it up a little bit to help me, but much more to help herself. A fall on the stairs wasn't newsworthy, whereas surviving an attack by a mad killer unquestionably was. If she caught wind of the story at all, Laurie Corvallis would no doubt discover Mandy and I had been out hiking together, but there would be nothing for Laurie to hear about, if Mandy stuck with her version of events. God knew I wasn't about to dispute them.

Morrison, however, gave me a gimlet eye. "Is it now."

I shrugged, willing enough to feed the party line to someone like Corvallis, but I'd made an unhealthy habit of telling my boss the truth. "No. It was the—"

"Wendigo," Coyote put in unexpectedly. I jolted around to gawk at him, then twitched back to face Morrison again and pretended like I hadn't missed a beat.

"It was the wendigo, and I had to do a soul retrieval to save her life. Which," I said much more softly, "I did put in danger, yeah. I drew its attention to her. If it's worth anything, I'm not sure it really wanted to kill her as much as it wanted to flush me out."

It didn't help. I could tell from Morrison's expression. But he snapped his attention from me to Coyote, clearly expecting to get more answers there. "What the hell's a wendigo?"

"A—" Billy and Coyote spoke at the same time, and I saw a little battle of will and surprise, mostly on Billy's part, before he gestured for Coyote to continue. "A man who's gone mad and developed the taste for human flesh," my mentor said. "It usually happens in times of famine, but sometimes other circumstances trigger it. He's becoming a monster, a physical transformation. The wendigo is drawn to the forests. That's why your victims are outdoorsmen."

Morrison shot me a look that said "How come you didn't know that?" and "How come this guy knows so much?" in equal parts. What he said aloud, though, was, "Captain Michael Morrison of the Seattle Police Department. And you are…?" as he offered his hand.

Coyote said, "Cyrano Bia of the Diné," and although he was flawlessly polite, I could have sworn he was laughing at Morrison. He arched an eyebrow at me, and added, "Jo might've mentioned me as 'Coyote.'"

For the countable space of a breath, there was goggle-eyed silence, and then all hell broke loose.

Morrison and Billy started trying to out-shout each other, both of them asking the same questions: "Walker's Coyote? The one who's dead? What are you doing here? Well, I guess that explains the scene at the Tillers' house. How did you get here? I thought you'd died! What the hell is going on? Joanie? What's going on? Walker, what the hell—"

I hadn't known that only two people could make that much

noise. Worse, Coyote started trying to answer them, not that they were listening, and finally somebody bellowed, *"Enough!"*

For some reason everybody looked at me after that. It took a few seconds to realize my throat was sore from the shout, and that my hands were fisted hard enough to ache. I said, "Enough," again, much more quietly this time, but my voice was trembling. "You know what, Morrison? Billy? You don't get to have the answers right now. *I* don't know how Coyote got here or how he's alive, and God knows I spend way too much time imagining it's all about me, but this time, you know what? This time it is. I get to find out first. He's my mentor, my friend, he's the one who was in *my* head, you don't know him, and you don't get to *have* him right now."

To my embarrassment, I was crying again. Real girl tears for the second time, these ones born out of frustration. That didn't happen to me very often, but I hated when it did. It was faulty wiring in the female body, tear ducts attached directly to the frustration meter. Trying to explain to men that no, I wasn't being manipulative, I just couldn't stop my eyes from leaking salt water, only added to the aggravation.

In this particular case, though, even if I hadn't been angling for it, Billy and Morrison backed down looking shamefaced and uncomfortable, and I was nothing but glad for it. I was exhausted all the way down to the bottom of my soul. Not just physical tiredness from being thrown down a mountain as an avalanche that morning, not just the shaky emotional collapse of Coyote's arrival, but fundamentally, flat-out spent.

Coyote, who was fast earning rank as the number one most fantastic man in the universe, took my hand and gently uncurled it from its fist before slipping his fingers through mine. "Jo's probably right. Not only do I owe her a lot of explanation, but she's just done her first full-fledged soul retrieval, which isn't something I'd usually suggest trying in an ambulance. She needs a sacred place and some food, so I'd like to take her home. It's good to finally meet you, Captain. Detective Holliday." He nodded at my partner, despite having not been introduced, then drew me away from the ambulance and hospital and pressure presented by my friends.

I went into the hospital and used one of their dial-a-cab phones to call a taxi company Gary didn't work for. We were both silent on the drive to my apartment, because the only cab driver on earth I'd have a "So you're back from the dead, how's that working for you?" conversation in front of was Gary. As much as I loved him, right then Gary fell into the same category as Morrison and Billy: I was not ready to share Coyote with anybody, not until I got a chance to hear and assimilate some answers on my own. The whole drive home I watched Coyote, half afraid he'd disappear if I took my eyes off him. I was so exhausted even the joy had drained out of me. Coyote had to guide me out of the taxi when we got to my apartment building, or I'd have sat there all night.

We took the world's slowest elevator up to my fifth-floor apartment because I couldn't face that many stairs. Once ensconced in my apartment, I handed Coyote the phone and a menu from Mrs. Li's Chinese restaurant on the Way, and he placed an order for what sounded like every item of food on the menu while I, mindful of his comment about sacred space, went to lie down in the middle of my living-room floor. The draft from under the front door turned my skin to goose bumps, but once down, I couldn't summon the will to move.

Coyote, who was bordering on suspiciously perfect, looked

at me, went and dragged the quilt off my bed, and lay down behind me, the cover draped over both of us.

I didn't remember falling asleep, but I woke up when the delivery guy rang the doorbell. Coyote got up again, paid the guy, and came back to sit on the floor with me and spread two paper grocery bags worth of Chinese food around us in a veritable moveable feast. I ate all the Mongolian beef, half the cashew chicken, two egg rolls, a carton and a half of white rice, eight slices of barbecue pork, and drank a sixteen-ounce glass of milk before I felt even vaguely stable enough to whisper, "I'm really, really glad you're okay. What, um…? The last time I saw you…really saw you…was when I went into the Dead Zone and fought that snake thing."

"Fought." Coyote ducked his head over a heap of rice and sweet-and-sour pork. "Is that what you call it?"

"I got you out of there, didn't I?" All of a sudden I wasn't sure. "Didn't I?"

He looked up, dark eyes tempered with sympathy. "You did. Not very well, Jo. You shouldn't have even been there in the first place, not without me or at least a guide like Raven. But you did get me out."

"And then?" I really didn't want a scolding about where I should or shouldn't have been, or what I should or shouldn't have done. I was sure I had plenty of those in store. But my hands were cramping around the chopsticks and my tummy was getting upset waiting to hear where my mentor had been the past six months. "You just never came back, Coyote. I thought…I don't know what I thought. That you were mad at me. Or in trouble."

Coyote sighed. "I wasn't well enough prepared when I met you in the Dead Zone—that's a terrible name for it, Jo."

"Do you have a better one?"

He shrugged his eyebrows and went on. "I'd been in too much of a hurry, maybe, to meet you, but I wasn't shielded well enough. When you threw me out I never woke up from the dream state, not entirely. I got...lost on my way back to my body."

I took a shaking breath and put my box of rice aside. "I'm sorry. I was afraid that snake was going to eat you."

"It was going to." His smile was bright and sudden and made me want to crawl over and hide in his arms. "You were doing your best. It was messy, but you did your best."

That didn't make me feel as much better as I hoped. "And with...what happened with Begochidi, Coyote? I was dreaming about you all the time, but I wasn't sure any of it was happening...then." That sounded so absurd I put my head in my hands, fingertips pressed hard against my hairline. "Every time I saw you in those dreams it seemed like another time, another place. Your memories, or even your dreams. Sometimes my dreams, from when I was a kid. And I *know* something happened there, a closed time loop of some kind, because I had to take all of my younger self's memories of studying with you and bring them forward so I could use them now. Time got all fucked up, Coyote, and then you—"

I jerked my gaze up, heart thudding again, but not in the nice way it had earlier. Now it just made me feel like I'd eaten way too much and should probably run to worship the porcelain god. "You let go so much power," I whispered. "You got me out of that amber place where the night had butterfly wings, but...you died. I thought you *died,* Coyote."

He sighed again, that explosive sound that I'd heard from his coyote form more than once. "I almost did, but I was betting on Begochidi never deliberately harming one of the

Diné. I thought it was worth the risk of drawing her attention to me, but she was stronger than I thought. Or maybe less strong, in the end, because if she'd been at her best, I think I would have woken up. Instead I've been sleeping all this time."

"There must be healers—"

"My grandfather," Coyote said. "He's a shaman, too. He spent every day at my side, keeping me strong, but what he saw when he tried a soul retrieval on me was Begochidi standing before the rainbow that lasts all day. It wasn't a path he could travel. He knew then that someone else would guide me home. She nodded to him once, though."

I whispered, "Her. I saw Begochidi as a man."

Coyote shrugged. "We see in the god what is different from ourselves. In her acknowledging him, my grandfather believed he was allowed to keep my body strong, so he did, and he waited for you."

"I didn't do a soul retrieval, Coyote…."

"Didn't you?" He looked up, strands of fine black hair falling across his face. "I heard you calling, and saw your raven guide me from the storm."

I stared at him slack-jawed. "That—in Mel's power circle? That was you? The one who went running the other direction?"

His smile broke again. "Guilty as charged. It wasn't a classic retrieval like you did today—the Tar Baby was a good idea, by the way—"

I mumbled, "It wasn't my idea," guiltily. "I got it from a seven-year-old."

"A sss—I'd like to meet that kid!"

"Her name's Ashley. She's kind of amazing." A little grin worked its way over my face as I thought about Ashley Hampton and her ambition to be a "peace ossifer." "I'll introduce you."

"I'd like that." Coyote shoveled a couple more bites of pork into his mouth. "So I woke up yesterday morning with my grandfather sitting beside me. He'd done well. I was a lot stronger than I should have been, after all that time. I spent about six hours in one of our own sacred places—" He broke off, eyeing my living room floor dubiously.

I snatched up a new box, feeling defensive as I investigated its contents. Ban mian, full of noodles and greens. I stuffed my chopsticks in and ate several bites before muttering, "It's all I've got, okay? It's where I do most of my work. I just usually put a blanket in the door so there's no draft."

"Whatever works." He gave me another one of his bright smiles and went on with his story. "Anyway, I spent the morning eating and sweating out the results of lying in bed for months, and in the afternoon I left to drive up here."

"You just took off? What about the rest of your family? Didn't they care?"

A wash of old, resigned pain sluiced across Coyote's features. "It's just me and my grandfather. My parents died a long time ago. I'll tell you about it, but it's not a happy story, and these should be happy times." He reached out like he'd catch my hand, but he was too far away, and dropped his hand before I could meet it with my own. "I was worried about you, so I came as fast as I could. Grandfather understood."

"I've been worried about you for months. I didn't even know where to go to try and find you. There's three hundred thousand people in the Navajo Nation." Guilt was spoiling the food I'd eaten. "I'm sorry."

"Hey." Coyote put his box of pork down and crawled over to me, loose hair sliding around his shoulders. Honestly, if just watching that didn't make me feel a little better, nothing would.

Fortunately, it did. Then the way he hopped around one of the depleted grocery bags reminded me of his Coyote form, and I laughed before he got to me. He sat at my side, knocking his shoulder into mine. "That's better. Jo, it's okay. I didn't expect you to come looking for me. You had things to do here. And judging from what I saw today, you've been doing all right."

I shook my head. "I've been scrambling to just keep my ass covered, Coyote. I've felt like a walking disaster. I really wish I'd had your help."

"Well." He looked abruptly serious. "You will now. And I hate to say it, but this time you're going to need it."

CHAPTER FIFTEEN

I hated for him to say it, too. If a wendigo was a nasty enough piece of work that I, who had fumbled along facing gods and demons, was going to have trouble with it, then I really just wanted to hide under the bed until it was gone. On the other hand, that approach hadn't worked in the past, and if I *had* fumbled through before, having Coyote actually at my side now ought to be a major confidence booster.

Somehow it wasn't. "Why is it so bad? I've gone up against some pretty powerful things, Coyote…"

"Gods," he said quietly. "Sorcerers. But the wendigo used to be human, Jo. It's easier to stand against the immortal and corrupt than it is to face a ruined human soul. And we're mean, humans are. When you put us in a corner there's no telling what we'll do. Wendigos are like that, too."

I wished I hadn't asked. "Okay, so is this a 'Joanne would get dead if Coyote wasn't here' scenario? Because I don't like those."

"No. No, nothing like that. I mean, maybe," Coyote said less than reassuringly. "But it's not what I meant. You can't wait for a wendigo to come to you. They take hunting, Jo. Not like a murder case, but real hunting."

"Like out in the woods with a rifle and an orange jacket hunting? I don't look so good in orange."

"More like out in the woods with a spear and—"

"Magic helmet?" I asked hopefully.

Coyote, exactly like his furry counter-self, whacked his shoulder against mine hard enough to hurt. "If you have one, wear it."

I rubbed my shoulder, too glad to experience that again to sulk about the pain. "Did you come up here because you knew I had a wendigo on my hands?"

"I thought you might be more willing to believe it was me if I showed up in the flesh. Besides, I haven't seen you in real life since you were about five. I wanted to see how your mental image stood up to the real thing."

My heart lurched with sudden nerves. "And?"

He leaned away so he could examine me, then smiled. "I haven't seen your astral self in half a year. There's no comparison. You were a mess then. Angry spikes shooting out of a wraith trying to stay unseen. Now…"

I thought of the spiderwebbed windshield that reflected the state of my soul. "I'm still a mess."

"Nah." Coyote traced a fingertip down the scar on my right cheek. I startled, then startled myself even more by closing my eyes and tipping my head into the touch. "You don't have this," he said. "I didn't know you had a scar."

"Sure you did. It's the one that didn't want to heal that very first day, when Cernunnos stuck a sword through me."

"Oh, yeah." He dropped his hand and I opened my eyes again to see him shrug thoughtfully. "Guess I didn't expect it to leave a real scar, since you don't have one in your image of yourself."

"Well, I did live twenty-six and a half years without one. And I don't really see it when I look in the mirror." I took a deep breath. "We're procrastinating, aren't we?"

"Are we?" Coyote sounded amused. "On what?"

I took a breath to say *on dealing with the wendigo,* and instead ran up against the disconcerting idea that he was flirting with me. I'd never considered the possibility that he might find me attractive. I found *him* attractive, but then, I figured anyone female, heterosexual and breathing probably would. For his hair, if nothing else, but it was only one of a number of what I considered to be very fine features.

Instead of answering, I blushed. Coyote's grin, of which I was becoming very fond, blossomed. He said, "Ah," in a very wise and sagely tone, "procrastinating on *that,*" and leaned in to kiss me.

We left the Chinese food to be cleaned up in the morning.

Thursday, December 22, 4:07 A.M.

My room was lit up by the glowing numbers on my alarm clock and their reflection in the shining ceramic of the bedside lamp. Coyote was a comfortable, steadily breathing lump between me and the light. His hair, braided—we'd twisted it into loose plaits before falling asleep—was wound over his shoulder, where I couldn't roll on it, and the red light made thick shadows of his eyelashes. I didn't know why men so frequently got to have lashes like mascara companies advertised, although the idea that it was to keep dust out of their eyes while they hunted antelope on the savannah popped to mind. It didn't matter. In modern terms they were just attractive, and I stopped myself from brushing a fingertip over them. I didn't want to wake him up. I just wanted to lie there for a while, head propped on my hand, and smile stupidly while I watched him.

Some vaguely rational part of my brain said this was not like me. That Joanne Walker, Reluctant Shaman, did not fall into bed with a guy a few hours after meeting him. That Joanne Walker didn't succumb to stupid, giddy, exciting infatuation.

Truth was, Joanne Walker couldn't think of a single reason why she shouldn't. I could even build a nice rationalization if I wanted to, because I'd technically known Coyote half my life, what with the shaman's training he'd given me in the dream world when we were both teens.

For once in my life, I wasn't even vaguely interested in rationalizations. I was just happy. I was iridescent bubble, fluffy bunny, rainbow sky happy. I was happy Coyote was alive. I was happy we'd saved Mandy. I was happy he thought I was pretty. I was happy—bizarrely—that this was one guy who was neither unduly interested in nor threatened by nor uncomfortable with my aggravatingly esoteric set of talents. I could be me with Cyrano Bia, even if I hardly knew who that was.

And this was a possibility that Suzanne Quinley hadn't shown me. I liked that. I'd become resigned to feeling like there was some kind of destiny awaiting me, something I didn't have much control over, but was going to have to face. The simple fact that there were still surprises in store, that there were paths untaken, even unimagined, made me feel like maybe I had a little bit of choice after all. For the first time that I could remember, I was just plain happy to see where the road took me. It felt good.

I lay back down, put my nose against Coyote's shoulder and my arm over his ribs, and went back to sleep.

Thursday, December 22, 7:58 A.M.

There was an Indian in my parking lot.

All right, technically there were three, if you wanted to count me and Cyrano, but I wasn't interested in us. I was interested in the low-slung, shiny green beauty that had no business at all being outdoors in a Seattle winter. I approached with the reverence due a vehicle old enough to be my grandfather, and knelt in the slush, not caring that my knees got soaked.

I knew cars, not motorcycles, but I also knew beautifully restored work when I saw it. "It's a, uh… What is it? Early forties? You didn't…drive it up here. Not through the mountains. Not in winter." I twisted to look over my shoulder at Coyote, who looked as nervous and hopeful as a six-year-old.

"It's a 1938 Chief. There's a sidecar, but I didn't want it to slow me down." He shook his head, all but digging his toe into the slurry on the ground. "I shouldn't have driven, I know. I should've flown. But…"

The idiotic grin that'd been peopling my face for a lot of the past twelve or fourteen hours popped back up. "But you wanted to show off, didn't you."

Sheepish little boy voice: "I thought you'd like it."

I turned back to the bike, smiling so widely my ears hurt. There was a fringe on its leather seat, and the rich forest green paint job was highlighted by white over the wheels. The poor thing's engine was exposed, fine for someone living in the Navajo Nation, but less than fantastic for December in Seattle. "How the hell did you get through the Rockies without killing yourself? Without freezing to death?"

He sounded guilty. Pleased, but guilty. "I shanghaied a friend with a pickup into driving me over into California and then came up the I-5 as fast as I could." We both looked at the Indian, and the guilt in his voice turned smug: "Which was pretty damned fast."

"You weren't on this yesterday when you showed up at Mandy's house. I'd have noticed." The world could have been ending and I'd have noticed. There was a small, indiscreet part of me that wanted to lick the bike. That's how gorgeous it was.

"No, I parked it here and took a cab to where I felt you. I didn't want to bring you home on this without the sidecar. Or at least a helmet."

"You knew where I lived?" That didn't bother me, for some reason, but I grinned over my shoulder at him again. "You were going to put *me* in a sidecar? Not you?" Okay, honestly, the idea of riding around in a sidecar built for a 1938 Indian Chief, wearing one of the old-fashioned leather motorcycle helmets, was pretty appealing. But I was used to being the driver, so I had to give him hell.

"The apartment building felt like you. You've lived here a long time, haven't you?" His smile broadened a bit, too. "I'll let you drive the Chief the minute you hand over Petite's keys."

I raised my hands and stood up, defeated. "You drive. Except not in this weather. C'mon, we're going to have to move him inside. You're lucky it didn't snow last night."

"Inside? Do you have a storage unit?"

I wrinkled my eyebrows. "No, I have an apartment. We can bring him over to Chelsea's garage tonight, and our beloved but impractical-for-winter vehicles can keep each other company until the weather breaks." Or until Coyote went home, but I didn't want to think about that just yet.

He said, "Your apartment will smell like gas and oil if we store him in there," but he was heading for the bike when he said it.

I beamed. "Yeah. It'll be great."

My apartment building was mostly filled with college students—Coyote was right; I'd lived there a long time, since I was one of them—and the few who were up at eight in the morning clearly thought nothing of someone wrestling a classic motorcycle into the slow-moving elevator, nor of wheeling it down the building hallway on the fifth floor. The Chief looked a lot bigger inside my apartment than it had in the parking lot, and we had to move my computer desk and the smaller couch to fit it in, but he was safer and warmer inside, so I was satisfied. Of course, doing that took all the extra time we'd bought by getting up early, and the bus delivered us to the precinct building ten minutes late. It wasn't the optimum way to start a day when I needed a favor from my boss.

Billy was already at work, head down over a stack of files, and though he glanced at his watch when we came in, he didn't say anything. Possibly he didn't say anything because it was *we,* and not just me, who came in, but I counted my blessings anyway, and made the introduction I'd failed to yesterday: "Coyote, this is my partner, Billy Holliday. Billy, this is Coyote. Cyrano. Cyrano Bia." I noticed I was holding Coyote's hand, and let go so he and Billy could shake.

Billy looked like he was swallowing back seven or eight hundred questions as he shook Coyote's hand. "It's good to meet you. I'm glad you're all right. Joanie's missed you a lot."

Coyote mouthed, "Joanie?" at me, and aloud said, "Good to meet you, too. She thinks a lot of you. Sorry about the melodramatics yesterday. Have you heard from Ms. Tiller?"

"She sent an e-mail late last night. She and Jake are home

and okay. Looks like the news didn't pick up on her adventure. Morrison still wants to see us."

Some of my good mood drained away. "Us, or me? Because this wasn't really your fault."

"Us, and it was as much mine as yours."

I started to argue, then subsided. We were both in trouble, and Billy apparently wasn't going to let me be the fall guy. "When's he want us?"

"About ten minutes ago."

I pulled a hand over my mouth, turned to Coyote, said, "Crap," turned back to Billy, then walked in three little circles while trying to figure out what to do with myself. "All right. He's going to kill me either way. I guess I should go get it over with. Hang tight, okay, Coyote? I'll be back soon, if I'm not dead."

"We don't have a lot of time, Jo. The wendigo knows there's someone of power hunting it now."

"Oh, it more than knows. It checked me out while we were at Mandy's." I bet that was an important detail I should've mentioned earlier. I tried for an apologetic smile, managed a grimace, and added, "But it ran away," hopefully. "Maybe it didn't think it could take me."

Coyote's expression suggested I definitely should have mentioned this earlier, and that I was probably also a moron for having made the hopeful suggestion. "If it's already retreated, Joanne, it's going to be all the harder to find. And it'll get worse the longer we let it run."

"Right. So I better go talk to Morrison." Who was going to kill me. Rightfully. I gave Coyote an impulsive kiss and scurried out of Homicide.

Billy caught up, looking between me and where we'd left

Coyote so sharply I thought he'd give himself whiplash. All he said, though, was, "'Jo'?"

My face wrinkled up entirely of its own accord. "Yeah. I didn't used to like it, so everybody calls me Joanie. Everybody but Gary. He started calling me Jo and I guess I got used to it."

"Cyrano," Billy said, as if he was afraid he was pointing out something dangerous, "isn't Gary."

The stupid little smile cranked the corner of my mouth up again. "I know."

Billy said, "I *see,*" and any further commentary was lost because Morrison flung his office door open and we slunk in.

The captain left us standing there long enough that my feet began to itch from holding still. Under almost any other circumstances it would have started to be funny, and I would've turned into a smart-ass, but I was vividly aware that I wasn't the only one in trouble. I was afraid to look away from Morrison, though I didn't much want to look at him, either. I fixed on his right shoulder, judging it close enough to meeting his eyes. I could certainly still see his face, which was florid.

"I don't know what to do with you two," he finally said. "I'm used to Walker being an idiot, but this is new territory for you, Holliday."

A modicum of wisdom suggested this was not the time to defend myself. Besides, it was a legitimate statement. I'd spent quite a bit of time making an idiot of myself in front of Morrison.

For some reason that made me think of Coyote, and I smiled, which wasn't really the smartest thing to do. Morrison snapped, "You think this is *funny,* Walker?"

"No, sir." I honestly didn't, except possibly in a "the tension is getting to me, I must either laugh or scream" way. I had the presence of mind—barely—not to say that. And to bite my cheek when another dippy smile started to come out of nowhere. I was hopeless.

That, at least, was a sentiment Morrison would agree with. "The only reason you're not both suspended is Mandy Tiller is alive and well. I should suspend you anyway." But there was a killer out there that only his paranormal detective duo was equipped to find, so he couldn't afford to draw attention to us or the department by suspending us from a case we pretty much had to work on anyway.

He didn't say any of that out loud. He didn't need to. Instead, he snapped, "You'd better goddamned well consider yourselves on probation. You will do *nothing* without clearing it with me first, and I mean nothing. I don't want you taking a coffee break without my permission."

Billy, sensibly, said, "Yes, sir." I, less sensibly, said, "Aw, hell, Captain, look, in that case I need permission to go haring off into the woods for a few days, because I'm going to anyway."

Morrison's eyebrows shot toward his silvering hairline, and I had the distinct impression Billy was trying to run away without actually moving a muscle. "You *what?*"

"This thing, the wendigo, Coyote and I are going to have to hunt it, but it's not a city creature. I can't stay here and report in and still do my job." There was a certain irony to that, but Morrison didn't look like he was buying.

"You're not going anywhere, Walker, and if you were, it wouldn't be with a stranger who's not on my force. I don't care how well you think you know this guy. All I know is he's showed up in the middle of a serial murder case claiming to know things about the killer that, frankly, I'm not sure he could know if he wasn't involved."

I laughed. It was bad form, but I laughed. "Are you serious?"

Morrison's ears turned red. "Walker, you told me your mentor was *dead*. And now this guy with all the answers just happens to show up, wrapped in a package only you can recognize? You tell me if that isn't suspicious."

Phrased that way, it was. Phrased that way, it also sounded just a little like jealousy, a trait which Morrison hadn't exhibited over Edward Johnson while I'd been dating him. I wrote it off as amusing but unlikely. "It's Coyote, boss. I know him. He taught me for months. He saved my life, for Pete's sake. I trust him. And we can stand here all morning going around on this, but in the end I'm going to do this, so you might as well give me permission so you can feel like you're retaining some kind of control."

Morrison's voice went very low: "I could fire you."

A pit of regrets opened up in my belly. "Are you going to?"

I heard Billy take a surreptitious breath and hold it, like he might not draw attention if he was utterly still. Morrison stared at me, the raging color gone from his face, and I stood there on the edge of a coin, waiting to see which way it, and my fate, fell.

The door opened behind us without so much as a knock of warning, and I caught Coyote's scent as it closed again. Morrison clenched his jaw, but Coyote beat him to the punch: "I'm sorry for the intrusion, Captain, but Joanne and I can't wait any longer. We really have to go."

CHAPTER SIXTEEN

I'd kind of gotten used to Morrison and Gary posturing at each other. It was a testosterone thing that made no sense, given that one was my boss and the other was forty-six years my elder. They'd also laid off the worst of it recently.

So I was really in no way prepared for the explosiveness of two young men with equal interest and stakes in me facing off. The air actually got heavy, like it did just before a storm, and I shot a compulsive glance out the window, wondering when Seattle had started featuring dead-of-winter thunderheads.

"Detective Joanne Walker is an officer under my command—"

"Cosmically," Coyote said, "I've got you trumped."

The way he said it reminded me, dismayingly, of me. I could never be that calm or casual, or manage to put that much weight behind a handful of on-the-surface silly words, but in terms of picking just the right thing to inflame Morrison, it could've come straight off my short list.

Equally dismaying, Morrison responded just like he would've to me. His whole head turned crimson and he stepped forward to invade Coyote's personal space, clearly expecting me and Billy to give way. Billy did. I almost did.

My knees locked up, though, and my core went solid with determination I didn't know I had. Gary and Morrison fluffing their feathers at each other was one thing. It was something else entirely with Coyote and Morrison, and I very much didn't want to see either of them take it in the teeth. I didn't want much of anybody fighting over me, but especially not these two, because God forbid somebody should lose, and someone would have to. I forgot I was a police detective and a shaman. For a minute I just ran with being a girl, and got between the men in my life. "Guys. Come on. Knock it off."

Standing between them was like getting into one of those static electricity balls. Morrison radiated challenge, sparks physically stinging me. The Sight reacted to all that aggressive emotion, awakening to show me vivid darts of red exploding through Morrison's usually purple-blue aura. Every time one of those jagged bolts zipped outward, I felt it against my skin, sharp and uncomfortable.

But if he was the lightning in the storm equation, Coyote was the thunder. I'd never Seen another shaman before. Even if I hadn't already, I'd have known instantly that this was someone of power. His aura was dune-colored, with slashes of desert-sky blue, and it rolled toward Morrison's like he'd flatten him and be done with it. I could all but hear his presence in the small bones of my ears.

Morrison was about the last person on earth, though, who

could be flattened easily. I said, "Guys," again, and lifted my hands, palms facing each of them. "That's enough."

My boss, who didn't often say stupid things, said, "Walker, this isn't about you. Back off."

Astonished, vaguely insulted, I said, "Really. Who exactly is it about, then?"

Coyote, very calmly, said, "Don't worry. We'll get it settled," which ranked pretty high up there in stupid things, too, as far as I was concerned. Neither of them was moving, and despite the fact that I was tall enough to be in their lines of vision, my presence between them didn't seem to be stopping them from a world-class stare-down. I was afraid that, given another few seconds, they were going to start peeing on things. I was not about to get peed on.

Billy, cautiously, said, "Joanie, maybe you should just get out of the way," which for some reason pissed me off beyond belief. What was I, the fragile female who needed protecting?

It was a good enough question that I repeated it out loud: "What the hell is wrong with you two? Do you think I need a big strong guy to take care of me, or something?"

"I said this isn't *about* you, Wal—"

I said, "Oh for Christ's sake," and made like Moses and the Red Sea.

A shimmering silvery-blue wash of magic flared on either side of me, right in Morrison's and Coyote's faces. I expected Coyote to see it. I was more surprised when Morrison's eyes widened, but I straight-armed both of them before he had a chance to speak. Sheets of magic pushed Coyote up against the door and Morrison all the way back to his desk, which hit him in the ass and stopped his backward slide. "Have I got your attention now, gentlemen?"

I pretty clearly had everybody's attention. Gratifyingly, both objects of my pique nodded obediently. So did Billy, for that matter. I felt a nudge of resistance against my magic from Coyote's quarters, and glared at him. The probe faded away and he looked genuinely contrite.

"Good. Let me make something clear. I don't require rescuing. I don't require protecting. I frequently require help, which this pissing-match behavior in no way qualifies as. Now understand something else. I found out the hard way that this power of mine doesn't cotton to being used as a weapon." *Cotton to.* Get my dander up and I fell just a smidge toward the Southern in my choice of dialect and dialogue. It wasn't my fault. Four years in North Carolina will do that to a girl.

Morrison was looking slightly relieved around the eyes, which wasn't what I was after. I stopped dissecting my own verbal tics and finished my explanation: "I'm pretty sure bashing the two of you up against the walls a few times wouldn't actually trigger a super-psychic alarm saying *oh my God, Joanne's using her powers for evil,* but I'd kind of like to see if I'm right. Anybody else interested?"

For some reason they all three shook their heads rapidly. I thought they weren't any fun at all. Still pissed off, I let the magic go. Morrison, whose posture had been extremely erect while I'd held him in place, sagged a little, then scowled at Coyote. "Couldn't you stop her?"

"Couldn't *you?*"

I'd become the common enemy. It wasn't exactly what I'd been going for, but it was better than the two of them at each other's throats. Billy just gaped at me like I'd sprouted another arm, or a second head. Apparently ostentatious displays of power were not what he'd come to expect from his partner in crime. Anti-crime. Whatever.

I turned to Morrison and said, "Sorry," with about as much emotional integrity as he could expect after behaving like a hormone-ridden teenager. "Boss, this hunting party is the best shot we've got at stopping this thing. *I'm* your best shot at it. We know I'm going anyway, so may I please have permission?"

Morrison suddenly looked older than his thirty-eight years. I probably would, too, if I had me to deal with on a regular basis. "How often are we going to do this, Walker? How many times are you going to walk into my office and tell me how it is, even if it's against every rule and regulation we stand by?"

"I don't know." I wasn't angry anymore. I wasn't bubbling over with goofy happies, either. I was almost sad, really, like I was losing something I barely recognized. "Until neither of us can take it anymore, I guess."

The captain looked between me and Coyote, and when he looked back at me again I wasn't sure we were still talking about the same thing, even though nothing more had been said to change the slant of what I'd just offered.

More, and worse, something subtle happened in Coyote's face, as if he'd heard and understood the change in subtext, too. My heart spasmed and I glanced away from both of them.

That might have been okay, except there was somebody else in the room, and he'd followed the unspoken conversation just as clearly as the rest of us had. Billy met my gaze with the deepest, most tempered expression of compassion I'd ever seen, and the small sadness inside me burgeoned into something so big I had a hard time swallowing around it.

Billy was the one who broke the silence, which hadn't dragged out for long, but a lot had been said inside it, and none of it had been easy to hear. "You want me along on this, Joanne?"

His timing was perfect. Half a second earlier I wouldn't have trusted my voice. Half a second later I'd have fallen over into a sniffle that would've belied my tough-girl antics. "I think it'll be just me and Cyrano on this one. Thanks, though." I looked in Morrison's general direction without actually going so far as to meet his eyes. "We'll rent a car, or something. Keep it off the department books entirely."

"Something happen to Petite?"

I hadn't fully realized Morrison knew my car's name. I mean, yes, her license plate said PETITE in big block letters, but given he felt my relationship with her was pathological, I wouldn't have expected to hear him call her by name. A pinprick hole released some of the ache inside me, and I crooked a smile. "She's in the garage. The insurance paid up after that Doherty guy came by in October, so I've got enough money to switch out her transmission to a manual. It's my winter project."

There was no way on earth Morrison cared about any of that. I'd never met an American male with less interest in cars than my boss. But he nodded like it meant something to him, then nodded a second time, this time at the door. Not at Coyote. At the door. And said, "Take care of yourself, Walker."

"Yes, sir." I left his office with Coyote on my trail, confusingly aware that last time I'd walked away from Morrison with another man, he'd told the guy to take care of *me*. I had the uncomfortable sensation that last time, he'd been willing to relinquish—ownership, for lack of a better word, though it wasn't a good one—because he hadn't seen Thor as a threat. This time I was responsible for myself, which suggested, awkwardly, that Morrison was still in the game.

My life had been a lot easier when I was emotionally stunted.

Coyote waited until we got all the way out to the parking lot before he said, "So. That's how it is with Morrison, huh?" like that should mean something to me.

Aggravatingly, it did. "It isn't any-how with Morrison. He's my boss." Butter wouldn't melt in my mouth.

"You called me Cyrano, back there."

My life had been a *lot* easier when I was emotionally stunted. I knotted my hands into balls and glared at the ground. "Okay, yes, fine. That's how it is with Morrison. Jesus Christ."

"What about last night, then?"

I did not want to do this. God, how I did not want to do this. I walked a dozen steps away, shoved a hand through my hair, and came back a few feet. Coyote, slim and lean and beautiful, just stood there watching me. His brown eyes had a gold tint to them: he was watching my aura, reading more from it than my body language would tell him. I wondered if it showed my heart as an aching, tender, beat-up point inside me, bleeding red through my usual colors.

"Why does there have to be some kind of big explanation for last night? I've had a crush on you since I was about thirteen. You came back from the dead and, I don't know, Coyote, I kind of like the idea of being stupid in love with you. You had me at hello. Why can't that be enough? Morrison's my boss. Nothing's going to happen there as long as he is, and I'm not planning to quit my job. So why does it have to matter?"

"Maybe because you just chose him over me." Coyote's voice was remote. I utterly refused to look at him with the Sight and find out how much or little of that was an act. I didn't want to see him hurting, too. I was confused enough already.

Except on one thing: "I didn't choose anybody, Cyrano. But you should have known better."

Coyote snapped his gaze up to mine, astonishment mixing with injury. "Me? *I* should've known better? Why me? Why not him?"

"Because you're on his territory. For that reason alone you shouldn't have walked into *his* office and tried laying down the law, and you know it. That wasn't about us needing to get going. It was about who gets to tell Joanne what to do, and honestly, Coyote, in the scheme of things, he does. If that's choosing him, then yeah, I choose him, because he's my *boss*. We have our issues, but we get it figured out, and we would've gotten this one figured out. So if nothing else, you should've respected being on somebody else's playing field. Instead you had to push it." *And spoil everything,* I didn't say out loud.

We stood there a long time. A wind came up, making my cheeks cold but failing to get under my jacket and wool sweater. Finally Coyote mumbled, "I'm sorry," and looked up with credible puppy-dog eyes.

It was more or less the last thing in the world I expected him to say, and the excessively mournful gaze was enough to break the tide of my anger. In fact, it was nearly enough to make me giggle, which I resented enough that it almost made me angry again. I said, "Stop that," with enough asperity that he did. "People who actually possess puppy-dog eyes in another shape aren't allowed to use them to get themselves out of trouble. I say so. It's the rules."

"Okay." Despite the promise inherent in the word he gave me another puppy-dog look, though this one more said "Am I forgiven?" than "I'm sorry."

I glowered at somebody's Jeep, trying hard not to fall for manipulative men with big brown eyes, and gave up with a snorted laugh. "Okay. You're forgiven. But if you do something that stupid again, Coyote, I swear to God…"

"I won't." He sidled up to put his arm around my waist and his nose on my shoulder. I fought off another giggle, and he repeated, "I won't. You're right. I was being a dick, and I'm sorry. You've changed a lot, Jo."

I eyed him, which was difficult given his proximity. "You mean, six months ago if you'd shown up and tried going to the mat with Morrison over what my responsibilities were, I'd have been delighted to let you play hero so I didn't have to face up to any of those decisions or responsibilities myself?"

He cleared his throat. "I wouldn't have said it like that, but yeah."

I turned in to him, catching his coat in my hands and bumping my nose against his. "You're right. I've changed. I'm a superhero now." I stole a kiss, then smiled against his mouth. "So let's go save the world."

CHAPTER SEVENTEEN

That kind of line needed a supersonic jet to swoop down and pick us up, just for the drama of it, but I was obliged, much more prosaically, to call Gary and wait fifteen minutes for him to pick us up. We spent most of the time taking turns being the one to lean our rear ends against the cold hoods of other people's cars, and being the one to warm up our hineys by getting to lean on each other. I was sure it was an affront to his masculine dignity, but we fit together better when Coyote leaned on me, since I had a two-inch height. Furthermore, my arms were slightly longer than his, so I could get a better grip on him than he could on me. I'd just stuck my cold nose in the corner of his neck and was holding him so he couldn't squirm away when Gary pulled up. His disgruntled, "Did I miss somethin'?" rose over the sound of his Chevy's engine, and I let Coyote go with a grin.

Gary gave us the fish eye through the rolled-down driver's side window. "Who's this, doll?"

If I'd been hanging on to any resentment, it dissipated. Gary was like my own personal cheer-o-meter. I jolted forward and whispered, "This is Coyote," like it was a tremendous secret. "He's not dead. He got better."

Gary gawked at me, then got out of the cab looking like he couldn't decide what to ask first. I interrupted with, "Coyote, this is Gary. My best friend. The best thing that's ever happened to me. I wouldn't have made it through the last year without him."

Coyote, looking unexpectedly nervous, stepped forward to shake Gary's hand. Gary seized his shoulders, looked him up and down, then hauled him into a rib-popping hug instead. "Heard a lot about you, son. Glad to see you alive. How the hell'd that happen?"

Coyote said, "Joanne set me on the path home during a spirit walk," like it was a perfectly rational thing to say, and I said, "'Son'? I get 'doll' and 'dame,' and he gets 'son'?", which *was* a perfectly rational thing to say.

"Ain't my fault. Language's got a lot more oddball words for women than men." Gary set Coyote back, hands on his shoulders again, and examined him for a second time. "Knew she was getting better at that spirit quest stuff. What're you two kids up to?"

"We need to go—" That was both of us. I said, "To Olympic National Park," and Coyote said, "Home," and we looked at each other while Gary ping-ponged between us. "I fought with it at the park," I said after a few seconds. "It's our best lead."

"If it came into the city to study you, it's smart enough to not return to the place you hunted it, Jo. We need to create a sacred space and search for it in the Lower World. That should help us pinpoint its location in this world."

"Don't you think I've been trying that?" I snapped off a description of my power circle adventure, and the Space Needle-based search of Seattle. "The power circle was how I rescued *you,* but I didn't get any kind of bead on where the thing was."

"Yes, but I'm here now," Coyote said with an air of authority all the more aggravating for being apropos.

I'd become aware of Gary drawing breath to speak every time one of us finished a sentence, and that we'd kept running over whatever it was he had to say. I finally looked at him, eyebrows arched, and he said, "You wanna go to Rainier National Park."

A flicker of polite patience crossed Coyote's face. "How do you know that?"

One of the many things I loved about Gary was his inability to bear fools. He gave Coyote a look that reminded me sharply of the throw-down in Morrison's office, but instead of turning it into a thing, he just said, "Because that's where the news just reported a new cannibal murder, kid."

Downgraded from *son* to *kid* in less than two minutes. Maybe it was some kind of throw down after all. Either way, Gary said, "I'm drivin'," and thirty seconds later we were on the road to Mount Rainier.

Thursday, December 22, 10:16 A.M.

It turned out we were actually on the way to my apartment. It took the drive over, plus time for Coyote and me to pack up some clothes and my drum, minus several minutes of Gary cooing over the Chief and heating toaster pastries while trying to find something in my apartment that would serve as on-the-road lunch, just to explain Coyote's return. Gary kept saying, "I'll be damned," in a tone that suggested being damned was about the niftiest thing possible. By the time we got back out the door, he and Coyote were old friends, and some of the explosive joy I'd felt earlier had returned. More quietly, maybe, but it still felt awfully good.

For a girl who'd grown up on the road and who loved driving as much as I did, I didn't get out into the countryside nearly enough. I'd driven out to western Washington to test the promise of some of its long straight stretches at high speeds, but I'd never headed south.

The road to Rainier National Park wasn't a speed demon's dream, but even in the dead of winter it was beautiful. Bare-armed trees reached over the black strip of road cutting through white countryside, every curve and hill promising more of the ever-changing same. Gary and Coyote rattled on about a variety of things, starting with Coyote's resurrection and touching on Gary's misspent youth as a saxophone player: things I knew about, by and large, which let me just slip into the thoughtless rhythm of the road.

It reminded me of being a kid, traveling all over America with my dad. He'd had an old boat of a Cadillac that never broke down, but we'd taken the engine apart eight or ten times I could remember, just so I could learn how to do it.

Those had been the good times. We'd stopped at junkyards all over the country, Dad chatting up the owners—he'd been good-looking, tall and rangy with hair almost as long as Coyote's—and getting them to let me, or teach me to, work on the old beasts they had lying around. I'd gotten into the bellies of cars most people my age didn't know existed. I'd loved it.

That wasn't something I remembered often. Mostly,

looking back at my childhood, I tended to focus on the changing schools every six weeks, the inability to make friends in such a short time, the weird period when I was seven or eight when Dad had been teaching me Cherokee, and I'd almost forgotten how to speak English. Since then I'd made up for it by almost forgetting how to speak Cherokee. But long car trips made me think about the good stuff, especially if I wasn't driving, and for the first time in a long while I wondered how Dad was doing. I hadn't talked to him in years. Last I'd known he was still in Cherokee County back in North Carolina, but it was hard to imagine he'd stayed on after I left for college. He'd grown up there, but he'd never given any impression of wanting to stay. He'd never given any impression of wanting to stay *anywhere,* particularly after a year-long stint in New York had given my mother a chance to relocate him and drop me on his metaphorical doorstep.

These days I suspected she would have found him if he'd been on the lam in Timbuktu, but I certainly hadn't known that growing up. Besides working on cars and moving around a lot, my real, lasting impression of childhood was that my father often looked like he neither knew how he'd ended up with a daughter, nor what to do with one now that he had it. He'd been the one who called me "Jo" in the first place, which was why I didn't like it. Once I'd gotten old enough to think about it, I'd suspected he'd used that nickname so he could pretend he was just talking to himself. It had more recently occurred to me that maybe he'd been trying to find another point of similarity for us to build on, but I hadn't been anything like that forgiving as a kid. In retrospect, I was probably lucky he hadn't drowned me. Thoughts like that slipped away at the speed limit, following hard on one another like the dashed lines on the road. It was as close to meditation as I ever got.

For some reason when we got to the park entrance Coyote and Gary both looked at me like they expected me to pay the fee for all three of us. I'd paid it at Olympic, but Mandy'd been doing me a huge favor. This time we were all in it together, although Gary was more all in for fear of missing something than for standing the line. Not that he wouldn't. He was a good guy to have at my back when things got rough, a fact I knew from experience.

Somehow that talked me into paying the fee, and we drove into the park with me feeling like I'd been Jedi-mind-tricked. "Wait a minute, where are we, anyway? Which entrance was that?"

"Nisqually." Coyote looked over his shoulder at me. "Weren't you listening? The body was found near the Longmire museum."

"Wouldn't the pickings be richer at Paradise?" That was the only section of the park I'd ever really heard about, mostly thanks to the occasional news story about the visitor's center. It looked like a flying saucer, and the roof kept threatening to collapse under the snowfall. They were going to build a new one any minute now.

"There's a lot of old growth forest around Longmire. The wendigo's probably drawn to it."

I said, "Ah," then squinted at him. "You're from Arizona. How can you possibly know this?"

He held up a PDA with a Wikipedia entry visible on its little square screen. "Oh. That's not very mystical of you."

"No, but it's handy." He flashed me a grin underscored by Gary's chuckle, and we fell into a companionable game of glimpse-the-mountain wherever there was a gap in the trees. Not too much later we pulled into the parking lot of what a sign proclaimed was the National Park Inn, which, from the outside, was a genuinely gorgeous rustic-looking building with the mountain serving as a dramatic backdrop.

Gary whistled. "Damn, that's something."

I said, "It is," except my eyes had fallen right off the vista and landed on a black 1967 Chevy Impala. It didn't belong up here in the woods any more than Petite might've, but it was a beautiful car. Gary parked a few spaces down from it and I got out to walk circles around it. Kansas license plates. I patted the Impala's hood and mumbled, "Long way from home, aren't you, baby?" before reluctantly turning away.

Laurie Corvallis, evening anchor for Channel Two News, stood right behind me with a smile as pointy as a crocodile's. "And so are you, Detective Walker."

In any other circumstances I'm sure I would've seen the news van another fifteen feet down the lot, and suggested to Coyote and Gary that we get the hell out of there. But I was weak in the face of classic cars, and truthfully, we couldn't have escaped anyway. This was where the job was, for us just as much as for Laurie Corvallis.

Which was hardly something I could say to her. I fished my best genuine smile out of somewhere and said, "Fancy meeting you here. You up for the Christmas break?"

"I'm not," she said, every bit as pleasantly. "And neither are you."

"Really? I thought I was. I'm going to be disappointed, then. So why am I here?" She didn't have a microphone, so I didn't much care that I sounded like a babbling idiot.

"You're up here following the Seattle Slaughterer, just like I am, Detective. And the fact that you're here makes me all the more certain I'm going to get my story. I'll be watching you."

"Ms. Corvallis." I rubbed a finger over my eye. I hadn't been smart enough to take my contacts out at the apartment. Three hours of staring out the window and forgetting to blink made me wish I had. Glasses were more forgiving of that behavior. "If I were up here on police business I'd be here with my partner, not friends. Call Captain Morrison, if you like. I'm here on my own."

"That doesn't mean you're not where the story is, Detective. I look forward to seeing more of you soon." She walked away, leaving me with an increasing pit of dread in my tummy.

Coyote caught up to me, carrying his own bag, but not, I noticed, mine. "Cute. Who is she?"

"The devil."

"Really. I thought the devil would be taller." He jogged into the lodge after Corvallis. I bent, scooped up a handful of snow, and caught him in the back of the head with it just before the doors closed behind him.

Gary, who *was* carrying my bag, stopped at my side. "What's the deal, Jo?"

"Nothing, it's just that woman is going to make this a lot more complicated."

His bushy eyebrows went up and he glanced after Coyote. I don't know how I knew he was looking at Coyote and not Corvallis, but I did. "Is that a *that woman* like a woman means it, or like a cop means it?"

I took my bag from him as an excuse to give him a hard, considering look. "Whoever said men don't understand women obviously never met you. It was a cop *that woman*. I don't care if Coyote thinks she's cute. She is cute. She's also going to get herself killed."

"Nah. She ain't the outdoorsy type." Gary, clearly satisfied with his line of reasoning, marched into the lodge. I stared after him, then, because there was nothing else I *could* do, shrugged assent and followed him.

Corvallis was at the front desk, trying to flirt with Coyote, who arched an eyebrow at me over her head. She looked to see who he was making eyes at, and her smile went flat. It went flatter still when I gave my name and the desk attendant pulled up our reservations. I saw no reason at all to tell Corvallis they'd been made from the phone on the drive down. Better to let her think we'd had them for weeks. Maybe it would throw her off the scent, although I didn't really think anything could.

Certainly she didn't fail to notice we were all staying in one room, which clearly, in her opinion, put the kibosh on any potential romance between me and Coyote. I sort of had to agree with her, but on the other hand, if we were going to fight monsters, I didn't want the team split up even for sleeping. That was how people got picked off in horror movies.

Corvallis, who wasn't privy to my line of thought, cozied up to Coyote a little more. I resisted the urge to drop my bag on her foot, but only because it was a soft-sided backpack that wouldn't do her any damage. Coyote gave me another look over her head. Gleeful, I said, "Cut it out, Corvallis. He's with Gary."

I couldn't decide which of the three looked more shocked, but it left me grinning as the girl behind the counter offered me room keys. "It's a bed-and-breakfast package. Just give them your room number in the morning. Welcome to the National Park Inn, and please let us know if there's anything we can do to make your visit more comfortable."

A blast of cold air dropped the lobby's temperature by about ten degrees. We all turned to see a petite park ranger with a grim expression holding them open. Her face was pale, cords standing out in her throat, but she lifted an extremely steady voice to say, "Ladies and gentlemen, I'm going to have to ask everyone to stay inside for a little while. I'm afraid we've had another incident."

Coyote, Gary, Laurie Corvallis and I all ran for the door.

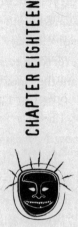

CHAPTER EIGHTEEN

I had to give Corvallis credit for chutzpah, anyway. She was easily the least physically threatening of the four of us, but she was quick on her feet, and got in the park ranger's face first. The poor woman took a breath to argue and the rest of us went galloping by like wolves to the slaughter.

I don't know what I was expecting. A gnawed-on body spread all over the parking lot, maybe, staining the snow red and fixing nightmares in holiday-makers minds for the rest of their lives. If I'd taken half a second to think I'd have known there'd be no such scene. If nothing else, we had yet to encounter a victim who'd actually been allowed to bleed out.

The only saving grace was Coyote and Gary both looked like they'd had expectations similar to mine. Coyote glowered around, dumbfounded, then turned on his heel to face me. "We're going to need to find out where the body is. The faster

I can get to one and take a look, the more likely I am to be able to track it."

A sting of possessive envy caught me in the gut and left me trying to catch my breath. For months I'd been wishing Coyote was on hand, metaphysically speaking, to show me the path. To take responsibility. Now, finally, he was, and I had the uncharitable thought that this was *my* territory, *my* game, and *I* should be the one taking charge.

I had the unpleasant sensation that I now knew just exactly how Morrison had felt a few hours earlier.

"I almost had it yesterday. Before we saved Mandy." I was trying really hard not to sound petulant. Judging from Gary's carefully neutral expression, I wasn't succeeding.

"Almost had it how?" Coyote either didn't care about or hadn't noticed my churlish tone. I wasn't sure what I thought of that, either. It was good, of course, except it sort of meant he either wasn't listening, or was blowing me off.

God, if I was going around in circles like that I'd blow me off, too. Exasperated with myself, I threw my head back and glared at the sky until I felt some modicum of rationality return. "I'd been about to follow it across the astral plane when—" When Morrison touched me and woke me up. I was glad for the cold. It made a legitimate excuse for my face to be pink. "When I got pulled back to the normal world. You showed up a minute later."

"What were you going to do when you found it?" The way he asked wasn't a good sign. It suggested I'd screwed up beyond belief without even knowing it. Given that that had been my modus operandi for most of the last year, it was a perfectly legitimate assumption, but it didn't sit well. I hunched my shoulders and turned my scowl at the snow.

"I was going to kick its ass. I don't know, Ro." I'd barely ever called him Cyrano, much less shortened it to "Ro," but it rhymed and I was childishly pleased with that. "I hadn't thought that far ahead."

"You've got to start." Now he was the stern, slightly worried teacher. I had no idea how he fit so many personalities into so few words, or so little time. "The astral plane's an incredibly dangerous place to take on a wendigo, Jo. It's its home turf. Out there it'd be simple for it to cut you away from your body, and for something like this creature, you'd be a seven-course meal. You can't afford that kind of mistake."

"Well, how was I supposed to know? It's not like you left me a shaman's primer to study! There's no fricking handbook for all of this! I'm doing my goddamned best!" Frustrated, I scooped up a handful of snow and whipped around to fling it across the parking lot with as much strength as I could muster.

It hit the defenseless Impala, twenty feet away. I said, *"Fuck,"* and went to wipe the marks of my temper tantrum away.

Coyote, very mildly, asked, "Would you have felt that bad if you'd hit me?"

"No." A better person than I would've apologized, but I was by definition not that person. "C'mon. Let's go find the body."

"I'll tell you where it is," Laurie Corvallis said from behind me, "but you have to take me with you."

I was really beginning to hate how she kept doing that, turning up behind me or off to one side with a pithy statement and a microphone. I snapped, "No," and then because I was *stupid,* added, "How do you know where it is?"

The park ranger came out of the inn looking a little like she'd been bulldozed, saw us, shook herself, and put purpose in her stride as she approached. I said, "Ah," under my breath, and turned back to Corvallis. "Why is this turning into a you'll-tag-along instead of us trying to sneak after you while you go get your story?"

She studied me for a long moment, during which the park ranger reached us and began, firmly, insisting that we return to the lodge, everything was under control, but it was imperative that we not be outdoors for the immediate future. I made accommodating noises and didn't move. Corvallis just ignored the woman entirely, no more interested in her than she might've been in a silent rock face. Eventually the ranger faltered, then went to try her spiel on Coyote and Gary.

Only when she was gone did Corvallis say, "Inexplicable things happen around you, Detective Walker. Inexplicable, dangerous things. We both know there's a story there, and someday I'm going to get it. But let's pretend for a minute that I'm not after that right now."

I rocked back, bemused at her frankness. "Okay…?"

"My job is to go somewhere and learn more about the situation. The best way to do that is to make some kind of connection with the people I'm investigating. Sometimes it's dangerous. I've done gangland exposé pieces, I've gone to the Middle East, I've—"

"I watch the news, Laurie. I don't need your résumé."

She shrugged her eyebrows, a more ordinary expression than I was used to seeing from her. "The point is, when you're following a story into a world you don't know a lot about, you try to make friends, or at least allies, with somebody who can show you the ropes. Somebody who's going to offer a degree of protection, because they've got a vested interest in the story being presented."

"And then you hang them out to dry."

"Less often than you think. You can't keep going into investigative situations and expecting to get your story, your truth, if you've built a reputation for selling out the people who open their doors to you."

"My door is not open to you, Corvallis."

"But it is. You have no idea how much research I've done on you, Siobhán."

Nausea ruptured inside me, backwash of acid climbing up my throat. Siobhán was the name my mother'd given me at birth. Siobhán Grainne MacNamarra Walkingstick. Dad took one look at Siobhán, determined nobody in America was ever going to say it correctly, and gave me a whole different usename, Joanne. Technically it was an Anglicization, as Siobhán more or less translated as Joanne, but nobody could tell that by looking at it.

I'd abandoned Walkingstick of my own accord, the day I graduated high school. It hadn't been much of a trick to hack the school records so I was Joanne Walker on them, and that's the name I'd used for more than ten years. I'd always known the full name was out there if somebody wanted to research it—Morrison had—but I'd never imagined anybody would want to. Moreover, recently I'd become aware of the power of true names, which made me particularly uncomfortable with anybody bandying mine about.

If Corvallis knew my full name, she certainly knew plenty of other things about me that I'd left, deliberately, on the eastern side of the Mississippi. I wanted them to stay there. I might've been growing up and getting in tune with myself and other garbage like that, but there was plenty I planned on leaving alone.

And Laurie Corvallis wasn't going to let that happen.

Carefully—very carefully, because I was honestly afraid of what I might do if I let go—I triggered the Sight. I did it because I wanted to see her aura, to see if I could read her intentions, and I did it forgetting that it made my eyes change color. Hazel to gold; I'd watched it happen in Coyote's eyes, and once in Billy's when I'd lent him the ability to See. I thought it wasn't half as disturbing as the blind bone-white that rolled over the eyes of people who could see the future.

Judging from how Corvallis blanched, it was disturbing enough. Her aura was yellow, incredibly clear and tightly focused, and for the second time I had to give her credit for *cajones*. Spikes of red panic, every bit as clear as the yellow, shot through her aura and made loops as she sucked them back down, controlling them. Her whole body was rigid, blue eyes round and lips pale, but shots of green rushed across her aura, like she was recording every second of her emotion. Recording it, mastering it, ultimately subsuming it: her whole range of flipping out lasted about a nanosecond, and then she was back to clear yellow.

And almost all I could read out of that was ambition. No urge to hurt people, but no particular desire not to, either. She wanted one thing above all else: the story. Maybe other things came to the fore when she was off duty, but I'd never seen her anything but on. I closed my eyes, letting the Sight go. "Sorry. I didn't mean to scare you."

She scoffed. "You didn't scare me."

I opened my eyes again, concentrating on not letting the Sight filter my vision. Concentrating on my eyes staying the color they belonged. "Yes. I did."

Discomfort flickered across her face and, like her spurt of

panic, was buried. "So we have a deal? I go with you to check out the body?"

A tiny bubble of amusement burst inside me, replacing the acid burn of sickness. "You think you're blackmailing me? Corvallis, the important people in my life—and that includes Captain Morrison, in terms of job security, in case you're wondering—already have the information you've dug up. There's no bandage to rip off. There's no wound to expose." That wasn't entirely accurate, but it was close enough to take the wind out of her sails. I hoped. "You still haven't told me why you're even making the offer. Is it to get a chance at that story you think I'm hiding?"

She gave me a long look that I interpreted as "Your eyes just changed color and you're still pretending there's no story there?" but what she said aloud was, "You've walked away from some extraordinary events, Detective. I want the Slaughterer story, but I'm not stupid. This guy's dangerous. I don't want to put myself on the line without some kind of backup, and you strike me as the right kind."

"Now, see, wouldn't it have just been easier to say that in the first place?"

"You wouldn't have agreed."

"Corvallis, the only reason I'm agreeing now is it's faster to hitch along with you than to go find out on my own where the victim is." I turned my wrist up, glancing at where my watch was hidden beneath the weight of my winter coat. "Or it would've been five minutes ago, anyway. The body's getting cold. We need to go."

The FBI had gotten there before us.

I didn't know why I was surprised. Up until that morning,

all the bodies had been found within the greater Seattle area jurisdiction, but these last two were on federal parkland. It was their case now, which meant I was going to have to avoid explaining the truth to a whole new branch of law enforcement. Other people had to worry about whether they'd remembered to feed the cat. I got to worry about telling lies to people who could throw me in jail for it.

There were only three agents, though I was sure there were more on the way. One, a woman, was down beside a body we were no doubt not allowed to see. The other two were men, one of whom was really tall and the other of whom was really cute. I waved at, and stomped toward, the cute one, while Corvallis and her camera guy, who'd joined us before we left the lodge, headed for the tall one. Coyote and Gary exchanged glances and stayed where they were. I thought Coyote should've tried to go chat up the woman, but she was on the other side of yellow cordoning tape, and he had no badge to legitimize himself.

I waved my SPD badge at the cute Fed, then left my hand up, palm toward him, in apology. "I know, I'm way out of my jurisdiction, but I've been on this case for weeks, and the last body before the ones up here was found in the park across from my apartment. I want to do what I can."

He jerked his thumb toward the woman. "Hey, I don't care if you're here. Just don't cross her, man. Can I help you?"

"Yeah, maybe. Are there any tracks?" I turned on the Sight and stood on my toes to look over his shoulder, which only caused me to sink into the snow. It was compacted from traffic, but not that much. I wished I still had Mandy's snowshoes.

There were marks deep under the snow, against the surface of the buried earth, but for the first time I could see indentations in the snow, too. They were barely there, like bird tracks, and my eyes crossed as I tried to See them more clearly. "Holy crap, there are."

"You've got real good vision." The Fed sounded less than thrilled, and I glanced back at him. His aura was flat and wary, like I'd done something unexpected and definitely not right. His voice dropped to a warning tone: "What are you?"

For a couple seconds I stared at him in bewilderment, then swore under my breath and pinched the bridge of my nose, deliberately hiding my eyes. Whoever'd had the bright idea of tying a physiological change to magic use was an idiot. "I'm a shaman, and I do have good vision, I can See things—"

I dropped my hand again, scowling, and his aura flared up into something more normal. The distrust fell out, replaced by a different kind of discomfort, like he'd gotten caught with his hand in the cookie jar. I blinked at that for a moment, trying to understand it, and it abruptly came clear.

He wasn't supposed to be there, in much the same way I wasn't. I smiled crookedly. "For example, I can See that you're lying, aren't you? You're not really a Fed."

His jaw tightened, not quite guilty, not quite defiant. "Yeah, well, not a Fed doesn't mean not supposed to be here. We didn't expect the real ones to get here so fast."

Auras made pretty good lie detectors, and what he said was absolutely true. He didn't have power, not like Coyote, not like me. Not even like Billy, but he still knew the score. He knew there were things that went bump in the night, and I was pretty damned sure that he bumped back.

Somehow that made my whole day, my whole world, a better place. I didn't know why. It just came as a load off my shoulders, a huge shocking relief that there were other people out there fighting the monsters. I mean, I'd kind of known there had to be, but I'd never expected to randomly encounter any of them while on the job. My mouth bypassed every mental roadblock I'd ever had and said, quietly, "We think it's a wendigo."

In any sane world, those weren't words to inspire a crooked little smile at one corner of his mouth, but one appeared. "Yeah, we know. We were heading into Seattle when the police scanner mentioned the kill up here. It's got the earmarks."

"More like the tooth marks."

His smile opened up to full-fledged. I had the nigh-irresistible urge to take him home and feed him. Instead, grinning back, I jerked my thumb toward the road. "Look, why don't you get out of here before somebody figures out you're not really with the Feds. At least I've got a genuine badge to wave. We've got this one under control."

"You sure?"

"Yeah, we're cool. Thanks."

"Figures. I meet a hot chick out hunting and she's already got a team." He blasted a piercing whistle that made both the tall not-a-Fed guy and the actual agent down by the body turn around. The man headed toward us, but my new pal swung his finger in a lasso and threw the motion down the road, and his friend took a sharp turn that way.

The woman stood up and I muttered, "Better scram."

"Scrammin'." He gave me another take-him-home-and-feed-him grin, then jogged after the taller guy, boots squeaking against the snow. Coyote and Gary shot curious looks after them, then at me, before the female agent reached my side.

"Is there a problem with my men? Who are y—" She swallowed the question, staring up at me, then yanked her hat off, like it would help her see me better. Dark honey hair collapsed around her shoulders in classic salon-commercial style, but there was nothing particularly inviting about her expression. *"Joanne?"*

There'd been a lot of things I wanted to leave east of the Mississippi. The woman standing in front of me had been one of them. We'd been best friends for about thirty seconds, about a million years ago, and it had gone all to hell over a boy. I scraped a few brain cells together and managed, eventually, to produce a witty response no doubt years in the making:

"Hi, Sara."

CHAPTER NINETEEN

"What are you doing here, Joanne? Where'd you send my men?"

"Your m—what'm I—what're *you* doing here? I live in Seattle. Don't tell me you live in Seattle. Your men? Really?" I turned to look after the duo beating feet down the road. "You brought them in?"

"No, they were here when I arrived, but I've got rank. What're you—"

I pulled out my SPD badge again and earned a credible sneer from the woman who'd once been my best friend. I said, "Oh come on now," sort of vaguely. "Don't tell me you're going to play that whole federal/state jurisdiction superiority thing."

"Not as long as you stay out of my way."

That had a peculiarly school-yard ring to it. I stood there watching snow melt in Sara's hair and reeling at the idea that we hadn't moved past that. I mean, I was no great shakes in terms of emotional maturity, but dwelling on rivalries that had exploded almost fifteen years earlier seemed a little much. It didn't mean I wanted to be bosom buddies again, but I could hardly fathom getting in jurisdictional fights because I'd nailed the boy she'd wanted in high school.

Coyote, a bit diffidently and from a safe distance, said, "You two know each other?"

I said, "Yes," and Sara said, "No," at the same time, and Coyote looked like he wished he hadn't asked. I said, "Yes," again more firmly. "We went to high school together. This is Sara Buch—"

"Isaac."

I wasn't moving, but my feet slipped anyway. I lurched upright again, clutching the air for support, and turned goggly eyes on Sara. "You're kidding. The same—?"

She drew herself up, all but hissing. She was taller than she'd been in school, though still quite a lot shorter than I was. I'd thought she was beautiful, back then. She'd grown up just as pretty, except for the pinch of anger between her eyebrows. She'd been buckwheat blonde in school, but the dark honey tones suited her better, playing up her cheekbones and skin tones. "Yes, the same Isaac. Just because you got everything you wanted in high school doesn't mean you—"

I lost the rest of what she said to gales of laughter. Her cheeks flushed and her eyes went bright, making her even prettier, but I couldn't stop laughing. I doubled over, still whooping, and finally braced my hands on my thighs so I could peer up at her. "I'm sorry. Are you serious? You really think I wanted to get pregnant and have twins at fifteen? I just wanted him to *like* me, Sara, and I was a moron. You said you didn't like him. I swear to God, I had no idea you were just playing it cool. I wasn't that good at reading people. I'd never had a real girlfriend before, with Dad moving us around all the time. I swear I didn't get it. I tried telling you this back then. I'm really sorry. I had no idea." I straightened up and offered a hand in peace. Handshakes were formal gestures, but I'd never felt like I was participating in ritual before when I initiated one. I'd been wanting to say that for a long time.

Sara didn't look like she'd been waiting to hear it a long time. "Oh, I'm not just talking about Lucas. It was you and that stupid drum you were so proud of, you and all your stories from all over the place, like you were some kind of hot shit because you'd traveled—"

I had never previously experienced the phrase *my head was spinning* in a literal sense, but I began to feel as if someone had taken a stick and was liberally stirring my brains. The world went zipping to the left and I clutched my skull with both hands, trying to steady it. "Wow. You're serious. That's…really not how I meant to come across."

If I'd meant anything, it had been to keep people from picking on me. I recognized now that I'd had a massive chip on my shoulder. I could see how it could've come across as arrogance, but the idea was—to me, anyway—laughable. "Sorry. I didn't mean to be a prick."

"Like it matters now."

Apparently it did, but I was smart enough not to say that. The smart part of me, in fact, thought I should maybe focus on the dead person a couple dozen feet away so that we could sort out what could be sorted, and then go inside and have Irish coffees to ward off the cold. The teenage girl inside me, though, said, "But he went back to Canada. How'd you guys get back in touch?"

Sara's pretty face went shifty. "We never lost touch. We wrote letters after he went home."

All the air whooshed out of me like I'd taken a solid gut-punch to the diaphragm. It wouldn't unknot enough for me to inhale again, even when I hunched over, trying to find a little more room to exhale so I could convince the whole breathing process to restart properly.

I hadn't really blamed Lucas for leaving. I'd never been sure that he wasn't supposed to be in North Carolina for just the one semester anyway, since he'd left at Christmas, which was a perfectly reasonable time to go back home. It also meant he was gone weeks before I'd started to visibly show, and because teenagers frequently aren't too smart, very few people had bandied his name around as the possible partner to my predicament. Nobody counted backward to figure out when the deed was done; they just gossiped and suggested names of boys I had no interest in. Sara and Lucas were the only two who actually knew. The idea that he'd just walked away, disappeared entirely, was one I was okay with. My mother had done more or less the same thing with me.

Somehow him walking away from me and keeping in touch with Sara was a whole lot less okay. I wasn't sure if I wanted to cry or throw up. So much for emotional maturity.

I don't know what Sara saw in my face, but it apparently fed whatever jealous beast she'd been keeping in her heart all these years, because what I saw in hers was a flash of triumph. Revenge, best served cold. I'd never cried over that particular fiasco in my life. For the first time I wanted to. Might have, if I could've gotten the breath, but my head was starting to hurt from a lack of oxygen, and my belly still wouldn't unknot.

Coyote put his hand on my shoulder, and a pulse of dry

desert air rolled through me. It unwound my stomach, letting me catch a breath and pull myself upright, and warmed my extremities a smidge. I'd given people little hits like that, but I'd never received one. It felt good, all strengthening and compassionate. I hoped that's what it was like when I was the healer, rather than the healed.

Once I was stable, Coyote put his hand out. Sara took it, which she hadn't done with me. "It's nice to meet you, Agent Isaac. I'm Cyrano Bia, and this is Gary Muldoon. We need to take a look at your victim."

"Seattle Police Department hasn't got jurisdiction here."

"That's okay," Coyote said easily. "We're not police." He stepped over the police line and ambled toward the body without waiting for a response. Sara shot me a withering look and went after him.

In most ways, that was helpful. It meant I could shake off astonishment and take a look at the marked earth again. Or it would have if I was the kind of person who had her shit that much together, but I never had, still didn't, and probably never would. Gary came up beside me and said, "Jo?" as tentatively as I'd ever heard him speak.

"Later, okay? I...later."

"Arright." The big old cab driver put an arm around my shoulders, squeezed carefully, and let go again. "See anything out there?"

Every answer I wanted to give revolved around Sara Isaac, formerly Buchanan, and the one-up she'd just pulled on me. I thought I would've been pleased, honestly. If she and Lucas had just managed to end up together, I would've thought it was kind of cool. Finding out they'd never lost touch was manifestly not cool, and I pretty much wanted to bury myself in snow and let the cold numb me while I worked myself up to dealing with it.

If I'd learned anything in the last year, it was that the world very rarely put itself on pause to let people cope. "It's getting realer," I said quietly. "When I faced it in Olympia Park it made marks in the snow, and now, here…there's blood on the snow down there. I can still see where it left prints on the earth, but it's getting realer."

"What is?" Laurie Corvallis had disappeared for a few minutes, maybe chasing the false Feds down, but she was back, and had been long enough to hear my faltering explanation. "How can something not real be doing this?"

"Do you believe in God, lady?" Gary asked unexpectedly. Corvallis looked around like she thought he must be talking to someone else, then wrinkled her eyebrows at me. I shrugged and tipped my head, inviting her to answer. I certainly wasn't going to. "Angels?" Gary asked. "Demons?"

"I believe there are good people and bad people and that there's some of both in everybody. I believe the world's got a lot of power to fuck us up." It was the second time she'd sworn, and I glanced toward her camera guy to see if he was recording. The little green light blipped at me, but presumably the whole thing would be edited for PG viewing. "Are you saying this is a demon?" She sounded skeptical in a sell-me-the-story way: not like she unconditionally disbelieved, but like she wasn't going to accept wooden nickels.

Gary shook his head. "Nah. Just curious. Wondered if that reporter's mind of yours kept itself open or if you made up your mind before you went in."

I heard myself say, "It's a spirit," and wondered what exactly I thought I was going to accomplish by telling Laurie Corvallis our hypothesis. "A very angry, hungry spirit who's either being controlled by, or who is, someone powerful. I'm sure you know there's been no blood at any of the scenes. I'm afraid the thing has been feeding psychically, maybe trying to strengthen or create a physical body. The stronger it gets the more it takes on the ability to chow down mass in the real world, which is why this one's messier. I don't know how bad it'll get if we don't stop it."

Corvallis's gape became a sharp scowl. "No wonder Morrison doesn't want you talking to me." She climbed over the police tape and stomped through the snow toward the body, cameraman trailing behind her.

I pursed my lips, watching them go. "Next time I wonder why I don't just tell people the truth, remind me of this."

"Doll, I didn't know you ever wondered that."

"Not often, and now I know why." Coyote, Corvallis and the cameraman were being hustled away from the murder site, none of them looking happy about it. Given the increasing number of FBI agents and forensics experts appearing on the scene, I thought they should be grateful none of us had been arrested yet. Sara was glaring at me from the dip where the body had been found, like the reporter and the nosy Indian were my fault. I shrugged and slipped my way back down toward the road, waiting for them to catch up.

"They're not going to recognize it as the same killer," Coyote said as soon as he did. "I got close enough to look at the cusp marks. It's more like a wild animal. That, and there's blood this time, and pieces of torn flesh in the snow around the body. It's getting more savage."

Corvallis all but lit up and pulled a sleek phone from the pocket of her coat. "A copycat killer? We can call it mountain madness. Christmas killer? No, that's been done." She hurried ahead of us, shaking her phone like that would help her pick up a signal.

Gary chuckled in her wake. "Think she ever met a story she couldn't tackle?"

"I think she's going to if she stays out here." I stopped in the snow and Coyote knocked me into motion again. "Ow. Look, I don't know if you saw anything, Ro, but—"

"Do you have to do that?"

"You call me Jo, I get to call you Ro."

"I like Coyote better."

"You don't look so much like a coyote in the real world. Did you see anything?"

He bared his teeth at me, the expression surprisingly close to that of his coyote-form self, then shook it off in much the same way I'd seen him do on the astral plane. "Aside from a body that doesn't fit the physical signs of the other murders, no. It *is* the wendigo," he said, like I'd been going to argue. "There's no hint of soul left to the corpse at all. Like Mandy was." His mouth thinned, eyes gone grim. "But much too late to save her."

"I believe you. I think every time it feeds it's getting more distorted." I puffed my cheeks and followed Corvallis down the mountain listlessly. "The bite marks on Charlie Groleski were rounder than the ones on Karin Newcomb. If it had managed to take Mandy out, it might've looked like a different case, too. Wait, what are we doing?" I stopped following Corvallis and frowned. "We're going the wrong way. Its tracks went up the mountain. We should get *them* out of here, but we should stay."

Gary, in a low rumble, said, "'Should' is one of those funny words that don't mean what you think it means," and pointed behind us.

CHAPTER TWENTY

A shadow paced on the snow, clearly watching us. Tooth and claw and red raging eyes; the rest was white and translucent and almost impossible to see. The Sight snapped on, making it more visible, though I instantly wished it hadn't.

Rivulets of blood dripped and flowed from its teeth, never falling far enough to stain the snow. Its claws were tangled with shredded souls. The tatters could have been anything from cobweb to gauze, fragile against the beast's bulk, but the healer's magic within me *knew* I was seeing the last vestiges of what had once been human beings. It was all much, much more clear than it had been on the mountain yesterday morning. Clearer, even, than it had been on Mandy's rooftop the evening before. I had the gut-sinking feeling that having sized me up, it had decided it was time to get serious about manifesting in the real world.

It was still nominally manlike, in that it had arms and legs, but its shoulders and neck had disappeared into a massive head with a wide-gaping, grinning mouth. Even the humanoid features were stunted: the arms were short, the chest incredibly thick, the legs seeming too small to carry its weight.

It *stank*. From thirty yards away, it smelled of rotten meat and offal. It had smelled like roses yesterday, by comparison. The transition toward more real wasn't doing it any favors.

Very, very quietly, I said, "Gary, what do you see?"

He said, "A bear," in a way that let me understand how utterly inadequate, how completely wrong, the description was, and yet that it was the best he could do. It was no more bearlike than I was, but with its shifting, fluid white form almost impossible to focus on, I thought *bear* was as close as any non-magically-gifted person was going to get.

"Coyote?"

"…not a bear." He sounded like Gary did: unable to express what he saw any more clearly. "What do you see?"

"A trap." The only problem was, I didn't know for whom. "Gary, back up really slowly. Just a few feet. I want to see if it…cares."

"That don't fill me with confidence, doll." He backed up anyway, a few slow steps down the road. The wendigo went very still, thick torso lifted like it was scenting the air. It cared, in other words. I swore under my breath, and Gary froze again. "That don't, either."

"It shouldn't. Don't move again." The wendigo relaxed when Gary stopped inching backward, though it began pacing back and forth, a few steps at a time, as it stared down the mountain at us. I had the unpleasant and probably accurate feeling it was assessing us in terms of easy pickings, and I very carefully began building a shield.

The heat of desert sand, delicious when I stood in the middle of a snow-covered forest, washed over me. Dune yellow and sky blue became a part of my shield, strengthening it beyond measure. I'd only ever made a weaving with so much power one other time, when I'd borrowed my dead mother's talent to fight a banshee. It felt terrific, and despite the wendigo I shot a smile toward Coyote. He didn't exactly smile back, but the heat of his magic intensified a moment, making me feel welcome.

The wendigo snarled, the same low threatening sound that had started an avalanche the day before. There were more trees along the road here, maybe enough to stabilize the snow, but it wasn't a risk I wanted to take. Not with a news crew and a couple dozen FBI agents who could be swept away.

Right on cue, they noticed the wendigo. Half a dozen people voiced variations on, "What the *hell?*" and Sara bellowed, "Jesus Christ, Joanne, what're you doing now?" like a semi-visible slavering monster was obviously all my fault.

I decided she would rather I kept her alive than give her an answer. Our shield stretched across the road, making a wall between ourselves and the wendigo, but I'd seen the thing jump. "The shield has to go over us, too."

"I can do that if you've got a plan for the wendigo." Coyote sounded strained, which surprised me. I was used to thinking of him as well-nigh omnipotent, but I could feel the intense concentration in his magic as he stretched the shield back in a wide curve. The whole investigative area, including the road, covered a good forty square yards, maybe a little more. I didn't think we needed a bubble unless the wendigo was smart enough to leap the shield and attack from behind, but I'd never dreamed that sustaining a shield that big might wear my mentor out.

Especially when I had plenty left to give. I poured more into the shield, feeling it strengthen, and turned some of Coyote's energy toward my favorite catch-all. Tight bands of magic wove together, creating a net with much greater holding capacity than the one I'd built yesterday. "I've got a plan."

It would've been a better plan if a net had worked the day before, but I saw no reason to burden Coyote with that knowledge. "If this works, I want you to try to get everybody off the mountain, Gary. Back down to the lodge, at least. I don't think Mister Stinky here cares much about whether he's noshing on outdoorsmen anymore."

"If what works?"

Crap. I'd forgotten he couldn't See what I was doing. "I'm going to try to catch it in a net. I just want to hold it in place until everybody's safe. It didn't work yesterday, but it's more real now and Coyote's backing me up."

"Joanne Walkingstick, what the hell are you doing?" Sara'd caught up to us, but I still didn't think it was a good time to answer her questions. I almost hoped she'd grab me. I had this idea that power would zot off me like an electrical arc, and she'd end up ten feet away in the snow with her hair all frazzled. It wasn't nice, but it was funny.

Gary was apparently down with ignoring the Feds, too. His voice dropped to a low enough grumble that it raised hairs on my nape: "And if it don't work?"

"Then we're all fucked."

"Gotcha. Just tell me when, darlin'."

Coyote eyed me. "Are you always this inspiring?"

"You should see me on a bad day. Ready?"

"Joanne, what are you *doing?*"

Nobody paid Sara any heed at all. Coyote nodded, tensing

in preparation. I launched the net and yelled, "Run!" at Gary as the wendigo leaped.

Time, as it so often did, collapsed into infinite slow motion as everything went to hell.

I understood immediately that my mistake had been in making the shield one-way. It was meant to keep wendigos out, not FBI agents in. Not, as it turned out, FBI agents and over-eager television news reporters. Laurie was there all of a sudden, cameraman in tow, two steps behind Sara and on the wrong side of the shield.

A part of me was given over to admiring Sara's weapon stance as she slapped her duty weapon from its holster and brought it up, firing repeatedly at the wendigo. Her honey-blond hair made her vivid and living against white snow and black trees, *real* in a way the wendigo wasn't. I saw flashes from the muzzle of her weapon, bright imprints in dilated time, and I could almost watch the bullets spin through the air.

I could without question see how they utterly failed to impress the wendigo. They didn't seem to strike it at all: no shudder of impact, no mist of blood, no slowing of its headlong rush. Middle World means clearly couldn't stop it, even if it was more connected than it had been yesterday.

Corvallis and her cameraman were Sara's civilian mirrors. The guy was on his knees, face stretched with enthusiasm and terror, but his camera light was flashing and the lens was angled to catch the wendigo's leap. Corvallis, as admirable and idiotic as Sara, shouted breathless commentary while five hundred pounds of monster barreled toward her.

I swear to God, people like them should've gotten my shiny weird power set. They were delighted to throw themselves into danger's face, ready and eager to take on the world, happy to do stupid, stupid things in the name of truth, justice, and getting the story. I had no desire for that much excitement in my life.

That was probably why I got it, and they didn't.

I flung my net forward, putting all my will behind it: it _had_ to hold. Its cables were steel, titanium, unobtanium, whatever couldn't be broken. I had held gods with that net. I could, by God, hold one nasty little demon spirit.

Wendigo and net collided, and the net stretched, pulled out of shape by the wendigo's need to feed. I let out a wordless roar that felt every bit as deep and earth-shattering as anything the wendigo had voiced, and surged forward a step, holding the line.

The net rebounded from its stretch, knocking the wendigo ass-over-teakettle back up the mountain road. It bumped and crashed and shuddered to a stop, thrashing and snarling as it fought the psychic bonds that held it. Over its screams I heard Sara shouting, "What the hell? _What the hell!?_" as she fired her gun again and again.

I yelled, "Get behind me! _Get behind me!_" Instead, a dozen more federal agents ran forward to join her in trying to shoot to death a creature that only barely had a corporeal body.

Exasperation erupted in my chest and I had sudden, bone-deep sympathy for Coyote and everybody else who'd dealt with me in the first months of my shamanistic career. The federal agents simply _would not accept_ that were facing something they were completely unprepared for, which was the moral equivalent of me utterly refusing to accept my talents. It was incredibly frustrating, and I made a note to apologize to everyone I knew.

Right after we got out of this alive.

I kept feeling pops in my power, like soap bubbles exploding in the air. A bit of the wendigo, an elbow or a claw or an ear or a tooth, broke through the net every time it happened. The net resealed itself, drawing more power each time, and I got a double-vision impression that the monster was slipping between its physical and psychic form. I had its tangible self under control, but if it pulled itself just a little farther into the spirit realm I wasn't sure I could hold it. The nets I'd cast in the past had held physical things, not spirits.

A small, weary part of myself thought I should probably be able to hold spirits, as well, and that we were going to pay heavily for my lack of skill. But slowed-down time or not, I didn't have the luxury of dwelling. "Coyote, can you kill it?"

"Me?" Incredulous horror spiked through the question, though he toned it back down with the next question: "With what?"

I shot a sideways glance at him. He looked like breathing and maintaining his part of the shield was just about the limit of his capability, which made my brain cramp again. He was my teacher, for pity's sake. I wasn't supposed to walk all over him in the sheer wattage department.

On the other hand, again, not such a good time to worry about it. I turned my attention back to the wendigo and the popping net. One hand fisted of its own accord, like I was holding on tighter, and the rest of me divorced itself from the wendigo just long enough to reach across space and seize my rapier.

It became real in my hand, a solid silver weight. I threw it to Coyote and hissed, "With this."

He caught it clumsily, and stood agog for what seemed like a horribly long time, maybe a whole second or so. Then he bolted forward, black braid bouncing against his spine, and I found myself the unhappy maintainer of both the entire shield and the net.

Screw it. We didn't need the shield as long as the net held. I let it go and focused on the rippling power containing the wendigo. The popping stopped, and relief lightened my heart. We were going to win.

The whine and roar of gunshots ceased abruptly as Coyote tore past the federal agents. Only Sara's protests followed him, unexpectedly thin after the world-shattering noise of the guns. The wendigo still howled, but the mountain was a bastion of silence, compared to what it had been an instant earlier.

Coyote's attack was cinematic. Two quick steps up the wendigo's bulk and he was on top of it, sword lifted in both hands. Power sparkled around him, dune yellow and sky blue connecting with the net, glimmering along the length of the sword, though I could See he hadn't infused the blade with power the way I'd once done. He froze there, captured in time like the Iwo Jima photo, and I Saw sudden gut-churning reluctance splash through his aura.

I was already roaring approval, a tremendous yawp of sound, and it hit him like a physical thing. He flinched and drove the blade downward.

The wendigo vanished.

Gary's whoop of triumph echoed mine. Coyote stood on air for the briefest instant, levitating before he crashed to the snow where the wendigo had been. The rapier plunged deep, leaving him kneeling over it like a king of old, and Gary snatched me up and spun me in a circle, both of us shrieking like idiots.

The others—the federal agents, the news crew—were less excited, their questions an endless round of *what the hell?*

Coyote stood up slowly, expression grim as he pulled my sword from the snow and came back to us. He offered me the blade and I took it happily, turning it this way and that to examine it. There was no blood, nothing but a shimmer of melted water against silver. Coyote, unexpectedly softly, said, "Where did that come from?"

"It's the one I got skewered with. I kept it. Spoils of war." I peeked toward Corvallis, trying to make sure the camera wasn't on me, and whispered it home again. It disappeared as readily as the wendigo had, sending a little thrill of glee through me. Healing powers were handy and all, but a magic sword was six kinds of awesome. I wanted one. I *had* one, and I still wanted one. That's how cool it was.

Laurie elbowed me in the ribs and shoved her microphone in Coyote's face. "Laurie Corvallis, Channel Two News. You are?"

Coyote gave me a genuinely panicked glance, and I insinuated myself between them. Her camera guy's light turned the world to a bright blur, but I figured I was too close to focus on, which was a small favor. "He's not part of your story, Laurie."

"The hell he isn't. He just killed that thing with a sword. A sword! Where'd he get a sword? Where'd it go? What was that thing? Where did *it* go? I could barely see it. Did you see how it bounced back during the attack? Like it hit an invisible wall—"

I was going to have to ask Gary what that whole thing had looked like with unSighted eyes. "Ms. Corvall—"

"This is not a case open for discussion." Sara got between me and Laurie, which more or less put her nose against the camera lens. She put her hand over it, too, blocking any hope of a picture, focused or not, and repeated, "I'm sorry, Ms. Corvallis, but this is a federal situation and I'm going to have to ask you to respect the on-going nature of the investigation. I'll be happy to release what information I can, when I can."

I stepped backward gratefully, removing myself from sight and, I hoped, from Corvallis's mind. All the major cases I'd been involved in so far had been cover-up-able with some kind of vaguely plausible story. I couldn't think of a damned thing to explain away the apparent reversal of certain laws of physics, like *an object in motion will remain in motion* after everybody'd seen the object in question hit an invisible wall and bounce off. Nor could I explain where Coyote'd gotten the sword, or even more importantly, how he'd slain a monster which disappeared upon being skewered.

As it turned out, I didn't have to. While I was worrying about it, the wendigo rose up out of the snow and snatched Gary.

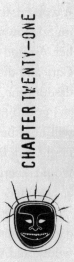

CHAPTER TWENTY-ONE

The old man roared louder than the wendigo did, though it sounded more like surprise than pain. I dived at them with no plan beyond *save Gary,* and passed right through both of them to face-plant in the snow beyond. I shoved up to my hands and knees, spitting ice, and twisted around to gape helplessly as an epic battle erupted.

The wendigo was in no way damaged from the sword thrust. It had to have gone incorporeal, losing cohesion just as Coyote drove the blade down. Either that or having a four-foot-long pointy thing stuck through it simply didn't have any effect at all, which was not a happy thought.

Sara had her damned gun out again. I wasn't sure I could help Gary, but I could at least keep him from getting shot. I flung up my shield again, this time willing it to be visible. I knew it *could* be—a few hundred partygoers had gotten an eyeful of it at Halloween—but visible wasn't its natural state. It worked, though. Sara cupped the gun's butt and pointed the muzzle toward the sky as silver-blue burst into being all around her. Around her and everybody else, in a sort of doughnut with Gary and the wendigo in its hollow center. Sara, for the hundredth time, yelled, "What the hell?"

I got to my feet. "Don't shoot. I don't know if the shield will hold bullets or ricochet them. And don't touch it. You might get fried." I was sure she wouldn't, but I hoped it would keep her out of the way while I figured how to answer her.

For something I'd fallen through, the wendigo looked pretty damned substantial. It seized Gary in its mouth and shook him wildly, and when he refused to bend or break, flung him to the ground again in a huge poof of snow. I cried out, but he just rolled to his feet, a slow pedantic action that went well with the way his shoulders gathered in a methodical hunch. He muttered, "Let's dance," and the wendigo paused a moment, like it was smart enough to be surprised at the phrase.

Gary charged it, a slow run that slammed a broad shoulder into its gut. They both went flying off the side of the road and bounced through the snow. Like everybody else, I rushed over to watch. They bashed into two pine trees, breaking first their fall, and then the trees, which creaked and shuddered and collapsed in a rain of snow and needles.

The wendigo was on its feet first, but Gary swung a fist up, catching the thing in its enormous jaw. The *crack* reverberated up the hillside and everybody around me hissed in a painful, impressed breath. Me, I wasn't breathing at all, and didn't know if I ever would again. Gary was a tough old coot, and still had the linebacker build of his youth, but it seemed utterly impossible that he could hold his own against a semi-embodied, soul-sucking, flesh-eating monster.

I flung power toward them, not even so much as a net. More like a lasso, just to find out if my magic had more effect than my physical attack had. It whistled through the wendigo harmlessly, which didn't surprise me, and whooshed through Gary as effortlessly, which did. I lurched toward the incline, heart hammering so hard I could barely see. If Gary was as unaffected by my magic as the wendigo was, I was horribly afraid he wasn't exactly alive anymore.

Coyote's hand on my shoulder stopped me. I jerked away, but he caught me again, pulling me around so I could see astonishment curving his lips into a smile. "Your friend's spirit is strong."

That sounded so much like hokey-jokey Indian crap that I nearly decked him. Then a tiny bit of cleverness caught up and I whipped around again, trying to See more clearly. I'd been using the Sight all along, but I'd been paying attention to the wendigo, not Gary.

Who was carrying a great big beautiful tortoise shell on his back. More than on his back: it was somehow larger than he was, solid plates protecting him all around. A tortoise's huge snapping jaws translated into enormous physical strength, far more than an ordinary man could command. He got to his feet ponderously, every action deliberate, and when the wendigo leaped at him again he ducked, caught it on his back, and did the nicest back-slam I'd ever seen outside of pro wrestling.

The wendigo screamed. Gary rolled over, unscathed by its tiny clawing arms, and lifted a heavy fist to drive it down, not fast, but implacably, into the beast's chest.

It wasn't bone that splintered, but souls. The fragments and tattered remains of the wendigo's meals contracted and shriveled, becoming part of its body as it tried frantically to repair itself. Gary hit it again, then again, and its screams turned to panicked squeals as it twisted, trying to escape. Gary held it where I couldn't, caught between corporeality and insubstantiality. Even now I couldn't get my magic to take hold, though a glimmer of understanding finally washed over me.

I was used to fighting in one realm at a time. There were frequently metaphysical manifestations that cropped up during physical battles, but mostly, I fought in the Middle World. I wasn't used to switching wholesale from one level of reality to another in the middle of a fight. The wendigo, though, was completely unconstrained in its ability to move from the physical world to the spirit. I couldn't catch the damned thing because I couldn't keep up. Watching Gary and his tortoise spirit, I thought maybe, _maybe,_ if I gave myself over to Raven entirely, I might be able to slide between realities as freely as Gary and the wendigo were now doing.

I wasn't sure I trusted Raven that much. I wasn't sure I trusted _anything_ that much. I admired the hell out of Gary, that he could let himself be so subsumed by the tortoise spirit. I'd asked the tortoise to protect him, but I didn't think either of us had anticipated just how far the totem animal would go to do that.

I also wondered, briefly, if giving myself to Raven that completely would be as effective as Gary's tortoise was against the wendigo. I didn't exactly think of tortoises as deadly predators, but their sheer size and strength made them worth reckoning with. Ravens were more likely to peck somebody to distraction than destroy them with slow relentless determination.

Determination that the wendigo couldn't stand against. It

broke free, shrieking with pain and terror, and Gary's lunge at it was just that much too slow. Hope springing eternal, I flung a net around both of them, encompassing whole yards of sky and earth within it, but the wendigo slipped to spirit form and disappeared through my lashings without a trace. "God damn it! Where'd it—is it coming back? Coyote? Is it going to—?"

"I don't know. Maybe it's too badly hurt."

I whispered a prayer to a deity I didn't entirely believe in, and slid down the mountainside until I reached Gary. He was on his knees, gray eyes wide and uncertain. His tortoise spirit was retreating, no longer needing to encompass him with its protective strength. I crashed into him, hugging him hard, and poured a pulse of my own healing magic through him. Even if the tortoise had taken the brunt of that fight, getting chewed on by a wendigo couldn't be good for anybody. "Gary, are you okay?"

"Right as rain, doll."

His eyes rolled up and he fell over in a faint.

He woke up again almost instantly, a face full of snow apparently just about as effective as smelling salts. I got myself under his arm and we clambered back up the hill, huffing and puffing like two old geezers. Well, like one old geezer and one young one. Close enough.

Somehow I was surprised to find a couple dozen federal agents and a news team waiting for us at the top. I said, "Don't ask," and of course everybody did anyway. Under their babbling, I said, "Mind playing up being fragile? At least some of them will volunteer to help get you back down the hill, and that leaves me fewer to deal with."

Gary whispered, "I donno," back. "Am I fragile?"

I snorted, trying not to let it turn into an out-loud laugh. "About as fragile as a bulldozer, I think."

"In that case I don't mind at all." He lifted his voice a little and put a convincing quaver in it, sounding more like a querulous old man than I'd ever heard him. "Somebody gimme a hand? I ain't feelin' so good. I think I hit my head…."

More Feds than I expected stepped forward. A few just looked like they wanted to be anywhere but here, but one, a woman about my age, looked a little starstruck. If Gary hooked up with a girl forty years his junior I was never going to hear the end of it. Either I'd lost my old silver stallion to a younger, prettier model, or I'd set him on the road to being a dirty, dirty old man. He came out ahead and I looked like a dork either way.

Oh well. It wasn't like I didn't have a lot of practice at that. About eight of them, including the young woman, opted to help carry him down the mountain. I didn't think any of them saw the roguish wink he gave me as they carted him off.

Sadly, eight still left me with about fifteen agents and two news reporters to deal with. Corvallis looked like her brain was collapsing in on itself as she tried to process what she'd seen, or maybe more accurately, hadn't quite seen.

Sara said, "Get back to work," to her team, then gave me a sharp look. "Is it safe?"

I wondered what it had cost her to ask, and wished I had a better answer than, "I think so."

She nodded, and her people reluctantly dispersed. I hated to think how much mess had been made of their crime scene, though on the positive side they weren't going to find anything useful anyway. When we were alone, she said, "What was it?"

"A wendigo." I mostly wanted to see if it meant anything

to her. It wouldn't have to me not that long ago—like, yesterday—but the skin around her eyes tightened a little, as if she at least recognized the word.

"Don't tell me you're still into that mystical crap, Joanne."

I started to say, "It's a soul-eating demon," only it came out "Woo-woob-wha? Mystical crap? Me? Into it?"

"You were totally into it. Freaky into it. You were always talking about these big meaningful dreams you had." She made quote marks around half the words in that sentence, while I reeled and tried to match my teenage memories with Sara's violently clashing ones. "Your 'spirit guide,'" she said. "Your 'shamanic training.' You were so full of shit."

I put away trying to reconcile disparate memories and looked down at her for a while. I was tall enough that just looking at people could get them to back off sometimes, but she had federal agent training and, more important, remembered me as an awkward teenager. One she apparently hadn't liked as much as I thought she had. That's what I said, actually. "Wow. You really didn't like me very much, did you? I had…no idea." It stung, the same way learning she and Lucas had kept in touch. I was willing to admit I'd screwed it up. Unintentionally, maybe, but I'd screwed it up. Still, the idea that we'd never really been friends cut a lot deeper than it should've, all these years later.

She glanced away, a trace of guilt slithering across her pretty features. It made me feel a little better, not because I wanted her to feel badly, but because maybe it meant we *had* been friends and she'd just heaped a lot of after-the-fact resentment onto the relationship. I was coming to realize I knew more than a little about that kind of behavior.

"It doesn't matter. I guess I am still into it." I had no recollection at all of being into mystical stuff in high school, and wondered if those memories had faded the same way my Coyote dreams had faded. Wondered, in fact, whether they'd had help in fading, which made me want to kick Coyote's shin just in case. "It's kind of what I'm doing now. It doesn't really matter if you believe in it or not, but you're not going to f…" I trailed off because Laurie Corvallis had worked her way into my line of vision, and was staring at us very nearly hard enough to set my hair on fire. I'd forgotten she was there. "Shit."

Sara glanced at her like she was of slightly less significance than a bug. "Don't worry. I can seize her tapes under the Patriot Act if I need to."

For the first and possibly the last time in history, Corvallis and I started spluttering in outrage for the same reason. Sara said, "Oh, great, you're still a bleeding-heart liberal, too," and grabbed my arm to haul me several steps away. Corvallis tried to follow, but two of Sara's agents materialized—a word I should've use more cautiously, given the wendigo's vanish-and-reappear act—between us. Corvallis bounced on her toes, trying to see what was going on. A mean little part of me snickered. Sadly, that part was attached to my voice box, so it happened out loud, but Sara only smirked and didn't chide me. "You were saying?"

"That you're not going to find a conventional killer. I know there's no point in asking you to step back, but unless the FBI has its own paranormal investigative team, you're not going to find an answer." A sudden childish hope sparked in me. "Do you? Is there really like an X-Files department? I would've made a great—"

"Mulder," Sara finished, which was not at all what I'd been going to say. "If we've got X-Files, I don't know about them."

And don't want to, her tone said. "Are you for real? You think there's some kind of mythological monster out here in the woods killing people?"

"Can you give me a logical explanation, a clear definition, of what you saw in the last half hour?" I raised a hand, blocking any answer she might give to what was effectively a rhetorical question. "Seriously, Sara, what did you see? Because I can hardly see this thing myself, and it's probably easier for me than most people." That sounded better than "for you."

Her upper lip curled and flattened again, almost invisible signal of frustration. "A wolf," she finally said, in much the same way Gary'd named it a bear. "I don't know, Joanne. I could barely focus on it. It had teeth, that's all I know, and all my victims have been eaten. Let's say I believe you."

Way, way, way under my breath, I mumbled, "I believe you," obediently. People hardly ever thought that was as funny as I did, though, so I hoped she hadn't heard, but mostly I wished life came with emoticons, so I could stamp a disembodied smiley face in the air next to me as an indication that other people should think I was funny, too.

"If I believe you, and this isn't something bullets can handle, what am I supposed to do? Go back to my bosses and say sorry, no idea what happened, but I promise it's over? What are *you* going to do? And how are you going to prove you're right if you kill this thing?"

"By Seattle not being the epicenter of cannibal killings anymore? Honestly, I don't know yet how to stop this thing." That was clearly the wrong thing to say. Sara's jaw tensed and she turned her shoulders in a way that indicated closing-off body language. I hurried along, words tumbling over each other. "It's coming at me from a different place than anything else I've gone up against, Sara. I'll take it down. I always have before. But it's a lot easier if I don't have civilians around to worry about."

I'd forgotten her quirky lifted eyebrow. She didn't raise it up high like most people did. She only twitched it just enough to indicate she was amused, and that hadn't changed in thirteen years. Hopeful, I smiled back just a little. "I use the word 'civilians' advisedly."

"You better. Look, Joanne. I can't pull out. You know that."

"Yeah, I do. Just…if you believe me at all, just drop when I say get down, okay?"

She sighed, the sound starting somewhere around her ankle bones. "Okay."

"Good," I said. "Great. *Get down!*"

Sara hit the deck, and the wendigo came tearing over us.

CHAPTER TWENTY-TWO

It smelled of desperation, a scent I'd only associated with humans before, and even that as a parable rather than an actual definable stink. But its stench was sour, and there was no method to its behavior, just a frenzied launch at those closest to it. Sara was facedown in six inches of snow, and the thing rebounded off me, sending me into a backward stagger.

I could feel the agents' life-pulses so clearly I didn't need to see them, and snapping fresh shields up was by now instinctive. The wendigo leaped from body to body, bouncing off, and finally, with a howl, turned back to me. Shields or not, it landed on me like a ton of bricks. I sank down but shot my hands upward, grabbing at its thick neck.

Thick, but smaller than it had been. Gary'd done a lot of damage in his brief battle, and I knew it was starving for lack of souls, for lack of flesh.

Given that it had backed off from me twice now, it *had* to be desperate to attack me when it had been weakened. It made sense: I could probably power it back up to its previous size, all in one tidy snack, but I didn't think it was happy about its range of choices. It swung its head, hot saliva spattering my face as it pressed down, trying to make my arms buckle. I wasn't about to falter, but neither did I know exactly what to do now that I had it by the throat. Using my magic as a weapon was a cosmic no-no, and I didn't dare let go so I could draw my sword. I had unpleasant visions of lying here in the snow for the rest of eternity, trying to throttle something that wasn't exactly alive.

Coyote appeared, a silhouette against the blue sky, and clobbered the wendigo with a tree branch. It howled, whacked him away, and fled. I heard Coyote hit the snow, and then silence broken only by the harsh breathing of those around us. Even that faded after a minute, and there was nothing but wind and the occasional plop of snow falling from trees to the ground. I ventured, "Sara?" and got a muffled grunt in reply.

"I think it's gone. I think maybe you and your people should go back down to the lodge and keep anybody from going hiking or skiing or whatever. What do you think?"

"I think that sounds like a good use of federal resources." She sounded almost like the girl I'd been friends with a lifetime ago. Snow squeaked as she got up, and I lay there listening to the brief, unconvinced and unconvincing arguments presented by her forensics team. A couple of them decided to stay behind, with a handful of others offering to stand guard while they worked. I didn't think any of them imagined they were going to find anything, but I admired their work ethic. The rest took Corvallis and her cameraman, the former complaining bitterly, and headed back to the hotel to keep tourists from getting themselves eaten.

I was pretty sure I should join them, but staring at the sky as I lay deep in what would be a snow angel if I could muster the energy to wave my arms and legs had its appeal, too. "So," I said eventually. "Nice job there at the end, scaring it off."

Coyote's voice drifted up out of the snow. "I think it was trying to escape and went after you because it was desperate. That wasn't a real attack."

"Yeah, I know. Still, you got it off me." I lay there awhile longer, replaying the last several minutes in my mind, and coming up repeatedly against Coyote's expression of distaste and terror as he struggled with the wendigo. In time, I repeated, "So. This fighting thing. You're not actually very good at it."

"No." Coyote sounded like he'd like to say a lot more, and yet like he knew absolutely none of it was of any use.

I nodded. Snow creaked under my head. "Interesting."

"It's not—"

"No," I said, "really. It's interesting. I'm not mad." I considered that, then decided it was true. "You're a teacher. You're a healer. A guide. Right after this all started I was told I was on a warrior's path. I'm guessing nobody ever said that to you."

He said, "No," again, and then, "People usually don't, to shamans. It's sort of anathema to the purpose."

"Yeah, no, I get that. It's cool. It's okay." I stared at the sky for another little while, making a half-hearted effort to formulate a plan, or an opinion about me being a fighter when my mentor wasn't, or in fact to do anything besides lie there in the snow. I was pretty content with lying there, really, except, "My butt is freezing."

Coyote let out a sharp, barklike laugh. "Mine, too."

I sat up, hunching my shoulders against snow falling down my spine. "I vote we regroup back at the hotel with hot soup and carbs and a boiling-temperature bath."

"Yeah." Coyote sat up, too. "All except those last three things. We've got some work to do first."

I whimpered, and we got up and went back to the hotel.

Gary was sitting by the fireplace in the hotel lobby with an enormous cup of tea in his hands and the twenty-five-year-old FBI agent perched on his knee. He spilled both in his haste to get up when we came in, but instead of looking abashed he gave me a broad wink and a wicked smile. I had to look away to keep from giggling, and when he got close enough I whispered, "You Lothario, you."

"Keeps me young, darlin'. Keeps me young. What happened after I left?" He waved goodbye to his FBI agent as we headed for the room, filling in details as we went. "You left 'em up there with no protection?"

I spread my hands, defenseless and helpless alike. "I think it's gone for now, and there are other things we need to do. You were the only one who even laid a hand on it out there, much less—" We got to the room and I stopped to gaze up at the old cabbie while Coyote unlocked the door. "I don't think I said it before, Gary. You were fantastic out there. You were amazing."

Red curdled along his cheeks and he all but dug a toe into the floor. "Wasn't me, mostly. It was that tortoise you found for me, Jo. I never felt him like that before. The way I figure it, you did all the heavy lifting. I was just the vehicle."

"No." We stepped into the room and I turned to give him a hard hug. "That was you, Gary. It was all you. You kicked ass, took names, and saved a lot of lives."

"You can thank your protector during our spirit journey," Coyote said. "He'll hear you. Jo, when was the last time you slept?"

I gave him a look. Gary peered between us all bright-eyed and curious. Coyote had the grace to blush, which warmed his already-warm skin tones attractively. "Right. It'd be better if we hadn't—"

I gave him another look, this one explaining how he was going to die unpleasantly if he came anywhere near suggesting the phrase *this was a mistake.* "If we hadn't *slept,*" he said firmly. Gary brightened up even more, his low-brow suspicions apparently confirmed. I averted my eyes so I wouldn't revert to grinning like an idiot, and grinned like an idiot anyway. Coyote, in his best superior teacher tone, said, "You should know by now that spirit journeys are easier when you're sleep deprived."

"Oh." Heh. I did know that. My stupid grin fell away in embarrassment, and I stared at nothing for a moment. "We could get high instead."

There was a little silence while we sat there, none of us quite believing I'd said that. First, as far as I knew, we had nothing to get high on except the overpriced alcohol in the hotel bar. Second, and far more importantly—

"That'd go over great with the random drug tests at work," Gary said. "You lost your mind, Jo?"

"I'm beginning to think so, yes."

"We did bring your drum," Coyote said tartly. "Unless that's not recreational enough for you."

"Oh, bite me. I don't know why I said that. It just popped out." I was a stick in the mud when it came to drug use, and had been long before I became a cop. I just flat-out didn't get why anybody would risk the high when there was always the very real possibility that the low would include sudden and permanent death. That, obscurely, reminded me that I couldn't remember the last time I'd snitched a cigarette, which somehow made me feel like I had the moral high ground. Satisfied, I got up to unwrap my drum and hand it over to Gary.

Coyote intercepted me halfway, his palms turned up and his expression unexpectedly shy. "May I? I've never seen it, and I remember how excited you were when you got it."

I almost tripped over my own feet fighting off the urge to cling to the instrument. It had been in my bedroom the night before, but we hadn't exactly stopped to admire it. I'd never imagined it might be an object of interest to my mentor, and I wasn't in the habit of letting people besides Gary handle it. Morrison had, a couple of times, and the first time he'd picked it up I'd felt it from across the room. I thought I would have felt it from across the world. Given that history, handing it to Coyote was a lesson in anticipation.

Magic spilled through me as he took it. Not like what I'd felt with Morrison: that had been warmth bordering on sensuality. With Coyote it was the heat and clarity of the desert, like the colors of his aura were pouring into me in short, intense bursts. Hairs stood up on my arms and his gaze, gone gold, jerked to mine. The wendigo—in fact, the entire world— faded from relevance, and I took a half step toward him.

Gary, very politely, cleared his throat. I jumped backward, cheeks flaming with teen-level angsty guilt. Coyote flinched, stared at Gary like he'd appeared from the ether, then hastily transferred his attention back to me. "What—?"

"The drum, it has, I guess it has—" Opinions. I couldn't quite bring myself to say that, and instead started whistling the

Matchmaker song from *Fiddler on the Roof.* Coyote's eyebrows went up and I stopped whistling to rub my face. I wondered if Morrison had felt anything when he'd picked up my drum. I wondered what would have happened if I'd let Thor handle it. I wondered if I really wanted to know in either case. "Look, just nevermind, okay? Can we just get on with it?"

Coyote's eyebrows remained elevated, which left me to imagine all sorts of things we might get on with, none of which were hunting down a wendigo. Gary, who had as dirty a mind as I did, gave an indiscreet snort that probably masked a much less discreet guffaw. I cast an exasperated glance skyward, then put my hand out for the drum. "Come on, Ro."

He put his eyebrows back down where they belonged and otherwise ignored me, concern creasing lines into his forehead as he examined the drumhead. "What happened?"

"The wolf—the—" I gave up and sat on the end of Gary's bed. "I always thought it was a wolf there. A wolf and a rat-tlesnake under the raven's wings." They were painted beauti-fully, raven wings following the drumhead's curves, and the colors were gorgeous, as bright as they'd been the day I received the drum. But the wolf was smeared, like it had gotten wet and was fading away. "But it started changing after you—died—and so I've been wondering for months if maybe it was a coyote, not a wolf at all. I don't know what it means, espe-cially since you're not dead."

"If it was a coyote, maybe it means I have less influence over your future than I used to." Coyote gave the drum a gentle shake, rattling its beads, then offered it to Gary. "Or maybe it just means the elders who gave it to you saw wrong, and it's changing itself so it's more in tune with your needs."

"It's an inanimate object, Coyote, it can't…" Logic held

sway in the completion of that sentence, but like it or lump it, my life encompassed a great deal more than just logic these days. "Yeah, okay, maybe. Can we get started?"

He gave me an odd little smile. "That's the third time you've said that. What happened to the woman who didn't want anything to do with magic?"

"She nearly got her mentor killed, and a lot of other people did die. Come on, Coyote. What are we doing here? Guide me."

His smile fell away into apology. "Right. Okay, so I've seen your—" he broke off, eyed Gary, and euphemized what he'd been about to say "—your spirit animal, so I—"

"My raven," I interrupted petulantly. The idea of excluding Gary from the small circle of people who knew what my spirit guide was seemed all wrong. I resented Coyote's attempt, even though the smarter part of me knew he was trying to protect me. Spirit animals, like true names, were not to be taken lightly.

Coyote gave me a brief, steady look, then corrected himself. "Your raven. So I know you've managed at least one successful spirit quest, which is heartening."

"You don't have to sound so surprised."

For some reason he ignored me. "You need a second for this, Joanne. The kind of soul retrieval we're looking at doing here is significant. The raven is a very good guide, but I want you to have something whose purpose is to protect you, as well."

Worry began to loose worms in my tummy. "I thought any spirit guide protected you in the astral realm."

"They do, so maybe you see my point. I don't think one's enough. I wish you had three, but this kind of quest usually only brings them one at a time."

"There were—" I swallowed, heat suddenly burning my

face. Three spirit animals had turned up when I'd done a quest with Judy Morningstar, but that entire situation had gone to hell in a handbasket. Odds weren't good that any of them had been real, even if a raven had legitimately chosen me later, as it had seemed to then. "Okay. One quest, one guide. Is that going to be—" I was having a hard time getting through sentences. That one was supposed to finish *enough?* but Coyote's tense-jawed expression made me swallow it.

He was afraid. My mentor, my golden-eyed, laughing Coyote, who had saved my life and taught me most of what I knew about shamanic magic, was scared of the monster in the woods. It was a bigger bad than he was accustomed to dealing with, and he'd only just woken up from a special kind of hell that had a lot in common with what the wendigo was doing to people. I'd been staggering along for months, desperate for reassurance, and now the guy I'd expected to provide it wasn't in any shape to do so.

"It'll be enough." I hardly recognized my own voice, though there was something vaguely familiar in the tone. "One guide, one shield, and besides, I've got these." I touched the silver necklace at my throat, garnering a smile from Gary and a look of incomprehension from Coyote. "Talismans of faith. They'll help. Trust me."

Coyote's shoulders relaxed a little and, bemused, I recognized the tone I'd taken. It was exactly the same one he'd used to convince the paramedics to let us help Mandy Tiller: utterly reasonable and calm and certain, even if the words themselves were preposterous. He gathered himself, then nodded, equilibrium regained. "This is dangerous, Jo. The wendigo is hunting in two worlds, so during a spirit quest you're going to be particularly vulnerable. For this journey, I'll be your protector as much as the raven."

God. No wonder he was freaked out. Hunting monsters was scary enough, but hanging around waiting for them to attack had a particular kind of nerve-wrackingness to it. "I'll try to hurry."

"It's not the kind of thing you can rush." He slid to the floor, making himself, by all appearances, less comfortable, and I reluctantly joined him. I didn't see why I couldn't sack out on the bed and do my spirit quest in comparative luxury, but I bet he'd argue that comfort invited complacency. Even I didn't want to invite complacency in the face of a soul-eating demon.

He said, "We should wake up naturally," to Gary, who nodded, lifted the drum, and began the familiar heartbeat cadence.

For the first time ever, I had instantaneous company in my journey to the other worlds.

CHAPTER TWENTY-THREE

Coyote was at my side, trotting along in his animal form. The sky above lingered between Middle World blue and Lower World red, shading to warm purple before we fully entered the Lower World.

I had no recollection of following a path, the other times I'd come here. It wasn't man-made, but more like some ancient streambed, rocks smoothed over until they were cobbles, patch-worked together by nature's hand. That was Coyote's presence, stabilizing my generally awkward entrance to other realms. I wondered if I'd ever be as competent.

We followed the streambed up a low mountainside, Coyote's tongue lolling as it got hotter. I said, "You could always switch out of the fur suit," idly, and he managed to slam his entire body weight into my knee without arresting his forward motion at all.

"Four feet are easier than two on this kind of surface. Besides, I'm a better hunter and protector in this form. You could try it."

"Being a coyote?"

"Or a raven."

I liked how he said that. Like it was not only within the bounds of reason, but in fact utterly reasonable. "I can't shape-shift."

"Not with that attitude you can't."

"I meant people can't shape-shift." This despite the obvious evidence to the contrary. But we were in the Lower World, where rules didn't hold true quite the same way they did in our world. "Or are you going to tell me you can do that at home, too?"

"I wouldn't dare." We crested the mountain and the Lower World spread out before us, a multicolored valley of forests and meadows. Mist took the distance even though the low sun burned steadily in the sky, but I doubted little things like terrestrial weather patterns meant anything here. Coyote sat, wagging his tail, and snapped at a seed dancing on the air. "Does anywhere call to you?"

"Just the local telephone exchange."

He snapped at me that time, and I raised my hands placatingly while I studied the view.

I honestly wanted somewhere to jump out at me, for some small hollow or meadow to brighten in invitation. I wanted to feel like I belonged somewhere here, that some place in this strange odd-colored world welcomed me. Nothing did. Yellow rivers cut their paths across orange-and-purple earth, blue trees stretched toward red skies, all of them disproportionately close to one another, but none of them said *c'mere, Jo, this is a safe place for your spirit quest.* I sighed and gestured a little ways down the mountain. "Nowhere, really. We might as well just use one of the hollers."

"One of the what?"

"The hollers, the…" I stumbled over the explanation,

having never imagined needing to give it. "The mountain hollers. One of the little valleys down there. You know, if you holler it echoes? It's a…it's a holler."

Coyote turned his face toward me to give me the direct upward look that made such effective puppy-dog eyes, except there was no soulful hope in his expression. It looked a lot more like "What the hell are you on about?"

The phrase *I shrank in on myself* was more literal in the Lower World than at home. I curved my shoulders defensively, becoming physically smaller with unhappiness. "It's what my dad calls them. I thought everybody did. Maybe it's just a North Carolina thing."

I didn't know why Coyote's disdain made me feel so bad. I just hadn't expected to be called out over a regionalism. He looked awfully big now, compared to me, and his furry eyebrows bunched together in the worried way that dogs had. He poked his head toward me, long tongue wrapping around my wrist, and although it should've been impossible for him to speak that way, he said, "I'm not a dog," very gently. "Sorry. I just never heard the phrase before. Mountain hollers."

"Doesn't matter." Still hunchy, I turned down the mountain, but Coyote tangled himself in my legs and wouldn't let me move.

"It does matter. This is supposed to be a spiritual journey, a peaceful one, not another tit for tat one-man-upmanship. I'm sorry. I didn't mean to make fun of you."

"Yeah, you did." I wasn't trying to be childish. I just figured if he was going to apologize it should be for the right things, or it didn't mean diddly-squat. He looked up at me for a moment and then his big pointy ears flopped over.

"Okay, you're right. I did. I shouldn't have. I'm sorry."

That sounded more sincere somehow, and I sat down to bash my head against his and hug him. "Okay."

"You've been doing a good job, Jo. I don't know if I said so. You've been doing all right without me."

"I've been a huge flailing mess without you." I got up again, feeling much better about the world, and we slipped and climbed our way down into the nearest holler, where I threw my head back and, well, hollered. "Halloo the reverberate hills!"

Echoes bounced back all around me, and Coyote, after throwing me a startled glance, tilted his sharp nose to the sky and howled. I joined him, shouting nonsense and howling myself, until we were both breathless and our ears rang with the shadows of our voices. Then, smiling and yet feeling strangely formal amidst all the noise, I oriented myself toward the north, where I bowed extravagantly. The other three directions got equal acknowledgment before I sat in the center of a power circle inscribed by echoes.

"All I've brought," I said to no one in particular, "is the song of our hearts. I'm sorry I haven't got any other gifts today, but liveliness and fun ought to count for something." It certainly did with my raven friend, who could be outright silly. I closed my eyes and, a little more solemnly, added, "I seek a second guide today, another spirit to protect me on the warrior's path. I'm grateful to anyone who considers me, and I'll do my best to honor one who might choose to walk with me. I'm pretty bad at that," I admitted, because it seemed like I ought to be honest, "but I'm getting a little better, and Raven means a lot to me even if I'm an ingrate."

I didn't dare open my eyes, for fear Coyote would be gaping at me. I wasn't exactly Ms. Formality, but my little speech was heartfelt, which was a long way from the bastion of refusal I'd been six or twelve months ago.

In the silence that followed I became aware of my drum, its rhythm steady enough that it seemed to define the boundaries of the world. The earth rattled softly with its thrum, mountains picking up the reverberations and rattling them through me. Even the air shimmered with the beat, dancing against my skin. Trees rustled in time with it, and I thought if I opened my eyes the sun itself would skip to the drum's sound.

Instead, though, I drew in closer to myself, concentrating on how my heart fell into time with the external beat. My blood pulsed with its time, red brightening and dimming in my eyelids, until slowly the dimmer aspect became black, and then so too did the bright. I could barely hear the drum anymore, could barely even hear my own heartbeat, assuming they weren't one and the same. Sparks danced against my eyelids, tiny colorless fireworks that were alien and familiar at the same time.

The drumbeat turned to hope in my chest, filling me until I had no sense of my body left. I floated, nothing more than a spark myself, and then the spirit animals came darting through the dark to investigate me.

Most came only once. A badger dug his way by, stopping to snuffle me and then move on. I thought I'd seen him before; he'd come to consider Gary as a companion. The fleet deer that leaped by me, though, had not, and I was unsurprised when its spirit-white form continued on. Solid stodgy badgers seemed a more likely fit for me than quick-hearted flighty deer.

Others came and went, spilling by in a river of possibility, and I became slowly aware of the one animal who returned again and again. It wound its way toward me as if it were the riverbed, long thin lines of white glowing and fading away.

Once, twice, three times, and the fourth it stayed. I said, "You—well, one of your brethren, anyway—came the first time, too. In the false quest."

A rattlesnake folded himself up to strike, narrow head held motionless as he met my gaze. "There isss no sssuch thing assss a falssse quessst, ssshaman. There are only falssse prophetsss. We come becausssse your ssspirit isss true, and alwaysss wasss, even when you were led assstray." He dipped his head and I mimicked the gesture, profound thanks sending a chill over me.

"I mussst tessst you," he said. "Sssee if you are worthy. Thisss will hurt," he warned, and struck.

Hurt didn't begin to cover it. I'd taken a sword through the gut more than once, had been punctured through the hand— also more than once, now that I thought about it, and overall any lifestyle that involved being gutted and stabbed repeatedly really needed a good hard look taken at it—and I'd fought off an ancient serpent's poison while in the form of a thunder-bird.

The rattler's bite managed to combine all of that into one excruciating wound. My hand, where his fangs had sunk into me, throbbed so hard I thought it would explode. Poison scored my veins, stripping them of blood. They shriveled inward, constricting my heart, and agonizing sickness threatened to split my belly open. I gasped for air and instead wheezed toxins, my throat burning raw.

I didn't know what the hell I was supposed to do to prove myself worthy. Playing the stoic seemed like the obvious answer, but with screams ripping my voice box to shreds, I was clearly not taking that road. A spasm seized me, flinging me down and arching my back until bone cracked, but when tears spilled along my cheeks they burned too, poisoned water. Stoic was right out.

That left me with two choices. I could heal myself, or I could die. I didn't think dying would prove anything, and I'd managed to survive poisonings before. It was a complex process involving separating blood from poison and pushing the venom out. Water in the gas line was how I thought of it, and it was time-consuming and uncomfortable.

I think I actually said, "Oh, fuck this shit," out loud instead of keeping it safely behind my teeth. Then again, my teeth were rotting and falling from my mouth thanks to the contamination swirling through me, so they weren't keeping much behind them anyway. I reached deep inside myself, past the belly-twisting bleak horror my life had become, and seized hold of the healing magic that was part and parcel of who I was now.

Nobody'd ever mentioned if shamans had any real use for spell working, for a focus of magic through words. Then again, nobody had mentioned a lot of things, and I'd found words to be handy a time or two. I set my raw bleeding gums together, snarled, "Physician, heal thyself!" and commanded my magic go.

It erupted through me, silver-blue light brilliant against the darkness. Poison splashed out of me and sizzled into nothing. Pain faded instantly, my bones whole again, my body no longer wracked with pain. Something glittered in my vision, a glimpse of fractured, spiderwebbed glass. Bits of the web were sealing up, coming closer to the center. Then the image faded, replaced by a growing sense of astonishment.

I'd known almost since the beginning that real shamanic healing didn't have to go through all the tiddly steps I took, all the metaphorical stretches that I used to convince myself any of it was possible. Knowing it, though, and experiencing the pure blowout of power, the instantaneous transformation from broken to whole, were two very different things. I took a deep breath, marveling at how it didn't hurt, how my lungs weren't melting inside my chest, and sat up beaming.

Snakes were not creatures well-known for their expressive faces, but my rattler managed to look pleased anyway. "That was sssatisssfactory. Ssstrength you have, ssshaman. Ssstrength, but little sssense. You would be wissse to heed the raven."

Bemused, I said, "Yeah? I'm trying. What do you bring to the table?" and winced at my own lack of gratitude. "I mean, um…"

"You mean asss you sssay. Sssnakesss, like you, are sssimple creaturesss. We ssstrike when it isss necsssessssssssary. It isss sssomething I like about you. Asss for my giftsss, they are plain to sssee, if you ussse a little sssenssse."

I wasn't sure I liked being a simple creature, but I did like how his forked tongue got all excited and tangled around a word like "necessary," with all those *ess* sounds. I bet if I could get him to do the "she sells sea shells" tongue twister he'd get such a hiss going he couldn't ever stop. I also bet he wouldn't appreciate it at all, and bit my lip against trying. "The healing," I said instead. "I couldn't do it like that before."

He inclined his head quite elegantly, and I reached out, tentatively, to see if snakes liked being scratched on the jaw. This one evidently did; he preened and tipped his head like a cat, leaning into the scritch. "There isss more. It will come to you when you need it mossst."

"More? Instantaneous healing is kind of a lot."

"Yesss, but it isss not all of what you are." His snaky eyes lidded contentedly and he began coiling down on himself, clearly ready for a nap. "Sssoon you will sssee."

"I can't wait to find out." I even sort of meant that. "One more question. How come you talk to me? Raven doesn't."

The rattler swayed his head to the side, examining me as if I were a fool. "Becaussse ravensss can talk in your world, sssilly ssshaman." He bumped me with his blunt nose, and I awakened to the Lower World, and chaos.

It wasn't the wendigo, if I wanted to count small favors. There was none of the blood stench, none of the bitter cold, none of the almost-human drive for food. Instead, Coyote staved off wolves, for a metaphorical if not literal description.

I had some familiarity with the demon denizens of the Lower World, having accidentally released them into Seattle one time. Coyote faced them and their brethren: chimeras of terrible form and shape ranging from vicious-toothed, segmented worms to giants whose bodies were twisted with hate. One of those, a stone giant called an *a-senee-ki-wakw,* locked gazes with me as I woke, and I saw from the depths of rage in its eyes that it knew me. I'd released it and then I'd put it back, and it intended on having its revenge. They all did, and knew they only had to go through Coyote to get to me.

Now would be a good time for whatever other gifts the rattlesnake had offered to show up. I drew my sword and rushed forward to join Coyote in battle. He was bleeding and his jaws were red, and my appearance at his side was shock enough that he snarled and turned on me for an instant before he knew who I was. Then relief sagged his features and he turned back to the demon spirits, hunched low in preparation for attack. "You need to get out of here. We can't kill them, not here, but they won't stop hunting until your spirit has been extinguished. You really pissed them off."

"It's a feature." I fell into step with him, backing up, but the holler wasn't built to scramble out of backward. "You go first. Get up there so you can give me a hand out."

He barked a protest and the twisted giant surged forward, slamming a huge first into the ground. The drumbeat faltered, then sped up, shaking the earth as if somewhere out in the real world, Gary knew what was happening and was trying to help. "Coyote, go! I've got the reach weapon!"

He snarled again, but my logic apparently swayed him, because he suddenly turned tail and raced up the back side of the holler. The demons, eager for their prey, leaped as one, converging on a single point.

Me.

I twitched to the side, faster and more graceful than I knew I could be. My sword lashed out, whipping like a saber, and blue power flared along it to score a mark against the giant's hide. One of the others, a flint-winged monstrosity, turned on a wing tip and jumped at me again. I flattened against the earth, rolled, and came up again in a fighting stance, all while my brain was still shrieking in panic and waiting to get crushed.

"I am not your enemy!" My staccato shout bounced off the holler's walls until the only word left was *enemy*. The *a-senee-ki-wakw* seemed to feed on it, getting stronger and taller with each repetition. I darted back and forth, avoiding scorpion tail stings and gnashing worm teeth sheerly by the grace of God, while Coyote stood above me barking his fool head off.

I wanted to scurry up the hill after him. I really did. But aside from the fact that I didn't think I'd make it, the blinding need to *do* something about these creatures, the simple wish to succeed in defeating *something,* since the wendigo kept kicking my ass, had grown stronger than the impulse to run. The misses got narrower, and I got angrier, until I flung down my rapier and bellowed, "Fine! You think you can take me? Come and get me, motherfuckers!"

It was awesome. I felt like Samuel L. Jackson, right up until the motherfuckers came and got me.

CHAPTER TWENTY-FOUR

I didn't know there was anywhere below the Lower World to get dragged down into. It turned out there was, and the best word I had for it was Hell.

The Lower World, for all its bizarre proportions and colors, was a comparatively friendly place. Dangerous, sure, but I'd yet to encounter a plane of existence that wasn't. The Lower World, though, didn't shove knives into my chest when I breathed. It didn't smell of sulfur and brimstone and fire, and it didn't reflect a gory sky in its obsidian surface. There was no sun, but where there was light, it shone dull red through dark translucent rock.

Demons roamed the gleaming black earth. They fought each other, they bled, they rose again. Some reached for the bleak sky, trying to claw their way free. There were rents where a few had succeeded: where a handful had been sufficiently inspired by my presence to tear through to another realm.

Peculiarly, now that they had me, they seemed reluctant to attack. My sword was lying on the ground in front of me, glowing so brightly it hurt my eyes. It struck me that the blade was really the only source of light. I could see the sky because of its brilliance, and where black stone looked red, the rapier also reflected there. I squatted to lift it, and the monsters shrank back, mewling and twisting their gazes away.

Demons didn't strike me as particularly smart, but my limited experience suggested they wouldn't, of their own volition, have brought me somewhere that I had the upper hand by dint of a glowy sword. Slowly, semi-consciously, I looked to my left. Followed the beat of my heart in that direction, half knowing, half dreading, what I would see.

A cavern, black maw in a black mountain, made one dark shadow against another. It looked warm, somehow. Warm and not exactly inviting, but more comfortable than a jagged plain filled with things that wanted to eat me.

"Oh no." My voice came out light and shaky, an alien thing in a world made for screams. "No. I'm dumb, but not that dumb. And I don't believe you're Lucifer, God damn it, even if this is Hell." I didn't believe it was the devil because I didn't believe there was any way, on any level of reality, that I could ever go head-to-head with The Devil Himself, and I knew someday I was going to have to face the thing under the mountain. Therefore, it couldn't be the devil. *Cogito, ergo sum.*

Rich laughter rolled from the cavern, deep enough to make glassy rock crack and shatter against the ground. I bared my teeth, feeling very much like a mouse facing down a lion, and repeated, *"No."*

The earth rumbled, a scrape of stone on stone. A trapped sound, I thought with a tiny surge of hope. My mother'd done a thorough job of kicking the Master's ass, if he couldn't wriggle free from his mountain cave even in what looked to me like the depths of Hell. It gave me a little confidence, and a little, compared to what I'd had, was a lot.

I didn't know what the creature in the stone was, besides an enemy. He commanded the banshees, feeding on the blood of their victims. Feeding on their souls, maybe, though I had the impression that was an act of desperation on his part, after my mother and I had thwarted his more usual dinner plans. He was weak, but he was interested in me, and I was going to have to deal with him someday.

Personally, I wanted that someday to be as far away as humanly possible. The monster in the mountain commissioned death cauldrons and frightened gods. I was in no way a match for him.

He knew it, of course. He'd caught my attention, or I'd caught his, the very first time I'd used any kind of power as an adult. I'd known instantly that I was part of some game to him, and that if he could destroy me while I was young and stupid he'd be happy to. He almost had, too, but my dead mother had taken him to the mat, and ever since he'd been lingering at the edges of my mind, unable to break through.

I didn't like that he kept turning up in the shadows. It made me think I was being investigated for weaknesses, and I had more than enough to show. It also made me afraid that Sheila MacNamarra's smackdown was losing its hold. If he worked his way free before I was up to full speed, I was pretty sure it wouldn't be just me who suffered.

On what constituted a positive side, the best he could do right now was send minions—assuming they were his minions, and not just foolish demons who hadn't thought through their attack clearly enough—to drag me around and try to scare me.

I was, by increments, becoming less scared and more pissed off. I leveled my sword at the cavern, willing power to carry my words to him. To weigh him down, too, as much as I could. Mom had pinned him. I should be able to reinforce that, at least. Silver and blue coalesced in the blade, almost humming, then leaped forward in a surge to rush the mountain like a locomotive. "You aren't ready for me yet, buster, and I'm not ready for you. One of us is going to pull a trump card sooner or later, but until then, quit dicking me around. I'm not in the mood."

His presence retreated under the weight of my power, and all the amusement I was accustomed to sensing from him went flat. Triumph blared through me.

And was followed hard by a tremendous heave from my bound enemy. The whole mountain range shook, earth roaring protest at rough treatment. Glass exploded everywhere as the Master's rage surged outward as if it were suddenly a living thing given body of its own. My own puny magic went thin and terrified, riding the upswell, trying frantically to pin it back down.

It couldn't, but neither could he quite break through my silvery power clinging furiously to the earth and keeping him from bursting through. All my bravado went up in smoke, and I whispered, "Raven, please, get me out of here."

The sky broke open under enormous talons. Red light bled through, sending demons squealing and scattering. My raven dived through the tear in the heavens and caught my shoulders to drag me back into the worlds I knew.

Coyote and Gary were both kneeling over me when I opened my eyes. Coyote had two black eyes, a split lip and a host of other small injuries I couldn't see. I felt them, though, as wrongnesses in his aura, in his power. Without thinking, I clapped my hand against his face.

His yowl of pain turned to a gurgle of astonishment as I pushed a torrent of healing power through him. The bruises cleared up, cuts sealing over, and it was only as a distant second that I thought of patching the paint job on a vehicle; the metaphor hadn't been necessary. He fell back on his rear, prodding at himself, and raised wide brown eyes to me. Gary did just the opposite, leaning forward all bright-eyed, like he couldn't wait to hear what had happened.

"A snake," I said before either of them asked. "A snake, like on my drum. They're symbols of healing, did you know that? It, I mean, he, it, um. Just cleared away all the cobwebs, kind of. Whoomp, no more messing around with metaphor. I can just do it." Oh God. I needed a swoosh, now.

"They're symbols of renewal," Coyote said in a deliberately pedantic tone. "They can also represent shape-shifting, Jo. The shedding of the old skin, coming into the new…."

I sat up. I didn't know when I'd fallen over, but I sat up. "He said there were other gifts I'd discover when I needed them. Maybe shape-shif…" Nope. I couldn't get through the sentence "Sorry. I just don't believe people can shape-shift, Ro. Maybe when you're traveling through the other worlds, yeah, okay, because I usually end up a mole or something when I'm trying to get to my garden, but not for real."

Muscle went tight along his jaw before he bobbed his eyebrows in a shrug. "All right, then. Some other gift, then, if he's offering more." I felt somehow chastised, and, contrary to the last, suddenly as if maybe I did so believe in shape-shifting, neener neener. Coyote, probably just as well for me, couldn't read my mind, and continued on with, "You should thank him for the healing, though." He glanced at himself, and muttered, "*I* should thank him."

"I should thank you. I had no idea those demons had come up, Coyote." Augh. He was right. I called him Coyote when I was trying to make an emotional connection and some variation on his real name when I was annoyed or trying to impart information. Good thing I never played poker. "I wasn't aware of anything except the quest. They'd have torn me apart if you hadn't been there. Thank you."

He said, "It's my job," but he sounded pleased. "But then what happened? You were playing them like a pro and then you threw down your sword and they jumped you and you disappeared."

I'd already forgotten it was my own moxy that had let the demons pull me into Hell. I wondered if the Master could've influenced me, made me pull a stupid stunt like that, but the sad truth was, I just wasn't too bright sometimes. It'd been all me. "Know anything about someone called the Master?"

"From about six different science fiction television shows, sure." Coyote's humor faded away when I didn't laugh. "Sorry. I didn't know it was important. Never heard of him. Who is he?"

"The bad guy." I shook my head. "I don't really know. My mother faced him a long time ago, and it's going to be my turn sooner or later."

"'Unto every generation a Slayer is born'?"

Gary, who was apparently more up on pop culture than I was, guffawed. I glared at them both, but mostly at Coyote. "You told me I was mixed up fresh. No baggage like whatever you're talking about. This isn't a generational thing, not like that." Actually, for all I knew, it could be.

Maybe the women in my family had been fighting monsters in the dark all the way back to the beginning of time. I hoped they'd generally been more competent than me, if that was the case.

"No, no, that's not how it works on B…nevermind. What about the Master?"

"He was trying to get my attention again. That's where I went. It doesn't matter that much right now. I don't think he's influencing the wendigo." I rolled that statement around in my mind, testing it for veracity. It seemed accurate: as far as I could tell, the wendigo was after flesh and soul for its own survival, not for someone else's benefit. I'd been afraid something had been controlling it, but there'd been no hint of a link to another entity in my encounters with it. Besides, a soul-eating demon working for itself was plenty bad enough. "We can talk about him later. Right now you tell me, Ro. Am I in good enough shape to try this soul retrieval now? Can we take this thing before it kills anybody else?"

He said exactly what I didn't want him to: "I don't know. That you found a second spirit animal is a good sign. That it's a snake is probably even better."

"The third one was a horse." I spoke without meaning to, and looked over my shoulder like I'd see someone else to blame. Or maybe like I'd see a horse, I wasn't sure. Coyote made a curious noise a lot like his dog-form snuffle, and I said, "When I did spirit quests with Judy. I know they weren't right, but two of the three animals I saw were a raven and a snake. A copperhead, not a rattlesnake like came to me today, but a snake, anyway. And the third was a horse. Do you think maybe that's right? That maybe I should…" I wasn't sure where that question ended, but Coyote got up to take my drum off the bed—Gary must've put it down while I was still under—and tapped his fingers against the smeared animal on its head.

"Raven and rattler. I don't know, Jo. If you're right, if this third animal was a coyote, then I don't think you'll find your third spirit guide until this has resolved."

"Or maybe it won't resolve until I find my third guide."

"Look, you kids are talkin' chicken and eggs here. It don't matter." Gary reached out to thunk the drum with a fingernail. "We work with what we got, and right now that's Jo's two spirit animals and whatever you bring to the table, son."

Coyote had upgraded to "son" again. I wondered if he'd gotten the promotion in the moment he'd picked up my drum and I'd almost thrown myself on him. It seemed possible. Gary worked hard at supporting my emotional well-being. Harder than I did, really. "It's gonna be enough," he went on, "'cause it's what we've got."

"Don't discount yourself," I said. "We'd have already lost, without you."

"Maybe so. So tell me what we know. It eats people, flesh and soul, and it ain't constrained to the physical world. What else do we know?"

Coyote and I exchanged glances, and I muttered, "Gary ought to be the detective here," before saying, "It's cold. Everything about this wendigo is cold and snowstormy. Is that normal? I should've brought a computer."

"My BlackBerry will do." Coyote got it from his coat and sat on a bed, poking at the tiny screen with the stylus. "Cold, wendigo, what else?"

"It didn't just try eating Mandy. It stole her spirit, but it could be retrieved. None of the other bodies have had ghosts, which isn't normal with violent death, so maybe theirs were too lost. Too eaten," I said grumpily. "Maybe she wasn't lost, just lucky there were still bits of my shield hanging around. Or maybe it was more interested in getting a look at me than finishing her off. Or may—"

Coyote said, "Lost souls," firmly. "Mine was lost and you found it in the snowstorm. We'll use it. I can always take it out again if it narrows the search parameters down too much. Give me a few minutes, okay?"

"Yeah." I finally got off the floor, which was less drafty than mine at home, and pulled my coat back on. I was hungry, but I didn't want to eat in case we had to do more spirit stuff in the near future. Instead I went out to the balcony and looked up at the stars, whose presence vaguely surprised me. It had still been daylight when we'd begun the journey to the other realms. I waved at the Big Dipper, then knocked snow off the balcony railing and put my forearms on it, weight leaned forward as I lowered my head and waited for the inevitable.

CHAPTER TWENTY-FIVE

It took almost five minutes before the sliding glass door opened behind me and Gary, tentatively, said, "Joanie?"

It wasn't a good sign that he called me Joanie. The only other time he'd done it, I'd been completely falling apart. I waggled my fingers, inviting him out to the balcony, and he took up a post next to me, weight on his forearms against the rail, just like I stood. I knew what he wanted, but I wasn't quite man enough to broach the topic myself, so we stood there in silence awhile before he took a deep breath, released it as fog, and said, "I don't mean to be nosy, Jo, but…"

I laughed even though I knew what was coming. "You do, too. You're dying to be nosy. It's killing you. I'm amazed you lasted this long before cornering me."

"We been kinda busy."

"That we have." I still wasn't quite ready to talk, but Gary was unfailingly discreet for approximately forever, giving me time to work up to speaking. "Dad moved us around a lot when I was a kid, so I'd kind of never been anywhere long enough to have real friends. We moved to Qualla Boundary right after I turned fourteen, because I told him I wanted to go to high school in one place. So we went home. To his home. Where he'd grown up. It wasn't my home. Anyway. We'd been there about a year, and I was…Sara was my best friend. My only friend, I guess, except that sounds pathetic. I'd known who she was my whole freshman year, and I thought she basically walked on water, so when we started hanging out that summer, the year I turned fifteen, I thought I was in heaven. That was when I got the drum, too." Those couple months there had been some of the happiest I could remember, in fact. Up until this past six months, I wasn't sure I'd ever been happier in my life. It was an interesting thought.

"Anyway, so that fall there was a new boy in school. Lucas. And I had the worst crush on him. I'd never really had a crush and I was just…man. Stupid. And Sara said she didn't like him, and I wasn't anywhere near smart enough to figure out she was playing it cool. I don't think I knew people really did that. It was like something that happened on TV, to me. Anyway, I was desperate for him to like me, so I did the number one stupid thing that girls do and I slept with him."

Gary took a breath like he was going to say something, and didn't. It was just as well. I was afraid I'd either get angry or burst into tears, no matter what he said, and I'd had enough of both lately. "It didn't work. I mean, he was okay with sleeping with me, but it didn't make him like me any better. And I got pregnant, and I told him and Sara, and he went back to Canada where he'd come from, and Sara never spoke to me again. Until today."

I really wanted that to be the end of it, but it wasn't. Rushing through it all didn't really help, not after twelve and a half years of never mentioning this to anybody. It wasn't like ripping a bandage off. It hurt. It hurt so much I had to hurry and try not to let myself feel anything, which was how I'd been coping with my whole life for thirteen years. "I planned from the beginning to give them up for adoption. My mom abandoned me when I was a baby and my dad didn't seem to want me much, either, so I wanted them to go somewhere they were wanted, and I was, I mean, I was fifteen and basically a mess even before I got pregnant. So I wasn't going to keep them. I wouldn't have been any good for them. I wasn't much good for me until recently. Anyway." I was saying that word a lot, using it like a wall between myself and my emotions. I honestly didn't regret my choices, but that didn't make thinking about them any easier.

"They were early, they were twins, and…the little girl, Ayita, she…died. She was so tiny, and she wasn't strong, and I…wasn't what I am now. I don't know if I could've saved her even if I was. The doctors couldn't." My hands had turned to claws around the balcony railing. I kept my gaze fixed ahead, but my vision was blurred, nearby trees swimming and the distant stars dancing. For some reason my voice remained very steady. "It always seemed to me that there just wasn't enough life force for both of them. That it was going to be one or neither, and that Ayita decided…I mean, I know she couldn't have, she wasn't even old enough to think, but I just always felt like she decided that okay, Aidan was stronger, he could make it if he just had a little more to draw on, so she…gave him hers."

"Oh, Jo…"

I shook my head, violent little motion that tangled tears in my eyelashes. Sympathy was more than I could handle. "It was like it made it almost okay. I mean, it wasn't okay, it was horrible, but it was like…her gift to him, the only thing she could do. And mine was to give him to a family who was ready for him. He's twelve now, and he doesn't believe in vampires."

"You keep in touch?" Gary sounded rightfully surprised.

I shook my head again. "No, I just…I had a vision of him a couple months ago, when Suzy was here. That's all." That's all. Like it was normal to have visions of anybody. "I found Petite in somebody's barn that summer," I added inanely.

Gary, very softly, said, "Ah," like that cleared everything up. "Anybody else know about this?"

I shrugged. "Sure. Everybody in Qualla Boundary. But nobody out here, no. Morrison, maybe. Probably. Maybe Laurie fucking Corvallis, since she's been looking me up. But no."

"Hell of a thing to keep secret, doll."

"Like it comes up in casual conversation? 'Oh, and by the way, did I mention I had twins when I was fifteen?' I never wanted to talk about it, Gary. I left that whole life behind a long time ago."

"What'd your dad think?"

"I never asked him."

Something in my tone warned Gary off pursuing that path any further, because he made another one of those *ah* sounds and there was a brief awkward silence before he rolled his head back toward the room and said, "Your pal in there know?"

"I doubt it. Not before today, anyway. I wasn't studying with him anymore by the time I got pregnant." I sounded tired and bitter and angry to my own ears. Just this summer, I'd reached through time and stolen my younger self's expertise, leaving her with nothing more than a vague memory or two of coyote dreams. I could see a cycle there, a closed loop through time:

I'd taken the one thing that a young Joanne Walkingstick thought made her special. Less than two months later that girl was pregnant, putting her well and truly on the path to becoming the adult woman who had to steal her own younger self's understanding of magic in order to deal with the world she'd been thrust into.

"Can I ask you somethin' else?"

"You going to anyway?" I smiled a little and invited the question with a nod.

"Think you ever woulda told me?"

"Yeah." That was about the weariest confession I'd ever made. I turned around and put my butt against the railing, arms folded under my breasts. "I actually almost did last summer when you were in the hospital. You said, um. You said something about wanting grandkids, and I…" Words were hard. I dropped my chin to my chest and reached down to grab the railing hard. "It was the first time in my whole life I ever even thought about telling somebody."

"Aw, Joanie." Gary put his arm around me and kissed my hair, and we stayed there, quiet and together, until a knock on the door forced us back into the now.

Thursday, December 22, 7:16 P.M.

Coyote slid the door open a few inches and latched his gaze downward, like he didn't want to intrude. "I think I found something. You, um, you want to come in?"

I felt bad for him. He had to have a pretty good idea of what we'd been talking about, and he'd decided he didn't belong in the conversation. Truth was, he probably belonged as much as Gary did, maybe more. On the other hand, Gary had been a real, solid person in my life for the past year, and Coyote'd been out of my life or mostly dead since I was a teen. Either way, I'd never heard him sound so diffident. I said, "Yeah," almost as carefully, then walked forward into him and put my forehead against his shoulder. I hadn't known I was going to. Neither had he, and he grunted quietly before putting his arms around me. Gary slipped past us into the room, and Coyote exhaled over my head, a small worried sound.

"You okay?"

"Not even a little." All I wanted was to crawl into bed and pull him up close behind me while I slept for about a week. The idea forced a tiny cough of laughter from my chest. "On the positive side, I'm emotionally drained and exhausted, which is practically like sleep deprived. Perfect for hunting monsters."

Coyote set me back a few inches and crooked a smile. "Great. Watch out, wendigo." He took my hand and led me inside. I sat down beside Gary so I could focus on Coyote, trying to push away melancholy and worry about the problem at hand.

He took his BlackBerry out again and glanced at it, though more as a prop than a prompt. "Okay. So there are Yu'pik stories about people who've been 'made cold by the universe.' It's something that happens in the winter, people get lost on the snow flats and they go…between. To this place that's not in any of the planes I'm familiar with. It's just described as a constant storm. Sometimes we can see them in our world, but they don't leave tracks and they're almost impossible to call back. They have to find their own way home, and while they're searching, they're neither dead nor alive."

"So they're like Schrödinger's People?" The idea amused me

enough that it actually did alleviate my moodiness. Coyote looked faintly exasperated, but Gary chuckled, so I called it a draw and went on. "Okay, sorry. But that sounds right, with the storm and no tracks and not being able to catch it with either magic or bullets. Do these things hunt people?"

"Not as far as the stories I can find say, but that doesn't mean it's not happening now. Especially if it's someone of power who became lost. Someone who might have had an understanding of what was happening, and who knew there was a path home if he could just find it."

I dropped my chin to my chest. "Score one small point for the home team. I thought it might be someone who knew what they were doing." Of course, I'd also thought it was someone using a power circle for nefarious ends, so it was only a very small point. "Tell me they have a reliable solution for rescuing or otherwise stopping these cold universe people."

"Nope."

I glanced up with a little smile. "Are spirit guides supposed to say 'nope'?"

I would never understand how he could look so much like his coyote self in his human form, but the grin he gave back was toothy and pointed like a coyote's. "Yep." Then he wrinkled his nose. "But no, they don't. These people either find their own way home or they don't. I think a soul retrieval is still our best option."

"A soul retrieval for someone whose body we don't have? How does that work?"

My mentor looked pained. "If we're lucky he'll find his way back to his body. If we're not..."

"If we're not, the body's long since dead and we've just got a spirit who won't die," Gary concluded. "That sound about right?"

Coyote nodded and we were all quiet a few seconds, contemplating that, until my stomach rumbled loudly enough to make Gary sit up straight. I clapped a hand over it, and must have looked unusually pathetic, because Coyote shook his head without me saying anything. "We shouldn't eat. I'd put this off until we'd been up a full twenty-four hours if I thought we had time, but I'm afraid that'll just give it a window to regain strength."

"You mean, to eat people." I didn't want to sugarcoat any of this, particularly if I was using it as an explanation for my belly as to why my throat had, from my stomach's perspective, apparently been cut. Also I hoped the idea of eating people might make me less hungry, but my stomach growled again. Guess not. Let's hear it for long pig.

Which was exactly what the wendigo was thinking. I picked up a pillow and hit myself in the head with it a few times, much to the bemusement of the men. I said, "Nevermind, forget it," into the pillow, then dropped it and scrubbed my hands through my hair. "Okay, if we have to do this thing, why don't we get it done so we can hit the hotel restaurant before it closes? I'm going to become very unreasonable if I don't get to eat until tomorrow."

Coyote, *sotto voce* but not very, said, "As opposed to how she usually is?" to Gary, who snorted laughter.

I hit them both with the pillow. "I don't know if you have any bright ideas, Ro, but I do." His eyebrows shot up skeptically, which I didn't think was very nice. Justified, maybe, but not very nice. "Soul retrieval happens in the Lower World, right? And it's dangerous for everybody. So we're going to want as much protection as we can get on every level."

He said, "Okay," in a dubious tone which suggested I was making sense but that he didn't quite believe I could be.

I got no respect. Fine. I was just going to have to be right. That would show him. "So we're going to want a power circle, and I think it needs to be drawn outside in the snow."

Coyote drew breath like he was going to argue, then let it out in a slow dismayed sound. "I think you're right."

"I think she better have some kinda good frostbite cure ready. Are you two nuts? It's ten degrees and fallin' out there, not to mention there's a man-eatin' monster roamin' around."

"I can handle the frostbite," I said with a blithe confidence I hadn't had a few hours ago. "And luring the man-eating monster out is kind of the point. Know anything about trapping demons in a power circle, Coyote? I figure if we limit its range of motion we're going to be in better shape than if it's able to run free. What happens if someone doesn't want his soul retrieved?"

"Ever tried picking two cats up out of a fight?"

"Er, no."

"Me either, but that's about what it sounds and looks like. Only the cats are as big as you are, in this case."

Whatever confidence I'd had turned tail and ran. "I definitely think a power circle is in order."

"You going to build it?"

I stood up, trying to look and sound like I knew what I was doing. "As a matter of fact, I am."

CHAPTER TWENTY-SIX

We tromped down to the hotel lobby armed for battle, which was to say bundled up like snowmen and Gary carting my drum in a pack over his shoulder. The lobby was deserted except for one floppy-haired desk attendant who raised his eyes despondently when we came in. "Checking out?"

I said, "Not even metaphorically," cheerfully, hoping to counter his Eeyore impression, but he looked at me with the emo gaze of a youth for whom all hope is gone. No sense of humor at all. I muttered, "Right, then," under my breath, and tried again. "We're just going out for a moonlight hike. We'll be back in a few hours. Why, have a lot of people left?"

"Everybody but the federal agents and you." The lobby wasn't deserted after all. Laurie Corvallis had been hidden in one of the chairs, its back to the front desk, but giving her a line of sight to the front door. She scooted the chair so she could see me, and so I could see her camera guy in the next chair beyond her. "Interesting decision," she said. "Going hiking out in the mountains in the middle of the night with a killer around."

"I'm an interesting person." I turned to the emo desk attendant. "I'll give you a hundred-dollar tip if you can keep her from following us."

Gary muttered, "Since when do you have a hundred bucks to be throwing around?" and I elbowed him. He grunted, but the kid missed it, his dull gaze lighting up as he looked at Corvallis.

She gave him one of her devastating barracuda smiles, and he shrank back behind the desk. "Sorry, ma'am, I can't stop the guests from coming and going."

"I can." Sara Buchanan—I had to stop thinking of her that way—came down the stairs in a thump of boots. "No one's going out there without my authorization. Joanne, one of my men didn't come back from the crime scene this afternoon."

"Shit."

"Shit? What does shit mean?"

I bit back a scatological explanation, pretty sure she wouldn't be amused. "It means he's probably dead. I'm sorry."

I had to hand it to her: she didn't even blink. "Probably?"

"Only one person's survived one of these attacks, and she…" Sudden hope seized my heart. The Sight flashed on, sending the whole room into surreal bright colors. Corvallis was about to fall out of her chair, she was so eager to hear what I had to say. Her aura stretched toward me like the borealis reaching for earth, like it would find the culmination of its being in touching me. Sara was tightly wound caution, afraid even to hope. Coyote blared with an unexpected combination of professionalism and awe, like he had a job to do but was a little overwhelmed. It was disconcerting to realize the awe was inspired by me. I was a mess, not somebody who should be able to impress a shaman with a whole lifetime's study behind him.

Gary, on the other hand, was his usual solid reliable eight-cylinder self. There was a fight out there and he was willing to take it on. I owed him more than I'd ever be able to express.

The desk attendant maintained his bored above-it-all expression, but his aura leaped and jumped with excitement. He didn't know what was going on, but he felt like he was a part of something big. I wanted to either pat him on the head or send him home to safety, maybe both, and fought back the snickering urge to do so. That wasn't in my bizarre job description.

Healing and protecting were, though, and everyone in the room except the desk attendant had traces of my magic lingering against their skin, just like Mandy Tiller had. I pressed my eyes closed, still able to See everyone in the room, and said, "Your guy, Sara. He was with us this afternoon?"

"We all were."

"Okay." I made myself meet her gaze. "Then maybe there's a very small chance he's still alive. He was there when I…" Corvallis was still leaning out of her chair, desperate to hear what could be heard. I said a word nice girls shouldn't know, then repeated it more loudly.

There was just no way this was going to end well. Short of clobbering her, which would get me up on assault charges, I couldn't see how to get rid of Corvallis. On the other hand, I had no doubt she would happily do a story on the Seattle Police Department's very own magic-using detective, and make me look like a complete fool.

Oddly enough, I didn't mind that. I was a believer these days, not because I particularly wanted to be, but because the world wouldn't have it any other way. The world, though, wasn't giving object lessons to most of its citizens. Even if Corvallis could be persuaded to do the most sympathetic possible story— which she wouldn't, because her point would be to make me look like an idiot, not to make herself look like a believer—I was going to come across as a complete kook. That was okay. I'd never wanted to make other people accept that magic was real. It was better if they just thought I was crazy. Hopefully the harmless kind of crazy, but crazy either way.

What I couldn't abide was the backlash Morrison would get. He couldn't come out of this alive. Either he knew he'd hired a detective who thought she worked magic, or he didn't. If he knew, I'd goddamned well *better* be the harmless kind of crazy, because otherwise my boss's neck was on the chopping block. And the truth was, people ended up dead around me a lot. Mostly they were bad guys, but not always. Marie D'Ambra and Henrietta Potter hadn't been bad guys. Neither had Colin Johannson, and Faye Kirkland had been…complicated. I knew the truth behind all of those stories, but on the surface, put those things together and I didn't look harmless at all.

And if Morrison *didn't* know he'd hired a dangerous detective who thought she could do magic, well, then, he was incompetent. Frankly, I'd prefer to force the world to believe in magic than to let them think my boss wasn't good at his job.

Sara folded her arms, waiting with impatience that wasn't so much ill-concealed as worn on her sleeve. She was my out: a federal agent in a country besieged with the Patriot Act. She could get Corvallis out of my hair, off my back, and out from under my feet, which was about as thorough a clichéd removal as I could come up with. And she would, too. Not because we were old high school buddies and not because she believed in magic, but because she wanted her man back, and if I said Corvallis couldn't be there or I couldn't get him back, Corvallis would be out on her ear faster than a fast thing.

And then the story would be about SPD Detective Joanne Walker getting a federal agent to oust a local news reporter from the heart of the action. The investigation would be about what I was hiding, and in the end, it would come out exactly the same way. Maybe magic wouldn't be involved, but the way people found themselves dead after not very long in my presence would be more than enough to screw me over and nail Morrison in the process.

Rock, meet hard place. I exhaled and finished my sentence: "He was there when I shielded everyone this afternoon. You have vestiges of the shielding clinging to you. The only person who's survived this thing did, too. It might not be enough, Sara."

She nodded once, sharply. "It's more than I've got right now. The rest of us will break up into teams of three to search—"

"Don't be stupid." That was probably not the most politic thing I could've said, and it wasn't likely to earn points for honesty, either. I barreled on before Sara had much chance to protest. "I can barely keep this thing off me. You saw how little effect bullets had. Everybody, and I mean you when I say that, is going to be a lot safer if you stay inside. The fact that your guy's gone missing should tell you that." My stomach lurched. "He *was* outside when he went missing, wasn't he?"

"Yes, he was. I have people on patrol, Joanne. I can't leave this thing—"

"You *have* to. Sara, you *can't* go out there—"

"Yes, I can."

"No, you can't."

"Yes I can!"

"No you ca—" Wow. We were, like, six. Clearly I was going to have to do something drastic for her own good. "Okay, fine."

I punched her in the jaw.

The Sara I knew would've dropped like a hot potato. Sadly for me, that girl had been a decade plus some federal training ago. Her head snapped to the right and tears glassed her eyes, but she didn't so much as stagger, much less fall. After a couple very long seconds she cranked her face back around to look at me, a red mark blossoming on her chin.

The emo desk attendant breathed, "Oh, this is gonna be good," and Coyote said "Ten bucks on the blonde," loudly enough for me to hear. Gary, wisely, didn't respond, only shuffled backward, getting out of the way.

Sara spun around and smashed a booted heel into my ribs.

I bet somewhere there was a really important law about not hitting federal agents. I bet there was an equally important one about federal agents only using necessary force. Lucky for Sara, my big poofy winter coat cushioned so much of the kick that she had all kinds of excuse to keep right on being forceful. I slammed into the registration desk, not quite winded, and she came after me with gut punches. I threw an elbow and hit her in the face. Padded or not, elbows were pointy, and she fell back with tears streaming down her cheeks. I swung around to put my weight on the desk, lifted both feet, and kicked her in the chest.

She went flying backward, slamming into one of the lobby chairs with a satisfying crash, and she came up with a girl-gladiator expression that belied her tears. That was okay. I knew they weren't oh-ow-woe-is-me tears. They were merely the by-product of being hit in the face twice. If I'd hoped that was enough to take her down—

Okay, realistically, although I'd thought the first punch might take her down, we weren't really hitting each other over the topic of who was or was not going out into the night to fight the monsters. The juvenile truth of the matter was I'd hit her mostly because Lucas had kept in touch with her after he left Qualla Boundary, and I was pretty sure she retaliated because I'd slept with him in the first place. Emotional maturity was overrated, anyway. I didn't think fighting over a boy was usually quite this literal, but right then it felt kind of good, so I didn't care. It'd been a long time coming.

All that introspection took place while Sara shoved herself out of the chair and rushed me. I waited until the last possible second and stepped aside, hoping for a real *Three Stooges* moment, but instead of bashing her head into the registration desk she flicked a hand out and caught me in the throat with its stiffened edge.

I went down clawing at my throat as I gagged for air. A tiny oxygen-deprived part of my brain thought to heal myself, and the power flat-out deserted me, which I no doubt richly deserved. Sara kicked me over and nudged my hands out of the way with her toe so she could put a booted foot on my throat. Then, with all the grace and time in the world, she withdrew her duty weapon and pointed it between my eyes.

I had never actually been at the business end of a .45 before. It turned out the scenes in films where the relatively small muzzle of a gun suddenly looked bigger than God Himself were pretty accurate. I didn't think she was really going to shoot me, but that was less reassuring than it might've been. I wheezed, "Okay. You win. You can come hunting with me," and put my hands above my head.

"Do you know what the penalty for assaulting a federal officer is, Joanne?"

"Two weeks' detention after school and a stern warning from the principal?"

Sara stared at me, and for a horrible moment I thought maybe I'd been the only one fighting over Lucas. That was bad, especially after I'd been all high-horse about her attitude earlier. But after a few more seconds she lowered her weapon a few inches and said, "Yeah. Something like that. Are we even?"

"No. I think you won across the board."

She pursed her lips, glanced skyward, and shrugged her eyebrows in a silent consideration that said, essentially, *hmm, well gosh, yeah, you're right, I did.* Words were overrated. Sometimes faces could say everything necessary. Hers also said I'd probably broken her nose, given how it was swollen and bleeding. The fact that she was still making expressions around it suggested some nerve damage, too, because otherwise it would've hurt too much. I put my hand up, just curious, and she put the gun away to pull me to my feet. I said, "Thanks. This is going to hurt like a son of a bitch," and pulled her nose straight with no other warning.

Her pained howl faded into a surprised squeak as I pulsed healing power right behind that yank. Fender bender, nothing worse, but I didn't have to go through the mental gymnastics of pounding the dents out. Her bruising faded, and when a little part of me wanted to leave a hint of yellow behind, Coyote hit me on the back of my head like he knew what I was thinking. He probably did, since he'd taught me a lot of what I knew.

Sara prodded her nose cautiously when I dropped my hand. "How the hell…?"

"It's easier when you don't know it's going to happen. There's no disbelief for me to fight. Healing's easy." I shrugged uncomfortably. "The body wants to be put right. I'm just speeding it along. Sorry about your nose."

She wriggled its tip with a finger. "I guess there's nothing to be sorry for. If you ever hit me again, Joanne…"

"Yeah, I know, straight to the principal's office with me." I was painfully aware of—well, several things, actually, ranging from my ribs to my kidneys to my throat, but mostly of Laurie Corvallis, who was on her feet. Her hands were working like she wanted to grab something but couldn't quite manage, and I felt a rare bolt of compassion. My world just didn't make any sense from the outside. I wondered if she would go away if I explained I was just trying to keep her out of a situation that she would never comprehend.

Probably not. For one, with the way my luck ran, it would turn out she was much more open to the possibility of and interested in the dynamics of magic than I was. For two, I suspected any time she was told "You wouldn't understand," it made her that much more determined to get to the guts of the thing, whatever it was.

I turned away, hoping out of sight was out of mind. That struck me as a good argument to keep people safe, and I pleaded my case to Sara. "You're the head of the squad, I get that. You have to go. Fine. But will you at least not send teams out? I can only be reasonably sure of protecting the people who are actually with me. I don't want you to lose anybody else."

"Wait a minute." Corvallis found her nerve and stalked over, catching my arm. "Wait a minute. What did I just see there? Her nose was *broken*."

I should have hit her, not Sara. It took a count of ten before I was confident I wouldn't rectify my mistake. She'd spent the afternoon watching people wrestle with a wendigo, but she was impressed by a broken nose getting unbroken. On the other hand, even I'd had a hard time seeing the wendigo with the Sight going full blazes. A healed nose was probably easier to both see and comprehend than a half-visible fight with a monster that couldn't be defined. I pulled my best smile out and presented it to her, not caring that it felt more like a death's head rictus than a real smile. "What'd I tell you during the blue flu?"

She reared back on her heels almost as if I *had* hit her, eyebrows drawing down. It took less than a heartbeat for her to answer: "You said it was magic."

"There you go, then." Sudden childish curiosity rose in me. "Tell you what, Laurie. Why don't you just go to sleep?"

Corvallis's eyes rolled up and she dropped to the floor.

CHAPTER TWENTY-SEVEN

I made it there a nanosecond before she did, but only because I was expecting her to fall. It was almost impossible to catch somebody if they really did drop into a dead faint, despite conventions of romantic literature. There was no swaying or fluttering involved, just collapse, and I'd have felt moderately bad if Corvallis had chipped a tooth on the hard floor because I put her to sleep while she was standing up.

I looked up to a ring of astonished faces. Mostly astonished. Gary and Sara and the emo kid and the cameraman were astonished. Coyote, however, was *pissed*. I said, "I didn't know it would work," feebly, but despite it being true it also clearly didn't hold any water.

"It shouldn't have. Even if it should have, you shouldn't have done it." He knelt at Corvallis's other side, his eyes flooding to gold, and a twinge of guilt stung me.

"She's fine. She's just sleeping. Look, Ro, what was I supposed to do? How the hell are we supposed to go wendigo-hunting with a news reporter on our asses? Besides, I didn't know it would work!"

I hadn't *known*. But I'd been pretty sure. Sleep was a healing agent, but more to the point, my magic hadn't retreated at the idea. It was very good about letting me know when I'd pushed the boundaries, so while knocking Corvallis out might've been morally gray in Coyote's terms, it was free and clear in mine. I was tempted to try it on Sara, too, partly for her safety and partly to see how far I could push my magic before it got annoyed with me and stopped playing.

That didn't really seem like a very good idea, once I'd thought about it. I nudged Coyote away and scooped Corvallis up, a feat which took more grunting than I'd anticipated. I was strong, but she was solid. I turned with my armful of reporter and handed her to the camera guy. "I'm sure the desk attendant will open her room for you."

He grunted, too, and eyed me over Corvallis's sleeping form. "She's gonna kill you when she wakes up. You know that, right?"

"Yep. But at least she won't have gotten eaten."

Apparently I made a convincing argument, because he shrugged at the emo kid, who mumbled, "Room number?" and scrambled for a key. They headed down the hall a few seconds later, but the camera guy glanced back.

"Hey. How'd you do this, anyway?"

I sighed, exasperated that the truth would never be enough. Ah, how the mighty had fallen. I said, "Hypnosis," which sounded just about as unlikely as magic, to me, but he said, "Huh," nodded, and went on his way.

Coyote got to his feet, eyes still golden in a bleak face. "We need to talk."

"We need to go hunting." I said it as gently as I could, but he grabbed my arm, much harder than Corvallis had, when I stepped by. I looked at his hand, then at him, and was just as glad when he let go. I'd already been in one fight in the past ten minutes, and he'd never forgive me for kicking his ass.

"We need to talk, Jo."

"'Jo,'" Sara put in, remarkably lightly. "She never used to let anybody call her that. It's her dad's name. She hated being called by it." She had Coyote's attention, a feat I wouldn't have put money on anybody accomplishing just then. I remembered the smile she used on him. It had worked on guys in high school, too, as had the touch to his arm. "Look," she said quietly. "I don't doubt that Joanne needs a good reaming, but I've got a man out there and he might still be alive. Can it wait?"

Not exactly the argument I'd have used, although I had to admit overall it was a pretty good one. It put Coyote in the right. Men liked that.

Okay, I didn't know anybody who didn't like that. He let out a long angry breath interspersed with a glare at me, but he nodded at Sara. "Yeah. It can wait."

"Thank you." Sara went from being soft and needy to tough and commanding inside the blink of an eye. "Then let's get going. I don't think we've got a lot of time."

She outfitted us all with FBI-marked snowshoes and reflective jackets, the latter of which Gary looked childishly pleased with. I let him fall back to walk with Coyote and took the lead with Sara, mostly because I was trying to avoid my mentor. It also let me drop my voice and say, on a frosty breath, "You're taking this all very well."

Sara shook her head, little more than a shadow in the dark. "I'm not. You haven't changed, that's all. You still hit things when you get pissed and you still think the world's full of mystical crap only you can see. What's to take?"

If she was right I was going to spend the next three months in a depressive funk. I thought I'd changed rather radically in the past year or so. "You know, I really don't remember that. Being into magic when I was a teenager."

She shot me a disbelieving look. "Seriously? You don't remember making me do a drum circle with you?"

"Not at al—oh, God. Maybe." I put the heels of my hands against my temples, a sluggish memory rising. "Maybe. Yeah. Right after I got my drum." Shaky relief slipped through me. I was pretty certain I hadn't been freaky into the magic thing, despite Sara's recollection. I had, though, been very excited about the drum, and maybe a little desperate to share it with someone. "You thought I was insane."

"You were trying to find my spirit animal." Sara glanced away again. "I even almost thought it was going to work. That it might make me more like you."

"Like me?" I said incredulously. "I wanted to be like you. Pretty. Smart. Everybody liked you. I was all elbows and knees."

"No, you were tall and strong, and you'd seen the whole country. I thought you were cool." That was a whole different slant on what she'd said earlier, and it gave me a little hope that maybe we had been friends after all. It shouldn't matter, but somehow it did. "I mean, you were a jerk," she added, "but man, you were brave. Never backed down from a fight, even after—" Whatever opening-up she'd been about to do, it shut down hard, with Lucas Isaac between us like he'd always been.

My shoulders slumped. "Well, it turned out I was right about the world being full of mystical crap only I can see, anyway. I'm sorry about the rest of it, Sara. I really am."

"Yeah, well, like I said. Nothing's changed. When we were kids you drummed up a badger and I couldn't explain it. Today you say there's a wendigo and I sure as hell can't say you're wrong, so there you are. Where Joanne Walker goes, so do outrageous answers."

I said, "A badger," rather quietly, and Sara looked uncomfortable. I ducked a smile at the snow, just barely smart enough not to push it any further. We creaked through the snow in comparative silence after that, breaking the cold night with curses when trees shivered snow from their loaded branches onto our shoulders.

I didn't have a plan, but my feet were taking me up toward the mountains. Off the beaten trail, so I was grateful for the snowshoes. I bet some pencil pusher somewhere would be surprised to find out the FBI was now providing winter gear to members of the Seattle Police Department and a couple of civilians. Well, hopefully nobody would get killed and there would be no missing snowshoes to account for.

Oh, what my life had come to, that I was casually hoping nobody would get killed. I stopped to thunk my head against a tree trunk, which was a tactical error on many levels. First, it rained snow on me. Second, it sent Sara on ahead without me. Third, and by far the worst, it gave Coyote a chance to catch up. "You can't do what you did back there, Jo."

"Apparently I can." I shook snow off myself and hurried after Sara. Gary got between me and her, leaving me to walk with Coyote. Some friend he was. Foolish friend, actually, since there was a good reason to have an—adept, as Sonny'd called us—paired up with a non-adept. Coyote and I could shield ourselves and a partner.

Or at least I could. It came naturally to me, and pretty clearly didn't come so naturally to Coyote. I let myself become aware of the Sight, its brilliance lighting the dark night as I slipped shielding forward to wrap around Sara and Gary. Coyote, grumpily, said, "That's not going to change my mind."

For a couple seconds I considered taking the low road and being the old me that Sara remembered so clearly. Belting my mentor was probably in no way the right choice, but it did have brief, glowy short-term satisfaction in its favor.

I took the high road, although doing so required letting a deep breath out through my nose before I dared speak. "I'm not trying to change your mind. You know what happens when I abuse my power, Ro? It bitch-slaps me. It stopped working entirely this summer when I screwed up with Colin and Faye. It knocked me on my ass when I used it as a weapon a few weeks ago. If putting Corvallis to sleep was out of bounds, I would've gotten a magical anvil dropped on my head. I'm not breaking any rules."

"Jo, this is serious. You can't—"

"Coyote, I'm *being* serious!" I stopped to face him. To get in his face, more accurately. To wave my hands in frustration, aware that with the winter coat and mittens, I looked more like a frenetic gingerbread man than a convincing orator. "Maybe you can't, Coyote. Maybe it's against your rules. But I'm not playing the same game you are. You can't do this easily." I gestured after Gary and Sara, meaning to highlight the shielding that encompassed them. "You can't fight. You're a hell of a lot better at the transitions to the other realms than I am, and you're worlds beyond me in dealing with what you find there, but maybe that's your *job*. Teach, heal, guide, con…con… consort, convert, con…" I rubbed a mitten over my face, trying to think of the word I wanted. "You know. Be the UN, in celestial terms. Talk to people."

Coyote, oh-so-drily, said, "Converse?"

Boy. Nothing ruined a good rant like your vocabulary failing you. I said, "Yeah, that's it," despondently. "You're my teacher, Coyote. You're not my boss."

His eyebrows went up a fraction of an inch. "Did you just use the infallible *you're not the boss of me* as an argument, Jo?"

My shoulders sagged. "Yeah."

"So who is the boss of you?"

"Morrison" sprang to mind, but it wasn't the right answer. Not under these circumstances. I could see Coyote waiting for it anyway, but I shook my head. "I don't know. You're the one who told me a Maker mixed me up fresh. Maybe that's my boss."

I was growing increasingly convinced that creating new souls for any purpose was just plain mean. Ordinary people didn't have active memories of past mistakes, maybe, but the impression I'd been given was that the choices made in previous lives did affect who people were this time around. Being told straight off that I had neither mistakes nor successes to draw from, consciously or not, could be a bit of a burden. Every single cock-up was one hundred percent me, no-holds-barred. I supposed it meant every single accomplishment was all me, too, but somehow that didn't seem as impressive. "Or maybe none of us have a boss at all."

"You believe that?"

"I don't know what I believe, Coyote. How about you?"

"I believe you're calling me Coyote again. That mean I'm back in your good graces, even if you're yelling at me?"

I scrunched my face and tilted it back to the sky, blinking into unshadowed moonlight. "I think it means I default to 'Coyote' when I'm thinking about you, but that it seems like a weird name to actually call you by." I tipped my chin back down, frowning around me. "Coyote...?"

"What?"

"...where did the trees go?"

He glanced around, glanced at me, and without saying anything else we rotated to stand back-to-back, eyeing the copse around us distrustfully.

We stood in the center of a mountain glade without so much as footprints speaking to how we'd arrived. The trees were present, but distant—a good stone's throw away, and I was certain we'd been surrounded by them when we'd started talking. I *knew* we had been. I still had snow on my shoulders from getting dumped on. Moonlight poured over us, undiminished by branches or clouds. Everything was colored as it should be, aside from the blue tint offered by the moon, and the sky wasn't unnaturally close or alarmingly distant, as it might have been in the Lower or Upper Worlds. We hadn't gone anywhere, then. Hadn't fallen from one plane of existence to another, at least. Whether we'd gone anywhere was debatable.

I thought about it carefully, then whispered, "This is new," to Coyote. "I never transported anywhere in the real world before." I'd been knocked out and slid from one realm of reality to another, had journeyed vast distances inside the gardens of people's souls, and had once chosen to physically get on a magical beast of burden and ride to another world, but the Middle World itself had never just up and changed on me.

Coyote whispered, "Me neither," which didn't surprise me. I seemed to have far more dramatic adventures than he did. I had more dramatic adventures than most people. I could have gotten a lot of angstful mileage out of that thought, but Coyote hissed, "So what do we do?" and yanked me out of it.

The glade was as silent a place as I'd ever been. Wind hissed over the snow, making the loose stuff on top dance, but beyond that it was so quiet my ears ached trying to hear something. Pine needles rustling against each other, the soft *paff* of snow falling from branches to hit the ground; the trees were too far away for those sounds to carry. And it was winter, and night, so any animal noises there might have been were already muffled or nonexistent. I had no easy way to tell if danger approached. Even the Sight told me nothing, just showed me a world ablaze with winter sleep, quiet black light offering nothing useful.

Mount Rainier was closer than it had been, a gorgeous cone rising winter blue and black toward a sky so brilliant with moonlight I could see for miles. Awed laughter caught in my lungs, and for a little while, I forgot to worry.

The stars only came clear near the edges of the world, cold moonlight swallowing them closer in. There were no city lights visible anywhere, no touch of humanity, and the snow-brisk wind smelled faintly of astringent sap. It seemed very possible that Coyote and I were the first, the only, human beings to have ever set foot on this particular bit of earth; that we had been brought somewhere utterly unspoiled so that someone might have a chance to marvel at its wonder. I said, "It's okay," as softly as I could, not wanting to disturb the quiet.

Coyote made an incredulous noise at the back of his throat, but I caught his hand and squeezed it reassuringly. "Really. It's all right." My breath fogged on the air, wisps drifting away, and, smiling, I brushed my fingers through that faint mark of my presence. "Normally I'd say we were in trouble, because we don't belong here, but this time I think we've been invited."

"Invited? Invited by—"

I raised my mittened fingers to my lips, the gesture meant to shush my mentor. "Invited by him."

I nodded into the woods, and was unsurprised when a god melted free of the trees and came to join us.

CHAPTER TWENTY-EIGHT

He was a woodland creature made of gnarled barky skin and dark tangling hair of knots and branches. His features were rough, little more than the impression of a face in a tree trunk, but his eyes were as I remembered them: brilliant emerald-green, like his father's before him. He said, "*Siobhán Walking-stick,*" and extended a thin-branched hand the way a human might, the gesture all the more alien for its familiarity.

"Herne." I took his hand, breathless with delight and surprised by that. "It's good to see you."

Amusement was a rare expression on a tree, but he wore it well. "Is it?" His voice was wind and rain on leaves, deep sound of eternity. "I think last time we met it was not so welcome."

"I was different then. You were different." The understatement forced a laugh from my throat. "Right. Hey, Coyote, I'd like you to meet the Green Man, Herne. He's, ah. Um." I stopped talking, because my mentor was trembling, with tears spilling down his cheeks.

"Spirit of the forest," he whispered, and dropped to his knees in the snow. "Soul of the world."

I don't know who was more appalled, me or Herne. Me, apparently, because Herne managed a kind chuckle, and put his leafy-fingered hands beneath Coyote's to draw him up. "Spirit of the forest," he agreed. "But I would not take on the burden of soul of the world, not for any reward you might offer. And I know something of rewards, and causes lost. There is an evil in the forest, shaman."

He hadn't taken his gaze off Coyote, but I knew he was talking to me. I said, "Only one?" under my breath.

He let go Coyote's hands with the sound of branches snapping, and turned my way with sorrow etched into his craggy visage. "Many, but most are the works of man, and for now can only be fought by other men. This is an older hurt than those, and needs an older touch."

"Older—" I seized on that, hoping it was profound intelligence regarding the thing we were facing, but optimism died a-borning. If I was the "older" solution, then he meant mystical, not ancient. I didn't qualify as old except by the standards of anyone under the age of eighteen. "Right. Older. I never heard anybody call magic 'old' before."

"Is it not easier in your day and age to follow the old ways rather than express it in laughable terms of magic and might?"

Just what I needed. A woodlands god telling me how to euphemize my way around the difficult topic of my talents. I stared at Herne a moment, then smiled. It *was* just what I needed, in fact. I could tell Laurie Corvallis I was following the old ways and she could sit and spin for months trying to figure that one out. It was perfect. "It is. It's a lot easier. I'll remember that. Thanks. When did you get so wise?"

What I really wanted to ask was when he'd gotten pompous, because he hadn't talked like this last time we'd met, but I figured I already knew the answer. Being a god automatically pomped a guy. Besides, there was something useful about the airs and high-minded speech patterns: they helped remind me I was dealing with something a long way from mortal.

As if him being a walking, talking tree wasn't reminder enough. Herne gave his odd gentle chuckle again, and shrugged rough shoulders that shed flakes of bark onto the snow. "At the same time, perhaps, that you became comfortable walking the old paths."

"Comfortable? I don't know that I'm ever going to be comf—oh." So maybe he wasn't so wise after all. I dipped a grin at my snow-shod feet, then looked up again. Kevin Sadler had been shorter than me, or at least, he'd come across that way. Herne seemed to be rather a lot taller, sort of oaklike in stature, except somehow he was compressed down to a less alarming size. I thought if I turned the Sight on him, he would overflow my vision as both his father and daughter had done. "Suzanne's doing well, by the way."

Pain blackened his face. "I'm pleased. Tell her, if the time is ever right, that I am sorry."

"I will." I fell silent, entirely at a loss as to how to proceed, then turned my palms up. "Why did you bring us here?"

"The demon hunts in my forests and leaves scars of wrongful death behind, holes in the fabric of life. It cannot be fought easily, not even with the magic and myth you command. To do battle with this demon requires strength bound to the earth and yet so flexible it can reach for the sky."

"Bound to the…I hope that's a really poetic way of describing a shaman, Herne, or we're screwed. All I've got is a pocketful of attitude. My sword's not even useful."

He blinked at me, slowly. "Swords are forged, Siobhán, not grown, and will do you no good. But here: at the least, I would have the beast drawn to where its only prey are those who might successfully stand against it."

I breathed a laugh. "At the least. Thanks." I reconsidered my tone and said, "Well, no, really, thanks. I mean that. But you know you left our friends out there to get eaten, right? Can you bring them here?"

He tilted his head, fey motion that made him look more animalistic. "Some are closer than others, and none are as attuned to the old ways as you. It will take time."

"Better that than letting them wander around while the wendigo's hunting. I don't even know how we're going to find our way back when this is over." I liked how I said that, making the assumption that it would be *we* who were returning, and not *it*.

"The forest will guide you." Herne moved back, and I took a hasty few steps after him, tripping over my own snowshoes.

"Hey. Hey, wait a second." I glanced at Coyote, but he stood rooted where he was, his hands knotted around the bits of branch Herne had left behind. That was okay, as I wanted a private conversation. I dropped my voice to murmur, "You're doing better, huh? The last time I saw you…"

"I was wounded." Gods, it seemed, had a gift for deprecation. Technically the last time I'd seen him he'd been dead, although that was only a mortal shackle he'd left behind. "I am still not well, Siobhán Walkingstick, not as well as I might be. Should the day ever come when I gain full strength, it may not be man who must fight man to set the forests aright."

"I look forward to it." I did, too, in a perverse kind of Jimmy-crack-corn way. "Is there anything I can do?"

A smile creased his woody features. "I think you, too, are 'doing better,' shaman. Rid this forest of its demon and you will have done enough."

A zing of doubt turned my lungs cold, even in comparison to the icy air. "Really?"

Silence drew out long enough that I became aware I couldn't even hear Coyote breathing. I was alone in the quiet of the woods, with its god standing over me to make judgment. "No," he finally said. "No. Our slate may not be yet wiped clean. We shall see, Siobhán. We shall see."

I nodded, and Herne afforded me a nod of his own, deep enough to almost be a bow. I returned the honor, and when I straightened he was gone.

Only then did I realize that, like the wendigo, he had left no tracks in the snow.

"Joanne." There was a strained note to Coyote's voice, and I figured he'd noticed the same thing I had about the tracks. I turned around, searching for some kind of reassurance, and swallowed anything I had to say.

Instead of the bits of broken branch he'd had, Coyote held a spear half again his own height in his hands. It was made of a white branch stripped of bark and polished, though knots and whorls marked its surface, so the haft wasn't a straight smooth shaft like I thought of spears as having. Its head was black wood, so dark and shining that moonlight reflected off it like metal. A feathered leather strip bound haft and head, but

I was quite certain that if the leather was taken away there would be a seamless transformation from the white wood to the black.

I, Joanne Walker, master of the obvious, said, "Holy crap, you've got a spear! Where'd that come from?"

From Herne, obviously, but not even Coyote's expression managed to say that much. He just shook his head, then wordlessly extended the weapon to me.

I actually backed up a few steps. "No way. He didn't give it to me."

He gave the spear a couple of shakes and came toward me, obviously trying to get rid of it. I tucked my hands behind my back. "When gods give you gifts, Coyote, you do not go around handing them off to the nearest sucker you can find." A lightbulb went off, and I almost ran forward to seize the spear regardless of what I'd just said. "Bound to the earth and able to reach for the sky. Trees. Duh. That thing's meant to fight the wendigo with, and he gave it to you."

"But this isn't what I do! I don't—I don't fight! I don't even know how to use this!"

"I think traditionally you stick the bad guy with the pointy end. My path's changed, Ro. Maybe yours is changing, too."

I swear to God, you'd think I'd said *maybe your grandmother has recently contracted syphilis* from the way he glared at me.

"Donno about his," Gary said from out of nowhere, "but ours sure as hell did. Where are we, doll? How'd we get here?" He broke through the trees a dozen yards away, and I lifted my hands with a squeak.

"Stop! Wait! We have all this unbroken snow, we should use it!"

Gary froze with Sara a step behind him, both of them wide-eyed as startled deer. I said, "Herne brought you here to keep you safe from the wendigo," like it was a perfectly normal explanation. The funny thing was Gary's eyes lit up and he went *ah* like it was, in fact, a perfectly normal explanation. Sara didn't look so understanding, but nor did she push it, for which I would thank her later. For the nonce I pointed imperiously in opposite directions. "Both of you go that way. Make a circle. But take a jump forward so your footsteps don't run into it."

There was a small kerfuffle while they got who was going which way sorted out, but peculiarly, they did as I ordered without asking why. I eyeballed the handful of steps Coyote and I had taken, then tromped a circumference slightly larger than that around them. "Mash everything inside this down, will you?"

Coyote eyeballed me, but did as I asked while I turned around, trying to get my bearings. I had no sense of direction; Rainier was off to my left, but that didn't mean anything, particularly under a sky too bright with moonshine to show me the North Star. After a second I stopped looking with my eyes and reached out with the Sight, trying to get the same sense of place in the Middle World that I could achieve in the Lower.

The earth itself gave a confident thump when I settled on true north. I said, "Thanks," out loud, and struck off that way, making a thick spoke in the snow. "Only walk inside these, okay, guys? I want the rest of it pristine."

Sara, more than forty feet away, muttered, "She's nuts. She's completely bonkers," and the snow carried it to me clear as day.

Carried it to Gary, too, who said, "Nah, she knows what she's doing," which heartened me more than I could've imagined. I marched back the other way, extending the line south, then ran around behind Sara to the most westerly point so I could make a cross-path to the east. I was sweating and panting by the time I was done, and everybody else was sitting in the middle admiring Coyote's spear. My eyebrows waggled entirely of their own volition, and I rejoined them, trying not to giggle.

Coyote looked up at me, eyes gold in the moonlight. "Is this circle meant to keep things in, or out?"

I swallowed the temptation to give him the same answer Melinda'd given me, and said, "Some of both," instead as I trod a little path at the outer edge of the inner circle. It was about ten feet across, plenty big for the four of us, and the snow was well-packed. I took my snowshoes off and stomped a smaller cross like the one I'd just beaten into the unbroken snow, only with the spokes at the lesser cardinal points. My footprints were deep, dark blue shadows—imperfect, but pretty. "Everybody, and when I say everybody I mean you, Sara, and then Gary and then Coyote, in that order, stay inside this circle. This is going to be the keep-things-out circle."

Sara, sounding very much like a petulant teen, said, "Why me most of all?" but also blew the question off with a raspberry, which I translated loosely as *because I'm not a magical fruitcake and the rest of you are.*

"The larger one will be the keep-things-in circle." I slipped mostly free of my body, letting my astral form rise up above the snow so I could see my circle's shape.

It was surprisingly—no, strike that—*unbelievably* perfect. I'd known I was keeping to straight lines with my spokes, but I had the advantage of following the earth's magnetic fields when I was doing that. Gary and Sara were just winging it, but they'd done an incredible job. There were tiny wavers in the circle's outer edges, but no obvious bulges or indentations. It felt strong and ready to accept whatever power I poured into it.

I dropped back into my body to beam foolishly at Gary and Sara. "You guys are amazing. The circle's amazing. Thank you. Okay. I've never really done this before…."

The truth was I'd never done it at all. Melinda's promise to teach me how to open a power circle loomed large, and I wished to high heaven that we'd had time to do that. That we'd made time to do it. I'd gone home and gone to bed two days ago when I could've gone back to her house to learn. That hadn't seemed like an oversight at the time, but it left me with a thimbleful of experience where I needed a vat-full. Accidentally reactivating Mel's power circle with Raven's help wasn't exactly in the same league as what I was about to try.

I knelt where I was, tugging my mittens off to place bare hands against the snow. It was very cold, almost ice, and despite having been mashed down, sharp edges poked my palms. I resisted the urge to stuff my hands into my armpits to warm them up, and instead reached inside myself, eyes closed as I whispered to my power.

Keep-things-out. I was good at that; I could build shields and sling them around with the best of them, these days. But I needed something more from the magic, now. I needed it to come alive outside of myself, to live within the circle until I called it back. I needed to not have to concentrate on it, to trust that the form I'd given it was strong enough to hold shape and protect my friends while I dealt with terrible things beyond its defensive walls.

Purpose came first, in waking it. I felt my needs sinking through the snow, sinking into the earth, where they were absorbed and considered. I recognized in its strength an aspect of my need, and asked that it share with me what it could.

I felt its pride in its own power, at the very idea that I should come to it and ask for help. There was spirit in all things; that was a tenet of shamanism, and I'd come to appreciate it more and more as time went on. Everything was imbued with purpose, and one of the many things the earth itself coveted was to give life. My desire to protect life wed nicely to that, and with a roar of silence, power rushed upward, greeting me, leaping into the boundaries set by my circle. My own power answered, containing it, tempering it, drawing vitality, until the two dancing magics balanced each other: my need and the earth's willingness to offer. Rich clay brown wove through silver-blue, pushing and pulling against one another in an endless, sustainable flux of magic. It would hold, robust and true, until I brought it down again with the same deliberation it had taken to raise it. It would keep things out as long as I needed it to.

I whispered, "Thank you," for the second time, and clenched my fists in the snow in an awkward attempt to hug the mountain itself. My hands were blue and my fingers didn't want to uncramp once I'd closed them.

Behind me, Gary said, cautiously, "Jo? You're…glowin'."

I glanced over my shoulder, realizing too late it might be a bad idea. Using magic made my eyes turn gold, and given how much I'd just called, I had no idea what "glowing" might constitute.

Then I did a double-take at my hands. They were still blue, but not from cold, after all. It was magic running through me, becoming my lifeblood. This had happened before, me pulling down enough power to see through my own skin. I hadn't thought anybody else could see it, though. "Sorry. Gimme just another minute and I'll be…" *Back to normal* seemed like asking a lot. I'd left normal behind a long time ago.

The second circle was easier. Keep-things-in. A net, a cage, a blockade. I knew those things pretty well, and the earth was, a second time, willing to give. It knew everything about closed mountain passes, about treacherous land that turned to silt beneath the feet, about all the tricks that could keep a man or a beast stuck where he was. Sides of a coin, keeping things out and keeping them in, and the world was willing to lend me its power on both sides. The larger circle closed with a flare so large that even on my hands and knees, I staggered, its sheer size taking more out of me than I'd expected to give. The burning power disappeared from beneath my skin, drained far enough to fade.

Not an ideal way to start a fight. I dropped my head until my forehead almost touched the ground. "Coyote?"

He was there beside me, offering a hand that I took gratefully. "Soul retrievals are supposed to happen in the Lower World, right?" He'd said so at least fourteen times, so I kept talking without waiting for an answer. "Can you open a door for me, if I need you to? You're a lot better at it than I am, and I'm a little…dizzy."

"I'm not surprised. I think I can, yes. Just ask."

I'd never heard him sound quite so grim, and cranked my head up to study what I'd done that worried him that much.

The circles I'd created danced like waterfalls from the heavens. Ever-shifting rainbows ran across them, my power mixed with all the hues the earth chose to offer. I could almost hear the magic hissing and crackling, eager to do as it had been bidden: keep things out, keep things in.

And in the distance, I felt it: deep in the forest, Herne released frozen trees from his willpower, letting them relax back into the root-deep places they knew best. I felt how they had been a maze, a thicket, a briar, confusing and confounding the wendigo: fairy-tale trees fighting against the dark, refusing to let it pass during the brief minutes it took for me to make a haven in the snow. How, with their rushing branches carrying the wind elsewhere, the beast couldn't scent us. I hadn't known that was in the woodland god's power, and I whispered thanks that he'd held the monster back as long as he could.

I took up my sword, and stepped beyond the inner circle to meet the wendigo in battle.

CHAPTER TWENTY-NINE

More accurately, I jumped out of the inner sanctum, not wanting to disrupt the power lines I'd drawn. I landed in an easy crouch a few feet beyond its edge, and Gary began to play the drum. Its reassuring thump was higher than usual in the cold air, but it was familiar. The circle walls shimmered with its music, embracing it and growing stronger. I caught glimpses of the magic's movement far above my head: the circles rose forever, ensuring the wendigo couldn't leap in or out.

It came for me in a straight line, unimpeded by trees, drawn by the drum's song and driven by Herne's command of the forest. It slipped in and out of moonlight, shadows rendering it black, but I could finally *see* it, a massive ruffed thing that ran lightly on the snow. It had regained its size, which boded poorly for Sara's agents. Regret slammed through me before I set it aside to better face the wendigo.

It was all tooth and fur and talon, with tiny crimson eyes. If it had anything left of humanity, it was buried under a raging animal. And that was a blessing: the beast disregarded the outer power circle's border, charging across without slowing. Magic sputtered, allowing it entrance, and I saw a vestige of rational thought break through. It skittered on the snow, making as tight a turn as it could, and rushed back the way it had come.

The circle held. Magic fluxed, colors intensifying where the wendigo hit, and it bounced back, knocked ass over teakettle by my wish to keep it there. I heard Sara very carefully *not* scream, the sound no more than a tiny sharp intake of breath. Apparently they could see it, too. That was…probably good. I told myself it was good, and waited for it to get back on its feet. It wasn't that I had any pride tangled up in a mano a mano fight with a wendigo. I just wanted to see how clearly it was thinking, or if it was at all.

It rolled over, breaking snow as it went, and fell back to nearly the edge of the circle, staying just far enough away that the circle's power couldn't electrify its fur. That suggested another hint of cognative capability, which gave me hope that there was a spirit worth rescuing somewhere in the beast.

A snarl broke from its throat, like it had heard my thought. It leaped sideways, not attacking, but exploring. Long loping steps took it halfway around the larger circle. I followed on the outer edge of the smaller, able to keep pace only because I had so much less distance to travel. Once the fight was met, I put all my money on it, speedwise, so even a few seconds to study its movements was a win for me.

Increasingly physical or not, it seemed barely constrained by the laws of gravity. Its legs lacked the power to drive it in the massive jumps it took, but that appeared to be supremely ir-relevant. It answered to someone else's physics.

Like the Lower World's. I'd known I had to take the battle to it there, where I might have a hope of performing the soul retrieval, but I hadn't quite thought of the wendigo itself as a denizen of that world. The idea struck me just before the creature did, and with almost as much force. Almost. Made physical, the beast had to weigh three hundred pounds, and it slammed me against the inner circle with all that weight plus momentum. We both grunted, and I choked on its fetid breath, but rather than attack again it skittered back, swinging its heavy head as it studied me, then the three behind me.

"You bastard. You weren't even trying to…"

"It wanted us," Coyote confirmed quietly.

"No," Sara said. "It just wanted to see if it could get to us. It's dangerous, Joanne."

I twisted around from where the wendigo had dumped me in the snow and gave her my best *no shit, Sherlock?* look before getting to my feet. The wendigo had circled almost all the way back around to where it had begun, and now paced, breath steaming in the cold air as it watched me. I slid around the inner circle's circumference and stepped toward the beast, lifting my free hand in invitation. "C'mon, you smelly son of a bitch. Let's go."

I didn't actually expect it to come for me, but it did, showing off its unearthly prowess for leaping once more. I flung myself forward to meet it, blade lifted, and saw confusion flash through its beady little eyes. I was clearly prey, and prey wasn't supposed to return attack. We collided midair, my sword sliding through its chest like there was nothing there, and I bellowed, "Coyote!"

A door opened, and the sky went red as the world went yellow.

We fell to earth in the Lower World, crashing to the too-close earth with more force than I expected. Dust rose up around us and we rolled apart, me dragging my sword with me. Its presence reassured me, as did the faint brush of wings that too-briefly cooled me beneath a nauseatingly hot sun. I was wearing my favored oily tank top and torn jeans rather than my winter gear, which brought me up short: I'd intended to enter the Lower World physically, actually leaving the Middle World behind for the duration of this fight. Moving into another plane shouldn't, I thought, change my clothes.

I raised my eyes, confused, and was caught with a jolt of understanding. There was a woman before me, stringy hair falling in her face, gaunt cheekbones making her eyes too large. Her teeth were filed into narrow points, an affectation that gave me the heebie-jeebies. I could only think of filed teeth as being fingernails on chalkboards to the umpteenth degree, and the very idea sent horror rushing up and down my spine and tap-dancing on my skin. I wanted to throw up, which was not the ideal way to begin a spiritual smackdown.

She pulled her lips back from her nasty, nasty teeth and hissed at me, breath as hideous as it had been in her wendigo form. It actually distracted me from her teeth, which probably hadn't been her intention, but I was grateful.

I was less grateful for the talons she had lashed to her hands. Two on each, between the fingers. She only had one each tied between her toes, but it was quite enough; she looked like a demented dinosaur, arms raised and feet kicked high as she lurched back and forth in front of me.

A demented, *starved* dinosaur. There was ropy muscle on her skinny arms and legs, but I could count the ribs above her starvation-bloated belly. This pathetic, mad-eyed woman was what lay at the wendigo's core. Traveling into the Lower World physically had stripped us to more fundamental versions of ourselves, the winter trappings taken from me and the monster torn away from this woman. My heart twisted, suddenly sorry for her, and I stepped back rather than close in. "I can help you, if you'll let me."

She bobbed back and forth, apparently taking that into consideration. Then she lashed forward, much, much faster than someone in her condition should have been able to move, and struck out with her taloned hand. It was a flawless hit, executed so fast I could barely see it, and it should have gutted me.

It missed by a hair's breadth. My gut sucked in to my spine as I curved backward, air whooshing from my lungs. She surged past me, carried by her own momentum, and whirled back with a shriek of angry surprise.

I was right there with her with regards to surprise. I knew myself. I'd spent most of the past year studying fencing, and my reflexes were better than they'd been. They were not, however, that good. Nobody was that good, in much the same way that the wendigo-woman couldn't be as fast as she was. It was inhuman, lightning fast, snakelike reflexes; name the cliché, and I'd just fulfilled it.

She struck again, this time with both fists raised, bringing them down in an X meant to slice me apart. I was too busy gawking at myself to parry, but for the second time I folded in on myself, taking my body just out of reach.

This time I snapped my rapier out, not so much for the kill as to gain space and time. It whipped toward her so quickly it vibrated, almost unfurling as though it were liquid or leather, and it cracked when I reached full extension. Power surged through me into the blade, making it a weapon worth reckoning, and the wendigo skittered back, avoiding the shining silver.

Impulse drove me forward in a series of quick attacks. She countered, catching the sword on her talons every time, all of it so fast my mind lagged behind what our bodies were doing. By the time we broke apart again I was panting through a grin splitting my face.

Snakelike reflexes. The rattler had promised me a second gift to be discovered when I needed it. The tremendous healing ability belonged to the Middle World, a place of physical bodies. But a significant percentage of the things I encountered belonged to spirit worlds, where the laws were defined by what they believed they could do.

Defined by what I believed *I* could do, and by what my power animals were willing to grant me as gifts. I felt a hiss of snakeskin over my own, and grinned wildly. I would never have dreamed of moving so fast, but to a rattlesnake, it was second nature. First nature, even, and so it became for me. I loved it.

The wendigo, on the other hand, didn't like it one little bit at all.

We came together again with a great crashing roar that was equal parts her shrieks and my laughter. I was sure I'd get over it soon enough—as soon as she landed a blow, for example— but in the first moments, the speed was glorious. I ducked under her claws and dragged my blade across her belly, dismayed when its silver edge drew no blood. Probably I wasn't supposed to be eviscerating people, but she hadn't seemed inclined to listen. Sometimes a sharp knife to the gut could get somebody's attention. At least, it had always gotten mine.

She somersaulted over the rapier and rolled to her feet, striking backward toward my unprotected spine. I snapped forward again, just avoiding her talons, then jerked around and grabbed her arm, trying to get a better look at the claws.

They'd belonged to a bear, once upon a time, or some similar massive predator. A mountain lion, maybe, but I thought their curve was too shallow for that. Certainly a creature of at least that size, though: they were black and as long as her fingers. They were strong, too, stronger than any mortal remains should be. My sword should have sliced through them, not bounced off.

I wasn't used to being Ms. Intuitive, but comprehension slid through me, a clear and bright rain. "Did they belong to your spirit guide?"

Rage turned her eyes red, ending our brief moment of arrest. She stuffed her free hand into my gut, the punch hard enough that I went cold with breathlessness, but we were both surprised when she pulled back unbloodied fingers. I looked down to see bloodless gashes closing in my torso, and clenched my fist around her wrist all the harder. She squealed and tried to pull away, but in a fit of morbid curiosity I slammed my forearm onto her black talons.

Cold sliced through my arm, making muscle cramp with its intensity. I drew back and the cold faded as the wounds sealed flawlessly. Nothing but an inexorable sense of rightness accompanied the healing, no rush of power, no silver-blue aura hurrying to fix what was wrong. I knew I could bleed in the Lower World; I'd done it before.

I'd done it before Raven and Rattler had come to protect me. Healing wasn't Raven's purview, but Rattler had already proven what his presence could offer. "Your spirit animals give you the weapons," I said slowly. "Mine protect me from the wounds." I let her go, and turned a considering look on my sword.

I'd struck her with it any number of times, in both her wendigo form in the Middle World, and her more-human shape here in the Lower. It wasn't precisely a power animal, but it did, unquestionably, represent my power. It was part of a circle of magics which protected me and offered me weaponry to fight with. It was a thing of spirit, whether it was an animal or not.

And it was useless to me in this fight. Her bear-spirit would drive her past whatever wounds I inflicted with it, the rapier's slim blade too delicate to disturb such a great force. Maybe if I managed a heart-shot, but I wasn't actually here to kill this woman. I was going to save her, if I could. I released the rapier from my thoughts, and it faded away. "C'mon, sister. It's just you and me."

She screamed and kneed me in the belly, which was more effective, overall, than her talons had been. I doubled over, coughing, and she brought her fisted hands down on the back of my neck. I hit the yellow earth teeth-first and came up spitting dust. Mandy had not put up this kind of fight, when I went after her soul. Then again, Mandy hadn't turned into a slavering flesh-eating monster, either. I said, "Oh my God, is that Chuck Norris?" and pointed dramatically past the wendigo's shoulder. To my amazement, she actually turned to look, and I knotted my hands together, swinging for her temple.

She dropped and I pounced on her, pinning her arms. She smelled worse than humanly possible, and flung herself up and down with a lot of enthusiasm for such a skinny thing. Still, I had the upper hand and shook her entire torso, not caring that her head bounced off the ground like a bowling ball. "I am trying to help you!"

Her eyes cleared for an instant. Triumph shot through me, sharp enough that I didn't care about her stench. "You're in there! Come on, let me—"

The dusty yellow earth turned white beneath her, and the broiling Lower World sun fled behind sudden thick clouds. Wind howled up around us, cutting through my flimsy summertime clothes and icing my skin. My nose hairs froze, and my eyebrows went stiff inside a single breath, the air colder than I'd ever felt. The wendigo's human shape warped, twisting under my hands to become the monster once again, as loose-jointed and dangerous as it had been when I'd entered the cold universe searching for Mandy's soul.

This time, though, its face was stretched in agony, and its voice was that of the storm's. It had been the predator, then; now it was something else, not even prey. It needed protecting, rescuing from the cold threatening to tear us both apart. I hauled myself closer to its face to shout, "Let me take you out of here! Let me take you away from the—"

From the storm was how that was supposed to end, but the last few words were already shouted into silence. Even without the wind, the cold intensified to a killing temperature so extreme it seemed malicious. My exposed skin went numb, and the breath I drew through an open mouth hurt my lungs, like cold lead had been poured down my throat.

I let the wendigo go and shoved to my feet. The storm still raged around us at a distance as great as the circle I'd made in the Middle World, but it was quiet now, its screams pushed away.

Loneliness crashed over me, a feeling of isolation that expanded beyond my most melodramatic childhood moments. There was no way free from the circle of silent snow, and its featureless blur made my gaze unfocus. Disoriented, I reeled around, bewildered at how the silence and lack of wind could be worse than the battering storm itself. I wanted to escape, but my body was failing me, thick icy limbs refusing to respond, frozen thoughts running evermore sluggishly.

Someone stepped through the storm, joining me in the relentless white circle.

The wendigo gave a gleeful shriek and rose up out of the snow, racing for the distant sky.

I tried to follow, and failed.

CHAPTER THIRTY

I was too cold to be afraid. Too cold to be surprised, even, like the oncoming storm had taken away my capacity for emotion. There were things I should be able to do. Command my healing aspect to heat my blood, to shake off the malaise of ice. Imagine myself in warmer clothes and have them appear. I'd done them, or things like them, in the past, but my thoughts were sluggish and my magic frozen, just a solid lump inside me where it should have been reassuringly alive.

If this was what the wendigo had experienced, then I had a hideous bleak appreciation for the sheer willpower that had brought her back into the mortal world to feed. I was lost and too numb to care. My rattlesnake friend could do nothing for me here; he would freeze even more quickly than I did, cold blood turning to slush in his veins. Maybe that was how the wendigo had survived, if her claws had been a bear's. Maybe she had the gift of hibernation, of holing up and storing energy until she'd conserved enough to break free. It wasn't how hibernation worked in the Middle World, but this place was something else entirely.

Someone else was here. Someone else had crossed into the circle. It was something to focus on, a way to force myself to move. My own safety, apparently, wasn't quite enough, but if someone else had wandered into the storm, they needed rescuing, and there was nobody but me to do the job.

"Here." My voice cracked in the cold like I'd been without water for a week. "Here, can you hear me? Can you see me?" The wendigo had left a dent in the snow when she'd fled. I tripped on it, my legs too heavy to move properly, and I splayed facedown in the ice.

It almost felt warm. That was wrong, dangerously wrong; my dull mind recognized that much. It meant I'd lost too much of my own heat. It meant, in fact, that I was dying, and while I had plenty of experience at dying, it was usually accompanied by a certain amount of anger which sparked me through the unpleasant parts and back out the other side.

This was not a place for fire of any kind. I was willing to let mine fade, just to evade the terrible cold. I sighed into the snow, my breath not even warm enough to melt it, and my eyes drifted shut as sound finally broke through the silence: squeaking, coming ever closer. My curiosity sputtered, then died again, frozen out of existence.

Hot hands rolled me over like a giant rag doll, and Laurie Corvallis put her face close to mine to whisper, "Detective? Is that you?"

Ice cracked at the back of my mind, like amazement had the strength to punch through cold. Of all the people I might have dreamed up to accompany me into a frozen hell, Corvallis was about the bottom of the list. It suggested she was real, which was both good and bad. Good because she was substantial, something to focus on. Bad because I was quite certain her physical body had crossed to this plane, just like mine had, and it was a short dash to death from where we currently stood.

At least she was still dressed for the weather. Her cheeks were reddened by cold, but her eyes were bright, and her face was framed by the soft fur of her expensive coat. It was fitted, but not so snugly she couldn't wear layers under it, and from the way her breath steamed warmly I figured she probably was. Her hands were mittened, which told me a lot about both the amount of heat she was putting out and how very cold I was: even through the mittens they'd been hot on my skin. She muttered, "Where'd your coat go?" and started to shrug hers off.

"No, don't." I was surprised I could talk, then relieved that I could be surprised. It was like her presence offered enough warmth and life to reawaken me. Given my peculiar talents, that seemed fairly probable. She stopped mid-action, her coat still on, and I shook my head against the snow. "It wouldn't fit anyway. Just stay close to me, okay? I'll get you out of here."

"Where's here? I was following you through the forest when it all went twisty and I got dumped in this field."

It all went twisty sounded like something I would say. I started to say so, then shoved up on my elbows, suddenly actually awake. Herne had said some were closer, others were farther away and would take longer to guide to the power circle. It hadn't occurred to me that he'd meant there were other people out there besides Gary and Sara. "You were following me? You were supposed to be asleep!"

"I woke up." Three little words shouldn't sound like portents of doom, but somehow they did. Well, there'd be time for a reckoning later, if we were lucky. I resisted the urge to hug her—for warmth, although I was kind of happy to see her, too—and instead blew into my hands, trying to get some feeling back.

"Did you see the others? Coyote and—" She was shaking her head no, and I echoed the motion, then said, "Shit. I wonder if that means you just got dropped directly between."

"Between what?"

"Between here and there. Between life and death. Between the cold." I sounded like an idiot. I felt like an idiot. "Don't worry about it. All right, look—"

"Don't *worry* about it? Don't worry about the fact that a minute ago I was in a snowy forest under a clear night and now I'm in a field someplace in the eye of a blizzard? Fine. I won't worry about it. I'll just figure out how to get out of here, since you're no use at all." She stood up, a small figure full of fire. Admiration, which was not an emotion I wanted to associate with Corvallis, bloomed in me. *She* wasn't a woman who would get trapped by the cold universe. She'd build a flamethrower out of snow and blast her way free.

I could hardly do less. I got up, ice crystals forming on my arms, and tried not to shiver too hard. "Can you hear a drum?"

Corvallis glared at me. "Of course I can't hear a drum. All I can hear is you. I can't even hear *that*." She jabbed a finger at the storm whirling outside the circle's boundaries. Then wariness came over her face and she said, "Why? Can *you* hear a drum?" like it would be a very bad sign if I could.

I envisioned *Police Detective Loses Mind!* as the headline, and sighed. "No. I wish I could." It would give me a direction to head in, or at least provide some kind of promise there was still a world outside this one. "Corvallis, come over here and put your arms around me, and whatever happens, don't let go."

She stayed right where she was. "Why?"

"Because I'm going to freeze to death if you don't." While true, that was less than half the reason I wanted her to hold on to me. It did, however, sound much more reasonable than the real explanation, and after a few seconds of looking for its flaws, Corvallis did as I asked.

Heat rushed through me so fast it hurt. I swallowed a whimper and did my best to not curl up around the smaller woman like she was a teddy bear. If I did, odds were we'd both find ourselves frozen lumps in no time. I doubted she could sustain enough warmth for one very long, much less two. Instead I mumbled, "Thanks," and folded my arms around her shoulders. It wasn't as warm as her hugging them against me, but I didn't trust she'd keep hanging on if this worked the way I hoped.

I said, "Raven, it's me again," over Laurie's head. She jerked like I'd stuck a pin in her, and I tightened my arms. "Shh. It's okay."

She hissed, "You're talking to ravens," which I had to agree sounded a little crazy, especially since there weren't actually any ravens around. On the other hand, stopping to explain just seemed tedious, so I didn't. I tilted my head back, concentrating on my heartbeat as a substitute for a drum.

"Raven, I know you were there when I entered the Lower World. I felt you. Raven and Rattler both. But I lost you when

I came here, and now I need you or I'll be lost, too. So will this woman, and she's only here because of me."

"That is *not true.* I'm following a story, a—" I felt Corvallis shift, turning her head to glance around the storm-bound circle before she muttered, "Fine. Being here, wherever here is, might be because of you. You owe me an explanation, Detective."

"I already gave you one." That was not helping. I made a disgusted sound in my throat and bared my teeth at the sky. Raven was out there somewhere, and he was good at storms and at passing through the flimsy barrier between life and death. I only had to give him a way to find me, and he'd come for us. There had to be a path somewhere.

I tipped my chin down and looked at the top of Corvallis's head. She didn't strike me as the type who would get stuck between, not by any natural means. In so far as *natural means* applied to my life or scenarios like this one, anyway. "Tell me exactly what happened when you came here."

"I already did," she said in exactly the same snappy, impatient tone I'd used on her a moment earlier. I swear to God, karma was not supposed to be an instant payback thing. I wanted to beat my head against something, but the only thing available was Corvallis's head, which I didn't think would help the situation.

"Laurie, please." People were supposed to respond well to the sound of their own names. I hoped it worked.

Corvallis gave me a look which suggested she knew exactly what I was doing. She probably did. News reporters probably used that kind of trick all the time. But she answered, which was all I asked for. "I told you. The forest twisted in on itself, and when it unfolded we were—"

"We?"

"Jeff and me. My cameraman."

"You brought your cam…" I reminded myself that this was not the time. "When it unfolded you were what?"

"We were here." She glanced around, and I could all but see the gears whirling in her little reporter mind. Then she closed her eyes, and when she spoke again she sounded like the woman on the six o'clock news every night, her voice crisp and concise. "We stepped out of the forest into a clearing about thirty yards across. There was a path of trodden snow right in front of us, and…four. Four people about halfway across the clearing. Jeff stepped across the path and I followed after. Then I was here, in the middle of this storm."

She opened her eyes again, looking up at me. "Back to you at the studio, Jo."

"You," I said, "are one hell of a reporter. When Jeff stepped across the path, did he scuff it?"

"It's snow." Corvallis managed to look pleased at the compliment and sound irritated all at the same time. "How can you scuff snow?" But she closed her eyes again, making me think she was rebuilding the image in her mind, then nodded. "His snowshoes left a line from the forest's edge to the path. Is that important?"

"Very." My circle had been broken, allowing the wendigo to escape and pulling Corvallis in to the between-place in its stead. I wished I had the luxury of panic, but I was starting to get cold again. It crystallized my thoughts, hurrying them to the necessary conclusions. "Look for a…lollipop, Raven. A lollipop in the snow." It sounded silly, but it was a better analogy than a steering wheel, and besides, it involved food. Raven liked food. "A lollipop with a really short handle and the biggest candy circle you've ever seen. Find that in the snow and you'll find us, and then I can bring you a lollipop just like that of your own." I sounded like I was cajoling a two-year-old.

Corvallis, almost reverently, asked, "Have you completely lost your mind?"

I was just about to admit I had when Raven plunged from the sky to our rescue.

The storm was a thing, not a sentient being. Not something that could recognize whether we were vulnerable or strong. I knew that, and yet it came to life, attacking as Raven plummeted down. Wind broke through the circular barrier, slashing at us with knives of ice carried in its invisible hands. Snow whipped around, moving so fast it became a weapon, tiny beads of cold driving into my face and exposed arms. I tucked Laurie's hooded head against my chest and turned eyes blinded with frozen tears toward the hidden sky.

There was no Sight to call here, no way to look beyond the blizzard and follow Raven's path. But I could feel him almost as if I flew with him, battered and driven by the storm. The cold didn't affect him the same way it did me, his existence a more supernatural thing than mine. But the wind did, and to my delight there was a part of himself given over to shrieking, gurgling laughter at being tossed around by the storm. He had a job to do, yes, and he knew it, and was dedicated to it, but he was of a breed known to go sledding down snowy hills, and to deliberately fold their wings so the wind off high bluffs could toss them to and fro. He worked his way through the snow toward us, but he had fun while he was doing it.

It was probably an extremely good life lesson. I put it on my list of things to think about after I was no longer a Jo-sicle and had saved the girl.

Which, if it didn't happen soon, wasn't going to happen at all. I raised my hand, skin stinging with the snow's impact, and bellowed, "Raven! Here! *Hurry!*" Corvallis was still warm, but I wasn't. Snow-shadows tore around us, making me think I was seeing our rescuer, but every time I grasped for him, he disappeared. My fingers were so cold I wasn't sure if I was clutching at ghosts or if I simply couldn't hold on to Raven long enough to be saved.

All I wanted was to escape the cold. I would do *anything* to escape the cold. I knew there was a world outside it, and clung desperately to the idea that Raven was on his way, but I could no longer feel him. I wasn't certain I felt anything; Corvallis's fur-wrapped self against my chest could have been a figment of my imagination. I kept holding on, just in case she wasn't, but no matter how hard I tried to hug her, I felt no pressure, no give, nothing but the endless snow. Dying seemed preferable to the cold. Even forcing myself out of this world as a wendigo seemed like a better fate—*anything* to be warm again. I'd had very little sympathy for the monster, but if it had begun as human and had faced the cold between, now I at least understood how it could reach for such extremes in order to avoid the cold.

Raven came out of the storm and sank his claws around my wrist, talons pinching far more sharply than the wendigo's had when I'd fought it. A sob caught in my throat, too cold to go farther. I was glad I could feel pain because it suggested I wasn't frostbitten from the marrow out, but I feared my blood would freeze as it fell to the snow, droplets forming a staircase for the cold to climb into the sky so it could chase me back to the warmer world.

My spirit guide cawed, a stern sound which broke through

the storm as he struggled to lug the weight of two mortals upward. I tried to think myself lighter, think myself as weightless as a snowflake, and relief burst through the raven's second cry. We soared upward, striving for the sky.

Halfway out of the storm, Laurie slipped from my numb grasp.

CHAPTER THIRTY-ONE

I hit the real world in a lunge, trying to catch a woman I didn't even like. Snow sprayed up in front of me and I surged to my feet, hoping against hope that Corvallis had somehow fallen to the Middle World, and not back into the storm.

She had. Laurie Corvallis's body was a dozen yards away, collapsed in the snow at the larger circle's inner edge. Aching relief tore away my ability to breathe. Healing a spirit torn asunder was far less terrifying than searching for her physical body in that god-awful storm. I ran toward her, and only too late began to hear and see the other things going on around me.

Gary and Sara were out of the protective inner circle, yards ahead of me in the race for Corvallis. Sara, younger, lighter, lither, got there before Gary and vaulted the woman to land on her other side. Gary crashed to his knees, both of them driving themselves under Corvallis's arms to get her up and haul her to safety. Their auras blazed, fear buried beneath the determination to rescue a fallen comrade. I had no time to stop, no time to love them or admire them, but my heart damned near ruptured my chest, full of awe at the nerve they displayed.

Somewhere behind me a man was bellowing, "What the fuck? What the *fuck!*" I wheeled around, working a sort of mental triage: Corvallis's lost soul could wait a little while. Not long, but a while, and I could use that time to deal with the wendigo. It would do. It would have to do.

Jeff, the camera guy, was the one shouting as he crabbed backward through the snow. I had to perversely admire his professionalism. The film would be all *Blair Witch Project,* but he had the camera at his shoulder and the green light flashed to indicate he was recording. He was still doing his job.

And he probably wouldn't die for it, because Coyote, spear clutched in both hands, stood between him and the wendigo. His hair was loose and flying, and he looked both terrified and like a warrior out of an imaginative history, eyes alight with gold power and the spear brandished at a terrible beast. The wendigo swiped at him and he dodged back, its blow glancing off the spear with a vibration that rattled the cold air.

I shot one despairing glance at the inner circle I'd gone to so much trouble to build. Empty and useless. Well, at least my friends were the kind you wanted to have your back in a fight. That was something. And they kind of deserved me to step up and do my part, so I cut across the circle toward Coyote, running as hard as I could in snowshoes and layered clothes.

I hit the wendigo in a flying tackle that knocked it well away from Coyote and the camera guy. "Go! Go! Get back inside!"

It was excellent advice. Neither of them took it, so far as I could tell while I flew backward across the larger circle again myself. I hadn't even seen the damned wendigo hit me, though I could feel the blow in my belly. Coyote charged forward, jabbing at the beast. It turned on him, snarling, and it struck me that probably two of us had a better chance against the thing than just one.

Better still if the others would get inside the inner circle. I yelled, "Go, go, inside!" again, not that "inside" was particularly helpful to Jeff, who hadn't been there when I'd built the inner circle and who no doubt saw nothing resembling indoors in the snowy landscape.

At least Gary and Sara knew what I was talking about. They rushed toward the circle's center with Laurie, and in a flawless moment of slapstick, bounced off it.

Because it was meant to keep things out. I finally hit the ground again, skidded backward, and doubled forward on myself to pound frustrated fists against the earth. My life was a Laurel and Hardy skit. Which would be fine if it were just *my* life, but other people were involved, and depending on me. A smart shaman probably would've tagged the good guys with some kind of "Let me in, let me in by the hairs of my chinny-chin-chin" thing so they could come and go from the safety of the inner circle, but I flat-out hadn't thought of it. Someday. Someday I would be good at this.

Assuming I managed to kick a wendigo's ass and get everybody to safety right now, anyway. I got over my three-second wallow and charged forward, confident, at least, that Gary and Sara could keep dragging Corvallis around the outer perimeter of the smaller circle, which would make it harder for the wendigo to get to her if it decided it needed a snack.

The wendigo was bleeding when I caught up to it again. I thought that was a great sign. Nothing I'd used on it had left a mark. Coyote, though, genuinely looked ill, all the certainty pouring away from his aura. A knot of worry bound up my lungs, and I breathed, "Do no harm."

Coyote went still, like he'd heard me, then turned toward me with hope and horror written in his golden eyes. I said, "It's okay," out loud, and did what I'd refused to do before: put my hand out for Herne's spear.

He winged it at me, throwing it lengthwise, so it spun a long horizontal arc across the snow. I caught it with a slap against my palm, audible even though I wore mittens, and Coyote sagged with relief. His aura strengthened instantly, like the weapon itself had drawn it down. I wanted to hug him.

"Go see if you can help Corvallis." I was oddly serene. The weapon fit in my hand like it was supposed to be there, and I already knew that fighting didn't do to me what it seemed to do to Coyote.

I hadn't known. I really hadn't known. Herne gave the spear to Coyote, not me, and when a god did something like that, I was inclined to follow his lead. And maybe he'd meant it as a test for Coyote, to see if my mentor had the warrior spirit in him. Or maybe he'd really just given him the spear to hold until it was time for me to use it. Those two things, in my opinion, weren't incompatible. But it was clear that my friend and mentor was never going to take up the metaphorical sword. We were not alike, he and I. I was a little sad about that, but in the end, it was okay. We weren't meant to walk the same path, and I could live with that.

Then the moment's glorious calm was gone. Coyote spun and ran for the inner circle. The wendigo, howling, tore after him, and I snapped myself forward, interceding faster than I should have been able to. I whispered thanks to my rattlesnake, and collided with the wendigo in a rush of fur and fury.

For the first time, we did damage to one another. I heard ribs crack and thought they were its, not mine, and caught a blow across my cheek that sent me spinning. When I whirled back, the wendigo was running. Not toward the broken outer circle, but toward the smaller one, where my friends sheltered on its far side. Coyote was there, but only just: he was beginning to kneel at Laurie's side while Gary and Sara got to their feet, the latter with her gun in hand. It wouldn't do anything to the wendigo, but it was the act of defiance that mattered.

I surged after it, fast, but not fast enough. I couldn't match its leaps, not even with my snake-offered speed. The damned wendigo slithered around the inner column, claws scraping and digging against the magic. Sara lifted her weapon and fired repeatedly, and to my surprise the wendigo shuddered with each impact, blood spattering across the snow. It collapsed, crashing down the circle toward Coyote, who flung his hands up in a desperate attempt to protect his charge.

When it came to rest, it became Laurie Corvallis.

The monster simply disappeared, misshapen form falling into nothing, and Corvallis arched up out of the snow screaming in its wake. Coyote surged back in shock, and for a microsecond I just stood there agape and childishly infuriated. It wasn't *fair*. It was just *not fair* that this goddamned monster could shuffle off its mortal coil faster than a thought; that its very body was so much a psychic construct that it could be discarded the moment something better came along. No wonder I couldn't hold the damned thing. Even gods were more constrained by physical form than the wendigo was.

I hated it. I hated it a lot, even knowing there was a woman somewhere inside there who needed rescuing. I hated that it was so slippery and that I wasn't fast enough; I hated its need to kill to survive; I hated its cold ruthless will that let it cling to a world it should have already passed beyond.

And I hated that Laurie Corvallis, whom I didn't like very much, was going to die if I didn't get my act together. Coyote shook off shock and slammed forward again, pinning her down as I skidded across the snow to join them.

"I got her out." My voice was so low and frustrated it sounded like it came from someone else. "I almost had her out of the storm, out of the cold between. I just couldn't hold on, Coyote. I was so cold, and she fell. She fell, and…"

Corvallis opened her eyes and dropped her jaw to hiss at me from the back of her throat. I toppled over with an undignified squeak, and Coyote, holding her shoulders down, gave me a look of pure disgust. Some great healer I was, when a little demon possession freaked me out, but Corvallis's blue eyes were bloodshot red, even the pupils. Her teeth, at least, hadn't undergone a transformation, and were nice and white and even rather than being filed points.

"How far did she fall? *How far did she fall, Jo?*"

"I don't know! Far enough to leave her body empty!" I clapped one hand on Corvallis's head and put the other, awkwardly, at her hip. Awkward because I still had the spear and didn't want to let it go, not because I had some kind of personal space issue going on. "Raven, guide me. If I have to go back into that storm to find her, I will, but that place scares the crap out of me. I need your help. I promise lollipops."

I felt the reassuring non-weight of my spirit guide on my shoulder, his unearthly talons squeezing tight muscle. I whispered, "Don't let us freeze to death, Yote," and for what seemed like the hundredth time, closed my eyes to risk the storm.

Corvallis slapped her hand up, fingers clawed inside their mitten, and hauled me back out.

The world shifted, all signs of winter melting away. I was in a concrete jungle: skyscrapers wound with ivy reached for the stars, streams ran over the dashed lines of asphalt streets, predators prowled grassy sidewalks and lurked in alleyways while herd animals raced ahead of them, in a rush to eat, to work, to play. I thought I made a rather magnificent addition to the surroundings, in my torn jeans and oily tank-top and with a tall wooden spear in my hand. I fit right in as one of the predators. Men and women in business suits avoided me, while young punks sized me up for potential battle. I shook my spear and shooed them away so I could look around in peace.

Billboards and electronic tickers were half destroyed by wilderness, though their remnants showed news images, one of them recurring over and over: Corvallis at a news anchor's desk, internationally famous eye symbol predominant behind her. There was something not quite right about her, hard to pinpoint from the fractured images.

She was tawnier than in real life, black hair streaked with blond, warm skin tones a little more golden. There was something feline about her, and I laughed as it came to me: king of the jungle. This was pretty, ambitious Laurie Corvallis's garden, a cityscape jungle, and she was its lioness. Which was way, way more than I'd ever wanted to know about her. Still, I kind of admired it. At least she knew what she wanted.

Though in this particular case, the fact that I was *here,* and not in the wendigo's storm, suggested that what she wanted was help. It also suggested she had some vestige of control left, which was good for both of us. All I had to do was find her, and maybe together we'd stand a chance against the demon. "Laurie? Hey, Laurie!"

Her name echoed off ruined buildings, but she didn't appear. I pursed my lips, then took off at a run through the streets, trusting Corvallis's subconscious to take me where I needed to go. The city bent and folded and presented me with the Channel Two News building within a few dozen strides. Unsurprised, I took the stairs up two at a time, and burst into the anchor room. "Laurie?"

"I can't come out." Her voice was a whisper, bouncing around so it seemed to come from nowhere. "It'll get me if I come out."

"I'm here to stop it." I thought I sounded remarkably confident. I hoped she thought so, too. "Where are you? Can you tell me what you remember?"

"There was a storm. I was lost." She sounded about six. "Someone tried to rescue me, but then I couldn't see her anymore. The storm came up and I started to run, and I ran until I came here. But now the storm is here, too, looking for me. I think it wants to kill me."

I'd pinpointed her by the end of her explanation, though I didn't want to let her know that. Instead I came to sit on the anchor's desk, pretty sure she was under it. I wondered if she always thought of herself as a kid who hid beneath desks.

If she did, that probably explained a lot about her aggressiveness. Talk about making up for perceived inadequacies in spades. "I think you're right. The storm is trying to get to you. But I can help you fight it, if you want."

"…you can?" She *looked* about six as she peeked out from under the desk, all big hopeful eyes and quivering lower lip. Given a set of whiskers, she'd be the world's most pathetic kitten. Man, if I got her out of this alive I would have all the blackmail material I'd ever need to keep myself off the news.

Not that I would ever, ever use my special magic powers to such a naughty, self-involved end. Of course not. That would be *wrong*. And more to the point, the gift I'd tried so hard to ignore and had finally grown comfortable with would no doubt depart at the least opportune moment in retaliation for my bad behavior. Look, I never said I was a good person. Sometimes threats to my own health and happiness were the best way to keep me on the straight and narrow.

"I can," I said firmly. "That's what I do. I help people."

Corvallis squinted suspiciously over the edge of the desk. It reduced the kitten aspect and aged her considerably, which was something of a relief. I did not want to introduce six-year-olds to fighting wendigos. Or anything else, for that matter. She inched farther up the desk, frown deepening. "How?"

"How? How do I help? Messily, usually, and you don't make it any easier." Probably this was not the time to scold her. I made a face and tried again. "I'm a shaman. I deal in sicknesses that doctors don't believe exist. Right now you're sick. A demon's taken over your body. I can help you get it back."

She got to her feet, an adult again, though still with the vaguely feline air. "A demon. Like in *The Omen?*"

"No, that was the Anti-Christ, wasn't it? More like…" My limited knowledge of pop culture failed me entirely. "Look, don't worry what it's like. That storm we were in was…Hell." It wasn't. Or at least I didn't think it was. But it was the closest shorthand I had.

Unfortunately, it also had a connotation I hadn't quite thought through. Corvallis's voice shot up: "You mean I'm *dead?*"

"No! Not yet." That was probably less than reassuring. "But you will be if we don't go deal with the demon, so if you don't mind, I think we should get out of here and go find it."

She folded her arms, fingers tapping rapidly against her biceps. "And just how do you propose we do that, Detective?"

Bully for me. I'd gotten the Corvallis I knew and loved back. Still, it was a damned sight better than a child. "If I were the wendigo I'd be working from the part of your mind that contained the images and thoughts and places you wanted least to remember. I'd figure you'd avoid those places, nevermind stride in and pick a fight."

"I don't back down from fights, Detective." Corvallis was hard as steel now, while the backdrop shifted to show images of her scrappy childhood self standing up to a school-yard fight even while her heart pounded with terror. She got a tooth knocked out that day, but by God she didn't back down.

I had the sudden appalling idea that I could like this woman. Disconcerted by the idea, I extended a hand and raised my eyebrows in mild challenge. "Great. Let's go find one, then."

CHAPTER THIRTY-TWO

She took my hand, and the building disappeared around us, though the ground stayed solid beneath our feet as it changed from carpet to asphalt. A parking lot somewhere, half the lights out, only a couple of cars in it, the sounds of glass breaking and rowdy men in the near distance. There was no proper life here, not the way there was in the other gardens I'd visited, but it was certainly a familiar scene. It put me instantly on edge, hairs on my neck standing up and an apprehensive chill rushing over my skin.

Despite holding a tall spear in one hand, I released the other from Corvallis's grasp and dug into my pocket for my keys. I'd want them out, in this situation. I'd want them because I'd want to get into Petite as quickly as I could, and because, grasped in the palm and stuck jagged-side-out between the fingers, they made a decent weapon. I was nearly six feet tall and disproportionately strong from working on cars all my life, and even so, alone in a parking lot at night, I was scared.

No. I was wary, in this situation. I'd never been *scared*. The *fear* was Laurie, who had neither my height nor my strength, and who was much, much prettier than I was. Her anxiety pervaded the scene, though beneath it there was anger, too. Anger that she *was* afraid, anger that there was reason to be, and anger, I suspected, at knowing what happened next. Anger at being unable to stop it. I glanced at her, and she said, tightly, "This is where I don't like to go." Her neck was stiff with strain, like she was resolutely refusing to look over her shoulder.

I looked.

What *I* saw was the wendigo, talons between her fingers like I held my keys. What *I* saw was the beast's loping form, her raging eyes, her starving soul now determined to hold on to the body it had taken. The unwilling dead were so greedy for life it hurt me, like a blade in the heart. The handful of people I'd met who had died well, or who had understood their fate, had slipped away comfortably enough, but those who had gone down fighting or in fear would do anything to reclaim what they'd lost. It was a terrible thing, that we lived in a world that made such unhappy souls. I took a step forward, half intending to intercept the miserable creature, but Laurie spun around, fear and frustration making her aura sour.

"David, leave me *alone!* How many times do I have to say it's over? You can't follow me like this. It freaks me out!"

I never heard what David said in return. The wendigo rushed her, so abrupt even Corvallis was surprised, which suggested that this wasn't in keeping with her memories of what had happened with David. She shrieked, an aborted little sound, and her head cracked against the pavement with a noise like a plastic bowl landing cup-side-down.

For the second time in a matter of minutes, the wendigo sank into Corvallis's body, leaving nothing of itself behind.

I fell back, horrified. In the Middle World, the possession had been bad, but it had suggested Laurie's soul was out for lunch, leaving the body empty to be occupied. Here, in Corvallis's garden, there was nothing *but* her soul to replace. The landscape started to shift, mountains and cedar trees ripping up from beneath the pavement. I staggered, using the spear for balance, and my eyes were drawn to it as an unpleasant reality hit.

I was actually going to have to kill her.

She folded her arms up to put her hands palm-down on either side of her head, and did a full body surge that drove her to her feet. I'd only ever seen anybody do that in movies, and thought it looked just as inefficient in real life as on film. Also, it meant she came at me ribs-first, body arched forward to get the momentum she needed to gain her feet.

I kicked her in the sternum.

I didn't know why nobody ever did that in movies. Corvallis slammed right back to the ground, hitting so hard *I* went breathless. But whether it was the wendigo in control or simply that it was Corvallis's garden, she didn't stay down. I'd never seen a more classic stop, drop and roll, in fact, overlooking the fact that the stop and drop had been initiated by a boot to the ribs rather than being on fire. Look, it had been a good analogy. It didn't need close examination.

She rolled to her feet a few yards away, which was a much better way of getting up. I went after her, bellowing, "Damn it, Corvallis, I don't want to kill you, but I will if I have to!"

I sounded like a parent threatening a child for its own good. I had yet to meet a kid who believed that. Either way, I brandished the spear, hoping it would cow her.

She grabbed it just beyond the head and yanked it toward her to capture the haft between her arm and ribs. I very nearly let go from surprise, then grunted and set my weight. I had at least forty pounds on her, and it should have been easy to knock her off her feet using the spear as leverage.

The bitch didn't so much as tilt. I did a credible wendigo-sounding growl and shoved forward, managing to slide the spear and get myself a couple feet closer to her. I had no plan after that, but the Corvallis-wendigo did: she bared fingers whose nails had gone very claw-y, and slashed at my face. I dodged back, then kicked her in the ribs again, booted foot connecting solidly. She wheezed and her grip on the spear loosened. I yanked it away and backed up, ready for her when she pounced.

I had to give the wendigo this much: it wasn't an original fighter. Even with me armed with a spear, its inclination was to come from on high and bear down its victim by weight. That was more effective when it was three hundred pounds, not a hundred and fifteen. I took a chance and swung the spear aside so it wouldn't impale her, and straight-armed her in the xyphoid process instead.

Honestly, I couldn't have done better if I were a professional wrestler. The heel of my hand caught her just above the gut and I let go the spear to grab her with my other hand and body-slam her to the earth. It would've been hugely more effective if we were still in the parking lot Corvallis had imagined up instead of in the wendigo's preferred forest, but even so, it wasn't half-bad. The blood rage faded from Corvallis's eyes, and for a bewildered instant she blinked at me through a spray of snow.

"Corvallis! Is that you?" Fighting the wendigo was one thing, but I had Laurie's weight pinned, and confidence, if necessary, in my own ability as a brawler over her barracuda-girl attitude.

I hadn't counted on the possibility she knew how to fight.

She brought her feet up, caught me in the belly, and threw me over her head. I flew spectacularly until freshly-grown trees stopped me, and I slithered down them under a rain of snow and pine needles.

Corvallis was on her feet again by the time I looked up, pretty features all snarly. "I *told* you, David. It's over. Don't make me hurt you."

Unwelcome comprehension unfolded a clear path before me. I had no idea at all what had happened with Corvallis and this David person, but everything about the scene had suggested something bad. That left me between a rock and a hard place, shamanically speaking, because if I kicked her ass now, whatever trauma she had to face might never get resolved. On the other hand, if it turned out she'd actually kicked *his* ass then, while reliving the victory would no doubt be good for her, it would be considerably less good for me.

And the truth was, there wasn't really much of a choice. Power fluttered behind my breastbone, eager to help. If Laurie herself had an incident in her past she needed to deal with, I pretty much literally couldn't refuse. I just hoped like hell that it was Corvallis, and not the wendigo, in charge of this particular boxing round.

That was all the time I had to think. She left the spear behind, for which I was grateful, but she delivered a roundhouse kick to my head when I pushed up from the trees. I was considerably less grateful for that, as I spun around to eat snow a second time.

Corvallis jumped on my spine, a hand fisted in my hair. I could have shoved her off, but I thought—hoped—she wasn't going to kill me. Or David, whichever of us she saw. She leaned down and put her mouth by my ear. "I'm not the same girl I was back then, David. I'm tougher now. I learned how to protect myself. If you want to hit somebody, you don't need to look for somebody your own size anymore. I'm willing to fight." Then she lifted my head by the hair and slammed my face forward into the snow. I hit a tree root and saw stars, but her weight came off my back and when I rolled over, dizzily, it was to see her standing above me in triumph.

Her expression fell into confusion, though, as I worked my way toward sitting up. "Detective? What are you—" She looked around, clearly only seeing her surroundings for the first time. "Where are—?"

"It's complicated. Laurie, you're possessed, you've got a—"

The wendigo came back, and any chance to explain disappeared.

On the plus side, I was almost certain I'd seen a pattern. Momentary confusion or a hard knock lent a chance for one or the other personality to take control. In theory if I could whack Corvallis alongside the head, she'd come back and I might have time to try to talk her out of killing me.

In practice, I was afraid that, having put David's head through the allegorical concrete, Corvallis herself might have accomplished what she needed to, and that her personality might be okay with stepping back for a breather and adjusting to a new world order. Unfortunately, that very likely meant she'd never wake up again. There weren't enough swear words in the universe to satisfy my frustration.

We met in a head-on collision, my major intent being to get past the monster and pick up the spear again. It seemed safer to hit the thing from a distance, if I could, and there were no rules I knew about that said I couldn't use a spear like a really long baseball bat. With any luck I could grand-slam Corvallis's skull and knock her back into control. If not, there was always the added bonus of having hit her with a metaphorical baseball bat. That was probably a bad attitude to take, but it had been a very long day.

She clobbered me, back to the wendigo's slash-and-burn fighting style. Unlike in the Lower World, these hits connected, leaving my ears ringing and my vision blurry. On the other hand, she didn't have actual talons with which to gut me, so overall I called it a wash and hit her temple with my elbow. Her crimson-eyed focus went woozy and I scrambled over her, lunging for the spear.

She caught my ankle and hauled me back, and for a horrified minute I had to kick her off to keep her from gnawing my ankle. Definitely the wendigo in control. Regardless of how often I called Corvallis a shark, I didn't think she actually went in for biting body parts off. I lost a shoe to her ravening hunger, but that was a lot better than losing my foot.

A little too late, she realized what I was doing. Claws pierced my calves as she tried crawling up my body, but by then I had the spear in hand. I hit her over the head and she reeled back, gaze gone fuzzy again. For the briefest moment, Corvallis looked out at me again, and whispered, "Do what it takes to get the story."

There was something profoundly perverse about that attitude when by all reasonable reckoning *she* was the story. Still, as a scream tore her throat and her eyes flashed from red to blue and back again, I couldn't help thinking that she would. She'd do what it took to get the story, even if the story was her and it ended very badly. It might even win her a posthumous Pulitzer or something, and I had the impression Laurie Corvallis would be satisfied with that.

I wasn't, but I was also running out of options. I could spend most of forever in here trying to win back a reporter I didn't much like, or I could roll the dice and see if it came up snake eyes.

Corvallis was on the ground, fighting herself. I surged to my feet, the spear clutched in both hands, and stood over her. "Sorry, Corvallis. I wish it had ended differently."

I drove the spear down with every ounce of force at my disposal.

I awakened to the real world, where I stood over Corvallis with the spear plunged through her fur coat and layers. I could feel her heartbeat through the spear, living wood carrying it to me: that's how close she was to death.

She opened her eyes, all the wendigo crimson flooding back to blue. We stayed where we were for a brief eternity, Corvallis breathing shallowly because a deep inhalation would puncture her. Then she caved her chest in, shoulders rising a little as she shrank back from the spear. "It's me."

I nodded once and pulled the spear away, setting it butt-down in the snow. Coyote snatched it as I knelt over Corvallis, though I had no idea what he thought he would do with it. Use it as a bludgeoning weapon, from the way he held it. I would be the target, and I had to agree that from his perspective that might seem wise. I had, after all, just very nearly skewered one of the nominal good guys.

I shucked my mittens to open Corvallis's fur coat with one hand, then to push aside the layers beneath it. A tiny hole just above her heart drooled blood over the top of her breast, discoloring her bra. She said nothing, just kept her gaze fixed on mine as I bared her skin. It was by far the most peculiar, intimate moment I'd ever had with a woman, and she refused to blink or look away to lessen its intensity. Under the circumstances, if she wouldn't, I didn't feel like I could.

Not until I put my hand over the wound did she move, catching my wrist. "Will it leave a scar?"

"No."

"Then don't."

The little puncture wound hurt. Hurt her, hurt me; I could feel it wanting to be whole again. It would be easy to ignore her wishes with a patch-up job that small. "You sure?"

"Very."

I rolled back on my heels and withdrew my hand, blood on my palm. "Get it looked at, then."

"I will. As soon as you're done here."

"Yeah." I stood up again, deliberately not wiping my palm clean as I extended my hand for the spear. "I'm going to need it to finish this."

Coyote's hands tightened around the weapon's haft. "We need to talk, Jo."

"No." My heart hurt with all kinds of regrets for the different paths we had to follow. "No, Yote, we don't. I'm sorry. I just need the spear and my drum, and another path to the Lower World, if you'll open one."

"What if I won't?"

I sighed. "Then I'll go my own way, and this will be drawn out that much longer."

His silence said a great deal and was punctuated by words that contained more than just their surface meaning: "God damn it, Joanne…"

"I know. I'm sorry. Please?"

He gestured sharply behind me, and I turned to see a yellow sand road break through the snow. Gary, wordlessly, handed me my drum, and I tucked it safely beneath my arm. "Thank you."

There was nothing else to say. I nodded, then left my friends behind once again.

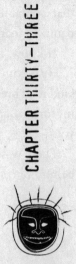

CHAPTER THIRTY-THREE

The truth was, I'd had enough. I'd fought gods, ghosts, demons and spirits in the past, and none of them had the staying power of the wendigo. I'd lost count of how many times we'd faced off, and pretty much every time, I'd come out with my ass in a sling. I was tired of it. I was flat-out tired, although to the best of my ability to remember, I'd only been up since that morning. Honestly, though, after being hauled in, out, around and over the Middle, Lower, Hell and snowstorm worlds, I didn't think I could be any more exhausted if I hadn't slept in a week.

The Lower World, with its too-hot, too-close sun, invited me to just curl up under the red sky and doze off. Instead I walked awhile, grateful for the silence, grateful to have left winter behind, grateful most of all that I had a little respite before fighting again. Sonata had explained in no uncertain terms that I was supposed to be the counterweight that made up for so many people of power dying a year ago in Seattle. I was willing to play that role, but there was a deep place inside me filling with envy for Coyote's gentler path. Not poisonous envy, but more a sort of appreciation for what it meant to be only a healer, and not a warrior as well. It was a good thing. Not that my duties were bad, but they were maybe more complicated. I'd actually been willing to sacrifice Corvallis, if necessary. I'd thought—I'd hoped—that the wendigo's desire to survive would send it skittering out of Corvallis before I struck the final blow, but I'd had to make it believe I'd kill her. In an astral world, where thoughts and intentions could be telegraphed even from behind shielded minds, that had meant *I* had to believe I'd kill her.

Coyote—Big Coyote, the Trickster himself—might have appreciated that ruthless game. My Coyote didn't, and I didn't blame him at all. I was afraid that in finding him again, I'd lost him for good.

A lush dark purple forest had come up around me as I walked. There were vines beneath my feet, leaves so dark they were almost black, and red sun filtered down through the trees above so shadows danced across my skin and played tricks with my vision. I wanted the forest; that was where a wendigo belonged, but I didn't know if winter ever came to the Lower World at all. Not that I had any desire to re-enter the storm, even with Raven at my side.

Which he was, skittering above the trees, diving through the branches so he was one of the objects mucking with my sight. I didn't mind. His presence made me more confident. I'd been walking without thought as to how I would end this thing, but a nugget of a plan formed at the back of my mind. I left it alone, afraid that if I focused on it too hard, it would disappear.

The forest broke abruptly, leaving me on a rock face in the full blasting sun. My rattlesnake was coiled there, baking away, and I sat beside him, eyes half-closed as I turned my face toward the sky. Despite the heat, I wasn't sweating. A gift, I supposed, from my cold-blooded spirit animal. I reached over to stroke his back, and he flattened out, scales rippling in the boiling light. Raven dropped on my other side and head-butted my knee, impatient as a cat, then quarked happily when I rubbed the top of his head, too.

They were the tools I needed. The snake, representative of healing and change, and the raven, able to wing between life and death. I tucked the spear by my thigh and took my drum into my lap, knocking it with my knuckles.

I had fought and fought and fought the wendigo, and each time it had been, at best, a draw, where "draw" really meant "Joanne lost, big-time." There *were* other paths open to me. I'd learned that, if nothing else, from Begochidi. All this time I'd been taking it to the wendigo's territory. This time I wanted her on mine, and for once—maybe for the first time—I was confident of what and where that territory was. Rattler and Raven helped define it, and with them beside me, I believed nothing could take it away.

Drum in hand, spirit guides at my side, I called the storm.

I knew it now. I'd been there often enough that I recognized the static scream warning me of its arrival long before the cold hit. There were so many voices in that storm, so many people lost beyond the boundaries of the worlds they'd belonged to. Most were echoes carried by shrieking wind, just a memory giving strength to the squall. I wondered if, with enough time, enough care, enough shamans, the whole of it might be dismantled, and if no one would ever be lost to the cold universe again.

And discarded the thought almost instantly. I believed it could be done. I also believed that the moment it was, the moment magic-users stepped away from the emptiness they'd left behind, a new soul would find its way through, and the storm would begin again. Nature abhorred a vacuum, even in levels of reality where nature seemed to play no part.

The cold wanted inside me, the way it had been accepted before. It slammed toward me and was rebuffed by the Lower World's warmth still clinging to my skin. I sat on the yellow stone cliff beneath the red sun's amazing heat while winter raged around me. Even my rattlesnake seemed undisturbed by the wind and weather, untouched when by all rights he should have frozen solid within moments. Raven, on my other side, hopped at the edges of our safe little circle, thrusting his head out to bite at flying snowflakes in an act that looked like pure silly defiance.

"There's a warmer world waiting for you, wendigo." I finally took up my drumstick, its raspberry-red rabbit fur end all bright and tasty as I turned the leather end against the drumhead. Raven lost interest in the storm and came to eye the waving fur hopefully, but I laughed and nudged him away with my elbow. "She'll need you, Raven. She'll need the cleverness you have to see her way out of the storm. But there'll be lollipops and shiny things when we're done. Will you watch for her?"

He *klok'd,* a huge self-important sound, and bounced back to the edge of our circle, wings half-spread in anticipation. I banged the drum properly for the first time, enchanted by the reverberation of leather hitting leather, and to my own surprise, began to sing.

I thought the idea came from Mandy, singing on solstice

morning. Singing in light and warmth and life, giving the sun a reason to return, like the star itself was a lost soul searching for its way back home. I wished I knew something about the woman who'd become the monster, something more than that she had a terrible will to live. But I sang to that, first just high notes in minor keys, where love songs from musicals always reached to twist the heart a little. They had some of the right idea, that touch of longing, but I wanted something more, something compelling. The drum provided a backbone to that, and after a while I found what I was looking for: wordless, atonal, urgent. Aboriginal song, like something the elders might have sung back in Qualla Boundary to teach the kids how to recognize their culture's music. I even managed to find a few phrases to call out in Cherokee, although it had been so long since I'd used that language I was sure I thoroughly mangled it.

But the song, or the willpower behind it, cut a path through the storm. Not quickly, but steadily, with Raven hopping forward eagerly with every inch it gave. He bounced far enough away I shouldn't have been able to see him, but we were bringing the Lower World into the heart of the blizzard. Proportions and distance were never quite right, in the Lower World, and he remained his full size even when he was hundreds of feet away.

The voices crying in the storm slowly faded away. They still hungered, they still wanted, but they seemed to understand I wasn't looking for them. As their howling shadows faded, a shape appeared at the far end of the path I was building. Raven got very excited, leaping around with his wings spread, and then suddenly dived into the storm itself, disappearing from view. The rattlesnake at my side finally stirred, lifting his head and flicking his tongue out in snaky interest. My heartbeat sped up and so did the pattern I thumped on the drum, like the two were intimately tied together.

Raven reappeared, another form stumbling behind him. It—she—stopped when she reached the yellow-earth path of the Lower World, its intrusion into the storm so astonishing I felt her amazement all the way down the road tying us together. Unlike Raven, she was tiny with distance, or her sense of self was so fragile, so lost, that she was nothing more than a speck on the horizon. I lifted my voice again, calling to her in song, and Raven, who had a distinctive but not beautiful voice, settled on her shoulder to flap encouragement.

The road closed up behind her, as if the storm was trying to take her back. I could feel her fear and confusion, and beneath that a thread of hope so thin it seemed impossible that it had sustained her as long as it had. Because I could only imagine hope *had* sustained her, a hope of returning home so very strong that it had made her into the wendigo. It was sheer cruelty that someone of such determination could be twisted into something of such horror, but if I was learning anything, it was that everyone had as much potential for dread as for beauty.

Even *I* did, which wasn't a comforting thought. Nobody who was purely full of lightness and fluff and goodness would have come so close to stuffing a spear through somebody's heart. That was, frankly, bleak as hell, and suggested I'd turned a corner somewhere. If I was capable of making that decision, I wasn't sure what other choices I might be able to make. I was even less sure I wanted to find out. I would have to talk to my disapproving mentor about the fine line between good and bad, and try like hell to stay on the right side of it while still acknowledging, even embracing, the need and ability to make the hard choices.

Maturity, I decided, sucked. On the other hand, the thought brought a warble of laughter into my song, and the woman on the pathway looked up at the sound. Something about her brightened, like she recognized laughter, and she came forward more eagerly, until I could see her clearly. She was still inhuman, but no longer in the way she'd been. No longer disjoined or falling apart, no longer a slavering monster of teeth and claws. She looked thin, not just physically but spiritually, like she'd almost faded away. I wasn't sure if the storm had done that to her, or if her attempts to break free had, but I was inclined to blame the storm.

I waited until she was only a few feet away, Raven whacking her on the head with his wings, before I set my drum aside so I could take up the spear and get to my feet. The rattlesnake finally uncoiled from his warm spot and slithered forward, wrapping around the woman's ankles. She looked down with alarm, and I shook my head. "It's all right. He's a friend. A guide, just like the raven. And I'm…"

For the first time I could remember, I wanted to hand over my full name, freely given. I wondered what that meant about this woman, about her fate, and what it meant about me, but I smiled and said, "I'm Siobhán. Siobhán Grainne MacNamarra Walkingstick, and I've come to take you home."

It sounded like such a gentle promise that it nearly broke my heart. I knotted my fingers around the spear's haft. "Home isn't back into the world you knew. I'm sorry. I don't know anything about you, but if we understand what happened, I'm afraid you've been lost to the cold for a long time. I think your body is probably dead, and I can't…"

She swayed a little, but stepped closer, like she was listening hard. I took a deep breath. "I can't let you go again unless I'm sure you'll return to your body. If there's no body to go back to, I'm afraid you'll become the wendigo again, trying to break free from the storm. I can't...let you do that. Too many people have already died. All I can do is bring you out of the storm and...set you free." It was such a stupid phrase. Free of what? Hope? Life? Chances? Those weren't things people sought to be set free from. We tried to escape prisons and bad situations, not gambles for survival.

Then again, if there was a worse situation than becoming a wendigo, I never wanted to encounter it. *I* would want to be freed from that, if for some hideous reason I ever became such a thing.

On the other hand, I wanted to be very, very clear about the limited options I was offering this woman, and so, voice low, I spelled it out. "You're going to die. It's the best I can offer you. But you'll die here, under the red sun, instead of out there in the storm. I wish I could give you more."

Something in her eyes suggested she still had words. Had the capacity to speak, but chose not to. A gift, maybe, for me. Something to make it easier, a pretense that she was nothing more than the animal she'd become. That was a kindness, and a lie: it took a thinking creature to do what she did next. She reached for the spear's neck, controlling it, and I let her. Let her bring it all the way down until the black wooden tip rested between her ribs, a certain kill shot. She lifted her gaze to mine, gave me a brief smile, and braced herself.

This was not how soul retrievals were supposed to end. They were meant to be a reunion of body and spirit, not a violent finish, not even if that finish was the closest thing to peace a lost soul might find. I hated it. There had to be another way. A promise I could make, a magic I could build. There had to be. The woman's gaze was clear on mine, waiting.

I whispered, "I'm sorry. I can't."

And shoved.

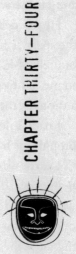

CHAPTER THIRTY-FOUR

The Lower World disappeared in a silent rush, leaving me standing cold and numb in the company of mortals. My spear was unbloodied, but I could feel the wendigo's weight against it, for all that I'd left her spirit behind in another realm. I also felt questions building up in the air, everyone around me wanting answers and not quite bold enough to ask for them. I was grateful for that. Grateful enough, in fact, that I reached for magic and brought down the power circles, hoping their fall would keep silence in place.

Corvallis inhaled sharply, and Coyote came to my side, everything about his presence uncertain. I offered the spear, and he took it cautiously. "Jo…"

I shook my head, trying to will him into quietness. I wasn't ready to talk. I didn't think I ever would be, even if I knew I'd have to sooner rather than later. Later: a little later, at least, because as he took the spear a whisper rifled the distant trees, and Herne was released into our midst.

He nodded once toward Coyote, whose hands fisted around the spear as he thrust it forward sideways, clearly trying to rid himself of it. Herne shook his head, then turned his attention to me, putting a branchy finger to his lips as I struggled to put a thought together aloud.

I hadn't needed to ask. Like he'd known what I wanted, he brought us home.

Laurie was right. The forest went all twisty. There was no better way to describe it: a violent twist of earth and trees, and we were a dozen yards from the hotel's back door instead of out in the far reaches of nowhere. I reached for a tree to steady myself as the others scattered for the hotel's warmth, safety and normalcy. I wanted to go with them. I wanted, really, to go close myself away somewhere silent and just *be* for a while. Just try to wrap my mind around the wendigo's death, and how I felt it as a loss in a way I'd felt nothing else over the past year. I wanted to step out of time and be safe and quiet until I felt ready to face the world again.

A breath of humor rushed through my lips. While that would be nice, it had no basis in reality. I stepped away from the hotel, closer to the forest. "Herne?"

The god stopped, and in his stillness was nothing more than a tree, all black branches in the moonlight. I waited for him to say something, then realized he wouldn't and blurted, "There was one other person we lost today, one of my friend's agents. Is he still out there?"

"I brought everyone who still walked the forest to you. If he is missing, there was no life to be found."

I slumped. "I was afraid of that. Okay. Thank you."

The tree bent a little, creaking as it did, and then was nothing *but* a tree, Herne's presence from it gone. I stood there alone for a moment, gazing at where he'd been, then twitched as Sara called my name. "What was that?"

I turned toward her, at a loss for anything but the truth. "That was…I thought you'd gone inside. It was a forest god. Sara, I'm sorry. He says your agent is dead."

She stared at me a long moment, then passed a hand over her face. "Yeah. You said he probably was." Another brief eternity passed before she shook herself. "All right. Thanks for telling me. You…you should go home for a while, Joanne."

Cold, not quite so bad as the storm, but abrupt and uncomfortable, clenched my gut. Sara scowled, reading denial in my face. "I'm serious. If this is what you're doing…you should go home. See your dad. Talk to the elders. You should do that."

Cold turned to ice and cracked in my voice. "Is he still there? Do you see him?"

"No, I live out here, but I go back sometimes. He was there last summer, anyway."

"You live here? In Seattle?" That was an easier thought than my dad back in North Carolina. "Maybe we should…" I thought of Lucas, and watching Sara's expression, said, "Or maybe not. I'll think about North Carolina."

Sara nodded and looked away, neither of us sure what to say next. We weren't friends, not anymore, but we were maybe less antagonistic than we'd been for years. Funny how rivalries could remain, even through time and distance and living only in memory. I didn't want to leave us with history as the last thing between us, and blurted, "What're you going to tell your bosses?"

She glanced back at me with a frustrated huff. "What *can* I tell them? Nothing. I'm going to spend the next six months or more working on this case, until it goes cold to their satisfaction. You're sure it's over?"

"Yeah. Look, I'm sorry about your man, Sara."

"Me, too." Sara fell a step back, precursor to escaping my presence. "I'll see you around, okay, Joanne?"

"Yeah." I didn't offer a hand, and neither did she. "I'll see you."

She walked away, and I waited until she was gone before following her in, and driving home to Seattle in time for Christmas.

Sunday, December 25, 5:20 A.M.

I had long since gotten over leaping out of bed bright and early on Christmas morning. Someone, though, apparently hadn't: pervasive thumping on my door dragged me out of a very nice sleep. I crawled over Coyote and into my fuzzy green robe half inclined to yell at the interloper who'd dragged me out of bed at such an unreasonable hour, but holiday cheer got the better of me before I even got to the door.

There wasn't even anyone there to be cheerful at. A gift-wrapped DVD-sized package sat outside my door, and I could hear somebody thudding down the apartment building's stairs. Coyote said, "What happened, Santa forgot where the chimney is?" I shot him a sleepy smile as I tore the wrapping paper open.

It was, in fact, a DVD. Not a popular movie sort, just a silver disc with a note that said "For Joanne" stuck to it. I shuffled to my computer and dropped it in. Coyote sat behind me and I pulled his arm around my waist as the disc spun up and began to play.

Jeff the cameraman, it turned out, was a dab hand with a video camera. Even his crab-walked retreat from the wendigo was surprisingly steady, and Coyote looked like a native god in the moonlight as he fought the thing. I blew in from offscreen, slamming into the wendigo hard enough that I grunted again, watching it. It and I flung each other back and forth, and Jeff's camerawork was only a half second behind as the wendigo leaped on Laurie Corvallis's prone body.

The next couple minutes were spent enthralled by the utter peculiarities of seeing what one of my psychic/real-world battles looked like from the outside. Every fight, every step, every gesture and every expression I made in Laurie's garden registered itself on my face and body in the Middle World. The wendigo wasn't visible. I just looked like the world's most dedicated mime, flying backward when something hit me, staggering around like a drunk after a bad blow. Not until I raised the spear and drove it down toward Corvallis, awakening her, did the fight have two participants. Moments later, Coyote opened a path to the Lower World for me, and I watched myself walk along it and disappear.

It looked, swear to God, like a magic trick. Like the audience should be peering around in search of the mirrors before applauding wildly. I was gone for a long time, long enough that Jeff panned around to the others. Coyote and Gary were all but leaning forward, both of them obviously—to me—offering strength and support and concern. Sara and Corvallis both looked grimly gobsmacked, and Laurie kept touching her breast where I'd very nearly impaled her. A clock came on in the screen's lower right-hand corner, then jumped ahead by half an hour, footage cut out before I finally returned.

The me on the recording looked so very sad. So tired, and so glad to hand the spear to someone else. I reached out to turn it off, and Coyote stopped me. I said, "C'mon," quietly. I'd already watched more than I wanted to, and all I could think was how utterly insane it was going to look on the evening news. Morrison would kill me.

The screen faded to black, then came up again in a news studio. Corvallis held a DVD between two fingers, turning it so it caught the light. "There are two copies. The one you've got, and this one."

She broke hers into pieces, and the screen went dark.

After what seemed like a long time, I cleared my throat and turned the computer off. "Guess we scored one for the home team there."

"So how come you don't sound thrilled?"

I shook my head. "Because I don't like making believers out of people. It's too big a thing to ask."

Coyote chuckled against my shoulder. "You went and grew up, Jo. While I wasn't looking. I didn't expect that."

"Oh, believe me, neither did I. I tried hard not to." I twisted, trying to see him, and he got to his feet, then pulled me to mine and herded me back toward the bedroom. I went, grateful he didn't have an overwhelming urge to be up at five in the morning either, even if it was Christmas. We tucked up together, me tracing idle patterns on his chest before I mashed my nose against his pectoral and mumbled, "I can't do things your way. You know that, right, Yote? I don't know if I'd have been able to even if I'd stuck with studying with you all those years ago, or if the past six months had gone differently. But I don't think so. You…you're a healer. I'm something else."

"Warrior's path." He put his mouth against my hair. "I don't envy that. But you've still got a lot you can learn. A lot I could teach you," he amended hesitantly. "If you want."

I pushed up on my elbow, feeling all serious suddenly. "I can't think of a better teacher."

The man had a smile like no other. I thought it had just been how happy I was to see him at first, but I'd had a few days to get used to it now, and it was definitely a grade-A smile. Bright and fleeting and all the more delicious for its quickness. He caught my hand and kissed the palm, then folded our fingers together on his chest. "Okay. I'll stop trying to remake you in my image, and you can…"

"Stop getting my ass kicked," I finished firmly. "I want the shamanic handbook, Yote. I want it all."

He laughed. "Oh how the mighty have fallen. It'd be easier if…" A crease appeared between his eyebrows and he sat up, exhaling a sharp breath that ended ruefully. "Okay, this is going to be harder than I thought."

Nerves seized my heart and I sat up, too, clutching my pillow. I didn't want him to say anything else, because I was pretty certain of what he'd say. We had, in fact, spent most of the past couple days not-quite-actively avoiding serious talk, which was made easier by me having to work. That made the hours we had together a little more precious, and neither of us had wanted to gum them up with anything other than living in the moment. It took everything I had to whisper, "What's going to be hard?"

"My grandfather bought me a plane ticket home last night, so I could be there for Christmas evening. It leaves SeaTac at ten-thirty." Coyote shot me an apologetic look and I shook it off even as a pang cut through me.

"You've been unconscious for months. I don't blame him for wanting you home for Christmas." I wanted him *here* for Christmas, but I wasn't quite selfish enough to say so aloud. Or maybe I wasn't quite brave enough. "That's not the hard part, is it."

"You're not supposed to know me that well. No, the hard part...it'd be easier to teach you if we were together. In the same place, I mean," he said hastily, and then, less certainly, "And maybe together, too. I know you can't today, but...but you could come with me, Jo."

I bent my head over the pillow, eyes closed. That was exactly what I'd thought he was going to say, and it made a hard little helpless place inside me. It took a long time to speak, and even then my voice was small and tight. "You're the shape of my dreams, Coyote. You came to me in my sleep when I was a girl and taught me magic, and now you're here and alive and beautiful and I—" I stumbled over the words so hard I almost swallowed my tongue, but I met his eyes so he could see me saying them: "I love you. You're my dreams come true. And this was going to happen," I said even more quietly, and mostly to myself. "Right from the moment you came back, this was going to happen. And it isn't fair, because it would break my heart to go and it'll break my heart to stay."

"But you're going to stay," Coyote said very softly. He glanced down as I slumped over my pillow. "I knew you would. I still had to ask." He touched my chin, making me raise my eyes, and offered a shaky smile. "Hey, I'll be back up here, you know. I've got to come back up when the weather clears so I can drive the Chief home. Maybe you won't be able to say no a second time."

"Maybe I won't." That idea hurt as much as the other. I snuffled and Coyote's gaze softened. He pulled me against his chest, and we stayed there, silent, until the alarm went off and it was time for me to go to work.

When I got out of the shower there was a flat rectangular black velvet box on my pillow. Not a ring box, but it didn't have to be: even as it was, it made my stomach lurch so hard I actually got dizzy. I hung on to the bathroom door frame for a couple seconds, just staring at the box before the penny dropped and I snatched it up to run into the living room shouting, "Coyote? Cyrano? *Cyrano!*"

He was gone. He was gone, and I'd known it on some level from the instant I saw the box. I knelt on the living room floor, wearing a towel and nothing else, working up the nerve to open the damned box. I was already late for work by the time I made myself do it.

Four earrings lay inside it. Two were gold wraps. One was a bird, so stylized you had to know me to know it was a raven. The other was more obviously a snake, with a rattle and all.

The other two were a wire pair, meant for pierced ears, which I'd never had. I got to my feet and went into the bathroom, stopping for a needle on my way.

Popping the needle through my lobes didn't hurt at all, nor did threading the earrings through the raw holes. It only took a whisper of healing power to seal the damage over, and then I stood looking at myself in the mirror like I was a stranger. Looking at the earrings, made of bone so smooth it seemed shaped, rather than carved.

Coyotes, crying for the moon.

Saturday, December 31, 11:48 P.M.

I had yet to get used to the earrings, which brushed my jaw and made me endlessly aware of their presence. Made me more aware of everything that had to do with my ears, for that matter, and that included the radio shouting in them. Its blaring countdown was the only human contact I'd had for hours.

There were better places to be—Billy and Melinda's, for example; a New Year's party was in full swing, and Billy had called twice to see where I was. I'd promised to be there by midnight, but at this late juncture, not even Petite would get me there in time.

I had paperwork spread all over my desk, Google results and newspaper clippings and police files from all over the country. Missing persons reports were shuffled together like puzzle pieces, scraps of data highlighted or circled with red and yellow pens. I needed a drink of water. My eyes were dry from scowling at so much paperwork.

The office door opened, sending me half out of my skin with fright. I clutched my chest, and Morrison, in the doorway, did a lousy job of covering a laugh. "What're you doing here, Walker?"

"Besides getting the life scared out of me?" I settled back down in my chair, gulping a couple deep breaths to calm my heart. "Just, ah. Just finishing up some paperwork. Sir."

"It's New Year's Eve. You're off duty. You're supposed to be at the Hollidays'." He let the door drift shut behind him as he wove his way through desks to reach mine. "What's so important?"

"It's just…" I gestured at my papers. "I was just trying to figure out who she was." "Just" implied I hadn't spent most of my off-hours since Coyote left at this very same task, although half the department had commented that I was showing a lot of dedication given that it was the holidays.

Morrison sat on the edge of my desk, arms folded across his chest. "Any luck?"

"I don't know. We're never going to know for certain." I straightened up and pulled a handful of papers to the fore. "But this woman, Liz Gregory…she was Tlingit, from up in the

Alaskan Panhandle near Juneau. She went missing last winter, during that cold snap in March. They never found her body, and…" I uncovered a newspaper photograph and handed it to Morrison. I'd long since memorized its image, a roundish, happy-faced woman sitting in front of a Native Alaskan-style block-print of a bear. She wore long black hair in a thick braid, and had a simple thong necklace with a claw pendant lying outside her T-shirt.

"Bear totem," he said after a moment. "Is that what I'm looking at?"

I nodded. "I think so. The newspaper stories about her…" I sighed. "She worked outdoors a lot, did a lot of living culture work within her community. There was no mention of her being a shaman or a mystic of any sort, but I'm not sure that would've been reported on even if it were true. And maybe it doesn't matter. Maybe she was just someone who had a big spirit and belonged outdoors, and when she got lost, the cold took her."

"The cold?"

I closed my eyes. "The place where her spirit was caught, Morrison…it was so cold. Cold enough to hurt. Cold enough that you'd do…anything. Anything at all, to get warm again. I didn't spend very long there, but you'd go mad, boss. Anybody would. I don't think very many people get out of there, once they're lost, and I'm not surprised you'd become something terrible in the trying." I shivered, trying to throw the memories off. "Anyway, the bear totem. I haven't contacted her family to ask about it yet, but…"

Morrison helped me change the subject, for which I was grateful. "What does this mean in practical terms, Walker? Are you going to try to pin the last two months of killings on a woman who disappeared nine months ago?"

"I wouldn't be able to. There's no evidence. I just wanted to know for myself. To see if I could find out who she was. Maybe at least tell her family she's at peace."

"Is she?"

"I have no idea." I pinched the bridge of my nose. "If it was her, she's more at peace than she was as a wendigo. That's all I know. It's something. Not a lot, maybe, but something."

Morrison nodded, not exactly satisfied, but accepting. That was just about how I felt, too. He handed the picture back. "If this woman's from Juneau, what was she doing down here? That's a long way to travel."

That was a question I'd been trying hard not to let myself think about. I had, of course, been thinking about it almost constantly as a result, and all the answers Morrison needed showed up on my face. "Because of you?"

"Right after Halloween, Morrison. The cannibal murders started right after Halloween. Right after I blew up the cauldron, after using all that power. I mean, I could be wrong, but I see it one of two ways. Either she thought I might be able to help her move on or she thought I might be a hefty enough snack to push her back into the world. She was getting closer to me, before we found her. Charlie Groleski? He used the same mechanic I do, Chelsea's Garage. And Karin Newcomb lived in my building. They're the only two connections I can find, and I know they're tenuous, but I can't help being afraid all those people are dead because of me."

"No." Morrison put his hand on my shoulder, making me look at him. "Don't do that to yourself, Walker. This thing would've hunted somewhere, and people would've died. That's outside your control. What matters is it's over. You stopped it. It's all any of us can do. We don't have the insight to stop killers before they strike, and maybe it wouldn't be a good thing if we did. This one's a victory. Take it."

I thinned my lips, then nodded. He was probably right. There was no cause without effect, but taking on the burden of being the cause and mitigating the effects would drive me crazy, especially since I couldn't *know* whether I'd drawn the wendigo to Seattle or not. On the other hand, having finally taken up the mantle of responsibility, I didn't want to find myself shirking it, either. There had to be a balance somewhere in there, but I was still a long way from finding it. "I'll try."

"Some days that's all I can ask for." Morrison gave me a brief, almost sympathetic smile.

I wrinkled my eyebrows at him. "What are you doing here, anyway?"

"Holliday sent me to get you."

"Really? You? Why?" I had a pretty good idea of why, but I was curious as to what he'd say.

"It was a toss-up between me and Muldoon, but he's three sheets to the wind and flirting with an FBI agent a quarter his age."

I did a brief calculation. "She can't possibly be. Even if you say he's seventy-four, which he won't be for—" I turned my wrist up to look at my watch "—for another three minutes, she wouldn't be old enough to be out of training camp. I mean, police academy takes months, wouldn't FBI training take at least twice as l…" Morrison was failing to fight off a grin. "Oh. You're teasing me."

"Yes." He stopped trying to beat the grin down, and tipped his head at the door. "I'm here because you should be at the party, and Holliday thought you might actually listen if I came to get you. Get your coat."

I got my coat, turned off my computer screen, and tugged Homicide's door closed behind me before chasing Morrison down the steps to the precinct's lobby.

Fireworks erupted in the sky as we pushed the doors open. Myriad colors bloomed against high clouds, reflecting the sparking streams of light as they popped and roared and whistled across the city. Distant music rang down the street, the strains of "Auld Lang Syne" played on radios and taken up by tuneless, exuberant voices. Morrison and I both stopped, taken aback by the sudden light and song show, then looked at one another.

There was really only one thing to do at midnight on New Year's Eve, and we both knew it. We stood there gazing at each other, eye to eye, neither with the height advantage. Neither breathing, as far as I could tell. Time hadn't stopped; I could feel my heart beating a little too hard as a blush started to climb my cheeks. But it felt like we were in a bubble, just me and Morrison, waiting to see what happened next.

The funny thing was that I thought if we'd been at Billy's party, I might've kissed him. A brief peck on the way to kissing someone else. It would've been impolite not to, in those circumstances, but standing there in the precinct building doors, fireworks raining colored light on us, a kiss was more than just a kiss.

I glanced up just to find somewhere else to look, and discovered some enterprising soul had hung mistletoe over the door. I breathed laughter, making Morrison look up, too.

Complicated amusement danced over his face, making his blue eyes bright. He said, "Ah," and took one judicious step out from under the door. "Happy New Year, Walker."

My heart filled up and turned my smile sad and stupid all at once. "Happy New Year, Captain."

"Come on." Morrison offered a hand. "We've got a party to go to."

There were probably a million reasons I shouldn't accept that gesture. A million reasons he shouldn't have offered it, for that matter. Right then, I didn't care. Still smiling, I put my hand in his and squeezed. "Yes, sir."

He squeezed back, released my fingers, and we went out into the new year together.

★ ★ ★ ★ ★

Does Joanne realize all the snake's gifts?
Don't miss the next adventure
SPIRIT DANCES
Coming April 2011

ACKNOWLEDGMENTS

My undying thanks to the Word War Writers, who are too many to name, but know who they are, for the daily word wars that helped me finish this book in a timely fashion. I would not have done it without you.

I'd also like to thank Heather Fagan for use of her name in this book, and for participating in the Brenda Novak Diabetes Research auction which led to her being a character in *Demon Hunts*. Information about the auction can be found at www.brendanovak.com.

And my thanks to the usual suspects: my agent, Jennifer Jackson, and my editor, Mary-Theresa Hussey, whose insights helped to shed light on the structural comment that Trent made which I had totally misinterpreted. The book is all the better for your help. Also, as far as I'm concerned, cover artist Hugh Syme and the Harlequin art department, headed by Kathleen Oudit, outdid themselves on the cover for this book. Imagine little heart shapes dancing around this paragraph.

I would say you can also imagine little hearts dancing around this paragraph, wherein I thank my husband Ted for being consistently wonderful, but that would be unbearably goopy and I could never say something like that in public without ruining my rep as a tough girl. :)